PINK MARGARINE

The Ultimate Conspiracy Theory

First Edition Published 2012

ISBN 978-0-9556928-2-6

Thanks to Pam for her encouragement
and to David, Joe, Lynn, Nick, Sue & Ulla
for their help in correcting the many errors

Contents

Introduction

This book is a work of fiction designed primarily to amuse and entertain.

I thought I'd better make that clear right away, since I don't want anyone to buy a copy in the belief that I have some amazing insight into the great conspiracy theories of our time. Unfortunately I don't, at least I don't think so. Not unless of course one of my far-fetched ideas is actually true.

The Americans really did land on the Moon, the Twin Towers really were brought down by a group of terrorists and Princess Diana died because she entrusted her safety to a drunk driver and what's more she didn't wear a seat belt.

But at least the inspiration for the book is founded on real life.

With Climate Change the current hot topic it seems strange that the main cause, and in fact the cause of most the problems faced by the Human Race, is rarely discussed.

I'm referring to over-population.

If we were to reduce the number of human beings on the planet most of these problems would disappear. Shortages of basic things like energy, food, water, etc., would probably not exist.

But more importantly, at least as far as global warming is concerned, even if countries can be persuaded to co-operate and reduce their dependence on fossil fuels, unless the human population is capped and then reduced we'll be in the same boat in a few years' time. Whatever savings we make now will be outweighed by the increase in the population in the future.

There must be a limit on the number of people the planet can comfortably support and that limit was probably exceeded during the last century.

And yet we hear virtually nothing from the politicians. A few countries, like China and India, have made attempts to control the growth of their populations but with limited success. Otherwise there's very little action, particularly in the West. In fact it always amazes me that politicians state that "this" or "that" policy must be introduced because the population is going to grow by this number over this timescale. Never do they seem to consider that there may be policies that could actually limit that growth.

So why is that? It's obvious that policies to limit population growth would be tricky to introduce, not the least because there are religious issues involved. I would have liked to have seen population control on the agenda at the Climate Change conference in Copenhagen. Someone could then have posed a question to the world's major religions along the lines of:

"Given that we need to keep a check on population growth and since you don't encourage contraception or abortion, have you got any other ideas?"

In particular, why is it that the Catholic Church can be so pre-occupied with preserving the life of a single human being without realising that it may end up helping to wipe out the whole of mankind in the process?

So this is the question. Why are politicians ignoring this issue?

The answer could be that they're not ignoring it at all, but since the issue of population control would be so contentious, one possibility is that they are taking action to address the problem, but without actually telling the population at large what's going on. Once you start considering this possibility things start to fall into place. When politicians appear to do really stupid things, that's perhaps because they can't let on what the real reasons are for their actions.

The alternative to this theory would be that there really are a lot of stupid, corrupt, selfish, power hungry people in politics who are willing to sacrifice the long term future of the planet for their own short term gain. This of course is also a possibility.

So the main thread of the book is to do with population control, or rather an apparent lack of control. What could be going on behind the scenes to combat the growth in the population?

The other issue that inspired me is the attitude of many individuals to the information fed to them by governments and companies. They seem to accept what they are told without much if any concern. Of course there are also those who don't believe anything that their government tells them no matter what it is, hence the proliferation of conspiracy theories.

I can understand people being complacent when it comes to things which have a marginal effect on their lives but I would have thought that when it comes to things like health, they might have more than a passing interest.

In the past year or so two simple things have occurred which caused me to ponder this issue and, together with population control, prompted me to write this book. The first concerns heart disease.

Some time ago, I had a cholesterol test as part of a general health check and was told that it was on the high side. Now since I had had my cholesterol tested regularly over the years, this came as a bit of a surprise. So I had another reading taken by my GP a week later and it was normal, but he did suggest that I should have the test repeated within six months in order to check that everything was OK.

I asked him what my options would be if in the future the reading was not below the recommended level. The answer was first to change my diet. He gave me a diet sheet and as far as I could see it involved giving up eating and drinking a lot of the things that I most enjoyed, e.g. red meat, cream, butter, wine and so on. In fact most of the things that, at least as far as food is concerned, make life worth living. And of course, the obligatory "and get plenty of exercise" phrase was thrown in.

For obvious reasons I wasn't too keen on this plan so I asked him whether there was an alternative option. There was. Apparently I could take cholesterol lowering drugs, i.e. Statins, for the rest of my life and this seemed to be a possible option except for one issue. I don't like the idea of taking medication every day for ever, particularly when the drug is not designed to cure a disease, but rather to manage a "symptom".

I wasn't very impressed by either of these options so I decided to look into the whole area of heart disease, cholesterol, saturated fat and Statins. I won't bore you with the details of what I discovered but I can say that I am not on medication. I eat plenty of meat, particularly the fatty cuts, butter, milk (full cream) and cheese. I have no idea what my cholesterol levels are like and what's more, I don't particularly care. (Since I originally wrote this section I have in fact had my cholesterol tested as part of a routine medical examination and it's now 5.0 (193mg/dL). It has dropped from 6.3 (244mg/dL) in the last 5 years. So much for saturated fat causing higher cholesterol levels, although I must concede that one person's experience does not prove anything)

Now this all seems to me to be a logical, sensible thing to do. A doctor tells you to take a drug every day for the rest of your life, even though you are not ill. Surely you would look into this situation so that you can make an informed decision.

Apparently not. I have spoken to a number of people who have had a cholesterol test and as a result have been put on Statins. And they appear to have gone ahead without question. They must be a drug company's dream customer. I refer to them as a customer since, as these people do not have an illness, they're not actually patients.

The same logic can be applied to food. I once went to stay with a friend who seemed to be particularly interested in healthy living. I saw that she was using a spread made from olive oil on her toast instead of butter. When I queried this, she justified it based on the fact that olive oil is healthy and butter isn't. I then read out to her the ingredients from the base of the spread.

It was a scary list.*

Now I naively thought that by highlighting the ingredients I would give her cause to reconsider her attitude but no, apparently not. Margarine Good, Butter Bad. Everyone knows. Well everyone except the French of course. (I must make it clear here that I am using margarine as a generic term since I'm not sure where the dividing line is between margarine and any other non-butter spread)

So this got me thinking. How is it that an intelligent and normally well informed person can have such a blinkered attitude? There must be a reason.

Of course, it is possible that butter is bad for you (very unlikely but it does depend on what you do with it) and that I have been misled by my own research. And that may well be the case, especially as most of the information I have gleaned has inevitably come from the Internet. You can find justification for just about anything on the Web if you look hard enough. So I can't be absolutely sure that I'm right. But I can console myself with the following little score chart.

If I'm right about the whole cholesterol/heart issue, I get a point for living a longer healthier life and another point for enjoying the food I like without worrying about what I am eating. If I'm wrong, I still get a point for enjoying my food, but no point for the long healthy life.

So I get a total of three points

You on the other hand may well believe the propaganda.

In that case if you're right, you get a point for the healthy life but no points for your enjoyment of food (unless of course you would actually prefer to eat margarine rather than butter) since you either avoid food you would love to eat or you eat it and feel guilty afterwards.

And if you're wrong you get no points at all since you'll give up the foods that you enjoy and shorten your life in the process.

* **Refined Olive Oils and Virgin Olive Oils, Rapeseed Oil, Water, Whey (from Milk), Vegetable Oils, Buttermilk, Salt (0.8%), Emulsifier: Mono- and Diglycerides of Fatty Acids, Preservative (Potassium Sorbate), Thickener (Sodium Alginate), Citric Acid, Vitamin E, Flavouring, Vitamins A & D, Colour: Carotene**

So I make that three-one to me.

Going back to the issue with the Internet, as I said at the start, this is a work of fiction but I have tried to use factual information for the background, particularly with the chronology of events. However, I have obtained a lot of the information from the Web, particularly Wikipedia. It's not that I particularly wanted to use it but if you search for anything on the Web, the Wikipedia entry is likely to come up near the top.

I did consider cross-referencing some of the health and nutrition bits in the book back to the original scientific papers but I decided that a) it was too much effort and b) anyone who is interested can quickly Google a topic to find the relevant information. However, I do think it's worth mentioning one particular piece of research which, bearing in mind the title of this book, is particularly relevant. I found this information following the appearance on TV of a doctor who was advocating a total ban on the sale of butter in the UK in order to cut the incidence of heart disease. I was so incensed that for the first time in my life I made a complaint to the BBC.

The scientific paper is based on research by Harvard Medical School and the Web address at the time of writing is:

http://www.ncbi.nlm.nih.gov/pubmed/9229205

In case you cannot trace the paper, here's the conclusion:

"These data offer modest support to the hypothesis that margarine intake increases the risk of coronary heart disease. Butter intake did not predict CHD incidence"

In summary, margarine increases the chance of a heart attack, butter doesn't. Just how brilliant is that!

This is an example of something that appears in the book and which I was aware of when I started writing. However there have been quite a few things that, at the time of writing, were an invention but have since been revealed as true. A couple of examples cropped up in the same week.

The first is that information regarding Area 51 has been declassified and some of the stuff that has come out includes the fact that the authorities did indeed encourage the belief that the site was somehow involved with aliens. A day later Goldman Sachs is accused of deliberately promoting derivatives based on sub-prime mortgages that they knew were doomed to fail. These sorts of things gave me the incentive to get on and finish the book, otherwise, if I were not careful, this would have been more of a history book rather than a work of fiction.

Two final points. Firstly, the action in the book involves a succession of American Presidents so it obviously takes place in the USA. However, I am British and I am conscious that, although I have tried to avoid it, I'm sure that as far as word usage is concerned I have mixed English and American/English in the narrative. For example, I have used "vacation" rather than "holiday" and "parking lot" for "car park" but I'm sure other references will have slipped through where I've used the English version. The spelling is however English, not American, hence there is a "u" in colour. Also, although Jack is an American, when I was writing some of his dialogue I couldn't help but hear it delivered in the style of Jeeves, the butler featured in the books of P G Wodehouse.

If you try to imagine that Jack's words are being spoken by Stephen Fry, perhaps you'll see what I mean.

Lastly, Pink Margarine did once exist but the enforced addition of dye by some US States was outlawed late in the nineteenth century. Since this is a work of fiction, I have moved this event to the nineteen-sixties when the last of the State laws regarding the sale of margarine in the USA was repealed. However, the last Federal law, which amongst other things restricted the size of a pack of margarine, was not repealed until 1996.

Truman

1950

January

Jack (A Presidential Aide) - Sir, I've just come from a meeting of the Strategic Issues Committee where we were discussing the current situation regarding population control. The consensus seems to be that our current plan to solve the problem of over-population isn't working.

I didn't realise that we had such a plan, Jack. What, does it involve?

- Well it's perhaps an exaggeration to say it's a plan; it's more of a by-product of the situation that we find ourselves in. For some time we have been monitoring the increase in the human population and that's because we have been concerned that the growth will become unsustainable. However, we did think that the military conflicts which have occurred in the last few years would have put the brakes on the growth.

You mean the fact that we seem to have a world war every 25 years?

- Yes, Sir, plus of course there have been many lesser conflicts, but no matter how high the death toll, people are breeding faster than wars can kill them. We are going to have to come up with another plan, otherwise, if we're not careful, soon there won't be enough resources to go round. The worst scenario is that it could herald the end of the human race.

Do you really think it's that serious?

- Well if you like, I can take you through the figures, Sir. You can judge for yourself. At the start of the 20th century there were around 1.6 billion people on Earth. That figure has since grown to 2.5 billion, an increase of nine hundred million in fifty years.

Well the numbers speak for themselves and so I dare say that you're right; something needs to be done, but can't we just start another war?

- Well, Sir, we could but it's very messy and quite expensive. Also, we had to use a lot of subterfuge in order to engineer the Japanese attack on Pearl Harbour. I'm not sure we could get away with it again so for that reason alone I don't think another world war is on the cards for some time to come. However small wars would still be an option, but they're not going to be a complete solution. I think that we have to come up with something else and that means that we need to either kill people off or stop them breeding.

But surely wars kill people off very efficiently. In fact, in that respect, the atomic bomb seems to have been particularly effective.

- Sir, I think we can forget using an atomic bomb for the foreseeable future. It's all very well deploying them when you're the only guy who owns one, but now there are other countries with nuclear weapons, I think we can forget that option. In any case I'm not talking about getting rid of people by the bucket load. We need to be operating under the radar and therefore we are going to have to pick them off one by one.

One by one? Isn't that going to take rather a long time?

- Well when I say that, what I actually mean is not all in the same place at the same time, otherwise people will start to notice. However, the total body count will still need to be huge.

Jack, are things really that urgent?

- Well, Sir, you need to consider the numbers and that is what the committee has been doing. As I said, the increase in population has been 900 million in fifty years. The body count from the two wars was between 80 and 90 million so by no means insignificant but still nowhere near enough to stabilise population growth.

So what do you recommend?

- Well as a first option, I would suggest some sort of birth control strategy. It will probably be an easier sell to the American people than our second option.

Which is?

- Mass murder, Sir, albeit using covert means.

In that case, you're right, we need to try the first option. You'd better get the scientists to commence work on the problem. In the meantime

I think that we start a few small wars, just to tide us over in the short term? Have a think about it and see if you can come up with a list of potential countries.

- Yes, Sir, Mr President.

And contact our allies in Europe to see if they'll buy in to the contraception plan.

- What about France?

OK, our allies and France. See if they have any ideas. And you'd better think of an option for reducing the population of the rest of the world. I can't see the Russians being co-operative if they know what we are trying to do.

- Yes, Sir.

February

- Mr President, the scientists have come up with a solution to the population problem.

Ah, I've been giving that some thought myself and I have come up with something that has the benefit of being very effective very quickly.

- Really, Sir? What is it?

We can perform a procedure on every new born male which will render them infertile.

- You mean castration? Good grief Sir, that sounds a bit drastic!

Well I don't mean that we actually chop the little fellow off. I'm sure that we can come up with something a little more subtle. And I can't help thinking that if we are going to come up with a solution we need to think the unthinkable and work our way backwards from there.

- OK, I'll get the marketing people onto it and see what they can come up with but I have a feeling that the American population will take a lot of convincing. Also, this isn't something that we could make compulsory, it would have to be left to personal choice in which case we may need to offer tax concessions in order to encourage people to take up the option.

Well that sounds like a potentially expensive option. I trust this plan would take some time to instigate.

- You mean like after your term of office has ended, Sir?

Exactly!

- Yes, Sir, I'm sure that could be arranged.

Good, but what about the war option? Do you have the list of countries?

- Yes, Sir, and so far we've come up with just three, North Korea, North Vietnam and Switzerland.

And which of those do you recommend?

- Well Switzerland is a land locked country with no navy and I believe that their soldiers wear skirts. What's more, it did not participate in the last big war.

How on earth did they get away with that?

- They claimed to be neutral and as a result Hitler left them alone.

I bet the Poles wish that they had thought of that one. OK, I guess that Switzerland sounds like the safest option so get the military to draw up a battle plan. In the meantime, we need to consider the options for the rest of the world.

- Yes, Sir.

The Next Day

- Sir, even with the tax incentives, the experts think that there could be some consumer resistance to the castration idea. Also the ad men are struggling to come up with a suitable slogan, so instead the scientists recommend a two prong attack, the main option being contraception, with homosexuality being very much a long shot.

Homosexuality? What's that?

- That's where a man prefers a man to a woman.

You mean as company when he's watching baseball?

- No, I mean in a sexual way. If we can encourage same sex relationships it would obviously decrease the options to breed.

Good grief, Jack, I think we need to keep that one as a back-up option. Let's stick with contraception for the time being. Do you think the pharmaceutical companies can come up with something?

- Yes, Sir, Mr President. I'm sure that if we give them enough money they'll deliver the goods.

March

- Good news, Sir, the pharmaceutical industry has come up with what they call the contraceptive pill. A man needs to take the pill once a year, give or take 6 months, and he won't be able to make a woman pregnant.

Good grief, Jack, you can't expect a man to remember to do something as complicated as that and in any case I can't see a women trusting a man to that extent. You'd better tell the scientists to come up with another option.

- Yes, Sir, I'll see what they can do. And there's something else you need to be aware of. We've received some interesting news from the British concerning smoking. Apparently, they think that it's bad for your health.

How can that be, Jack? It has always seemed to me to be such a pleasant activity.

- That may be, Sir, but in fact it's causing health problems. The Brits reckon it damages the lungs and causes cancer.

Surely Jack, if that were the case we'd have spotted it before now, after all people have been smoking for years. If cigarettes are really that bad we'd have bodies piling up in the streets.

- Not if the effects are long term. The research says that it can take on average 20 years to kill you. Smoking really picked up at the start of the 20th century and lung cancer was virtually unknown before the 1920's. Since then, the number of smokers and the incidence of the disease have mirrored one another, if you allow for the 20 year time lag.

So what do we do? Presumably, the first thing will be to stop this information getting out.

- Well it's too late for that, Sir, since the information is already in the public domain. But it was published in the British Medical Journal and it's not the most widely read publication. We just need to make sure that none of the mainstream newspapers pick up on the story.

OK, try to do that. In the meantime we need to start a campaign to promote smoking. Get the ad men onto it.

- Sir, I think the ad men are already very much onto it. Cigarettes are one of the most widely advertised commodities in the USA. No, if we are going to boost smoking we need to come up with something else.

OK, Jack, see what you can do.

June

- Mr President, we have another situation. There is a religious sect based in Italy which says that it is very much against the idea of contraception.

But surely the sect must include married men, in which case what do they do about contraception? Can't they understand the problem?

- Apparently the sect does not advocate marriage for its leaders so presumably they don't have the problem.

Well, I don't think they should be advocating sex outside marriage.

- Sir, they don't advocate sexual relations at all.

So what do they propose we do to solve the problem of population control?

- I'm not sure that they've ever considered that issue but as far as the leaders are concerned they use abstinence.

So you're telling me that the leaders of the sect do not get married nor do they have sexual relations.

- That's correct, Sir, they do not, at least not officially. Our intelligence reports suggest that there is some sort of mass hypnosis going on. Trainees are taken away to secret locations for years on end and come out as converts to the cause.

So do we need to concern ourselves with this group?

- Sir, I think they could become very influential. I don't believe that we can leave them alone to spread their dangerous ideology.

Well, can't we invade Italy and sort them out? I'm sure they were on the opposing side in the last war. In fact, I seem to remember that we passed through the place on the way to Berlin.

- Well the sect is holed up in a fortified enclave and they are well protected by a group of armed mercenaries from Switzerland.

In that case we may be able to kill two birds with one stone. If we invade Switzerland, the armed guards may be withdrawn and we can capture the leaders of the religious sect.

- OK, I'll get the military on to it.

July

- Bad news Mr President. It appears that most of the business leaders in the USA have bank accounts in Switzerland. They are pretty much opposed to an invasion at this time.

Well, where does that leave us?

- It looks like it's got to be North Korea or North Vietnam.

How do we choose?

- I've got a coin. Heads North Korea, tails North Vietnam. Do you want to toss the coin, Sir?

I think so, don't you? Something this important should not be left to a subordinate.

Brief Pause

- I think it went under the desk, Sir. I'll get down and look for it.

Another Brief Pause

- It's heads, Sir.

Which one was that?

- I think it was North Korea, Sir.

Are you sure?

- I believe so, Sir.

In that case we'd better get started.

- I'll brief the military.

OK, keep me posted. What about the rest of the world?

- Well, there the news is better. As for the Russians, the experts say we need do nothing. Their style of government leads to a great deal of poverty and that in turn leads to bad health and food shortages. They also ship dissenters off to detention camps and kill them by the thousand so I don't think we need to worry about a population explosion any time soon in any of the Communist countries.

Are you sure?

- Pretty sure, Sir. But just in case, the experts have suggested we get them involved in a space race.

What would that involve?

- Well, it would involve developing the technology to launch a man into space. It would be an expensive option, which is why it could be useful since economically, it would certainly stretch the Russians. They would have less to spend on food, health and heating for the masses. They'll end up dropping like flies.

But surely they would quickly realise that, up against the industrial and technological might of the USA, they'd stand no chance.

- Yes, Sir, you're right, which is where we need to be clever and start by giving them a few "wins".

Like what?

- We'll start by letting them launch the first satellite into space.

I'm not sure I like the sound of that, Jack.

- It's OK, Sir. It would have no practical significance.

Why is that? What would it do exactly?

- It would just orbit the Earth a few times making bleeping noises. The only purpose it would serve would be for the prestige and we can live with that. In the meantime, we'll develop a satellite which is actually useful but whatever happens we need to keep them thinking that they can beat us. Then on the final stretch, we'll race ahead.

What's the final stretch?

- That's where we land a man on the moon.

Now I do like the sound of that!

- So can we go ahead, Sir?

Yes, Jack. But going back to the basic issue which is what are we going to do about the rest of the world and population control?

- Well, if we exclude Europe, the other countries are in the main very poor and the life expectancy is not that great. However, to be on the safe side, the military have suggested that we send them simple weapons.

You mean bows and arrows?

- No, not quite that simple. No, you know guns and stuff, but nothing too dangerous. We don't want them to threaten us, but they will be able to do harm to one another.

OK, press ahead with that. Is there anything else?

- Just one final thing. We have a number of experts involved in our various projects and it is becoming increasingly difficult to keep their work a secret. We really need a place where we can get them all together and maintain the secrecy.

Where are they at this moment?

- They're in my spare bedroom, Sir.

What? That's terrible. Doesn't it cause problems?

- Well it has been a bit tricky trying to explain their presence to my wife.

No I didn't mean for you, I meant for them. Surely they need to be moved somewhere else. Do you have any ideas?

- Yes, Sir, it's a disused military installation on the sea bed in the North Atlantic, at the mid-point between Bermuda, Miami and Puerto Rico. It was used for top secret scientific experiments in the Second World War.

What sort of experiments?

- I don't know, Sir, they were top secret.

But it sounds pretty inaccessible. How will we get our people to this site?

- By submarine, Sir. We have plenty of them left over from the war.

OK, go ahead and keep me posted. Is there anything else?

- Well there is one thing, Sir. We really need a name for this plan. We can't keep calling it "the project".

Do you have any ideas?

- No, Sir, not at this time. But I'll give it some thought.
I'll do the same, Jack.

1951

February

Jack, this business with the religious sect in Italy, it's given me an idea.

- If it's to do with putting something in their water supply, I do believe we've already got someone looking at that option.

No, no, it's nothing like that. It's more to do with one of the basic principles of a religion and that's the fact that, in general, the followers do and believe what the leaders tell them.

- That's true, Sir, but that's why the various religions give us a problem, particularly so where contraception is concerned.

I realise that, Jack and that's why I think it will be a good idea to have our own religion.

- Our own religion, Sir?

Yes, why not? As an example of what's possible we could then tell the converts that uncontrolled breeding is wrong. It's so obvious and it should be a much easier sell than banning contraception, which is what this Italian sect does.

- Well, Sir, you may well be right but I'm not sure that it will be easy to just start a religion. I think that most religions, at least those that have any significant numbers of followers, have been around for some time.

I realise that, Jack. That's why I think that the best plan will be to take over an existing religion. That way, most of the work is done.

- That may well be true, Sir, but I can see a few problems with that plan.

Only a few?

- Well OK, there are no doubt many problems but the two that spring immediately to mind are, firstly, how do we take over a church? They're not like companies where their shares are traded on the stock exchange. In fact I can't think of a single case where a religion has been taken over as such. I'm not sure what that would involve. And then there's another more basic problem.

What's that?

- Well the fact that for most if not all religions, their beliefs are ingrained. They form the basis of the organisation. I can't see how we could go in and change them for our own benefit, no matter how honourable our intensions are.

These are valid points but do have a think about it. See if you can come up with something.

- Yes, Sir.

March

- Sir, we've considered the tobacco issue and we think that it would be a good idea to get Hollywood involved.

What, you mean make a promotional film?

- No, Sir, I'm not sure that will do any good. We need something a bit more subtle than that. Also, we need to make sure that no-one in government can be seen to actively promote smoking, just in case the information gets out about just how dangerous it can be.

So what have you got in mind?

- The plan is to recruit actors and actresses to actively promote cigarettes in their films.

Well that doesn't sound very subtle. You can't have them stopping the action mid-scene to do a commercial can you.

- Again, Sir, we will be a bit more subtle than that. We will just get the actors to smoke on screen.

But don't they do that already?

- Yes, but we need to make it happen more often. And we need to make the situation in the film look more attractive to the audience.

And how would we do that?

- Well for example, you can have the hero smoking a cigarette while he's chatting up the girl. When he's successful and gets her into bed, the inference will be that it was down to the fact he smokes.

That sounds a bit ridiculous to me. Do you really think it can work?

- Well that's where Hollywood comes in. They will have to make it all look believable.

OK, but how are we going to sign up these movie stars? We can't have a load of film actors on the government payroll.

- Oh no, Sir, this won't be down to us. It'll be the tobacco companies who do the signing up and make the payments. There won't be any cost to the US government.

Now that's the sort of plan I like, Jack, so let's go ahead. And incidentally, have you come up with a name for our little plan?

- All I've come up with so far is STOP. It stands for Strategy Targeting Over-Population.

Well I can't think of anything better so let's go with that.

July

- Sir, I have given some thought to your idea on religion.

I suppose it's a no go?

- No, Sir, that's not entirely the case.

Don't tell me you've found some takers.

- Well I did put out some feelers and there was some interest but I quickly realised that there's a significant problem that we haven't considered.

What's that?

- Well for this plan to work we need a large membership and that was the main problem since the only potential takers were all small fry. There's no point in taking over a religious bunch with one church and 50 people in the congregation. Even if we try to expand, it's not often the case that a person will convert from one religion to another. No, if the plan is to work, it has to be one of the main religions and let's be realistic, that's not going to happen.

Have you tried the Methodists?

- Well I haven't approached them directly but I can't imagine they would be an option.

No, I guess you're right. So, Jack, where does that leave us?

- There's only one option left to us and on paper it's a solution to all the problems. We need to start our own religion from scratch.

Can we really do that?

- Well we can certainly try. For a start we can make up whatever rules we want, so that immediately makes it an attractive proposition.

But how do we get people to convert to our religion? As you said, people don't often do that, at least not in the numbers that we would need.

- Ah, that's where we also solve another problem. There are a lot of people out there who don't follow a particular religion, at least not in practice. They will be our potential congregation.

You mean the atheists and agnostics?

- More like the complacent ones. Even the agnostics are probably too set in their ways for our purposes.

And how do we come up with a religion that will attract such people?

- We're still working on that, Sir.

I bet you are, Jack. I can't wait to see what you come up with.

1952

April

Jack, I've been hearing about a number of strange things going on in the North Atlantic. Is it anything I need to be concerned about?

- In what respect, Sir.

Well, I hear stories about ships and aeroplanes disappearing in the area. I believe that it's become known as the Bermuda Triangle. Is it something we need to look into?

- Not really, Sir. I already know what's happening.

And exactly what is happening, Jack? I assume it's to do with our secret site for STOP.

- Yes, Sir, it is, and there are several issues. The first is that we need to protect the site from curious sailors and airmen. That means that when someone gets too close we have to take action.

What sort of action?

- We intercept the craft, either in the air or on the water.

And then what happens?

- If they are in a plane than I'm afraid there's nothing to do but to shoot them down. There's no other way. But if it's a ship, we land a boarding party and take over the boat. We do it under the guise of the Customs Service, so they do not feel the need to alert anyone before we have control of the boat, and particularly the radio.

And then what do you do with them.

- We sink the boat and take the people to the STOP base so that there's no trace.

Isn't it getting a bit crowded down there on the sea bed?

- Well no, Sir, we have a steady turnover of such people because we use them to test our various experiments. Needless to say, there is a certain amount of wastage.

You mean they're used as guinea pigs?

- Yes, Sir. We need to test our theories to make sure they have the desired effect.

And by "desired effect" you mean it kills them.

- Not necessarily, Sir, at least not right away. We don't want them dropping like flies. No, we need the effects to be much longer term.

So if the test proves fatal straight away, that would be regarded as a failure?

- Yes, Sir, in the broadest sense, but of course we are in fact adding to the body count in a small way.

Yes, I suppose we are. But how come I've never heard of this "guinea pig" issue before?

- I don't know, Sir. How do you think we test the ideas that we come up with?

I don't know, I guess I never thought about it. But in future Jack, make sure I'm fully briefed on these sorts of matters.

- Yes, Sir.

August

Jack, how is the religion thing coming along? I haven't heard anything from you for a while.

- Well, Sir, things are progressing, albeit slowly. We have decided the basis of the religion and we know what sort of person we need to get the thing off the ground. We just haven't put a name to him yet.

Or "her".

- What do you mean?

You say we haven't put a name to him, but in the name of sex equality it could be a "her".

- I think in terms of equal rights for the sexes you're getting ahead of yourself by several decades, Sir. There are no religions, at least none that I am aware of, that feature a female as the leader. It's going to be a hard enough sell to people as it is without that particular handicap.

OK, I guess you're right but where does that leave us?

- Well, Sir, we have come up with a basis for the religion. We feel that in order to attract a different type of follower we need to bring things up to date and to make it more science based.

Isn't that a bit of a contradiction in terms? You know, science and religion somehow coming together?

- Well by doing that we hope that it will have more credibility with the modern generation and they're the ones we need to attract.

OK, that seems to make sense, but who is going to draw up the principles and lead the organisation?

- We don't have a name yet but we are thinking that a science fiction writer would be the ideal candidate. He, and I do mean he, would have the science background, and hopefully the imagination, to come up with something.

And do we yet have a name for this new religion?

- We haven't settled on anything yet but the working title is Techology. It combines a theological sound with a modern slant.

Well it sounds good to me. Keep me informed of any developments.

- Yes, Sir.

Eisenhower

1953

January

- Good morning, Sir, and welcome to the Oval Office. I have a few things to go through with you.

Anything urgent?

- Well there's currently an on-going project aimed at avoiding the demise of the human race.

So let's start there.

Five minutes later

So where do we stand?

- Well, after your predecessor rejected the male contraceptive pill, the scientists went back to the drawing board and they have now come up with a contraceptive pill for women. The only problem is that the women have to take it every day.

Well at least that's a better option than their first effort. What about the religious group in Italy?

- It's not good news there either. They are more widespread than we thought. In fact, many Americans are members.

So the option of wiping them out with a pre-emptive strike is no longer an option.

- No, Sir, it isn't.

Well they sound a dangerous bunch. See if you can come up with another option.

March

- Mr President, the scientists have come up with an option regarding the religious sect. We said that there are two options for birth control; contraception and homosexuality.

Yes, and my predecessor said go ahead with the contraception idea.

- Well I know he said concentrate on that but I thought it would be a good idea to follow up both ideas just in case and after a lot of work we've come up with a compound which we believe is likely to give a man homosexual tendencies. With any luck it'll be contagious. If it works, the male members of the sect may not be too keen on breeding. We intend to put it into the biscuits and the female contraceptive into the special water that's used by the sect. I know it's a long term plan but if we can stop them breeding, they'll eventually be wiped out.

But I thought you said that the sect does not advocate sex?

- That only applies to the leaders. For the members, the opposite is true. They are positively encouraged to breed like rabbits.

OK, go ahead and keep me posted.

July

- Sir, the peace treaty ending the Korean War has been signed.

And what was the final body count?

- Including civilians, about three and a half million.

Not bad, but what are we going to do next?

- Well, Sir, we can keep some small scale wars ticking over, but I think we need to wait a while until we have another big one.

Yes, you're probably right, but keep an eye out for another anti-commie opportunity. They're the easiest ones to sell to the American public.

- I'll keep on the lookout, Sir.

September

- Sir, regarding Techology, I've got some good news. I believe we've found our man.

Have you indeed. It's about time. Why has it taken so long?

- Well it has proved tricky trying to find the right person. By that I mean someone who, in terms of the knowledge and philosophy, could combine the scientific aspects of the problem with the religious ones. As I've come to realise, that's not a common combination.

So who is it?

- Sir, he would prefer to remain anonymous at this stage. But the important thing to remember is that he is willing to work with us and, more significantly, he has already done a lot of the ground work. It shouldn't take too long before we can be up and running.

So that's good news, but let's not forget what we are trying to do here. We need to get some of our basic aims included in the belief system of this new religion.

- Our man is well aware of that, Sir.

1954

April

Jack, this religious sect in Italy, does it have a name?

- What do you mean, Sir?

I mean exactly what I say, does it have a name? Whenever you mention it, you always refer to them as "the sect". So I wondered if they had a name. Like for instance, The Catholic Church.

- Ah yes, Sir, that's the group that I'm referring to.

And when you said that you would target their water, that was Holy Water that you were referring to was it?

- Yes, Sir, it was.

And the biscuits, can I assume that those are in fact communion wafers?

- Er, yes, Sir.

So when you set in motion a plan to get rid of, and I quote "a religious sect in based in Rome", you actually meant The Catholic Church.

- Well I don't suppose we can actually get rid of all of them.

Of course you can't get rid of all of them! In fact, you can't try and get rid of any of them. I insist that you call off the plan at once. If the Catholic Church finds out what we are trying to do, there'll be hell to pay.

- But what about their opposition to contraception?

We'll manage that problem somehow, but not by trying to wipe out the entire membership of the Catholic Church. Stop the plan right away.

- It may be too late for that, Sir. I believe the first delivery has already taken place.

That had better not be the case, Jack.

31

May

- Sir, regarding the Catholic Church, I have some good news and some bad news.

Get to the point Jack. Did you stop the delivery?

- Well I've stopped the delivery of the water.

And what about the biscuits? Have you stopped the delivery of those?

- Strictly speaking, Sir, no.

So what could possibly be the good news?

- Instead of the biscuits being delivered to Rome they've in fact ended up in down town San Francisco.

Good grief, how did that happen?

- Well the delivery paper work said "The Vatican" and by chance that is the name of a bar in the Castro district of the city. It's a rather unfortunate coincidence or, in the circumstances, should I say it's a lucky mistake.

And what's going to happen to them now?

- I believe that they're being used as bar snacks, Sir.

Well, Jack, it was certainly your lucky mistake. Just make sure you don't try and pull the wool over my eyes again.

- Yes, Sir. But there is an upside to this.

And what would that be?

- Well if we notice a significant increase in the number of homosexuals in the San Francisco area, we'll know the compound works.

OK, Jack, keep me posted.

1955

February

- Sir, we need to have a chat about the French.

Oh dear, what have they done this time, Jack?

- Actually, it's something positive for once since they are actually fighting a war.

You mean Algeria?

- Yes, Sir.

I'm already aware of that and as I understand it, it's a pretty bloody affair.

- It is indeed, Sir, and there's no sign of a settlement. But that's not the main issue. It's the underlying situation that's more interesting.

In what respect?

- Well it's a war for independence.

That I know, Jack.

- Algeria is a French colony and they want to be free from control by the French. France in turn does not want to see an independent Algeria. They feel it will diminish their power and standing in the world.

I thought that had already happened when they slunk out of Vietnam.

- Exactly, so they don't want to be seen to give up too easily this time.

But what's your point?

- My point, Sir, is that there are going to be many situations like this cropping up in the near future.

I didn't realise that the French had that many colonies.

- Well they have a swathe across West Africa but it's not that great compared to the British.

Again, what's your point, Jack?

- My point, Sir, is that we have an opportunity here, not with the

French but instead with the British. The plan would be to encourage them to resist the independence movements in each of their colonies. I'm sure that the resultant conflicts will deliver a decent body count.

Do you think they'll fall for it?

- It's worth a try.

OK, well get onto them and see what they say.

- Yes, Sir.

March

- Sir, I've spoken to the Brits about the independence issue. They don't seem too keen on the conflict option.

Well can't we talk them round?

- No, Sir, I don't think so and in any case we probably don't need to. The Brits have obviously given this some thought.

You mean they've come up with a plan of their own? What are they going to do?

- They're not actually going to do anything, Sir.

Well presumably they are at least going to grant independence to these colonies of theirs.

- Oh yes, when I said they're not going to do anything, I assumed that independence was a given. But beyond that they don't think they need to do anything because they think that the natives will do it themselves, especially if we supply the weapons.

But why should they start killing one another? What reason would there be for one of these newly established countries to wage war against another one?

- Sir, in general this won't be a cross border conflict, instead this will be within a given country. We're talking about civil war.

But what would be the catalyst for that?

- Well the borders of these countries were established by the colonial invaders years ago. They often followed geographic features like rivers and mountains but they had little to do with the ethnic make-up of the local population. Consequently, in most of the countries, and we're mainly talking about Africa here, there is more than one ethnic group. As part of the British Empire, they have a common target in the British, so currently they present a united front. However, once the Brits step down, there's the potential for internal conflict.

But supposing there is no conflict, after all they may all get on like a house on fire.

- That's an appropriate comparison, since if things go according to plan the whole of Africa will be on fire. Mind you, I've never really understood the origin of that phrase. It's supposed to mean that things are going well but I'm not sure that I can see how a house being on fire can be a good thing.

Not unless it's your enemy's house. But then I suppose that if everything goes according to plan, everybody's house will be on fire.

- That's bound to happen since there's little chance of them all getting on with one another. On the off chance that they do co-exist peacefully, I'm sure that we can step in to encourage a little conflict here and there. And there's always the natural wealth of the continent, you know, oil, diamonds and other valuable minerals. I'm sure there will always be something to fight over.

But if we're supplying the weapons, it could be very costly.

- Well we won't be giving them away. We'll be swapping them for something we need like…

Like oil, diamonds and other valuable minerals!

- Exactly, Sir.

Ok, Jack, tell the Brits that we'll go along with their idea. Let's hope we get results.

- Oh, I don't think we'll have a problem with this plan, Sir. I think that this one will run and run.

October

Jack, how is our new religion coming along?

- I think that we're on track, Sir.

I'm sure we are, but on track for what exactly?

- Well as you know the basic religion is up and running, but we lack some of the detail at this stage. But I've been assured that things will be fleshed out very shortly.

Well I hope so.

1956

January

- Sir, we may have come up with something regarding the killing off of people to reduce the population and like all the best plans, it's so simple.

Yes, it's amazing what these scientists can come up with.

- Actually, in this instance it wasn't the scientists, it was Rachael in Accounts Payable.

Good grief, these plans are supposed to be top secret. How did she find out?

- Well, she processed the invoice for the delivery of the water treatment to The Vatican and of course, after the initial problem with the delivery address, I could not authorise the payment and she said she couldn't delay payment without a reason code, as you know it's part of the new system we put in place to control costs, and so....

Oh for goodness sake Jack, never mind the details. What was the idea?

- Well, she said that if you want to kill people, surely the best way is to poison them. And that got me thinking. During the last war, we couldn't produce all the real food we needed so we persuaded the population to eat substitute food.

Like what?

- Well like dried eggs and of course margarine. There wasn't enough butter, so we got the scientists to come up with a substitute.

Yes, I remember trying some once. It looked and tasted awful. It seemed more suited to greasing a squeaking axle.

- Yes, Sir, you are right in that it is more suited to an industrial application but it's been around for a long time. In fact, I believe the French invented it, but recently the scientists have managed to make it more palatable. However, for our purposes that's irrelevant. What's important is that it can be dangerous since most margarine is made from vegetable oil which is liquid at room temperature. In order to make it solid, it needs to be partially hydrogenated and this produces Trans Fats which are dangerous to humans.

That sounds like bad news, Jack.

- Or good news, Sir, depending on where you're coming from.

I guess so, but what else do they put into margarine?

- Well because there are many different recipes it can vary a lot. They could add water so they'll need an emulsifier. As you know, oil and water don't mix too well. Then they'll need a preservative, otherwise it'll go off quickly. Oh, and an anti-oxidant, otherwise there could be cell damage in the human body.

If we're aiming to kill people off, Jack, isn't that what we want?

- Well yes, but we don't want to make it too obvious. That's why we add some vitamins.

Don't the ingredients have any vitamins or minerals?

- Well the vegetable oil had some before it went through an industrial process.

But not afterwards?

- No, certainly not afterwards.

Anything else?

- Well lastly there's flavour and colour. The finished product not only tastes like axle grease it looks like it so they add something like beta-carotene to make it look more palatable.

And what is beta-carotene?

- It comes from a carrot. It's what gives it colour.

But surely carrots are good for you.

- The scientists have that covered. By the time the carrots have been processed to make the colouring there's nothing nutritious left.

But surely people already eat margarine so why do we need to encourage them to eat even more?

- Well some people do eat the stuff, but it's mainly the poorest members of the population. That's because it's usually an issue of cost so the rest of the population are unlikely to choose margarine over butter.

I can understand why.

- Exactly. So our challenge is to persuade the rest of the population to eat the stuff.

OK, it sounds like if we can persuade most people to stop eating butter and start eating margarine, then that would be a start. Get the ad men onto it. However, we need more than just margarine, no matter how dangerous it is. We need a list of other foods.

- I realise that, Sir. I've got a team of scientists on it as we speak.

April

- Sir, there's yet another report from the Brits concerning smoking.

I hope that they've not decided it's good for you after all. Now that we've got Hollywood on side, I hate to think it's all been to no avail.

- No, Sir, quite the reverse. This latest report confirms the original findings in that smoking is definitely bad for your health. The problem we have is that it's yet another survey that's in the public domain. At this rate the lowdown on smoking is bound to get out to the public at large.

Well why are the Brits allowing such research to continue? Can't they stop it?

- Not very easily, Sir, at least not without explaining to a lot of people the reason why. We just have to hope that we can keep the lid on the thing for the time being.

You and me both, Jack. If this gets out, it could be very serious.

June

- Sir, you remember we discussed the option of poisoning the population.

I think I can recall the conversation, Jack. What about it?

- Well it seems that we're already doing it.

What! Someone's beaten us to it? How did that happen? Who's responsible?

- Well there's no cause for alarm, Sir, since we're the ones who are doing it.

What, and then we forgot?

- No, we didn't forget and what's more it's not being done deliberately. It's to do with the new chemicals that we've developed to treat crops. They're the ones that kill off all the insects and diseases. It turns out that most of them, and in particular DDT, are not all that good for one's health.

How long have we known this?

- It first came to light in the 1940's. The chemical has been around for a long time but it only started to be used as an insecticide fairly recently. It didn't take long to realise that it could be dangerous.

So why is it still being used? Is it already part of our grand plan?

- No, Sir, that's not it. Rather it's the fact that it's so effective against mosquitoes and hence malaria. It has been very successful in cutting the number of deaths due to the disease.

Well that doesn't sound like good news does it.

- No, Sir, it doesn't. But it's a bit tricky deciding whether, at least as far as our plans are concerned, DDT is good or bad. So I've got the team looking at the various scenarios. They'll report back soon.

Let me know as soon as they do.

- Yes, Sir.

Ten Minutes Later

- Sir, I've heard back from the team regarding DDT.

What, already? That was quick.

- Well it turned out that it was a no brainer. We need to stop using DDT.

And the logic is?

- Well we know for sure that malaria kills thousands, if not millions of people each year. Those numbers are reducing rapidly as the use of DDT continues. However, in terms of a future body count, the dangerous effects of DDT are unknown. We know that it's dangerous but in terms of our plan, we don't know exactly how dangerous so the preferred option would be to ban it. Also, there are plenty of other chemicals, both existing and in the pipeline, which will be just as dangerous. But we won't use them on mosquitoes so it will be a win-win situation.

And these new chemicals are available now?

- Yes, Sir. One particularly promising group are the organophosphates.

How do we know they will work?

- Because they've been around for a while. They were developed by the Germans as a nerve gas in the last war.

And you think we can spray them onto crops without someone objecting?

- Well I think the nerve gas thing is something we should keep quiet about, Sir.

So we won't be printing "as recommended by Hitler" on the packaging.

- No, Sir, we won't.

October

- Sir, I've been following up on something we covered recently. It's to do with scientific research. If you remember, we discussed the information to do with smoking which has been released by the British.

Ah yes. I asked you why they don't put a stop to it.

- Exactly, Sir, and that got me thinking about whether there is any way we can keep a lid on some of this stuff. We need to monitor what's going on and try to keep it out of the public domain. As of now, by the time we hear about it we're often too late. We need to get involved at a much earlier stage.

Is that possible?

- We think it is, Sir, and it's all to do with money.

What, you mean we're going to bribe the scientists?

- No, Sir, well not exactly. But how do you think most research takes place? Where does the money come from?

I'm not sure. I guess I've never really given it any thought. Research is just something that happens, a bit like breakfast.

- Sir, are you comparing scientific research to breakfast? In what way are they similar?

Well I come down from my bedroom each morning and there it is. Breakfast, all laid out. But it's never occurred to me to wonder how it got there.

- I'm sure if you give it enough time, Sir, you'll be able to work out where your breakfast comes from.

Of course I can work it out, Jack. The point is that until now I've never given it any thought and likewise with research. But now I come to think about it there must be companies who do research.

- Correct.

And government departments I guess.

- Correct again, although the actual research is normally carried out by universities but the funding comes from the government. But this means that we should be able to influence what research is being carried out and to some extent what the results will be.

But how about the companies? How do we influence them?

- I'm not sure that we need to, Sir. If you take heart disease as an example, we could get research carried out that says that baldness is the cause. Whether or not it's true is not the issue. Then it's over to the drug companies who can then do the research into a drug that will cure baldness, and hence reduce the number of heart attacks. Our research is more to do with the theory, theirs is the practical.

Well it all seems a bit of a long shot Jack, but if you think we can pull it off by all means give it a shot.

- Yes, Sir.

1957

January

Jack, I've been giving some thought to that discussion we had about baldness causing heart attacks.

- You do know that baldness was just a hypothetical example don't you?

Well I did at the time but after thinking about it I'm not so sure. After all, people who are bald are normally men who are middle aged or older and they are the ones who also get the most heart attacks.

- Yes, Sir, but one doesn't necessarily cause the other. After all if we got all bald men to wear wigs the number of heart attacks wouldn't reduce would it?

No, I suppose not.

- So in this instance one doesn't cause the other.

Well if you say so, I'll take your word for it.

February

- Sir, the French are not at all happy with the idea of margarine. They say that they'd prefer to stick to butter.

But I thought you said that the French invented it.

- They did, Sir, but that was back in Napoleon's time and he used it to feed his army. These days, the French aren't so keen on it.

And is it just margarine they have a problem with?

- No, Sir, they're not too keen on any of the alternative foods we're coming up with. It could be a big problem.

Well we'll just have to persuade them to fall into line.

- We have had problems with the French in the past but we have always come up with a strategy which has persuaded them to co-operate.

Can we try the same thing this time?

- Not really, Sir, since it normally involves being invaded by Germany.

What, you mean World War 2? I thought that was Hitler's idea,

- Well yes and no, Sir. The point is we cannot do that this time.

Why not?

- Because the Germans are siding with the French, in fact six countries are getting together to form a "common market".

What's that?

- I'm not sure, Sir, but I assume it's where people get together to buy and sell fruit, vegetables and other foods.

But not margarine?

- No, Sir, not margarine.

Well, this is obviously a bit of a setback. I trust the British are still on board.

- Yes, Sir.

And, Jack.

- Yes, Sir?

We need to go back to the issue of World War 2 at some stage. I think you have some explaining to do.

- Yes, Sir, but in the meantime I've given some more thought to your point about baldness and heart disease.

Good grief, Jack, don't tell me you've found a link!

- Well, Sir, I believe that you were the first to mention a link, but no, it's still the case that one does not cause the other. But baldness could be said to be a risk factor for heart disease, even though they are not directly related. I can't help but think that we could put this principal to some use at some stage.

Well it's good to know that I can be of use, Jack.

- I'm sure there was never any doubt about that, Sir.

June

- Sir, we've got something back from our science fiction writer.

I should hope so. This whole process seems to have taken ages.

- Sir, it appears that starting up a religion can be a time consuming process.

Well it has been done before and a darn sight quicker. In fact I believe it was just seven days, and that included one day off.

- If you're referring to the creation of the Earth, I'm not sure that involved religion.

Well whatever the details, it seems to me to have taken a very long time to get to this stage. Just leave a copy for me and I'll take a look at it this evening.

- You don't want me to point you in the direction of a few highlights, Sir?

No, I want to see what it is that we've been waiting for all this time.

- OK, Sir. Let me know how you get on.

I certainly will, Jack.

The Next Day

Jack, I've taken a look at this religious tome of yours.

- How far did you get, Sir?

Page twelve.

- That's further than me then.

But that's because it's impenetrable. I didn't understand a word of it. And in the bit I did manage to read I didn't see anything that seems to reflect our agenda. Where's the mention of butter?

- I'm not sure that we are going to mention butter specifically by name.

And why not? I thought that was the whole point of the exercise. You know: butter is evil and if you eat it you will go to Hell.

- I believe that we need to be a bit more subtle than that, Sir. I'm not sure that we will gain much credibility if we mention butter specifically by name. And as for Hell, I'm not sure whether we've included that in our operating manual yet.

Well if eating butter isn't going to be a mortal sin, then what are we going to mention, specifically.

- I've been assured that all will be revealed in due course. I believe that the chap heading up the organisation has it in mind to attack the medical side of our problem rather than a specific food stuff.

But why's that? Other religions don't seem to have a problem with that approach. There are the Muslims with their pork, the Catholics with their fish, and as for the Jews, where do I start?

- To be fair, regarding the fish I think that only applies to Fridays, Sir.

As if that makes a difference, Jack! The point I'm making is that if we can't ban butter altogether we could at least frown upon it at weekends.

- I take your point, Sir, but just for the moment let's see what else this chap comes up with. And as to the document being difficult to understand, I believe that's the general idea. The plan is that potential converts will have to join the religion and attend centres where the meaning will be explained. That way we can do a thorough job of enlisting them to the cause. In fact initially new recruits won't be told about the ultimate aims of the organisation at all. It'll be like a good novel in that we don't want to reveal the ending. That would spoil the enjoyment of the overall story.

Well that sounds a bit more complicated than I thought it would be. Are we sure this will work?

- Well we can't be absolutely sure, but in this day and age, it was thought that this would be the best approach.

And what about our agenda?

- That I believe will be explained when you attend the induction session.

Well perhaps you could explain to me now.

- I can't really do that, Sir.

And why not?

- Because I haven't attended the induction course yet.

What! You mean that we don't get to find out about our own religion until we've been on the course?

- Something like that, Sir. It appears that this chap is taking it all very seriously.

Well I suggest that you get on this course pretty damn quick.
- Yes, Sir.

1958

January

- Sir, we have a problem with margarine.

I know we have a problem, Jack, after all it is dangerous.

- No, Sir, that's not a problem, that's an opportunity, and it's one which farmers in some States are trying to stop us using.

How are they doing that?

- Well, Sir, it's to do with the colour.

I didn't think that margarine had any colour.

- No, Sir, in its raw form it doesn't, which is where we have a problem. We want to put a dye into the margarine to make it look more palatable, something like butter.

I can see why we would want to do that. When I've seen it, it looks pretty unappetising. I think in the past that you've mentioned using beta-carotene.

- Exactly, Sir. But the dairy farmers are not happy with this approach since they see it as a threat to their livelihood.

Well since our plan is to get people to stop eating butter, they may have a point.

- They will still be able to sell milk, Sir.

Only after it has been processed to remove the goodness, I hope.

- We're still working on that one, Sir, but in the meantime their business will still suffer if the market for butter declines. That's why some states are banning the use of a dye in margarine.

Well what can we do?

- In the long term, we'll have to lean on these States to persuade them to change the law. In the meantime, in the States where dyeing the margarine is illegal, some manufacturers have come up with a novel idea. They are supplying a small amount of yellow dye in a separate container so that the consumer can mix it in with the margarine themselves.

But that's hardly a solution, Jack. After all the margarine on the shelf in the shops still won't look very appealing.

- Yes, Sir, I know. We'll just have to persuade these States to change the law as soon as possible.

February

- Sir, regarding margarine, we have some good news and some not so good news.

Let's have the good news first.

- Well, we have persuaded a number of States to repeal their margarine laws. The producers can now add a dye which will make it more palatable. The bad news is that those States which are resisting have come up with a plan to stop people dyeing their own margarine.

And how have they done that?

- They are insisting that the manufacturers put a dye into the margarine during the production process.

But isn't that what we want them to do?

- That depends on the colour that they use.

And what colour have they chosen?

- Pink, Sir.

Pink! Why would they choose that?

- Well, it's the States that have chosen the colour and the effect will be two fold. Firstly, it looks even less palatable in the shop and secondly, if someone does have the stomach to buy it, they cannot dye it a yellowish colour so that it looks like butter.

That's very clever, Jack. You need to get onto the remaining States and try to convince them of the error of their ways.

- Yes, Sir.

March

- Sir, regarding the Pink Margarine, I may have made a break through with some of the States. They are willing to change the law, but there is one condition.

Oh, and what is that?

- They want the government to take the existing stock of Pink Margarine off their hands. They don't want the problem of getting rid of it.

Well I don't see that as an issue. Go ahead and agree to their demand.

- Yes, Sir.

July

Jack, there you are. I've been quite concerned. Where on Earth have you been?

- I told you, Sir. I went for my induction into Techology.

But that was weeks ago.

- It did take a bit longer than I thought.

But I contacted your family and they said that they hadn't heard from you. Was there a problem?

- There was, Sir. In fact there were several problems.

But you've been away for two months. That's a long induction process.

- I believe that the whole process is a bit longer than that, Sir.

What do you mean by you believe it's a bit longer? Don't you know?

- No, Sir. I didn't finish the course. In fact I rather got the impression that the process would never end.

So were they happy that you dropped out?

- I'm not sure, Sir. My guess is that they will be a bit peeved.

But what did they say when you told them?

- I didn't exactly tell them, Sir. It would have spoilt the escape plan.

Escape plan!

- Yes, Sir. It appears that once you are ensnared it's very difficult to get away.

Good grief, that's worrying.

- Well it is if you don't escape. But for us, that may be a good thing. It means that we should have a low dropout rate.

But did you stay long enough to discover what elements of our agenda have been adopted.

- Er, well I did attend a session where they castigated a particular area of medicine.

Good, what are they targeting? Something juicy I hope.

- Psychiatry, Sir.

Psychiatry! Is that the best they can do?

- Well I can't be sure because I didn't stay until the end. But I'm afraid that may be it.

And what good will that do? I can't see bodies mounting up in the street just because people can't see a shrink.

- That was my first reaction, but there may be some mileage in the situation, especially if we add guns into the mix.

Well it all sounds very unlikely to me. It seems that we've put a lot of effort into this exercise and most of it has been wasted.

- I'm afraid you may be right there, Sir. None the less I think we need to see it through. Perhaps if we find out what happens at the end of the induction process things may become clearer.

I hope that you're not intending to go back there.

- Oh no, Sir. I'll get one of the White House staff to go along.

Make sure it's someone expendable, just in case.

- Yes, Sir.

November

Jack, have you seen the Vice President recently?

- No, Sir, I believe he's on an induction course.

What sort of course?

- The one you suggested I send him on.

You mean you've sent him on the Techology course! I told you to send someone expendable!

- And your point, Sir, is what?

Don't be cheeky, Jack. You know what I mean.

- I wasn't being disrespectful, Sir. With all due respect, the Vice-President is in fact expendable but he's also fairly intelligent and loyal. We had to send someone who was bright enough to understand what was being said and to be able to report back.

Well how long has he been gone?

- Three months, Sir.

Three months! Why didn't I notice?

- Perhaps that's because he's expendable, Sir.

I think that you're confusing expendable with insignificant, Jack. But whatever, when is he due back?

- As I said before, we don't know how long the process takes so we don't know when he will return.

But how have we explained his absence to the press?

- Nobody in the press has noticed his absence yet, Sir.

But they will do eventually.

- Yes, Sir, and at that stage we'll have to go and get him out, but I don't envisage that happening for some time.

December

- Sir, the Vice-President has returned from the Techology course. I've just come out of a debriefing session with him.

Did he finish the course?

- Yes, Sir.

And what did he say? I don't suppose there was any mention of butter, was there?

- No, Sir. I don't think that was ever a realistic expectation. And as far as other items on our agenda are concerned, there's nothing to report there either.

So we just have Psychiatry.

- Yes, Sir.

Not much of a return on our investment is it.

- And there are a couple of other things, Sir. Apparently the course finished some weeks before we got the Vice-President out.

So he didn't come out of his own accord?

- No, Sir. It seems that he was happy to stay.

In which case I suggest that we keep a keen eye on him.

- Yes, Sir.

What's the other thing?

- Well it appears that once you have gone through the whole process you are made aware of the most sacred secret which forms the basis of the religion.

And what is that exactly?

- Aliens, Sir. It's all to do with aliens.

Aliens? Do you mean immigrants?

No, aliens from outer-space.

Good grief, Jack, this is all down to you. It's what you get when you employ a science fiction writer. Is there any upside to all this?

- I haven't come up with anything yet, Sir, but that's not to say that it won't come in useful in the future.

Let's hope so, Jack.

1959

February

- Mr President, Sir, I've got some good news. I think we may have hit the jackpot.

That's what we pay these scientists for.

- Well no, it wasn't the scientists who came up with it.

Good grief, it wasn't Rachael in Accounts Payable, was it.

- No, Sir, it wasn't Rachael. And in any case, she's now in charge of Personnel.

Thank God for that. Who was it?

- It was Rachael's friend Monica. Apparently, they were chatting over coffee.....

This is all supposed to be top secret, Jack. Can't we offer them something to keep quiet about all this?

- Sir, we've already taken care of that. That's why Rachael's now in charge of personnel.

And Monica?

- She's now working at the Pentagon.

Well at least she's out of harm's way. So what was the idea?

- Monica says that it's not enough just to say that margarine is good. No matter what the ad men come up with it's not going to work to the extent that we need it to. We've got to dish the dirt on butter.

OK, so what do you suggest? I suppose we could home in on one of the ingredients. How do they make butter?

- It's made from cream.

Yes, I know that, but what else?

- Well they sometimes add a bit of salt but otherwise that's pretty much it.

What, nothing else?

- No, Sir

What about a preservative?

- No, it doesn't need any, nor does it need an anti-oxidant.

And I suppose you're going to tell me that the colour is natural and it doesn't need added vitamins and minerals.

- That's right, Sir.

My God, these ad men must be good if they can persuade people to eat margarine instead of butter.

- Yes, thankfully they are, Sir.

So what do we do?

- Well since the only ingredient in butter is cream then that's got to be our target.

OK, get the scientists onto it.

- Well it's not really a general science problem. It's more of a medical thing.

Whatever you say, just get someone onto it.

- Yes, Sir.

June

- Sir, I think we've cracked the butter problem

What have you come up with?

- Well since there's only the one ingredient in butter we were not spoilt for choice.

So it's got to be the cream.

- Exactly, Sir. However, the PR people say we can't attack cream as such since it sounds too nice. But in scientific terms cream is actually a saturated fat and so that is how we are going to refer to it in future. And the beauty is that there's saturated fat in a lot of food, so if we dish the dirt on butter it will also give us a lot more targets.

Like what?

- Well milk for instance. If we convince people that saturated fat is bad for them, we could justify taking it out of the milk.

And what good would that do?

- Well most of the vitamins and minerals are in the cream....

Don't you mean in the saturated fat?

- Yes, Sir, sorry, what I meant to say is that most of the goodness is in the saturated fat.

And the taste, surely that has disappeared as well. Don't you end up with something like water?

- Well yes, it is like water in that it tastes like water, but the important thing from our point of view is that it looks like milk. However, the ad men do concede that it will be difficult to get everyone to switch to fat free milk so the scientists have come up with a process called homogenization for those people that still want cream in their milk. You squirt the milk through a series of small holes and it changes the structure of the fat. As a result, we're thinking that it will cause health problems, but you will still have the cream.

Why should it cause health problems?

- Apparently it's to do with the way that the fat is absorbed into the blood stream. The smaller the molecules, the more easily it is absorbed.

That's all well and good but how can we sell it to the public? What's in it for them?

- Well the cream won't separate out and float to the top.

Yes, and?

- That's it.

So where's the benefit to the consumer?

- They won't have to shake the bottle to mix in the cream.

What? All that effort and that's it?

- Yes.

Well if you think you can sell it to the public you're welcome to try. But there are going to be a lot of people who will still want to drink the stuff straight from the cow.

- Yes I know that, Sir, which is why we have one more ace up our sleeve and that's E-Coli.

I don't know what it is but it certainly doesn't sound good.

- No, Sir, it isn't, at least not the version that we are talking about. Most E-Coli are perfectly safe but the one that we are interested in is a nasty bug that can cause illness or even death and you can sometimes find it in milk. So we're going to treat the milk with heat to remove it.

But surely we'd be better off leaving it in there if it's that dangerous.

- In milk, E-Coli doesn't cause that many deaths so for our purposes it is better to remove it, since by heating the milk we will also destroy some of the goodness. In any case, if you get E-Coli, you tend to keel over right away. We need something more subtle and long term. Also, there are many other foods that can contain E-Coli and they are far more likely to kill you.

Like what?

- Like hot dogs, Sir.

I hear what you say Jack, but I don't want you messing with hot dogs. Leave the hot dogs alone.

- At this stage, yes, Sir.

July

- Sir, with all the different groups of scientists engaged in the food aspect of the STOP, we are having trouble keeping tabs on the different overlapping strands.

Well, how many people are we talking about?

- Many hundreds, Sir.

Good grief, are there really that many? How many different teams are there?

- Several dozen, Sir. There's the Margarine team, with a Butter sub-group, Milk, Eggs, Meat and Fish, Carbohydrates, Vegetables and Fruit.....

Yes, yes, I get the picture. But I don't seem to remember hearing anything from the Fruit and Vegetable people yet.

- No, Sir, we don't need to do anything on that front just yet. We've got them covered with the pesticides and insecticides. They're having all sorts of side effects. In fact far from dishing the dirt on vegetables, we may want people to eat more of them. And then there's the water team, with a fluoride sub-group.

What's fluoride got to do with anything? And how has this whole issue caused a problem?

- Well we'll leave fluoride for now but as for the rest, take milk and butter. On the one hand, the milk people were advocating that we take the cream out in order to reduce the nutritional value. But one of the main uses for cream is in the production of butter.

Ah, I see the problem. We are trying to stop people eating butter.

- Exactly. We now have a problem of what to do with all the cream. And that will be one of the first things that this committee can consider.

As I said, Jack, I get the picture. What do you propose we do about it?

- Well, Sir, I think we need to set up a committee to oversee all the different activities so that we don't get our wires crossed.

Ok, Jack. And do we have a name for this group yet?

- Sir, the working title is 'UNC'.

'UNC'?

- Yes, Sir, the Undermine Nutrition Committee.

Well that's an ugly sounding name. How about 'JUNC'? That sounds a bit better.

- Yes, Sir, it does, but what does it stand for?

Jack's Undermine Nutrition Committee!

- Well thank you, Sir, I'm very flattered.

October

Jack, how are we getting on with the different food types?

- Do you have anything particular in mind, Sir?

No, it's just that I haven't heard anything for a while. What have you got for me?

- How about carbohydrates, Sir? We haven't really covered them in any detail yet.

By carbohydrates, Jack, you mean what?

- Things like pasta, sugar, flour and potatoes. They all come under the "carbs" banner.

OK, and what have we come up with? Are they good or bad?

- Well let's take sugar as an example. Too much of it is bad for you.

I don't think I need a team of scientists to come up with that little nugget. Tell me something I don't know.

- How long have you got, Sir?

I'm sorry, Jack? Oh, right, very funny. Just what I need to brighten my day. But can we please get back to the subject of carbohydrates.

- Yes, Sir, of course. Like most basic food stuffs, carbs are all right in moderation. We all need them to keep going, since they provide a lot of our energy. However, we do have great hopes for carbs on several levels.

Like what?

- Well over a period of time the carbohydrates that we eat have been refined so that they contain less goodness.

That sounds like good planning. Which of our guys were responsible for that idea?

- In this case I'm afraid we can't take the credit. This process has been going on for a while. Take flour for example. It used to be a pale brownish colour and it would contain all the bits of the wheat and therefore include all the goodness. Then the millers came up with the plan to take all the rough bits out which would leave just white flour.

But why would they do that? I know it helps our cause but it doesn't sound like the best of ideas.

- Well at the time they really didn't have much of an idea about the nutrients in food stuff so they didn't realise that they were doing any harm.

Yes, but what was the benefit? And surely if you get rid of some of the flour, what is left is going to be more expensive.

- That's correct, Sir. But the benefit to them was that the processed flour would last a lot longer and to some extent this advantage outweighed the increase in cost. I think that it was something to do with the fact that the white flour would last until the next crop of wheat was ready. Anyway, whatever the reason, the millers have done us a favour. Unfortunately, it's not all good news. Some time ago the government realised that the white flour was deficient in many basic nutrients and passed legislation to force bakers to add vitamins and minerals to the flour. Hence the loaves of bread we get to day are somewhat more nutritious that we would like.

When on earth did this take place?

- Before the last War, Sir.

But surely they realised that by doing that they'd be saving many lives. That's hardly helping the cause.

- I think that during the Great Depression the Government had other things to worry about.

Like preventing the complete breakdown of society in the USA.

- Something like that.

But can't we revoke the regulations?

- We could, Sir, but it's difficult to see what excuse we could have. I think we're going to have to leave things as they are for the time being. However, things aren't all bad. The modern loaf contains a lot of extra "goodies" that help to extend the shelf-life of the product.

When you say "goodies", Jack, I assume that there isn't much that's good about them.

- Well I wouldn't say that, Sir. The fact that modern loaf can last for a week or more must be a good thing, surely.

And do all white loaves have these additives?

- Most mass produced loaves do, Sir. At least they do in the USA and I believe the UK. However, in other parts of Europe, and in particular France, things are a bit trickier.

I take that as read Jack. What have they done?

- Well I believe that there, laws exist that dictate what you can put into a loaf, particularly their beloved baguette. They don't allow a lot of the stuff that we do to go into their bread and that means that the shelf-life of a typical French loaf is somewhat shorter than it is in the USA.

So if our loaves last a week or two, how long do theirs last. How short is "shorter".

- I believe it's somewhere between 2 and 4 hours, Sir.

Good Lord, Jack. Is that why, whenever we see pictures of Frenchmen, they're got a baguette under their arm?

- Could be, Sir. I dare say by the time they've got it home it's time to eat it before it goes stale, at which point they have to go and buy another one.

So that could be the reason why they have so little time to work, Jack.

- It certainly could be one of the reasons, Sir. However, let's get back to the point. As far as carbohydrates are concerned, there's nothing we need to do about the production side of things. Flour isn't the only one that's been processed to take the goodness out. And of course, being a crop, there is always the usual assortment of chemicals being added to the mix by the farmers. But we have come up with a few interesting issues about the consumption of carbs.

Like what?

- Like the fact that, in general, the body can digest carbohydrates more quickly than protein, particularly meat. That means that a person eating carbs will get hungrier quicker and would therefore consume at lot more food, or at least they could if it wasn't for one small point.

Which is?

- People don't have enough time to eat all the stuff we'd like to feed to them.

Sorry, Jack, I don't follow you.

- Let's imagine someone has lunch and they fill themselves up with food. If it's mainly carbohydrates, they'll be hungry again by mid to late afternoon. But they won't be having another meal until the evening.

Well I realise that, Jack, since it happens to me. But I can just get out a candy bar. That'll normally see me through until supper.

- That's true, Sir, but we'd like there to be many more food options for people to consume to satisfy their hunger.

Well if you're thinking of increasing the number of coffee breaks people have at work, I'd certainly be in favour of that. That would certainly help them to eat more chow.

- This wouldn't have anything to do with being re-elected would it, Sir? After all, nobody is going to lose votes by advocating a shorter working week. No, don't answer that, it's academic. But without wishing to disappoint you, no we don't intend to increase the number of coffee breaks. In any case, that would only solve the problem at work. We need a solution 24/7.

And what have you come up with.

- The FAST team are working on it as we speak, Sir.

FAST?

Yes, it stands for...

No, Jack, don't tell me. Let me see if I can guess. F has got to be "food". Correct?

Yes, Sir.

And "S" is often "strategy" or "strategic".

Correct again.

So it's "Food" something "Strategy" something. No, I give up.

"Food Access Strategy Taskforce", Sir.

Of course. Let me know when they've come up with some ideas for FAST food.

- Of course, Sir.

1960

March

- Mr President, we have a situation. The contraceptive pill option is not going to work.

But I thought that we'd tested it.

- No I don't mean that it doesn't work as a contraceptive, instead I mean that it won't solve the problem of over-population. The experts think that people will still have the choice as to whether they have children and the population will continue to grow too fast. And of course there will be many people in the Third World who won't have access to the Pill. All things considered we need to come up with another solution.

So what are the options?

- Well if we can't stop people breeding we'll have to find even more ways to kill them off.

What? You mean hit squads in our cities? I don't think I could approve of that, after all I'm up for re-election next year. Perhaps when I'm serving my second term we can revisit that idea.

- No, Sir, not hit squads. We need to come up with something more subtle. I'll get the scientists to come up with something.

Ok, but keep the hit squad idea as a back-up. In the meantime, why don't you have a word with the Chinese. They seem to be killing off their population by the millions.

- Yes, I know, Sir. It's called the "Great Leap Forward". Initially I thought that they had come up with a stroke of genius, but it turns out that it's due to something we probably can't implement in the USA.

Why's that?

- Because it's Communism that's doing the damage.

That's no surprise. Their ideas on collective farming and state control of industry were never going to work.

- Well, you're right there, Sir. Agricultural output has dropped, but that's not the main problem.

What is, then?

- Fear, Sir.

Fear? How does that work? Do they frighten people to death?

- Not exactly, Sir. From what I can gather, in order to cover their backs, the various levels in the Party hierarchy have been falsifying the figures so it appears that production is increasing. They are afraid that they will be sacked if production falls. The leaders think productivity is increasing and are therefore taking more of the food from the farmers for their own consumption and for export. The farmers are not left with enough to eat. They are starving to death in droves.

So, this "Great Leap Forward", it's not some sort of clever plan after all.

- No, Sir, I think it's just fear and incompetence.

Well I'm sure our government could be just as incompetent, if we tried.

- I think that a plan to control population of the USA by having millions of people starve to death somewhat lacks the subtlety that we require.

So it's a non-starter?

- I think so, Sir, don't you?

Yes, I guess you're right. Is there anything else?

- There is one other problem, Sir. It's the secret base in the North Atlantic. We've outgrown the available space and in any case it's a bugger to get to.

So what do you suggest?

- Sir, we need a dedicated site in a remote location, one that's big enough to house many hundreds of staff, even thousands in the future. The military has come up with 60 possible locations. Here's the list.

Well, I can't look through all 60. Which one looks the most

promising?

- Site number 51, Sir. It's in Lincoln County, Nevada.

Later that month

- Sir, the Brits have a bit of a problem with the idea of removing most of the goodness from milk. Apparently, that's going to include getting rid of the calcium.

And what is wrong with that?

- Well calcium is good for your teeth and bones and the Brits are concerned because they think that the population is going to get more tooth decay.

They're probably right but why is that a problem? If people's teeth fall out they won't be able to eat. From our point of view, that can only be a good thing, surely. Why are they concerned?

- It's because dental treatment in the UK is free, Sir.

What? Are you saying people in the UK don't have to pay for dental treatment? I suppose if they need a filling they just walk in off the street!

- No, Sir, I do believe they have to make an appointment. And of course it's not free in the long term since it's paid for through taxes. But that means that more tooth decay means more dental treatment: more dental treatment, higher taxes.

What do they want me to do about it?

- Well, Sir, there are a small number of private dentists in the UK. I've suggested to the UK government that they start increasing the waiting time before you can get an appointment for free dental treatment. People can either wait or pay to have the treatment carried out privately.

How did they take that suggestion?

- They were very keen; in fact they may extend the principle to the whole National Health Service.

What's a National Health Service?

- It's where everyone gets free medical treatment.

!!

May

- Sir, the British want something in return for the deal on milk. They want to win the World Cup.

I didn't realise they played baseball.

- No, Sir, not The World Series, I'm talking about The World Cup.

What's the difference?

- Well, Sir, the World Series is for baseball and, despite its name, is contested by teams from just two countries, the USA and Canada. The World Cup is for football and is contested by most of the countries in the world, hence its name.

Canada? I didn't know that they had a baseball team.

- I only mentioned Canada because I thought that a World Series involving just one country sounded a bit ridiculous. They don't have a team just now but they could have.

Really? I didn't know that. Anyway, the World Cup is for football you say, so don't we always win? After all we do have some very good football players.

- No, not American football, Sir. It's what the rest of the world calls football. We call it soccer.

What's the difference?

- Well, Sir, in what everyone else calls football the player uses his feet, hence the name, whereas in American football, the player does not use his feet. The ball is passed from player to player with the hands.

Then why is it called football?

- Not sure, Sir.

Well, don't the British play American football?

- They play a similar game called rugby.

How is it similar?

- Well you score with a touch down.

Isn't that the same as American football?

- Not exactly, Sir. In rugby you have to actually touch the ball down on the ground in order to score, whereas in American football, a touchdown involves not touching the ball down.

So why is it called a touchdown?

- Er, I don't know that either. But I do think we're getting off the point, Sir. The Brits want to win the soccer World Cup.

Well let's give them what they want.

- That may not be easy, Sir. First they have to win through the qualifying rounds to get to the finals. We can't fix all the games.

Is there no way we can at least fast track them to the finals?

- Well the country which hosts the tournament gets to qualify automatically, so perhaps that's the solution. We'll fix it so that the British host the next World Cup.

Sounds good, get onto it as soon as possible.

- Yes, Sir.

June

- Sir, it's about the soccer World Cup. The next one is in 1962 but the host country for that has already been decided. So it looks like the British will have to wait until 1966.

And is there a problem with that?

- Well the British were hoping for something a bit sooner.

Well they'll just have to wait. And while you're here Jack, I've been giving some thought to the discussion we had about coffee breaks.

- I dare say you have, Sir. And the closer we get to the election the more thoughts you'll no doubt be having. However I feel that you're destined to be disappointed, Sir. We may have come up with a solution to our little problem.

You mean FAST food? Oh dear, I was afraid that would happen. This had better be good.

- I think so, Sir. The conclusion we came to was that we need to come up with a plan which will enable people to eat all the time, no matter what they are doing.

What, you mean a sort of plate that you hang round your neck?

- Believe it or not, Sir, I don't think we actually considered that option. No, the whole point of the solution that we have come up with is that people need to be able to eat food without the need for a plate or come to that, a knife and fork. The whole "meal" needs to be self-contained.

Like a candy bar.

- Exactly so, Sir, like a candy bar. Also, the main wrapping we use must also ideally be edible.

I'm sorry, Jack. Are you expecting people to eat paper? I'm not sure we can swing that.

- No, no, Sir. We're not coming up with anything radical here. These sorts of things already exist. For example, imagine a hot dog.

Does it have mustard on it?

- If it helps, Sir.

And onions?

- Sir, if it helps to move this conversation on, it can have a dollop of ice cream on top.

What flavour?

- Sir!

Sorry, I'm just joshing with you Jack. Carry on.

- Thank you, Sir. Well as I was saying, if you take the hot dog as an example, the meat is in the sausage and the carb is the bun which is the wrapping that enables you to hold and eat it the meat content. And you can eat it on the move. The same applies to a burger and of course a slice of pizza.

These are all hot items, Jack. Where's the cold version.

- Have you ever heard of a sandwich, Sir?

Sorry, Jack, of course I have.

- And in that case we think they can be sold from vending machines.

Won't they go stale?

- Not if they're made from white bread, Sir.

Of course, Jack, silly me. Well I have to say you seem to have all the angles covered.

- There's more. Most of these items will contain processed food, particularly meat. It'll give us carte-blanch when it comes to the sort of stuff we can add to the mix. It'll be a better option than the processed foods that are sold in the shops which have to have labels detailing the contents. When you buy a hot dog there's no such requirement.

Yes, Jack, you're right. I sometimes wonder what's in my hot dog. Is there any way to find out?

- I dare say I could ask on your behalf but I think it's better that you remain ignorant, Sir.

I dare say. So to summarise, everything's a win/win.

- Well not necessarily.

Why? Who's the potential loser?

- Er, that could be you, Sir.

Me! Apart from me finding out what goes into my hot dog, how can there be a downside?

- It's to do with coffee breaks, Sir.

I've already accepted the fact that we aren't going to be able to increase their number.

- Yes, Sir, but how about if we hatch a plan to decrease them?

Decrease them? Why would we want to do that?

- Well it's not exactly the coffee breaks that we want to target. It's meal breaks in general.

Do you mean that you want to mess with my lunch break?

- Sir, you don't have a lunch break.

Yes I know that, but if I wanted one I'd like to think that I could.

- Well I'm sure that our plans won't affect you personally but it is important for our overall plan. We've covered the meals that people will have at home but there are a significant number of them who eat at work, in the company restaurant. We need to stop that since those sorts of meals could be quite nutritious. And of course that's where our long life pre-packed sandwiches come in.

And will the companies play ball?

- It'll mean more time spent working, Sir, so what do you think.

But surely this'll only work in an office situation. I can't see the workers in a factory putting up with it, especially the unions.

- There I suspect you're right but it's better than nothing and bear in mind it's the middle classes we want to hit. The working classes already eat a crap diet.

Fair point, Jack, but let's make sure we don't start implementing this plan for a few months.

- That'll be after your second term has finished, Sir.

So it is, Jack.

Kennedy

1961

January

- Good morning, Sir, welcome to the Oval Office. I have a few things to go through with you.

Sorry, but I have a very important meeting with an actress which cannot be changed. Can it wait until tomorrow?

- Yes, I dare say it can, Sir.

The Following Day

So what have you got for me?

- Well, there's the special project called STOP.

Well let's start there.

February

Jack, I've been thinking about STOP and just in case we do not come up with a solution, I think that we need to have a contingency plan. In your briefing you said that we have two options; stop breeding or kill people off. There is a third option and that is to get more living space.

- You mean invade Poland? I think someone tried that once and it didn't turn out too well for them.

No, I don't mean just for us, I mean for all mankind, in other words another planet. We need to accelerate the investment in space travel and start by going to the Moon.

Your timing may be spot on, Sir, since I believe the Russians are about to launch a man into space.

Really? I'm not sure I'm happy about that. You said that we'd let them have a few little wins but I think that launching the first man into space is a bit more than that. Let's get things moving.

- I'll get the military onto it.

OK, keep me posted. And while you're about it, ask them about the war option.

- Yes, Sir.

March

- Mr President, I've been on to a number of aerospace companies and they say it is possible to get a man to the moon by the end of the decade. But it's going to cost a lot of money.

That's OK, this matter is very important so we need to give them whatever they want. In the meantime, I'll announce it to the nation; it'll give them something to think about. And, Jack, on a different subject, how are the Chinese doing with their "Great Leap Forward".

- I'm afraid it's come to a grinding halt, Sir. Apparently people began to realise that millions were dying.

I'm surprised it took them so long to notice.

- Well, China is a large country and communications are not that good. The press is controlled by the state, which means that the government can censor bad news.

It's a pity we can't do that here!

- We have tried, Sir, but without much success.

So the Chinese have abandoned their operation to kill off people by starvation.

- For the time being, but I suspect they'll come up with another equally productive plan to reduce their population.

And what about the war option. Have the military come up with anything?

- Well, Sir, as we've discussed before, the easiest targets are Communist regimes in far off places.

Like Korea.

- Exactly, and the best option at this stage is North Vietnam. It's almost a carbon copy of the Korean situation, you know, a country divided by conflict, the Communists in the North and our allies in the South. And what's more, it's a very long way from here.

So what do we do?

- Well the plan started some time ago and the two countries are already in conflict but it's probably too early for the USA to get involved. These things take time.

So what do we do in the meantime?

- Well, Sir, there's the possibility of a little war on our own door step.

Where?

- Cuba, Sir.

That's a bit close to home. What if it all goes wrong?

- According to the CIA that's not likely, Sir. And there is a bonus in that our side will be made up of Cuban exiles, so no American blood will be spilt. What's more, when it's a success we'll get rid of an embarrassment. It's not good for our reputation to have a communist state so close to our border.

Good point, Jack. OK, if you think it's feasible let's go ahead with that, but keep the Vietnam option under review.

- Yes, Sir.

April

Jack, that little excursion into Cuba seems to have turned into a fiasco.

- I must admit that there aren't many positives to be had from the experience.

I'm having trouble finding anything positive, although I suppose that the fact that there have been no American casualties is some consolation.

- Well that's not strictly true, Sir. There were a few losses I'm afraid, mainly pilots.

But I thought that we weren't supposed to be directly involved in the invasion and that all the manpower was going to be supplied by the Cuban exiles.

- That was the plan and the exiles provided most of the manpower on the ground but when it comes to air power, it proved a bit difficult to find the necessary experience. In any case, we didn't particularly fancy the idea of giving a fighter aircraft to any old Cuban exile. The body count is also a bit disappointing, although it's difficult to assess the enemy's losses. After all, their record keeping isn't particularly good.

Jack, in the scheme of things, the body count is irrelevant. We've been made to look ridiculous and the only thing we seem to have achieved is that Castro is even more popular. We need to learn a serious lesson from this whole sorry business.

- I'm sure that there are quite a few lessons to learn, Sir. Did you have anything in particular in mind?

Yes. Next time we want to start a war we'll do it ourselves and not rely on someone else to do the dirty work. And as for the CIA...

- Sir, they seem to be keeping a very low profile just now.

I bet they are, Jack.

October

- Sir, we've been discussing the FAST food options with the British.

I take it that they're keen.

- Oh yes, in fact they've added a few things to the list.

Like what?

- Like a doner kebab.

Well I know what a kebab is. What's so special about this one?

- I believe it's of Turkish origin. It's basically hot sliced meat with a few bits of greenery wrapped in pitta bread.

What sort of meat?

- Ah there's where it starts to get interesting. Or should I say alarming. The "meat" is a large sausage...

Like a hot dog?

- Oh no, Sir. It's a slab of meat perhaps two feet high by a foot wide. It rotates on a spit while it cooks. The cooked meat is carved from the slab as required.

Don't they have to wait until it's cooked through?

- Apparently not, Sir. Since the outside cooks first, this part can be used while the inside is still raw.

Isn't there a hygiene problem? I mean they could be selling raw meat.

- Well I don't think it will be completely raw and in any case it's not all meat. There are other ingredients.

But what proportion of it is meat?

- We believe that it's no more than about 10%.

And the rest?

- Ah, now that's where it got a bit tricky.

You mean it's like a hot dog and the recipe is a secret.

- Not exactly. Someone somewhere knows what goes into a hot dog but it appears that nobody knows what goes into the meat that's used in a doner kebab, or at least nobody is prepared to own up.

Amazing! So the doner kebab sounds very promising.

- And it'll be even more so if we can get the Brits to leave out the salad bits.

Have a word with them about that. And what else have the Brits come up with?

- Just one other thing before we move on. Most of the doner kebabs in the UK are sold from mobile premises.

You mean like a hot dog stall?

- No, from a motorised vehicle like a van. I assume it's so that they can travel around and attract more customers.

I dare say you're right but check with the Brits to make sure.

- Yes, Sir.

What else is there?

- Well of course there's fish with French fries, or as the Brits would say, fish and chips.

But don't they eat that at a table as a proper meal?

- Yes, Sir, they do, but it can also be consumed on the hoof, so to speak.

Isn't that a bit messy?

- You'd have thought so, Sir, especially when they add something called "mushy peas". It was the British Ambassador who briefed me on the matter. When I cast doubt on the whole process he gave me a demonstration and judging by the state of his shirt at the end it can get very messy, take it from me. I'll spare you the details. But the whole thing does go against our design specification which says that you should be able to eat FAST food with one hand.

I know that I should be able to work this out for myself but why the one handed rule?

- That's so that the other hand is there to hold the can of soda.

Of course it is, sorry. But returning to the subject, you're saying that these fish and chips, they're not wrapped up in something edible.

- I believe that the fish is covered in batter but the meal as a whole is wrapped up in newspaper.

Newspaper? But surely the Brits don't eat the paper.

- I don't believe so, Sir, at least not deliberately.

Let's be thankful for that small mercy. Anything else?

- There is a variation on the fish and chips. It's pie and chips.

What sort of pie?

- Steak and kidney, chicken and mushroom, that sort of thing.

And do they have them with or without mushy peas?

- Without, I believe, Sir.

So it won't be so messy to eat.

- That depends, Sir.

On what?

- On whether they add gravy, Sir.

Hang on Jack. You're telling me that these people eat this stuff out of newspaper and yet they put gravy on it.

- Yes, Sir, that's what I'm told.

Well I think I've heard enough of this. Let's move on. What about the rest of Europe?

- Well there are a few other countries, like Germany and Belgium, which have embraced the doner kebab. And of course the Italians have their pizza.

And what do the French have up their sleeve?

- I'm not sure yet, but knowing the French and their food, it's bound to be something special.

November

- Sir, I've done a bit of digging regarding the French and their hot dog/burger/sandwich options.

And what have you come up with?

- Just one item. It's called a croque monsieur. It's a type of sandwich.

Ah, now that sounds promising. I assume that they could sell them in vending machines if necessary.

- No really, Sir. They're made of ham and cheese and they're toasted so they'll be hot. Not suitable for vending machines I'm afraid.

I suppose at least you can eat them on the move, a bit like hot dogs.

- You would have thought so but here the French have a little trick up their sleeve. It appears that as a finishing touch the French put a sauce on top of the sandwich.

Bloody hell, Jack! Do those people put sauce on everything? Next you'll be telling me that they put sauce on their cornflakes.

- I'm not sure that they eat cornflakes, Sir.

So what do they have for breakfast? Bacon? Pancakes? Waffles?

- None of those, Sir, just croissants, which are a type of bread.

And do they put sauce on their croissants?

- As far as I am aware, Sir, no.

If that's all they eat for breakfast then no wonder they can manage a four course lunch. But back to this toasted sandwich, what sort of sauce do they put on top?

- I'm not sure that the type of sauce is relevant, Sir.

Well it may be if it improves the flavour. I may even be tempted to try one!

- In that case, I believe it's called a Béchamel sauce, Sir.

And what tasty little tit-bits do the French put in a Béchamel sauce, Jack?

- Mainly flour and milk, Sir.

Flour and milk! What's the point of that?

- Well presumably it does nothing for the flavour of the toasted sandwich but it does mean that it has to be eaten off of a plate with a knife and fork.

And no doubt washed down with a nice glass of Claret I suppose.

- More likely a vin ordinaire, Sir, but you get the general idea.

So have they added the sauce so as to make this croque monsieur difficult to eat on the move? Are the French being deliberately difficult?

- It wouldn't be the first time, Sir. In this particular case it does seem that they're deliberately trying to stop people snacking on FAST food.

I think that you need to have another word with them, Jack.

- Yes, Sir.

Later

- Sir, I have spoken to the French ambassador.

This is about FAST food?

- Yes, Sir.

And how did you get on?

- Well it was as if I was talking a foreign language.

And what language were you talking, Jack.

- English of course.

You are silly, Jack. To him English is a foreign language. Are you sure he understood?

- Well of course to start with he made out he couldn't understand a word of English but he couldn't keep it up for long. Not after I pointed out to him that it is a requirement of the job that foreign ambassadors to the USA speak English. No, this wasn't a language issue.

What was it then?

- More of a cultural thing. I started to explain the principle of snacking when you get hungry between meals. He had difficulty understanding this concept. He couldn't see how someone who has a four course lunch plus wine and coffee could possibly be hungry before dinner time.

Good lord, Jack. It would take two to three hours to eat a four course lunch with drinks. How long are their lunch breaks?

- Two to three hours, Sir.

Well that's the basic problem. Until we can persuade the French to take shorter lunch breaks, FAST food is going to be irrelevant to them.

- I agree, Sir, but I did get one concession out of him. The French are prepared to come up with a simpler version of the croque monsieur. That will be one that does not have a dollop of sauce on top. It's not a lot but as far as the French are concerned it's the best we can achieve at this stage.

1962

February

- Sir, we have a bit of a problem.

Have you asked Rachael or Monica for their advice?

- No, Sir, do you want me to?

It was just a joke, Jack. Now what's the problem?

- Well, Sir, we have moved the team of experts to Area 51 but the whole exercise has created a lot of interest locally. People are turning up to take a look at what we are doing.

Well they can't get in can they? I saw the plans and there's a high security fence around the site.

- That's to keep the experts in, not the locals out. Some of our workers are not too happy about being confined to the site for years on end in the middle of nowhere.

Well why did they volunteer in the first place?

- Sir, you'll need to define what you mean by "volunteer".

What do you think I mean?

- Well most of them "volunteered" to go on an all-expenses paid vacation to a new Disney resort in the Nevada desert. By the time they had unpacked and put their Bermuda shorts on, it was too late to change their minds. That's why we need the fence.

But don't they have their families with them?

- No, Sir, and for most of them, to get away from their families was the attraction. In fact, the longer they'd been married and the more children they have, the keener they seemed to be. And from our point of view, they were the people we wanted. We didn't want them pining for their loved ones.

OK, so what's the problem?

- We need to mislead the local population into thinking that something else is going on at Area 51, something that is nothing to do with STOP.

Presumably you've got something in mind.

- Yes, Sir. In fact the locals gave us the idea. The flights carrying the experts into Area 51 take place at night and the locals have been curious as to what's been going on. One chap with a vivid imagination thinks it's something to do with an alien space craft.

Why would he believe that?

- He thinks it's something to do with an unidentified flying object that came down near Roswell, New Mexico. His idea is that the whole south west corner of the USA is of interest to aliens and that the US military has built the base at Area 51 to counter any invasion from outer space.

Are you telling me there was a genuine UFO in New Mexico?

- Oh no, Sir, it wasn't genuine, it was just a spy balloon. But a combination of a vivid imagination by some members of the public and inconsistent information from the military has led some people to believe that there actually was an alien spacecraft of some sort.

But how does that help us?

- We will encourage people to think exactly that.

But without further sightings of alien spacecraft, they'll start to suspect something.

- Then we'll just have to simulate something.

OK, go ahead. Is there anything else?

- Yes, Sir, there is. You already know that we've come up with the plan to promote the idea that saturated fat is bad. That will give us the opportunity to promote our "healthy" alternatives.

What? You mean things like margarine?

- Yes, Sir, but what we've done is come up with something physiological that can show the average person how unhealthy saturated fat can be.

What do you mean?

- Saturated fat has to be seen to have some measurable effect on the body. It's got to affect something that everyone has.

What? Like blood?

- No, Sir, not something quite as basic as that.

So skin's not an option either.

- Yes, not skin, and before you ask not bone either, Sir. No, what we've come up with something called cholesterol.

I've never heard of it.

- Exactly, Sir, and outside of the medical profession not many people have. That's what makes it useful.

Well what does it do?

- It's a substance that can be found in every cell in the human body; it's part of the body's immune system in that it's used in the healing process; it's needed to produce hormones and a whole lot more.

It sounds like pretty important stuff.

- Yes, it is, Sir. In which case, what do you think would happen if we tried to get rid of it.

What, all of it!

- Well, no, Sir, not all of it. But we could try to lower the levels of cholesterol in the body.

I'm not sure what would happen, Jack, but it can't be good.

- No, Sir, I don't think it will be. You see the body produces all the cholesterol it needs to stay healthy. It's a function of the liver.

So you can't eat it.

- Well, in fact you can. Various food items, like eggs, contain some but if you consume cholesterol, the body will need to make less so the balance is maintained.

So, the more cholesterol in my body, the better.

- It's not quite as simple as that, Sir. The body produces what it needs. If it's producing a lot, it may be because it needs it to fight infection or repair cell damage. Also, as you get older, your cholesterol level tends to go up.

You mean as things start to fall apart.

- Put crudely, yes, Sir. The body will need more cholesterol in order to stay healthy.

Well it sounds promising but we are going to need some "science" to back it up. Anything else?

- Well, how would you like an omelette made with just egg whites, Sir?

It sounds horrible, but aren't we getting off the point.

- No, not really. I mentioned that eggs contain cholesterol. We can try to put people off eating them by using cholesterol as the reason.

But didn't you say that eating the stuff does not increase your body's cholesterol levels?

- Yes, Sir, but the public don't need to know that. Just as they don't need to know that eating saturated fat doesn't affect cholesterol levels. In fact, by eating saturated fat you are likely to be healthier, so it may actually lower them. A healthy body won't need so much.

And why do we need to stop people eating eggs?

- Because they are just about the most nutritious food you can eat. If you think about it, everything a little chick needs to develop from an embryo is inside the shell of an egg. In some respects, it's more remarkable than the development of a human baby. There, the baby grows inside the body and can get all the nutrients it needs from the mother. The chick doesn't have that luxury.

OK, Jack, I'm convinced, but where does the omelette made with egg white come in?

- Well, most of the goodness is in the yolk, so for those people that can't give up eggs completely, we could suggest that they just eat the white bit. Monica said it would be a good idea if the scientists could come up with an example, such as an omelette made without the yolk, just to see if it's possible.

Why an omelette?

- Well, a boiled, fried or poached egg without the yolk is definitely a non-starter, so an omelette is all we have left.

How can you be sure?

- Well, following our success with margarine, we looked for other food stuffs that were used in the War and powdered egg was the next option.

And?

- And nothing, Sir. We're not sure what it was used for in the War. You cannot make a boiled, fried or poached egg with powdered egg, nor even an omelette.

Are you sure?

- Oh yes, Sir, believe me we tried. We can only assume it was used for cooking, you know, cakes and things. So we have had some experience with the options for cooking with eggs which weren't real eggs.

- So where do we stand with the omelette made with just egg white?

Well, we have a version ready for you to sample.

- What, now?

Yes, Sir.

- OK let's try it.

A Few Moments Later

Ugh, that's awful. What does everyone else think of it?

- We haven't found anyone else prepared to try it yet, Sir.

Really! Very funny. Tell me, Jack, do you discuss everything with Monica before I hear about it.

- What do you mean, Sir?

She came up with the omelette thing, so you must have discussed eggs with her before telling me.

- Yes, Sir.

When was this?

- At the coffee morning that she has once a week.

And who attends this coffee morning.

- Oh, just the regular crowd, Sir.

You mean Monica and Rachael.

- Yes, Sir, how did you guess?

Well it wasn't that difficult was it?

- No, Sir, I suppose it wasn't.

Is there anything else Jack?

- Yes, Sir, on a different matter, the European "common market" seems to be a bit more significant than we thought.

You mean that it's a bit more than a few fruit and vegetable stalls.

- Yes, Sir, it appears to be much bigger than that. It seems that it now involves the trade between nations and ultimately their political links.

Well that seems pretty significant. Do we have any details about their intentions?

- No, Sir, not yet. The participating countries are all pretty tight lipped about their long term aims.

Well, what can we do?

- One option would be to get the British involved. They have already expressed concern that they may be missing out on something. If we can get them admitted to the Common Market, it's just possible that they could get information from the inside and report back to us.

That seems a good idea. Tell the British to go ahead and apply for membership.

May

- Sir, we have another issue to do with fat.

What is it this time, Jack? I thought we had it covered.

- Well we have, Sir, when it comes to the fat we eat. But we have discovered that there is also an issue to do with the fat in the body. Well not so much "in" as "on". We've discovered that fat people live longer that thin people.

Well, that's no surprise surely. Fat people have more "food" stored in the body so I could imagine that it would make them healthier. And they must be warmer, with all that in-built insulation.

- Well, Sir, I'm not sure it's as simple as that. All we know is that the fatter you are, the less you suffer from diseases such as cancer, heart disease, infections, diabetes, the list goes on. It's just that we're not sure why. Of course you can be too fat and then you start to put a strain on the body.

Well, we'd better get the experts on it and find out what's going on.

- I don't think we need to do that, Sir. We don't have to know why at this stage fat people are healthier, just the fact that they are.

So what are we going to do with this information?

- Well, Sir, what we need to do is persuade people that fat, i.e. body fat, is bad, and then we need to encourage them to get thin.

That may not be easy. Fatter people have always appeared to be attractive, especially women. Look at the old paintings by artists such as Rubens. The women are always voluptuous.

- Yes, Sir, I know. And it's continued on to this day with actresses such as Sophia Loren. And just look at Marilyn Monroe. Can you imagine what she looks like in the flesh?

I don't have to imagine, Jack!

- Sorry, Sir. You don't have to what?

Never mind.

- Anyway, Sir, you yourself admire such curvy women and you're not the only one. That makes them role models for people.

So how are we going to get the population to come round to the idea that "thin" is better?

- I'm not sure yet, Sir, but we're going to need a plan of some sort.

Perhaps Monica and her friends can come up with something.

- I've already arranged a meeting with them this afternoon.

Let me know how things go.

- Yes, Sir

July

- Sir, I've spoken to Monica's group about our plan to make "thin" appealing and we quickly realised that we have to attack the problem using the fashion industry. We have to make it look as though thin people are more attractive than fat people. However, it looks like we're going to have to get the British involved.

Why the Brits? Surely they are the last people on Earth that we should be talking to about fashion.

- Yes, Sir, that was my reaction but they got wind of the idea and they think that they can come up with something. They want to link it to popular culture, particularly pop music. They reckon that if we can get the youngsters to hear our message about "thin" being good, we can get them hooked while they're young. As we've discussed before, the younger they are when we try to make them ill, the better it is all round. Of course the best result would be to kill them off before they start breeding.

But do the British have their own pop music?

- I believe so, Sir. For example, they have someone called Cliff Richards who I believe is a cross between Elvis Presley and Billy Graham.

Good grief, that's hard to imagine.

- Yes, Sir, it is. And what's more he's the most popular pop singer in the UK. That's why it's been difficult for any British pop music to become popular in the USA.

OK, get onto the Brits and see what they come up with. But I have to say it's hard to imagine the Brits leading the world in fashion and pop music.

- It is indeed, Sir.

Is there anything else Jack?

- Yes, Sir, there is. The scientists at Area 51 have been trying to come up with a plan to use up the stock of Pink Margarine.

Haven't they got better things to do with their time? I assumed that we just put it in a cupboard and forgot about it.

- I don't think that it will fit in a cupboard.

Why, how much is there?

- About ten thousand tons.

Good Grief, Jack, ten thousand tons! What are we going to do with it all?

- Well, Sir, the basic problem is the colour. We've got to use it to make something that looks nice to eat even though it's pink. Tell me, Sir, what would you think is the most common pink coloured food?

I guess something strawberry flavoured, like ice cream.

- Yes, that's what the experts have said. So they are trying to turn the margarine into ice cream.

I can't imagine that's an easy task.

- No, Sir, it's proving to be a bit tricky. They have been working on the problem for some time but at last they have come up with a prototype. I have a sample here in this large tub marked "Luxury Strawberry Flavour Ice Cream".

So it's got strawberries in it.

- Oh no, Sir. We tried that and the result was a terrible mess. It seems that mixing real fruit with something like margarine, which is a man-made substance, just doesn't work. We had to find a man-made flavour.

But the label says "Strawberry Flavour".

- Yes, "Flavour" not "Flavoured". There is a subtle difference.

Too subtle for me, obviously. What's the difference?

- Well "Strawberry Flavoured" means that the flavour comes from strawberries, but "Strawberry Flavour" just means it tastes like strawberries but without actually containing any.

Isn't that a bit misleading?

- Yes, Sir.

In which case, well done. Can I have a sample?

- Well, you can't have this tub; it's still in the experimental stage. We don't want to take any chances do we?

No we don't.

- I'll send a tub of it over to your apartments when the product is finalised.

August

- Sir, Sir!

What is it Jack? I've never seen you in such a state. What's happened?

- It's the Pink Margarine. I sent a tub of the experimental strawberry ice cream over to your private apartment this afternoon. Have you tried it yet?

No, I haven't been back to my room yet. Why do you ask?

- Because we've discovered at a late stage that the stuff is dangerous.

Well we've always known that margarine is dangerous, Jack.

- Yes, but only if consumed over a long period of time. Remember that people tend to eat margarine in small doses. But with the ice cream, people are going to consume a lot more in a short space of time. It is likely to prove fatal immediately. I'll go over to your rooms now to retrieve it.

No, you can't do that. I have a guest.

- Do you mean the actress?

Yes.

- I hope she's not partial to ice cream!

Oh no! I'd better get over there.

The Following Day

- Are you OK, Sir?

Yes thanks, Jack. And I'm very grateful to you for sorting out the mess with the actress. The poor girl must have eaten the whole tub.

- I know, Sir. She didn't stand a chance.

Where did you take the body?

- Back to her house. We arranged for a doctor to find the body. We left a few opened bottles of tablets lying around. It should look like an overdose. He'll make sure there are no problems with the autopsy. It's a terrible thing to have happened.

I know. It could have been me.

- Well yes, Sir, there is that, but I meant that all that research has been wasted. Now we'll have to think of something else to do with the Pink Margarine.

1963

January

- Sir, we have a bit of a problem with the French.

Not the margarine thing again?

- No, Sir, it's the fashion business. The French are a bit miffed that we asked the British to promote the idea that "thin" is fashionable. They say that the French are at the forefront of fashion and it should be up to them to decide what is fashionable, not the Brits.

Well what do you think?

- Well it certainly used to be the case; you know "haut-couture" and all that. But if we are going to target the young, it probably needs to be the British.

OK, I agree. Tell the French what we've decided. Let's hope they don't get too upset.

Later That Week

- Sir, it's the French again.

What have they done this time?

- Well, you know when you said you hoped they wouldn't get too upset about the fashion thing.

You mean promoting "thin".

- Yes, Sir. Well they obviously take their fashion more seriously than we thought. In retaliation, they've vetoed the idea of the British joining the Common Market.

Oh, that's pretty serious. Now how are we going to know what's going on?

- Our only option is going to be the Germans. The Italians are still pretty sore about that business with the holy water and we don't know anyone from Luxembourg. In fact, we're not even sure where it is. And as for the Belgians.....

So that leaves the Germans.

- And the Dutch, Sir.

Well I think we'll go with the Germans.

- Yes, Sir. But we're going to have to "butter" them up a bit.

Shouldn't that be "margarine" them up!

- Oh yes, Sir. Ha, Ha. Good one.

Thank you, Jack. Either way, what will it involve?

- Well, I think you should go to Europe and make a big deal of the Germans, you know, put on a good show.

Like what?

- I'll write a speech for you that should do the trick.

A speech! Exactly what good will that do?

- You'll see.

OK, Jack, I'll leave it to you to sort out. But in the long term, we need the Brits to be in the Common Market. What can we do?

- Well the main stumbling block seems to be the French President, De Gaulle.

Well can't we get rid of him?

- I'll keep an eye on the situation, Sir, but it's going to take some time. He's still a hero to the French for getting rid of the Nazis.

I thought we did that.

- Not the way De Gaulle tells it.

Well even if it takes a long time, let's get rid of him.

- Yes, Sir.

April

- Sir, the situation regarding smoking is getting out of control.

In what way, Jack?

- Well, Sir, the public at large is becoming aware of the issues to do with smoking and health, particularly lung cancer. It's no longer going to be possible to ignore the situation. We have to do something, or at least we need to be seen to be doing something.

Well I guess there's only one option.

- You mean set up a committee.

Exactly! It'll buy us some time and you never know, they may come to the conclusion that smoking is good for you.

- Sir, please remember that we don't want them to come to that conclusion. We are relying on the fact that smoking kills hundreds of thousands of people each year, in fact millions worldwide.

Do you mean we want the committee to verify the research?

- We don't want them to but I don't see that we have any choice. There's just too much information out there in the public domain. We just need to come up with a plan of action so that when they do, we're ready.

Well you'd better get a team onto it.

- We don't need to, Sir. The tobacco industry is already on the case. They have a lot to lose if, or rather when, this gets out.

I guess so. Thanks, Jack, and keep me posted.

- Yes, Sir.

June

Well, Jack, the Germans are on board. The speech that you wrote went down very well. Especially the "Ich bin ein Berliner" bit. That seemed to really get the crowd going.

- Yes, Sir.

Why was that, do you think?

- Maybe it was the only bit they could understand, Sir.

Johnson

1963

November

- Welcome to the White House Mr President. I'm your personal advisor.

Thank you but I'd rather it hadn't been in such tragic circumstances.

- Yes, Sir, very.

Let no stone be unturned in an effort to find the perpetrators.

- Er, I don't think that will be necessary.

What do you mean? And why are you here? I have my own staff.

- Well Mr President, I'm here because there is an on-going Project about which few people are aware. It is felt that, during the transition from one administration to another, some continuity is required.

Exactly who thought so?

- Her name's Monica and she works in the Pentagon.

Well I think you'd better explain.

Several Hours Later

- So there you are, Sir, that's where we stand regarding STOP.

But how does that affect our need to search for the assassin?

- Well the idea of hit squads was put on the back burner but not before the adverts had appeared.

You advertised for hit men?

- No, not exactly. We advertised for gardeners but we mentioned that some use of firearms would be involved. We had just two replies, one from a Mr Oswald and one from a Mr Ruby.

Only two?

- The advert was in Gardeners Weekly, Sir.

OK, then what happened.

- Well they were given training and then issued with guns and ammunition.

And what did this training consist of?

- We had to show them how to fill in a time sheet and an expenses claims form. They already knew how to fire a gun.

And how long did this training take?

- About a week, Sir.

A week!!

- The forms are quite complicated, Sir.

OK, then what happened?

- Well, since they had been trained and were ready for action, it was decided to try them out. After all, the original argument against hit squads was that they would not be acceptable to the public. However, the effects of just two hit men would go largely unnoticed. There are already a lot of murders perpetrated using fire arms.

Then what happened?

- We sent them into action and told them to wait for instructions. We decided it would be best if we were to choose the first target. When we were ready, we sent a message to Mr Oswald and this is where things went a bit wrong. The message should have ended "don't forget The President is relying on you". Unfortunately, due to a transmission error, all he got was "get The President". Before we realised what had happened, Oswald was in Dallas and, well, you know the rest. We decided to abandon the idea of hit squads and told Mr Ruby to shoot Mr Oswald. That way there would be no loose ends.

Good grief, this is awful.

- It gets even worse. Neither of them completed their expense forms before they died. The paper work involved was horrendous.

No, I don't mean that.

- No, Sir, I'm sorry, you mean the death of a President.

No, not that either. I mean the fact that you have dropped the idea of hit squads. After all, guns are a pretty good way or getting rid of people. Give it another chance. See what you can come up with.

- Yes, Sir.

Is that all?

- No, Sir, I'm afraid there's something else. It's the space program. We said that we would put a man on the moon by the end of this decade.

Yes and a very brave statement it was.

- Well it has turned out to be more foolhardy than brave.

What do you mean?

- We are not going to be able to do it.

What!

- Well, Sir, we made the promise in the heat of the moment when the Russians were beating us in the space race. So we sort of got carried away.

But didn't you check with the defence industry before making the commitment?

- Yes, and we gave them a pot of money which they have spent. But they say it's just too complicated to send a man to the moon and bring him back safely.

What if we just send him there and don't bring him back. Would that make the problem easier, or should I say cheaper?

- Sir, I think the commitment included bringing him back.

Well, we have to come up with something. See what you can do.

- I'll get onto it straight away.

And don't forget the guns option.

- No, Sir.

A Week Later

Hi, Jack, what have you come up with?

- Well it's good and bad news really. The good news is that we have come up with an idea on the guns. In fact it was something you said that triggered it.

Is that some sort of gun joke?

- Is what some sort of gun joke?

Never mind. What have you come up with?

- Well, we can't risk the hit squads but we could encourage people to kill one another. As you said, there's already a lot of gun crime. We just need to increase it.

And how do you propose to do that?

- For a start, we can deal with the people that want to restrict the availability of guns. If we want people to kill one another, they must be able to get hold of the means to do so. Also, we need to promote the ownership of guns. There's a group called the NRA and I'm sure they'd be very willing to help.

Who are they?

- They're the National Rifle Association, Sir. They promote the use of guns in the USA.

OK, let's go with that. In the meantime, what about the space program? What's the situation there?

- Well, I've been back to the defence companies and they are adamant that it cannot be done, at least not without a lot more money and time. So we either have to abandon the project or we fake it.

What, you mean pretend to go to the moon? How are we going to do that?

- It's not as difficult as it sounds. We will have to actually launch the rockets since everyone can see that, but the astronauts will just orbit the earth. We will then simulate the moon landing.

But aren't the public expecting to see the moon landing on their TV?

- Yes, but if we make the pictures grainy enough, they won't be able to see the detail. It should work.

But what about the future? Surely mankind will eventually go to the moon? They'll find out that we haven't been there at all.

- Yes, but once this phase of the space program is complete, we'll make sure that there are no more manned trips to the moon for, say, 50 years.

Why 50 years? And if we can get to the moon surely the public will expect us to get to Mars within 50 years.

- You and I won't be around in 50 years, Sir.

So you think that you have it all covered.

- We're getting there, Sir.

December

- I have investigated the fake moon landing option and it seems that we are going to have to get Hollywood involved. They have the expertise we need.

OK, get in touch with the main players.

- I've already done that and there appears to be a bit of a problem. They want something from us in return.

You mean money?

- No, it's something a bit trickier than that. The people in Hollywood want one of their number to become President.

President of what?

- President of the United States of America.

What! You mean they want my job?

- Yes, Sir. Not right away of course, but some time in the next 20 years. And they want a commitment in writing.

And do they have someone in mind?

- Yes, Sir. It's Charlton Heston.

That figures. I can just picture him in the job. OK, draw up the necessary paperwork.

- Yes, Sir.

Anything else, Jack?

- Yes, there is one thing. There are several prongs to our attack on the problem of population control. There are our attempts to kill off people with a bad diet, the gun option, the fake moon landing. It's a lot for the public to believe. We need to do something to make the public more gullible.

And have you come up with something?

- Yes, Sir, we have. We quickly realised that we would need to somehow treat the population en-masse and the best way to do that is through drinking water. We have discovered a substance which can make a person gullible, even in small quantities. It's called fluoride.

But we can't just add a chemical to the drinking water without giving the public some sort of explanation.

- Yes I realise that, and that's the beauty of fluoride. It does have a beneficial effect.

Not too beneficial I hope. What is it?

- Well, Sir, after the Second World War, we noticed that the Germans had very little tooth decay. After some time we realised it was because they had been drinking water with fluoride added.

Why had they been doing that?

- Because we had been adding fluoride to their water supply for years.

And why on earth would we do that?

- To make the Germans gullible so that they would believe in what Hitler was telling them.

I'm sorry, Jack, you've lost me now.

- We realised it was going to be difficult to get Germany involved in another war so we had to make them gullible enough to believe that they had a chance of winning.

But surely that was down to Hitler.

- Yes, Sir, to some extent. But when we eventually came across Hitler, we realised that it would be a difficult job to convince the German people to accept him, especially as he was Austrian by birth.

Hang on a minute, what do you mean "when we came across Hitler"? I think you need to go back a bit in time and explain what happened.

- Ok, Sir, how far back do you want me to go? The First World War?

The First World War? Where does that come into things?

- Well that was the start of our efforts at population control.

But we didn't start that war.

- Didn't we?

No, it started when Arch Duke Franz Ferdinand was shot.

- And who do you think shot him?

Well it can't have been us; we weren't involved until the war had been underway for a couple of years.

- You mean a bit like the Second World War? That was all part of the grand plan since if we weren't involved in the fighting from the beginning it would make it less likely anyone would think we were involved in starting the conflict. In any case, it was also a safer option, joining the fray when the existing parties were already weakened. Anyway we're getting off the main subject. The point is we discovered that fluoride is good for the teeth and that is the excuse we can use to get it added to the water supply, creating "G-Water".

G-Water?

- Gullibility Water, Sir.

Ah! And you think that will help our cause?

- Well, we need something. And as a politician, I don't think it will harm your cause if the public are suffering from an attack of the "gullibilities".

No, I guess not.

- Anything else, Sir?

No, not at this moment, but I will want to go back to this Hitler thing at some stage.

- Yes, Sir, I thought you might.

And, Jack.

- Yes, Sir.

Let the British know about fluoride and the teeth thing. In the past they seem to have been a bit concerned about tooth decay.

- I've already done that, Sir. They seem very keen on fluoride.

I'm not surprised. It may solve their problem concerning the provision of free dental treatment.

- I think that they are more interested in the gullibility option, Sir.

1964

January

Jack, that announcement from the Surgeon General. It was a bit strong, wasn't it?

- What do you mean, Sir?

Well, as I understand it, he's told the American public that smoking is bad for your health and that they should stop.

- Well I'm not sure that he was quite as concise as that, but yes, in essence that's what he said.

But could you not have got him to tone it down a bit. This could be bad news for us.

- There wasn't much we could do, Sir. The information is out there and it would have looked a bit odd if we had done nothing. Smoking kills, it's as simple as that.

So what do we do? Have the tobacco companies come up with anything yet?

- Well we've had a bit of a problem there, Sir.

Why's that?

- Well they want to continue to sell cigarettes, so they are trying to come up with a safe cigarette, which is exactly what we don't want them to do.

No, quite. So where does that leave us?

- Well I've sent them back to the drawing board. I've told them to come up with something that achieves both our aims.

Is that possible?

- I hope so, Sir.

February

- Sir we have a problem in Europe. I'm afraid it's the French again.

What a surprise. What is it now?

- It's to do with G-Water. It appears that the French don't drink tap water.

I hope you're not going to tell me that they just drink wine.

- No, Sir, they do in fact drink water, but mainly from bottles.

Where do they get the bottles from?

- They get them from a shop.

What, you mean that they pay for them?

- Yes, Sir. The French could get their drinking water from the tap in the kitchen, but they choose to pay to get it in bottles from a shop.

But surely the shop has just filled the bottle from the local mains water tap.

- Oh no, Sir, the water comes from special water sources around the country, like underground springs. It's then shipped all over France by road, so you can see the problem. We won't be able to get the French to drink G-Water.

Sounds like the French don't need to, they seem pretty gullible already. Surely there must be more to this, Jack. Has anyone in the White House ever been to France?

- I shouldn't think so, but I'll ask around.

That Afternoon

- Sir, regarding the French and their tap water, I couldn't find any Americans who have been to France but there is a chap in the foreign language department. He speaks six foreign languages including French and he has been to France several times.

What nationality is he?

- English.

An Englishman who speaks six foreign languages. What are the chances of that?

- Not very high, Sir.

But not as unlikely as an American who speaks six languages, eh Jack!

- No, Sir, not when you consider the rate at which we're getting through the margarine!

You're right there, Jack. Anyway, what did he say?

- Well it was all a bit strange. I asked him to confirm that he had been to France and he just tapped the side of his nose and said 'don't drink the water'. I'm not quite sure what to make of it.

This is a bit worrying. You don't suppose he knows about G-Water do you?

- I don't see how he could. Unless of course, he's a friend of Monica's.

Well you'd better check. And see if you can get some better intelligence on French tap water.

- Yes, Sir.

The Following Week

- About the French tap water, Sir, I think we've shed some light on the situation. It seems that it's not very good quality, at least that's the perception. That's why the French drink bottled water.

That gives us a bit of a problem.

- Yes it does, Sir. Apparently, the tap water can make you ill but since the French don't drink it, it affects mainly foreign tourists.

Does it kill them?

- No, I don't think so.

That's a pity. Well in that case we have to persuade the French to improve the quality of the tap water and then encourage their population to drink it.

- And by "improve", you're including the addition of fluoride?

I think so don't you, Jack. And there's one other thing I need to discuss with you. It's about the alien spacecraft and Area 51. How's that coming along? I know we wanted to get the public to start believing in them but I haven't heard anything for a while. Have we come up with a solution?

- We have, Sir.

I suppose it's going to cost us a fortune. It's not going to be cheap to design and build flying saucers.

- It's not going to cost us anything, Sir.

What? Nothing at all?

- No, Sir.

How can that be?

- Well it was the original Roswell story that gave me the idea. One of the problems which made the situation worse was that the military kept giving out contradictory and erroneous information. The locals became convinced that the government had something to hide. But we didn't, it was just incompetence. We think that we can use the same ploy again.

For example?

- Well the locals see one of our night flights coming into to land at Area 51. We can stick some coloured flashing lights on the side of the plane and then get the pilot to do some strange manoeuvres. Some local idiot will see the lights and think it's something sinister, like a UFO. We'll say there were no flights or anything else in the area at that time and the rumour will spread that someone has seen a flying saucer. When we eventually say that, actually there was a flight, the population will think it's just a cover-up.

So there is a cost involved.

- Is there?

The coloured lights, Jack. Someone has got to pay for them.

- Sir, in the scheme of things I hardly think...

Steady on, Jack, I'm only joking. But getting back to the problem, won't people get suspicious when we keep coming up with the same type of story?

- Well there are plenty of people around who want to believe in flying saucers and we'll vary the story each time in order to keep them hooked. For instance, we'll say we can't comment due to national security or we'll deny that we're testing a new plane. We just need to keep them believing all sorts of rubbish so that they don't stumble on the real purpose of Area 51.

And how are we going to explain to the low lives in the military why they are misleading the public?

- If past experience is anything to go by, we won't have to. Their lines of communication are normally so tangled that they can achieve our aims without even knowing what they're doing.

As in Roswell?

- Exactly, Sir.

Well I still think we need something more tangible. Stay on the lookout for anything else we can use.

- Yes, Sir.

April

- You called, Sir?

Too right I called. Have you seen the newspapers?

- Which particular one, Sir?

Don't play games, Jack, you know what I'm talking about. It's the Beatles of course. According to Billboard, they occupy the top 5 places on the hit parade.

- Apparently so, Sir.

Well it's an unprecedented situation. What are we going to do about it? My phone has been ringing off its hook. The US music industry is not impressed.

- Well we have to look at the bigger picture, the one that links pop music to fashion, which in turn promotes being thin. I mentioned it in my initial briefing when you took office.

You mentioned a lot of things, Jack, but a British group topping the US chart wasn't one of them. I just remember something about the French being upset.

- Well having the top five records in the US pop music chart was an unforeseen event that's not likely to be repeated. When the Beatles became successful in the US, they already had a back catalogue of UK hits. These were all released in the US at the same time, hence the current situation. It's not likely to happen again.

Well I hope it's worthwhile. And just where do we stand with the "bigger picture", Jack?

- It's going very well, Sir. Just take a look at these photographs.

Who are these people?

- Well the first person is Twiggy.

Hence the name, I suppose.

- I guess so, Sir. In any case, right now she's relatively unknown but the Brits seem to think that she will become the top fashion model in the world. She will also be one of the thinnest.

I should say so. I've got pipe cleaners thicker than those legs.

- But you don't smoke a pipe, Sir.

Just a figure of speech, Jack. Who's in the other photos?

- There's Jean Shrimpton. She's also hoping to be a model. The others are Sandie Shaw and Cilla Black. They are both singers.

Sorry, Jack, I still don't see the connection between models and singers.

- Well you know we want to promote thinness and to do that we need to use the fashion industry.

Yes, that bit I understand.

- Well people have to believe that the fashion industry is right and that is going to be difficult to do if their idols in the pop music industry are not adopting the latest fashion.

I'm sure you're right, Jack. But what about the success of the British pop industry? I don't like the idea that it's a permanent thing.

- I'm sure it's just a passing phase, Sir.

June

- Sir, we seem to have another issue regarding our plan for birth control.

What, you mean in addition to the Catholics?

- Yes, Sir. We have discovered that the French actually have a law that makes birth control illegal and I believe it's the same in Italy.

Well that's just unacceptable. You need to have a quiet word and get them to put their house in order.

- I have already done that, Sir, and they came back with a more than reasonable point.

I can't see how they can possibly argue against such a plan. What excuse could they possibly use?

- It's quite a good one really. They say that since birth control is illegal in the USA, why should it be any different in France.

I hope you put them right, Jack.

- In what respect, Sir?

I hope you told them that they're wrong.

- But they're not, Sir, at least not exactly. There are still some states in the US where contraception is illegal and getting the legislation changed could prove difficult.

Well I don't care how we do it; it's got to be done. Have a think about it Jack, and come up with some options.

- Yes, Sir.

August

- Sir, regarding the issue of birth control, there appears to be only one option, that is, if we want to implement any changes in any sort of reasonable timescale. We are going to have to get the Supreme Court involved. That way all the states will have to comply with any decision they come up with. If we deal with it on a state by state basis it could take years.

OK, Jack, do whatever it is that you need to do.

- Yes, Sir.

1965

January

- Sir, JUNC has been studying the various food groups and they have come up with a significant problem.

Now, Jack, is it a problem? Or is it really one of your opportunities?

- It's a problem of the opportunistic variety, Sir.

Good, you know I like opportunities Jack, especially when it comes to JUNC food. What have you got?

- Well, Sir, our best efforts so far have been have been with processed foods.

You mean like margarine?

- Yes, exactly. Processed foods give us so many more options to influence the food the people eat. When it comes to the raw stuff, for instance meat and vegetables, it can be quite tricky. And wild caught fish are perhaps the worst of the lot. We can't inject them or spray them to make them unhealthy which is why we are trying to reduce the stocks as far as possible.

And how's that going?

- Pretty well, Sir. We've been concentrating on the larger fish to start with.

Well I suppose that makes sense, Jack. After all they're a bigger target.

- Yes, there is that, but we have discovered another issue and that's something called omega-3. It's a fatty acid that's important for our health.

And where do the fish come into the picture, Jack?

- It's because the main source of omega-3 is seafood, particularly fish. And some fish are richer in omega-3 that others, particularly the bigger ones, so the sooner we wipe them out the better.

What sort of fish are we talking about?

- There's tuna and salmon for starters. If we can get rid of them the sources of omega-3 for human consumption would be greatly diminished. And of course as far as salmon is concerned, the less wild stuff there is the more people will have to eat the farmed salmon. And you really don't want to know what we are going to pump into farmed salmon.

Like what?

- No, Sir, when I say you don't want to know, I really mean you don't want to know.

So it goes without saying that forcing people onto the farmed stuff is a good thing, Jack?

- As you say, Sir, it goes without saying. But getting back to the main issue, apart from margarine we haven't got many other significant processed foods. We really need to come up with something soon. We are looking at other substitute foods following the example of margarine.

Which is a butter alternative, Jack. So what we should be looking for are substitutes for other staple foods which we know are good for you, like meat for instance. And milk.

- That's been our starting point, but we still don't think that's good enough. After all, if you add in fats and sugar, what other basic food items can we replace? It's not like we can come up with a substitute Brussels sprout.

Jack, people don't like eating real Brussels sprouts, let alone fake ones.

- OK, that was perhaps a bad example, but it's still the case that we need to come up with something radical.

And soon.

- Yes, Sir, and soon.

February

Jack, thanks for coming in. I need to have a quick word with you. I've been thinking about the food problem. You know, to do with processed foods. I've come up with an idea.

- I hope it's a good one, Sir.

Well you tell me. It came to me when Lady Bird was serving up the meal last night. We had meat loaf again and it occurred to me that I have no idea what actually goes into it. She could put almost anything in the mix and I'd probably be none the wiser.

- That's true, Sir, but where are we going with this? Are you suggesting that we get the First Lady to rustle up meat loaf for the entire nation!

No, at least not personally. But just imagine how many more options we would have if we concentrated on the end product rather than the ingredients. We could put anything into the pot.

- That's true, but I'm still not sure how we would successfully achieve this. Even if we had centralised production, the problem of distributing the end result to tens of thousands of shops would be insurmountable.

Are you saying that this is a problem that JUNC can't find a solution for?

- No, I didn't say that, Sir. It's just that the solution doesn't readily spring to mind.

Then perhaps you'd better get JUNC onto it straight away.

- Yes, Sir.

March

- Sir, the French have agreed to initiate a project which involves modernising their drinking water supply system.

Good, I'm glad to hear it. How long is it going to take?

- About 20 years.

20 Years! But that's terrible.

- Yes, Sir, I know. We could have problems with the French for many years to come.

In that case, Jack, I need cheering up. Have you made any progress on the MLC?

- MLC Sir?

The meat loaf challenge, Jack.

- Perhaps one acronym too far, Sir.

Noted, Jack, but where do we stand?

- We're making progress but we haven't come up with a definitive answer. We're going down two routes at the moment.

Which are what?

- The first is to do with ingredients. Even if we were to be able to produce pre-prepared food, what are we going to put into it? After all we can't just put anything into the mix; it has to be there for a reason, otherwise we could use arsenic as an ingredient and we'd achieve our goal pretty quickly. But as to how we would explain its presence I'm not sure.

Well perhaps we need to start off with your gently-gently approach. Once the public have taken up the idea of buying pre-prepared food, well then we can start slipping them the hard stuff.

- Exactly, Sir. One step at a time, eh? But going back to the point, we have looked at the main ingredients of most meals.

Good, you're sticking to main meals. I don't like the idea of messing around with apple pie.

- But you're happy for us to mess with meat loaf?

Yes please. Anything would be an improvement of the version I currently have to endure.

- I'm sorry to say this, Sir, but if we do come up with a super-duper improved meat loaf, you certainly won't be having any, at least not while you're still in office. But back to the point, what we've come up with is a core list of ingredients: fat, salt, sugar, milk and flour. Now we need to decide what to do about each of them. If possible we need to come up with our own versions.

For example?

- Well for fat we already have a solution. We'll use hydrogenated vegetable oil instead of natural products like butter and lard.

And what about salt?

- We haven't yet decided what to do with salt, or indeed the other items. We're still working on them. In each case we need to decide whether the basic ingredient is good or bad. If it's good we must definitely replace it, but even if it's bad there's every chance that we can come up with a substitute that's even worse.

OK, so this all sounds very promising. Where do we go from here?

- Just hang on a minute, Sir. We haven't solved the main problem and that's to do with distribution. If we can't deliver our special recipe meat loaf to the consumer, then it doesn't matter how many substitute ingredients we come up with, the plan won't work.

And you haven't come up with anything yet.

- No, Sir, not yet.

June

- Sir, regarding birth control, the Supreme Court has come up with a ruling in our favour. State legislation banning contraception has been outlawed.

What excuse did they use?

- Well in principle the ruling said that the state should not interfere in matters relating to the marital bed.

Well I hope that covers everything.

- What do you mean, Sir?

Well what if a married couple have sex in the back of a car? Or an unmarried couple have sex anywhere? Will contraception still be illegal?

- I'm not sure that the judges went into the specifics, Sir. Their actual wording refers to the "right to marital privacy". I'll admit that the term doesn't specifically mention unmarried couples but my understanding is that in future contraception can be used anywhere and by anybody.

Steady on, Jack, we don't want to encourage public displays of excessive affection.

- I'm sure that's not on the cards, Sir

So does this mean that France will follow suit?

- I have been assured by the French government that it will lift the ban on contraception very soon and certainly by the end of the year. The Italians of course are still a problem since the Catholic Church is so set against it. There it will take a bit longer.

August

Hi, Jack, thanks for coming.

- Well when you called, it sounded urgent.

I think it is, Jack. It's about the heart disease issue you mentioned in my initial briefing.

- Which part of it concerns you, Sir?

All of it, really. I've come across a study that seems to contradict your theory.

- This wouldn't be the one by Ancel Keys, would it?

Oh, so you know of it?

- Yes, Sir.

Well it seems to contradict your theory that saturated fat is good for you. His study clearly shows that countries that consume the most saturated fat have the highest incidents of heart disease. Just look at this graph. There's Japan at the bottom. They consume the least fat and they have the lowest number of deaths from heart disease. Needless to say, we're at the top of the chart. We eat the most fat and we have the highest rates of heart disease.

- That certainly seems to be the case, but if you give me a few minutes, I'll just go and fetch something that you should see.

A Few Minutes Later

- Sir would you take a look at this.

What is it?

- It's another chart, Sir. It plots the same things; fat consumption against heart disease.

But it's the opposite of my one. On yours, Chile is the country with the highest fat consumption, but has the lowest number of deaths from heart disease. And Norway has the lowest fat consumption but the greatest number of deaths.

- Yes, Sir.

So the first one is wrong?

- Well it depends on what you mean by "wrong". Both graphs are accurate, but the conclusions drawn from the graphs are certainly wrong. It's just a question of what you are trying to achieve. Now have a look at this chart.

It looks the same as my one, Jack.

- It is except for one thing. This graph is plotting sugar consumption against heart disease. It shows the same thing; the more sugar is consumed the high the rate of heart disease. The only difference is that this relationship will tend to be true no matter how many different countries you include on the chart. If you do the same for the cholesterol one there will be no pattern. The points on the graph will look like snowflakes in a blizzard.

So what was this chap Keys trying to achieve?

- He was trying to achieve exactly what we wanted him to achieve, Sir.

What do you mean "we"? Are you saying that you were party to this deception?

- Well, Sir, I wouldn't call it a deception exactly. It's all part of the grand plan. And I prefer the term "we" rather than "you" when referring to STOP.

But I thought that the whole cholesterol/fat/heart disease thing was a recent discovery.

- We've only recently started to act on the plan, but we started to plant the false research some time ago.

Like when?

- 1953, Sir.

That's a long time ago.

- Some seeds take a long time to germinate, Sir.

That's assuming you're right about cholesterol.

- Trust me, Sir, I'm right, or should I say "we" are right.

November

- I think we've come up with something on the distribution front.

With regard to what exactly, Jack?

- You know, Sir, processed food.

Ah right, sorry but it's been a while since we discussed the matter. I'm with you now and I trust you've come up with a solution. What have you got?

- Well our plan would solve many problems, if only we can get it to work. Originally we had been trying to tackle the problem of centralised production with distribution to the existing small local shops and we never solved that one. So the only option is to address the issue of too many local shops. We need to have a lot fewer, but much bigger, supermarkets.

But we already have supermarkets.

- Yes, Sir, but we need to have bigger ones and preferably just a few large chains with national coverage. That's the only way our plan can work.

But how will we persuade people to shop at these places.

- Well what would make you use them?

I never have cause to use them, Jack. I leave all that to the First Lady.

- Yes, I realise that, Sir. But try to imagine, if you did do the food shop each week, what would persuade you to use one shop rather than another?

Convenience I guess.

- Anything else?

Well the range of products on offer would come into it.

- Try to imagine that you're poor, Sir.

I'd rather not, Jack!

- Humour me, Sir.

Ah right, yes in that case I guess price would come into it.

- Yes, Sir, I think it would and what's more, everything about our plan fits the bill. The site will be out of town so the running costs will be lower. And there will be an economy of scale on the supply side meaning that the prices to the customers can be lower. And to meet your requirements the size of these stores will mean that the variety of goods on offer will be greater. Stick a parking lot on the site and the local stores will find it difficult to compete.

So where's the problem?

- It's one of timescale. This sort of thing won't be achieved overnight but if we pull it off, the rewards could be great. Just imagine, if only we could get the food production and distribution into the hands of just a few big players, we'd be spoilt for choice when it comes to JUNC food.

You're right there. In the meantime let me know when you come up with something regarding the other ingredients, particularly sugar.

- Yes, Sir. And one other minor point, Sir. I don't think that the First Lady shops in a supermarket. I believe that she has staff to do that for her.

Well what does she do every Tuesday afternoon if it isn't the shopping?

- I really don't know, Sir.

1966

January

Jack, I haven't heard anything on the processed food front for a while.

- Well there hasn't been a lot to report. The move towards larger supermarkets is progressing but the Brits have come up with a couple of issues.

Like what?

- The main issue they have is to do with planning permission at the local level. It appears that some people don't like the idea of having large supermarkets on their doorstep, but they think that they can sort that out.

By greasing a few palms, eh, Jack.

- I find that normally works, Sir.

So do I, Jack. And what's the other problem?

- Well, Sir, if you're going to go to an out of town supermarket, what do you need?

Well you'd need money and I suppose a shopping list.

- What about car keys?

Well that's a given, Jack.

- Not if you don't have a car, Sir.

Of course I have a car. Otherwise how am I going to get to the out of town supermarket?

Exactly, Sir. Apparently in the UK, car ownership is not as widespread as it is here in the USA.

But how do people get around without a car?

- By public transport, that is by bus or train, and of course on foot. I believe that the same problem exists throughout Europe.

Well they're all going to have to get their act together otherwise this whole plan is doomed, at least for them. What are they going to do?

- Well if we can get the supermarkets built the problem may solve itself. People will have to get themselves a car if they want to take advantage of the low prices.

Let's hope so. And what about the other issue regarding the core ingredients? What's the position there?

- I'll have something to report back on shortly, Sir. Perhaps we can have another discussion next month.

I look forward to that, Jack.

February

- Sir, I can report back on the progress we have made regarding the core ingredients.

Good, what have you got?

- Where do you want to start, Sir?

Let's start with salt. What have we come up with for an alternative?

- Nothing, Sir.

And why is that?

- Because as far as salt is concerned we haven't been trying that hard. We've been concentrating on the other targets. However, we still have a strategy regarding salt. We reckon that consuming too much salt will be bad so if we can increase the salt intake of the population by putting more of it into our processed food, then we don't need to find an alternative.

That's all well and good, Jack but I still think that we need to find an alternative. And how are we going to get people to accept saltier food.

- We'll increase the salt levels gradually over a period of time. And remember, most foods contain a degree of salt so it won't be a problem to overdose the average person.

OK, next one. How about sugar? That's not in all foods.

- No, and this is why we've come up with a replacement. It's High Fructose Corn Syrup or HFCS for short.

What's it going to do for us?

- Well we know it's bad for your liver and we also think it's going to increase insulin resistance and this will result in many more cases of diabetes in the USA. But the best part is that we think that it will cause people to over-eat.

How can it do that, Jack?

- Because when we have consumed enough real sugar for our current energy requirements, the body sends a message to brain. We then know to stop eating. HFCS doesn't have the same effect so the person will keep on eating even though they don't need to.

So they'll get fat and that's not healthy.

- Remember that we need them to get not just fat but very fat to make them unhealthy and we think we can do that. But that's not the main point. We're hoping that when they over-eat, it'll be our processed stuff that they're chewing on and that'll be good for us.

But not for them, Jack!

- Not if we've done our sums, Sir, no.

OK, let's move on. What about milk?

- We've already done something about that by removing most of the goodness, but that doesn't make what's left actually bad for you so we're working on a replacement. But that's not important for our processed foods since we've already taken out the cream, so any recipe that needs fat will have to have Trans Fats added.

Hang on, Jack. You're now saying milk isn't bad for you? I thought that we'd done something to make it bad for your heart.

- You mean homogenization, Sir. Well our initial tests did seem to show an effect but now we're not sure. However, the good news is that we think that the long term effect will be to cause more people to be lactose intolerant.

And what does that mean?

- It means that they won't be able to drink milk and therefore they'll have to resort to something else.

Like what?

- We have come up with anything yet but I'm sure we will.

And I'm assuming that we're not talking about a healthy alternative, are we.

- No, Sir, we're not.

OK, but good work on the other stuff.

- Thank you, Sir.

May

Jack, there seems to be a bit of unrest in China. Is it anything we need to worry about?

- Not really, Sir. It's just the successor to the "Great Leap Forward". This time it's the "Cultural Revolution".

And what's the difference?

- Well, Sir, in the first, the state managed to kill off millions of Chinese by chance. Their ideologically flawed plans engineered a fall in food production and hence mass starvation. Now they plan to kill off vast numbers of people but this time it's deliberate.

But aren't the population going to notice?

- That's the beauty of the plan, Sir. They are going to stir up trouble in the population at large and people will start killing off one another.

How are they going to do that? And can we follow the same plan here?

- I'm afraid not, Sir. They plan to blame the problem of food shortages on the Bourgeoisie.

Is that some sort of plant disease?

- No, Sir. It's a collective term for the elite in the country, teachers, scientists, religious leaders, etc. The government plan is to blame these people and incite the peasants to attack them.

And do you think it will work?

- We'll have to wait and see.

July

- Sir, England has won the World Cup.

God Grief, Jack, that's a bit of a shock. I didn't know that they played baseball.

(And so on for some time)

So everything went according to plan?

- Not entirely, Sir. The West Germans reneged on the deal at literally the last minute.

What do you mean?

- Apparently, not all the team had been briefed on what was supposed to happen.

You mean the plan that meant that if they let England win the World Cup, West Germany will win all subsequent matches against England.

- Yes, Sir, that one.

So what happened?

- Well one of the team who had not been briefed on the plan scored an equalising goal in the last minute.

So what happened then?

- We had to play our ace card.

Which was what?

- Not "What", Sir, but "Who".

Alright, "Who"?

- Tofik Bahkramov.

Who's he?

- He was the Russian linesman. In extra time, he awarded a goal to England when the ball had not in fact crossed the line. It was fortunate that England scored again otherwise that third "goal" could have been the decider. We could have had some tricky questions to answer.

And how are we going to get the Russian linesman to keep quiet?

- We've promised him a lifetime's supply of vodka.

Well if he lives to be a hundred, that could prove costly.

- I know, Sir. That's why I'm throwing in some margarine as well.

Good idea, Jack.

- Thank you, Sir.

August

Jack, I seem to remember a conversation we had a while ago. I expressed some concern about the success of British pop music in the US charts. I seem to remember you used the words "it's just a passing phase".

- Er, well I can't remember the exact phrase I used.

Well I wouldn't be able to either if it wasn't for the fact that the main players in the music industry are reminding me of the fact on a daily basis. Unfortunately, I used the same phrase when I tried to reassure them about the time the problem first arose. And before you say anything, please don't include the words "bigger picture".

- But, Sir, it's difficult not to. The plan to make "thin" fashionable has succeeded beyond our wildest expectations.

Well you're right there. It's difficult to avoid pictures of thin models in the papers and magazines. And yes, you were right. Twiggy is now a household name.

October

Jack, I've been thinking about the problems we are having in Europe.

- In what respect, Sir?

In respect of the fact that it seems to be a bit difficult to get them to toe the line.

- Do you mean the French, Sir?

Well it's not just them is it, although they do appear to be the ring leaders. This Common Market thing seems to be a right pain in the butt. By getting together to chat about things they seem to come up with policies which suit them but not us.

- Well that's not surprising is it? And it's as much to do with democracy as it is to do with the Common Market.

That's as may be, but we need to do something; give them a bit of a shock in order to bring them into line.

- What did you have in mind, Sir, an invasion of France? We could overthrow the elected government and put in our own people.

Really? It would solve a lot of our problems in that area.

- I think I was joking, Sir!

Well don't. I don't want my hopes raised only for them to be quickly dashed.

- No, Sir, of course not. Sorry, Sir.

So you should be, Jack. But that means that you need to come up with something, and quickly.

- Yes, Sir.

November

- Sir, I've given some thought to your problem of Europe and I've come up with something.

I hope it's nothing to do with invading France. I don't want my hopes dashed again.

- Well in fact we did give that option some consideration but in the end we rejected it.

And why was that? Too difficult to carry out?

- No, not really. When it comes to being invaded, the French don't have a particularly good track record recently. They normally roll over and surrender pretty quickly.

And then we have to go over and get them out of a hole.

- And there lies the problem, Sir. If we are the ones to take over, there will be nobody to help the French.

Well that's a good thing isn't it?

- Well that depends on whether you like the idea of being responsible for the French indefinitely.

Oh, I see what you mean.

- Exactly! It would be a nightmare. It's bad enough when they're on our side. Can you imagine what they'd be like if we were to invade.

I'm not sure the French have ever been on our side, Jack.

- Fair point, Sir. The only side the French are on is their own side.

We can't criticise them for protecting their own interests, can we. It's just that they often fail to see the bigger picture.

- Exactly, Sir, and that's where they need a bit of gentle persuasion.

What do you have in mind?

- Well the French don't know that we wouldn't invade France. They regard the place as the next best thing to Heaven and they probably think that everyone feels the same. So we need to fire a warning shot over their bows.

And how do you propose to do that?

- We'll invade Greece.

Invade Greece! What good will that do? And why Greece?

- Well the French government needs to understand that it is not invincible and that it has to take responsibility for its actions. If we show what we are prepared to do by setting them an example, perhaps they start playing ball.

And Greece is your best option?

- It is, Sir. The Greek army is pretty weak and we don't think it would put up much opposition. What's more it has a long coast line which will make the invasion a lot easier. For example we wouldn't want to choose Austria.

Yes I can see that, but why not Italy?

- What, antagonise the Mafia! I don't think so, Sir.

And Spain?

- Spain isn't a democracy, Sir.

Really?

- Not as far as I know.

OK, so we'll go with Greece. Have you discussed this plan with the military? And do we have an estimated body count?

- Yes, Sir, they're looking to start the campaign in April. As for the body count, unfortunately we're probably talking low thousands.

OK, but why wait until April?

- Apparently the weather's at its nicest at that time of year.

Jack, this is supposed to be a military operation, not a vacation.

- I'm sure the military chiefs know that, Sir.

I hope so. Well keep me informed.

- Yes, Sir.

1967

March

- Sir, we seem to have a problem with the plan to invade Greece.

In what way?

- The Greek military have found out about our plan.

What! How did that happen? That's an absolute disaster.

- Well, Sir, as to how it happened, we're not sure and it's certainly something that we need to investigate. If such information is leaking out, then that could be a problem.

What do you mean "could be"? Surely it's a problem now?

- Not necessarily, Sir.

Why's that?

- Because the Greek army, or at least those in charge, have offered to do the job for us.

What! Invade their own country? Can they really do that?

- Not invade, Sir. But they can overthrow the elected government.

You mean stage a coup?

- Yes, Sir.

Why would they do that?

- Well think of the options that they have. If we invade Greece, they will have to fight us to defend their country. Militarily, they're at a significant disadvantage so they'll either die fighting or they'll surrender and risk the wrath of their fellow countrymen. On the other hand, if they stage a coup there will be little or no fighting so no danger of being killed. What's more they may end up in power with all that that would entail. As far as they are concerned it's a no brainer.

And what will that do for us? You know, regarding the French problem. After all that's the whole point of this exercise.

- Well that's where we need to be careful. We need to make sure that

127

the French understand that we are behind the coup and that it's taking place because the elected Greek government is not doing what we want.

And the inference will be that we could do the same elsewhere.

- Exactly.

But how about the body count? That doesn't sound so promising.

- No, Sir, it doesn't, but as I've said before we need to look at the bigger picture.

And in this case, what is the bigger picture?

- The fact that the Communists could come to power in the forthcoming Greek elections. Or at least they may hold the balance of power.

Good grief! Well we certainly don't want that.

- No we don't, and that can be the excuse that the Greek military will use to justify the coup.

I guess so. OK, we'll go with the coup option but make doubly sure the French know we're behind it.

- Yes, Sir.

May

Jack, I see that the British have re-applied for membership of the Common Market. Does that mean that De Gaulle is no longer a problem?

- No, Sir, he's still there.

So what's the point?

- Well, Sir, with the Greek coup under our belt, the Europeans realise we mean business and so the Brits think that the time is right. Also, it takes a lot of time to negotiate the terms and it's not just the British. There are three other countries involved.

So what will happen?

- We're hoping that De Gaulle will be gone by the time the negotiations are completed.

Well I assume that we're doing more than just hoping.

- It's all under control, Sir.

I hope so.

June

- Sir, we need to have a discussion about Area 51.

What's happened now? If it's anything to do with UFOs, I don't want to hear about it.

- No, Sir, it's nothing to do with UFOs.

Nor flying saucers, alien abductions…

- No, Sir, it's none of those, please let me explain. It's a practical problem. We may need somewhere else to house our staff.

What, all of them?

- No, Sir, not all of them.

But the place is huge. Surely we can't be running out of space.

- It's not a matter of space, Sir. It's more to do with the fact that it's getting difficult to find people who are willing to work in the middle of nowhere.

But surely we didn't have a problem at the start.

- If you remember, Sir, in the beginning we weren't exactly honest as to where and why the staff were being relocated. Also, the fact that the previous STOP headquarters was on the sea bed did help our cause since the staff were so keen to move away from there. Now we have to recruit new people and it's difficult to hide the fact that the place is in the middle of the desert.

But where can we house so many people while keeping the facility secure? It needs to be somewhere attractive to new recruits so it can't be another place in the middle of nowhere.

- Well that's something were looking at now. I'll let you know what we come up with.

August

- Sir, we have a bit of an issue regarding water.

What is it this time? Not the French again?

- No, not the French, at least not directly. No, it's the fact that it can be difficult for people to get water to drink while they are at work. Often, the only water taps will be in the rest rooms and people don't particularly want to drink that water in that sort of environment. If we want people to drink a lot of tap water, we need to take some action.

So what can we do?

- Well, the scientists at Area 51 have suggested that each place of work should have one or more taps that dispense drinking water.

It took a team of scientists to come up with that? How much do we pay these guys? I could have told you that in ten seconds.

- Yes, Sir, I know that. That's not the whole solution. We need to encourage people to drink the water, so we need to provide a container to hold the water, preferably a disposable plastic or paper cup, the water needs to be refrigerated, and the tap needs to be sited in a convenient location, i.e. in the office area, not in a kitchen area or a rest room.

Go on.

- Well that's it, Sir.

I can't see this proving popular. Just think of the logistics involved in installing the plumbing and a sink, a cupboard for the cups, etc. No, I can't see this working.

- I know, Sir, which is why the guys have come up with a machine that combines all these features in one unit. It's called a water cooler. All you need is a water supply and electricity.

Well it sounds promising but you'll need to get a few manufacturers involved. I don't want the guys at Area 51 turning the place into a factory.

- No, Sir, that won't happen. We've already got a number of companies lined up. If it's successful, the production volumes will be huge.

I can imagine.

- And on another matter, Sir, we've taken advice and it appears that we are going to have to house some of our staff in one of the big cities, preferably Washington or New York. They are the sort of places that staff will find attractive.

How many people are we talking about?

- I guess to start with somewhere between three and five hundred. Ultimately it would be more.

Good grief, what are all these people doing?

- Well I don't know that this is the time or place to go over the whole Project again, but I'm sure we can at some stage. If you want to make staffing cuts, that can be considered.

Every time we talk about cuts you end up convincing me we need more staff, not less.

- And I'm sure now would be no different, Sir.

Well it's hard to imagine where we could hide that number of people, whilst keeping prying eyes out.

- We've considered that problem, Sir, and it appears we only have one option. We need to build upwards.

Why is that?

- There are two main reasons. One is that, in a big city, we won't be able to find an area of land big enough unless we do. The other reason is security. The further off the ground we are, the more difficult it will be for someone to gain unauthorised access.

Do you have somewhere in mind?

- There is a site in central New York. The basic design for the building is done and I'm sure we could get things constructed to our requirements in terms of security. It just needs a bit of impetus to get things going.

You mean they need money.

- Yes, Sir.

But wait a minute here, we can't have it known that we are involved in this project. I can just imagine a sign on the lift door "Top Floors High Security - Out of Bounds". It would attract every nutcase in the country.

- Well of course we couldn't do that. We'd have to have a front operation.

Like what?

- Like an investment bank or a computer software company. They're the sorts of companies that could afford such office accommodation.

And how long will it take to get this thing ready for occupation?

- Two to three years, Sir.

OK, if you think we need to adopt such a drastic plan, we'd better go ahead.

- Yes, Sir. If you could just sign off this purchase order, we'll start the work.

What's the figure bottom line?

- It's 335 million dollars, Sir.

A sum that large can only be lost in one way.

- You mean the defence budget, Sir.

Of course, Jack. And so what is this place going to be called?

- It's called the World Trade Centre, Sir.

1968

March

- Sir, regarding the distribution of G-Water. The roll out of the water coolers is going well, in fact the French are rather keen on the idea. It may tide them over until they get their water supply system upgraded.

Yes, I gather they are proving very popular. In fact I saw one in the office of my lawyer.

- I hope you didn't drink any water from it, Sir.

Certainly not, but it did get me thinking. It's so convenient it's a shame we can't have one here.

- Well you understand that's not a good idea. You need to stick with the bottled water.

Yes I know, but wouldn't it be possible to modify the machine to take bottles of mineral water, rather than be fed from the mains?

- I don't know, Sir. I suppose it's feasible. I'll get one of the guys at Area 51 to rig up a version.

Thanks, Jack.

Later That Month

- Sir, how's your personalised water cooler?

Great, Jack, it's really good. There is one thing though. I keep having to replace the bottle since they don't last long. Would it not be possible to get the mineral water supplied in much larger bottles?

- I can certainly make enquiries, Sir. But I'm not sure it would be a good idea. I'd have to explain why.

And is that a problem?

- Because the supplier may ask why you're not using the standard model of water cooler.

Oh, right, I see what you mean. We don't want any rumours about G-Water do we, so leave it for the moment.

- Yes, Sir.

May

Jack, there seems to be a spot of bother in France at the moment. The students seem to be causing a bit of a stir.

- Well it's more than a bit of a stir. The whole country has ground to a halt. The trade unions have come out in support of the students.

Well what was it that triggered the conflict?

- Water coolers, Sir.

What?

- Water coolers. I told you that the French government was keen on them. Since the French people don't like drinking tap water, it's the only option the French have got to get their population to drink G-Water. Well they started by installing them in government and public premises, including universities. The students weren't keen when they found out that it was just tap water, so they wouldn't drink it. The universities stopped the in-house bars and restaurants from selling the bottled stuff but the students just brought the stuff in from home. When the authorities tried to stop them doing that, the whole thing escalated and that's where we stand.

Well, what's going to happen now?

- Well the water coolers have been removed from the universities.

Was that wise? It just shows weakness on the part of the government.

- Not really, Sir, they were removed in a skip. There wasn't much left of the water coolers after the students had vented their anger on them. Hopefully that whole conflict will die down soon, however I can't see the French messing with the water in France for a long time to come.

No, I guess not, but I'm surprised that the French even tried to address this water problem, after all it may lead to the fall of their government.

- Yes, Sir, that was the plan.

You mean that this is all part of the plan to get De Gaulle out?

- We're keeping our fingers crossed, Sir.

June

Well, Jack, so much for your plan.

- Which particular plan is that, Sir?

The De Gaulle plan. Far from getting rid of him, he's gone and won the election with a large majority.

- Ah, yes, Sir, that was a bit unfortunate.

So what do we do now?

- I'm not sure yet, Sir.

Well come up with something soon.

- Yes, Sir. Is there anything else?

Yes, there is one other thing Jack. When we talked some time ago about our core ingredients, I believe that you briefed me on all of them except flour.

- Sorry Sir, that may well be the case since I couldn't cover everything in one session. With regards to flour we've more or less come to the same conclusion that we did with salt; that is we're not going to do much since most of the goodness is removed from the flour before it's used.

So this is the stuff we'll be using in our processed foods?

- That's the plan, Sir and again, it won't be difficult to persuade the manufacturers to play ball. It's the cheapest stuff they can get their hands on.

I dare say it is, Jack. So it sounds like we've got all the bases covered, fats, milk, flour, salt and sugar.

- Well that's true for now, but we will keep up the research. You never know, we may come up with something that's even worse.

We can only hope, Jack!

July

Jack, it has occurred to me that it's all very well coming up with these new-fangled foods but how are we going to encourage the public to actually consume them?

- I'm not sure what you mean, Sir. We're making regular

announcements about various aspects of the stuff that we want to promote, and of course there is the price issue. Our JUNC food is normally cheaper and more convenient than the real stuff. Sales are increasing so I'm not sure whether we need to do anything else.

Yes, Jack, I realise that but I can't help thinking that it's all a bit piecemeal and I think we need to do something about that.

- Do you have anything in mind, Sir?

Yes, I do. I think we should set up a committee to study nutrition in general and come up with some dietary recommendations. That way we could get all our ideas out there in one concise message.

- Well I must admit there is some merit in the idea. Shall I see what I can come up with?

No, Jack, that won't be necessary. I have already set the wheels in motion.

- Really, Sir?

Yes, Jack, It does happen occasionally, you know.

- Apparently so, Sir. What's your plan?

I intend to set up a congressional committee and I already have someone in mind to head it up.

- And what will they do?

My plan is that they will interview various nutritional and health professionals in order to come up with dietary recommendations for the nation.

- And who would actually prepare the final draft of this document, Sir?

The guy in charge owes me a few favours so I don't see any problems on that score.

- Well I'm not sure I like the sound of this. We normally have complete control over all aspects of STOP.

Jack, you worry too much. Let's wait and see how things progress before we start to panic.

- Whatever you say, Sir. Do you have any sort of timescale in mind?

I think six months should be enough, Jack.

September

- Sir we have a bit of a sticky situation developing in Europe. It's all to do with chocolate.

Thank you for that, Jack. You know I always appreciate a good confectionery joke to start the day.

- I know, Sir, but unfortunately it's all downhill from here.

This isn't going to involve the French is it?

- Well yes, it is, but with the Germans, Italians and all the usual suspects thrown in. It could scupper the British attempt to join the Common Market. The Europeans are in the process of throwing their Hershey bars out of the pram, metaphorically speaking.

Well if it's to do with chocolate it can't be that serious, after all we all like our Hershey bars.

- Not the Europeans, apparently.

But why not?

- Because, according to their definition, a Hershey bar can't be described as chocolate.

Well that's ridiculous, of course it's chocolate. What else could it be?

- Let me ask you, Sir. What percentage of a Hershey bar do you think is actually chocolate?

Well all of it, naturally. Unless it's the one with almonds, in which case there's nuts in it.

- So if I say there's around eleven per cent chocolate, I guess that would come as a surprise.

Eleven per cent! Good lord, if that's the case I can see where the Europeans are coming from. Even I wouldn't class that as chocolate. Don't we have rules about that sort of thing?

- We certainly do, Sir. The minimum amount of chocolate that must be in a chocolate bar is ten per cent.

Well that's disgraceful. Surely we have to do something about this.

- I don't think so, Sir. Pure chocolate is quite a healthy substance when consumed in moderation. It contains anti-oxidants which are thought to be useful in reducing heart disease. The last thing we want to do is make our version of the stuff healthier.

Oh dear, I see your point. So what do the Europeans want us to do?

- Well it's not really us that they have the problem with. It's the Brits and, in this instance, the Irish.

I guess they want the percentage increased from ten per cent.

- Oh, it's not ten per cent in the UK. It's more like twenty, and in Europe it's thirty-five per cent. But that's not their main gripe. The Brits also put vegetable oil into their chocolate, something that the Europeans abhor. They say that chocolate should only contain fats from cocoa butter and in the case of milk chocolate, from cream. And that takes me onto another issue. The British put more milk into their chocolate than the Europeans, which also reduces the percentage cocoa solids in the mix. The Europeans aren't happy with that either. And of course, we don't want them to reduce the milk content. It's one of the ways that the Brits have managed to get rid of the stuff, now that we've put people off drinking it.

But surely if they consume milk in chocolate, for us that's just as bad.

- Not when you consider all the other things that go into the mix.

Like what?

- Well there's sugar for a start, and emulsifiers. I can see why the Europeans have a problem.

Well surely this matter can't scupper the whole process, can it?

- Sir, the Europeans take their chocolate very seriously. They don't appear to be prepared to back down.

Well we can't let this matter stop the negotiations from being successful. What would we do in a similar situation?

- We'd set up a committee, Sir.

Exactly! Tell the Brits it's what they need to do, assuming that the Europeans will play ball.

- Yes, Sir.

And Jack, get me some of this European style chocolate. I'd like to see what all the fuss is about.

- Certainly, Sir.

December

- Sir, your committee idea seems to have done the trick in the chocolate showdown. The Europeans have agreed to set up a working party to study the problem.

So the negotiations are progressing well?

- As well as can be expected, given that De Gaulle is still around.

And what about my chocolate bars?

- Ah yes, Sir. I have a couple of samples. Try this. It's a bar of 70% Belgian dark chocolate.

Pause for chewing.

Er, what's that strange flavour, Jack?

- I believe what you are referring to, Sir, is the flavour of chocolate.

But I'm not sure I like it.

- Well try this one. It's milk chocolate, but there are still 25% cocoa solids in it.

Another pause for chewing

Well it's better than the last stuff but it still has that strange "chocolaty" taste.

- OK, last one, Sir. Try this.

Another pause

Ah, that's better. What is it?

- That's a Hershey bar, Sir.

Well that's what I'm going to stick to in future.

- So we finish as we started, Sir.

What?

- With a confectionary joke, Sir.

19th January 1969

- Sir, before you go, can I ask how are we getting on with the dietary recommendations? I was under the impression that we would see something within six months.

That was my original plan but the chap heading up the committee seems to be taking things a bit more seriously than I thought he would. However, I do believe that we can expect something soon.

- I hope so, Sir.

And one last thing, Jack. Can you please get the water cooler uninstalled and crated up. I'm going to take it with me.

- Yes, Sir.

Nixon

1969

20th January

- Good Morning, Sir. Welcome to the Whitehouse.

Good Morning.

- Sir, my name is Jack and I am going to brief you on STOP.

Well before you do that, there is an important issue.

- Yes, Sir, what is it?

What's happened to the water cooler? When I came for my hand over session, I seem to remember that there was one in the corner over there.

- Your predecessor took it with him, Sir.

Why on earth did he do that?

- It was a special model, Sir.

Special in what way?

- Well, Sir, if I can explain project STOP, perhaps it will become clear.

Some Hours Later

- So you see, Sir, the water cooler was one of a kind.

Well, Jack, it's going to be two of a kind. I'd like one.

- Yes, Sir, I'll get the guys at Area 51 to get one made up for you right away.

Thank you, Jack. You seem to have everything under control, except perhaps for this dietary recommendations committee. How on earth did you let that one slip through?

- Unfortunately, Sir, your predecessor thought he could manage a part of the STOP project without my input and as a result we've landed ourselves with a bit of a problem.

Well what are we going to do? This can't go on forever.

- In fact it appears that it can. The committee members are taking it all very seriously and as a result they are travelling far and wide in order to get a complete picture of what our population is eating and what effect it is having on their health. It's a big job and I can see no end in sight.

So that's your plan? We just let them get on with it?

- For the time being, until they get bored. Then we'll have to come up with something in order to make sure that the recommendations are as required by STOP.

Absolutely! You'd better get a set of draft dietary recommendations drawn up right away.

- There's no need to do that, Sir, we have one already. I took the precaution of preparing such a document as soon as I heard of the committee idea from your predecessor, just in case things did not go according to plan.

Which they haven't.

- That was never likely, Sir.

OK, so for the time being we just wait.

- Yes Sir. In the meantime, Sir, we have a situation in the UK. It appears that the government there is giving free milk to school children.

What, like a birthday present?

- No, Sir, they give it away free every school day. And worse still it's the full cream variety.

Good grief, Jack, from what you've just explained to me about STOP, that's a serious situation. If these youngsters grow up fit and healthy, it'll be that much more difficult to kill them off when they get older. So what can we do?

- We have already had some success in the UK when we got them to stop giving milk to older children. But since then there's been a change of government and when it comes to co-operation, the latest person with responsibility for the free milk is proving difficult.

Can't we offer something in return?

- We have, Sir. It turns out that the person concerned wants to become the British Prime Minister.

That could be a bit tricky.

- It'll be trickier than you think, Sir. The person in question is a woman.

The Next Day

Jack, I've been thinking about this diet problem and I think I may have come up with an idea. And before you say anything, I know that the last time you heard that from a President we ended up in a right mess, but hear me out.

- Of course, Sir.

I've been looking at the paperwork and it seems that the committee was set up to study malnutrition.

- I believe so, Sir.

Well supposing we change the remit to one which we can be pretty certain will come up with the recommendations that we would like.

- I'm not sure what sort of remit would achieve that, Sir, unless it's one that's designed to put the dairy industry out of business.

How about we ask them to tackle over-nutrition? We can point them in the right direction, i.e. fat is bad, and let them run from there. What do you think? Is there a problem with my idea?

Pause

Jack?

- I'm giving the idea some thought, Sir.

A Further Pause

And?

- And I can't see that there is any problem with it, except for the fact that I never thought of it first.

Well if that's the worst thing, Jack, then there is no real problem, is there.

- Not for you, Sir, but there may be for me. I'm not used to having a boss that's smarter than me.

Get used to it, Jack.

April

Well done, Jack!

- Thank you, Sir. But why am I being congratulated?

De Gaulle. He has resigned at last! How did you do it?

- Well, Sir, as much as I would like to take the credit, in this case it was nothing to do with me. It was his ego.

And who on earth is Hisego? He sounds Spanish.

- No, no, Sir, not a person. I mean his ego. He was too confident of his own power over the French. He staked his reputation on a referendum and he lost. He said he would resign and he did. I think the French people had had enough.

Well whatever the reason, it's good news. Let's hope his replacement is more accommodating.

- I'm sure he will be, Sir.

Do you mean he's one of ours?

- I'm not sure that any French person will ever be "one of ours", Sir, but let's say I don't anticipate any problems.

July

Ah, Jack, I see the Apollo 9 moon mission has been a success.

- That depends on what you mean by "success". If you mean that we have been able to pull off a big hoax on the American public, then I suppose you're right.

You're sounding rather bitter, Jack. That's not like you.

- Well, Sir, I was around when we first committed to landing a man on the Moon. I'm a bit disappointed that after handing out all that money to NASA, we had to get Hollywood to fake it.

Yes, I can see what you mean. But since we seem to have pulled it off, it makes me wonder whether we can't use the same principle again in other situations.

- What did you have in mind?

I mean we could use Hollywood to help us with STOP. I'm not sure quite how but it's something to think about.

- Yes, Sir.

September

- Sir, some time ago we came up with the idea that we could try and influence the scientific research that takes place, both the subject matter and results.

Ah yes, so we did. Have we had any success?

- Well to some extent we have, but not necessarily in the way we expected.

Well we either have or we haven't. Which is it?

- It's in the "doesn't matter" category.

Which means what?

- It means that the situation appears to be taking care of itself, and for several reasons. The first is that in many cases the scientists can be pretty woolly when it comes to conclusions, especially if it goes against the received wisdom.

Received wisdom? By that I assume you mean if they don't come up with the answer we want.

- Precisely, Sir. If you were a researcher and you came to the end of a particular piece of work and didn't come up with the right answer, what would be your options? Of course you could start on a completely new topic but for that you would need funding.

Which wouldn't be forthcoming?

- Let's say that they may find it difficult.

Or?

- Or you can use what appears to be the most common conclusion at the end of any bit of research no matter what the subject. That's the phrase "more research is required". This way the researchers stand a chance of getting further funding in order to continue with the same topic and we get what appears to be an inconclusive result.

But supposing a researcher comes up with the answer that we want?

- Well bearing in mind that we are generally trying to mislead the public, that situation doesn't often arise.

But what if it does?

- If it does, the researcher will have no trouble getting funding for their next project.

OK, so that's one angle. What else is there?

- Well if someone does come up with the wrong answer and comes out and says as much, it's not just the funding for their next project that would be difficult. They'd have trouble getting any sort of job. After all, who would want to employ someone who goes against RW.

Who's "RW".

- It's received wisdom again, Sir. It's how we generally refer to the truth, these days.

Or at least our version of it?

- Yes, Sir. And there is also one really useful twist to the whole research thing and that's in the detail. It probably eclipses all the other issues on the subject.

Well that sounds good. What have you come up with?

- Well we've realised that with most research we're normally interested in a very general outcome. Will it shorten their lives or won't it? For example, do people who drink red wine live longer healthier lives than those who don't. But the actual research tends to be more specific. To take the same example, the question for the researchers will be, does drinking red wine cause liver cancer?

I'm not sure where you're going with this Jack.

- Bear with me, Sir, since this is very important. We've been assuming that if we want to influence the research we need to do it through funding and that is certainly an issue. But we can also achieve our end and leave the scientists with a clear conscience if only we ask the right question to start with, preferably one we already know the answer to.

Sorry, Jack, I'm still not with you.

- Let's take my example. We ask someone to do research into whether drinking red wine increases the chance of getting liver cancer. We already know, or at least suspect, that the answer is yes. The research confirms our theory. The headlines will read "Red Wine Causes Cancer" and the inference is that drinking red wine is bad. Of course what we don't do, and what we don't want the research to even consider, is whether people who drink red wine actually live longer healthier lives than those who don't.

Oh, I get the picture, and presumably the opposite is also true. For example we could say something positive about margarine without highlighting the downside.

- Good point, Sir.

Well I think you have something here Jack. It all sounds very positive.

- But there's more, Sir. We also have another trick up our sleeves when it comes to the underlying statistics.

Now, Jack, you know I'm not very good with numbers.

- I know, Sir, so I'll try to keep it simple. For example, if I were to say that someone who consumes a lot of saturated fat is fifty per cent move likely to die of a heart attack than someone who has a low fat diet, what would you say?

I'd say that I've been seriously misled, Jack, mainly by you.

- No, Sir, this is not a true example, it's just to make the point about statistics.

Well OK, in which case I'd say that it was a very impressive figure.

- Exactly, I think that most people would. But in fact the actual numbers behind that stat would be that, in a given group of people being tested, those on a high fat diet have a three per cent chance of dying from a heart attack whereas for those on a low fat diet the figure is two per cent. This is the real percentage difference.

But hang on a minute, the difference there is just one per cent. Even I can see that.

- Yes, but three is fifty per cent bigger than two so strictly speaking what I said is true. But if we want to put people off eating fat, it stands to reason that they would ignore a difference of one per cent, which is the actual difference, but they will sit up and take notice if we say it's fifty per cent, which is the relative difference. Of course in practice, if you look at the raw numbers, neither group should be particularly worried. In fact the margin of error that would probably exist in this sort of research could well mean that the opposite is true.

But doesn't that make the stats rather meaningless.

- Well not from our point of view it doesn't. We can use these sorts of figures to make our propaganda stick in the minds of the population at large. And of course, we can use a different version of the percentage game depending on what we want to achieve. If we don't like the research, we'll use the real percentage; if the results are in our favour, we'll use the relative value.

It sounds like I need to be very careful when I study the results of some of this research.

- I think it would be best, Sir, if I just give you the edited highlights.

You may be right there, Jack.

1970

January

- How's the water cooler.

Well it was a long time coming but it's working fine.

- I'm glad of that, Sir, because it's causing us a bit of a problem.

How can it be, it's just sitting in the corner of the office. And the extra-large bottles are a great idea.

- Well, Sir, I can't take the credit for that. Your predecessor had the idea first. But I told him it was not good news, what with the secrecy surrounding G-Water.

So why have we gone ahead with it now?

- Well we didn't, Sir. Your predecessor did. Once he left office, he contacted the manufacturer of bottled water and asked for a special delivery. When the company realised the reason for the request, they saw a commercial opportunity. They are now supplying water coolers that take large bottles of mineral water. They've supplied thousands. Apparently, they're very popular because you don't need the plumbing, just an electricity socket.

But can't we get the supplier to just fill the bottles with tap water?

- Apparently not, Sir. The customers are willing to pay a premium to get mineral water. They think it's better for them.

Well they're right there aren't they, so what are we going to do?

- I'm not sure that there is anything we can do in the short term. But we'll keep it under consideration in case circumstances change.

OK, Jack, do that.

February

Jack, I've had Mrs Thatcher on the phone and she seems to be a bit upset about the whole school milk thing. She seems to have been under the impression free school milk is something that is a problem unique to the UK. Unfortunately, she's now found out that it's a common practice in the USA and in fact many States have a free school milk program.

- Who told her that?

Never mind how she found out, Jack. It appears that she's right and she wants to know why she was the one to be put on the spot by doing away with free school milk when we weren't prepared to do the same. And in fact, since it seems to be such a good idea, I'd also like to know why we haven't followed suit. But first I'd like to know whether she has been deliberately misled.

- Well to be fair, Sir, she never asked about free school milk in the USA. She just assumed that the problem only existed in the UK.

As did I, Jack. And I suppose we were happy for her to go on believing that?

- It suited our purpose, Sir. We wanted to see what sort of flak she would receive for carrying out the policy before we attempted to do the same thing.

Oh, I see, and when she did receive a lot of "flak", you decided it was too risky to try it here.

- That just about sums it up, Sir, but there wasn't really any option. Here, free milk is not a Federal issue and there's no way that State Governors are going to risk their popularity by getting rid of it.

So where does that leave us?

- We're looking at a different solution. We've realised that, even though we can't stop the free milk, we can at least make it less healthy and we're going to do that by offering flavoured milk. The excuse will be that we're trying to make it more attractive to students but in practice it means that we can add all sorts of interesting things to the drink. Of course, we'll start with sugar but we don't need to stop there.

I guess that you're talking about things like strawberry and chocolate flavours, in which case I hope I can safely assume that there won't be a trace of real strawberries or chocolate in the mix.

- No, none whatsoever, Sir.

Good. But in the meantime, what do I do about Mrs Thatcher?

- You can explain our dilemma and point out that, since we've already promised that she can become Prime Minister in return for her co-operation, we don't feel the need to do anything else at this stage, and that includes making an apology.

I think that sort of thing would sound better coming from you, Jack.

- As you wish, Sir.

April

- Sir we have a situation. It's concerning Apollo 13.

I saw the lift-off myself. It looked very convincing.

- So it should, Sir. This one is the real thing.

What do you mean?

- Well, as you know, normally the rocket is launched and the Apollo capsule is put into orbit round the earth. When they get to go to the moon, that's when Hollywood takes over.

Yes, I know all that. What are you trying to say?

- Well, Sir, this time they are actually heading for the Moon.

How did that happen?

- I don't know all the details yet but it appears that there was a party of school children who were visiting mission control at the time and just for a joke, one of them pressed the button marked "Head For The Moon".

If we are not actually going there, why did we need the button?

- Well the mission control room needs to look as realistic as possible. Surely, Jack, the question we need to ask is why was it actually connected to anything?

- That I haven't established yet.

So what's going to happen? Can we turn the spaceship around?

- No, Sir, we can't do that. We are going to have to let the astronauts go to the moon, swing round the back and head for home.

And what chance do they stand?

- Well, Sir, when the money ran out, the lunar landing module was pretty much finished, but the command module was in a state of flux.

What does that mean?

- It means that it wasn't finished. So far nothing has gone wrong but it's unlikely they'll get all the way to the moon and back without something happening. We'll just have to wait and see.

Can't we get Hollywood to come up with a happy ending?

- No, I don't think that'll be necessary, Sir. Whatever happens, it can only give credibility to the whole moon landing saga.

OK, Jack, keep me posted.

- I don't think I'll need to, Sir. It'll be on all the TV channels.

Two Days Later

- Sir, as expected, something has gone wrong with the Apollo 13 mission. There's been an explosion on board.

Yes, I know, it's on the TV. What happened?

- The oxygen tank exploded.

What does that mean to the mission?

- Well the astronauts cannot use the command module any more. They have moved to the lunar module.

Will they be safe there?

- The air supply is the problem but luckily they have some bits and pieces on board that will help them put together something to purify the air.

Like what?

- Well they have things like sticky backed plastic, empty washing up liquid bottles, toilet rolls, milk bottle tops and empty cardboard egg boxes.

Good grief, why do they take stuff like that on a mission to the moon.

- Remember, Sir, this wasn't supposed to be a mission to the moon. It's part of a Hollywood film set and so everything is cobbled together from everyday items.

Just as well.

- Yes, Sir.

Three Days Later

I see on the TV that it looks like the Apollo 13 astronauts will get back safely. I think it would be a good idea if I meet the astronauts personally when they land.

- I think that would be a good idea, Sir.

Which lot do I go to?

- Lot, Sir?

Yes, film lot. You know, Hollywood.

- Sir, please remember that this one is real life, not a film set. In any case, the landing on Earth is always real. It's the landings on the Moon that are faked.

Sorry, Jack, sometimes it's difficult to remember.

- I can appreciate that, Sir.

September

- Sir, we have finally persuaded Italy to change the law that made contraception illegal.

Well it's about time. And has the Catholic Church bought into this change?

- No, Sir, there's no movement on that front.

I assume that most people in Italy are Catholic so what'll happen?

- I think that common sense will prevail. Contraceptives will now be available and Catholics will use them but they'll no doubt feel guilty and feel the need to go to confession. I wouldn't be at all surprised if the queues aren't already forming outside the confessional.

So where does that leave us?

- Ireland is still a problem, for the same reason as Italy. It's a mainly Catholic country.

But you're not thinking of intervening are you, Jack?

- No, Sir. I'm aware that you value the Irish vote and would not wish to jeopardize your chance of re-election.

Too right, Jack!

1971

February

Jack, what's this I hear about a mass sterilization program in India?

- What about it?

I mean is it anything we can use in the USA?

- Well, the Indian government has launched a plan to encourage men and women to volunteer to be sterilized. They have considered other methods of contraception but they are not keen on any of them.

Why not?

- Two main reasons. First, sterilization is the most reliable. If you use any other method, you are relying on individuals bothering or remembering to take some action, like use a condom or take a birth control pill. And that takes us to the other reason.

Cost?

- Exactly, cost. With all other methods, there is an on-going cost involved, but with sterilization, there is just the one off cost. So in the long term it's cheaper by far.

But how do they encourage people to get sterilized in the first place?

- They give them incentives.

Like what?

- Well, I believe the going rate just now for a vasectomy is $6, a bag of food and a sari.

Sari?

- An Indian dress. It's not for the man, it's for his wife.

Well it's doesn't sound like very much of an incentive.

- Maybe not here, Sir, but in India, $6 is a lot of money.

So do you think the plan would work here?

- I don't think so, Sir.

Not even in the Bronx?

- No, Sir.

Not even if we make it $10, 2 hot dogs and a pair of trainers?

- No, Sir!!

May

- Sir, the tobacco companies have come up with something regarding safer smoking.

It's about time. How long have they been working on it?

- About 7 years, Sir. I think that it's the fact that adverts are now banned on TV and radio that has spurred them into action. They know that the health issues concerning cigarettes are now a burning issue.

And what have they come up with?

- A safer cigarette.

I thought that was the last thing we wanted them to do.

- Wait until you see what they have produced. I have one here.

It looks the same as a normal cigarette. Have they done something to the tobacco?

- No, Sir. They found they couldn't do that since they need to retain the addiction and therefore the nicotine. No, Sir, it's the filter. If you look closely you'll see that there are holes in paper around the filter.

I can't see them, but I'll take your word for it. What good do they do?

- Well, when the smoker inhales, they draw in some air through the holes and therefore dilute the tobacco smoke.

Clever idea, but how much safer is it. We still want them to kill people.

- In reality, Sir, there's no difference between these cigarettes and the normal ones.

But how can that be?

- Well, for a start just hold the cigarette. That's it. Now can you see, the fingers cover many of the holes, rendering them ineffective.

But there are still a few holes allowing air in.

- Yes, but we've discovered in tests that the average smoker inhales more strongly in order to get the same "fix". The net result is the same as if they smoke a regular cigarette.

Sounds like good news, but I trust that this is not going to be something the tobacco companies will mention in their adverts.

- No, Sir, I'm sure they won't. But in the meantime, there appears to be nothing we can do to stop congress approving the law to put health warnings on cigarette packets.

No, I think that's a foregone conclusion. But the tobacco companies are still challenging the medical research in the courts.

- Yes, Sir, but again, I feel it's going to be a lost cause.

What, even though the tobacco companies are awash with money?

- Sir, there is only so much an expensive army of lawyers can do. It's mainly a delaying tactic.

Well we need to come up with something fast. Millions of Americans have quit smoking in the last few years which means that we have to keep finding other ways of killing them off.

1972

April

- Sir, I came as soon as you called. Is it something urgent?

It may well be, Jack.

- Concerning STOP, Sir?

Yes. I've had a message from the White House press office. Someone from the Washington Post has asked whether I have any comment to make about "water".

- What about water?

Exactly, what about water! That's all I've got, as yet there is no more information. What do you think they mean, Jack?

- I'm not sure, Sir, but if they are talking about tap water, we may have a big problem.

You don't need to tell me, Jack, since G-Water is one of the mainstays of the whole STOP project. We need to keep the population, or at least most of them, in a state of gullibility in order for all our other plans to work. You'd better start digging. See if you can find out what this journalist knows. I reckon that if he knew any details, the question would have been more specific.

- Yes, Sir, I'm sure you're right. I'll start looking into it right away.

May

- Sir, I've looked into the issue to do with the journalist and the "water" question.

What have you come up with?

- It's both good and bad news, Sir.

Let's start with the good.

- Well you were right. He doesn't know any details. The question was a fishing expedition.

And what's the bad news.

- He appears to know that there is a secret project that has something to do with water.

And how did he come to that conclusion?

- I believe that he overheard someone talking in a coffee shop.

But that's terrible. Do we know who was doing the talking?

- No, Sir, not at this stage. But in one respect, it's good news.

Why's that?

- Well, it means that the incident was an accident. It would be much worse if someone was deliberately leaking information. In that case, there would be little that we could do. As it is, we may be able to stop this going any further.

I'm not sure how we could do that.

- Neither do I yet, Sir, but he doesn't know anything about STOP except that it involves water. Perhaps we need to come up with an alternative fictitious scenario that also involves water in order to throw him off the scent.

Well that could work, but I'm not sure what such a scenario would entail. See what you can come up with and in particular, try to find out who was blabbing in the coffee shop.

- Sir, we certainly need to do that since if this cover story is to have any credibility, it may need to come from the same source.

What do you mean?

- Well if the source was person A, then there's no point in try to get person B to lead to journalist off the scent. Ideally, the misinformation should also come from person A.

Yes, I see what you mean. You'd better get on the case.

- Yes, Sir.

The Following Week

- Sir, I think we've found the source of the "water" leak. It was probably a chap called Ross. He's friendly with Rachel.

And what was he doing blabbing about one of our projects? He can only have got it from Rachel.

- I know, Sir. It's a serious breach of security. But at least we know

159

the extent of the problem.

How's that?

- Well I've questioned him and he maintains that the only thing he mentioned was the fact that a friend of his is working on the "water project". That's all.

There's nothing else?

- He says not.

So why is the journalist so convinced that there is something important going on?

- I think that's down to our initial response to his query. We didn't give a straight answer so he thinks there's something going on.

That sounds a bit like our responses to UFO sightings, where it works to our advantage. Except in this case, of course, it's working against us but none the less the plan to create a diversion could work.

- Yes, Sir.

And have you come up with anything?

- Not yet, Sir, but we're working on it.

And who's "we".

- Me and Rachel, Sir. She got us into this mess so it's in her interest to get us out of it.

June

- Sir, I think we've come up with something regarding the "water" leak.

Jack, can you stop referring to the "water leak". It sounds like there's a problem with the central heating.

- Exactly, Sir. If anyone overhears the conversation, they won't realise what we're talking about.

We're in the Oval Office, Jack. Who do you think is going to hear us talking?

- You never know, Sir.

Well as President, I think perhaps I should know. Is there anything you need to tell me, Jack?

- No, Sir, I'm just being careful.

So what have you come up with?

- Watergate, Sir.

And what is a "water gate", Jack?

- It's an office complex in Washington which is being used as the Democratic National Committee headquarters for the presidential election.

And how does that help us?

- We think that we can come up with something that connects us to the Watergate building.

Like what?

- Like a plan to bug the offices.

That's a bit drastic, isn't it? Not to say illegal.

- Maybe so, but it's got to be something significant, otherwise the journalist won't bite.

Well I want to be kept at arm's length on this. It could get messy. Make sure you line up a fall guy in case it all goes pear-shaped.

- That's already been covered, Sir.

Good. Go ahead and keep me informed.

- Yes, Sir.

1973

January

I see that the Brits have finally been allowed to join the Common Market. It's been a long time coming, in fact I've forgotten why it was important.

- Well originally it was because we didn't understand what it was all about and we thought we needed some inside information.

And now?

- And now we're pretty sure it just has two purposes.

Which are?

- To make the French farmers rich and the give the political ruling classes in Europe a lucrative exit route when they lose power in their own country.

You mean a gravy train.

- Yes, Sir.

So there's nothing for us to worry about?

- Not yet, Sir.

April

Jack, how are we going with the relocation of staff to New York?

- Well, Sir, we took possession of the top 10 floors of the South Tower last month.

And how many staff are now located there?

- As of today, Sir?

Of course, as of today.

- Three, Sir.

Three! That works out at 100 million dollars per person.

- Er, no, Sir. It's more like 300 million dollars per person.

What!

- The original estimates were a little on the low side, Sir.

And where has all the extra money come from?

- The defence budget, as authorised by your predecessor, Sir.

I've looked at the purchase order and it says 335 million dollars.

- Ah, but the small print on the back authorises payment of any legitimate additional costs. Did you read the small print, Sir?

I don't read small print, Jack.

- I'll bear that in mind, Sir.

Anyway, regardless of all that, why so few people?

- The numbers will increase, but so far the building only houses new recruits. We haven't transferred anyone from Area 51.

Why not?

- Because if we did there would be no-one left. We held a ballot of all 2,500 staff there to ask whether they wanted to transfer to New York.

And how many accepted?

- 2,610.

What!

- We think there may have been a problem with the ballot.

Oh really!

- We believe that in order to increase their chance of being moved some staff put their name into the hat more than once.

So what are you going to do?

- Nothing, Sir. The current staff will stay where they are. As they drop out, their replacements will be located in New York.

Can we do that?

- What do you mean?

Can we keep them locked up in Area 51?

- If you remember, it was always the case that the fences at Area 51 were designed to keep the staff in. Of course, it now serves a dual purpose by keeping the public out.

So the answer is "yes".

- Yes.

And do we have a name for this place?

- It's the World Trade Centre, Sir.

I know that, but we'll need a name for our part of it. I thought perhaps "Area 52".

- Area 52?

Yes, you see the previous place was Area 51 and.....

- Yes, I can see where you are coming from, Sir.

So we'll use it?

- Unless we can come up with something better.

Good.

July

Jack, how are we getting on with the relocation of staff to Area 52?

- It's progressing very slowly, Sir. And as I explained before, it's not really a relocation.

Yes, I know we haven't moved anyone from Area 51, but what about the other staff.

- What other staff?

Well there's Monica and Rachael for a start. Where are they based?

- At the Pentagon, Sir.

Well couldn't we move them to New York?

- We could, Sir, but I do have regular meetings with them. It would be inconvenient.

Have you heard of the telephone, Jack?

- Of course I have, Sir, but there's also the fact that much of what we do comes out of the defence budget. It's useful to have a presence in the Pentagon.

I can't see that it would make much difference, Jack. No, let's move them to Area 52.

- Yes, Sir.

August

Jack, I was under the impression that Monica had moved to Area 52.

- Er, yes, Sir.

Well how come I saw her at the Pentagon yesterday.

- She must have been visiting someone, Sir.

She was in an office which had her name on the door.

- I didn't know that you were going to visit the Pentagon, Sir.

Well it just goes to show that you don't know everything, Jack.

- Apparently not, Sir.

So?

- So what, Sir?

Why is she still there?

- At this stage, she is based on both sites. But all her staff are based at Area 52.

Staff? I thought it was just her and Rachael.

- Er, no, Sir. She has a couple of dozen staff.

A couple of dozen! What do they all do?

- They come up with ideas, Sir.

So when you say that Monica has come up with an idea, you really mean her team?

- Well of course, Sir. You didn't think that she came up with all that stuff on her own, did you?

Er, well now I come to think about it, I guess not. After all, they have come up with some good stuff over the years.

- Yes they have, Sir.

Well what about the rest of Area 52? Is it being fully utilised?

- Yes, Sir, it is now full.

Good. And you still think that it is secure?

- Yes, Sir, I do.

September

- Sir, we still have a bit of a problem with the "water leak". The journalists are not yet convinced about our cover story.

Journalists? I thought there was only one of them.

- No, Sir, apparently there are two, Bob Woodward and Carl Bernstein. And they're very sceptical.

So what do we do?

- I've already come up with something. We are going to suggest that the plan to bug the Watergate offices was recorded.

Recorded where?

- In the Oval Office.

But who could do that?

- You, Sir.

Me! Why would I record my own meetings?

- For posterity, Sir.

I don't know anyone called posterity.

- You know very well what I mean, Sir. It would be for the sake of historical record. It would be useful for future generations to be able to listen to the sorts off discussions you have. It would help people to understand how government works.

And you think that would be a good thing?

- No, Sir, of course it wouldn't, at least not in the short term. But these tapes would only be released after we are long gone.

Well if this is to be credible, I would have to tape more than just the discussions concerning Watergate.

- That's correct, Sir. We'll need to fabricate some previous conversations and then tape current and future ones. That should be convincing.

And how are these journalists going to find out about the tapes.

- We'll have to plant an informer.

And again I trust you've got someone in mind?

- Yes, Sir. He works for the FBI.

FBI! How on earth are they going to get in on the act?

- Well if there is a criminal investigation, they're bound to be involved.

This is all sounding a bit dodgy. And there is just one slight problem with this plan.

- And what's that, Sir?

Well, if these tapes are incriminating, why don't I just erase them?

- That's a good point, Sir. Let's hope they don't think of that.

November

- Sir, Mrs Thatcher is pressing us for progress on the promise we made.

Sorry, who are you referring to, Jack.

- Mrs Thatcher, Sir. She's a British politician. In order to ensure her co-operation over the milk issue, we promised that we would help her to become Prime Minister. She now wants to know what progress we've made.

And what progress have we made?

- Not a great deal, Sir.

And what progress have we tried to make?

- Not a lot, Sir.

Is that the same as none, Jack?

- Yes, Sir.

And why is that?

- Well, Sir, once we got what we wanted…..

Which was what?

- That the Brits stop giving out free milk in UK schools, Sir. You remember that we decided that it was too healthy and wanted the practice stopped. Thatcher was the minister responsible for education at the time.

And now she wants payback.

- I guess so, Sir.

So she wants to be Prime Minister. What does this entail?

- Well there are really two stages. The Prime Minster is the leader of the majority party in the House of Commons, which in Thatcher's case are the Conservatives, so ultimately they will have to win a general election.

But first, she needs to become leader.

- Yes, Sir.

How are we going to fix that, Jack?

- While the Tories are in power, there's not a lot we can do. We can't unseat their existing leader. We'll have to wait until the General Election has taken place. If the Labour party wins, then we can start working on a plan.

And if not?

- Then Thatcher may have a long wait.

1974

January

So what's happening about the dietary recommendations, Jack?

- Things are much the same, Sir.

So you're telling me that things are just rolling along with no sign of a conclusion.

- That's correct, Sir. Of course, the fact that we changed the remit has had a significant effect.

But surely it must come to a halt at some stage, after all the costs are spiralling.

- Exactly, Sir, and we intend to let that situation continue. As far as I can see the only way that we can call a halt to this whole thing is by using the cost card. We'll let, or should I say encourage, the committee to rack up the expenses and then we can use the excuse of cost savings to close them down.

OK, but we still have to work out a plan to get our own version of the dietary recommendations adopted, just in case they don't come up with the right answers.

- I don't think that there's any danger of that, Sir. Now that we've pointed them in the right direction we should get the result we need.

February

- Sir, there has been a breakout at Area 51.

How many people are involved?

- I believe that initially there were eight, but five were immediately apprehended, so that means there are still three on the loose. But we don't think they will get far.

But how did this happen? I thought it was a very secure location.

- It's about as secure as we can make it, but with the best will in the world, no site can be 100% secure. However, the site and size of the

169

complex makes it very difficult for anyone to get very far. It's not a particularly hospitable place.

No, I guess not. Keep me updated and let me know as soon as they are recaptured.

- Yes, Sir.

The Following Week

- Sir, the remaining three escapees have been recaptured. They were hiding in a remote area less than a mile from Area 51. As we suspected, they didn't get far.

Good, but I bet this isn't the last time there's an attempt to escape.

- No, I suspect you're right. And on another matter, Sir, the Labour party has won the British general election.

So that's good news for Thatcher.

- Not necessarily. In fact, when I say won, they've gained more seats than any other party, but not a majority. The expectation is that there'll be another election soon so the Tories are unlikely to change leadership just yet.

I guess Mrs Thatcher will have to wait.

- Yes, Sir, I guess she will.

July

- Sir, we need to do something about Greece.

You mean the military junta?

- Yes, Sir. I think that it's served its purpose. They seem to be getting a bit trigger happy.

I thought that the invasion of Cyprus by the Greeks was a good thing, you know, body count wise. You always tell me that we can never have too many dead bodies.

- Well I'm not sure I used those exact words, Sir. But in any case, in the short term bodies are not the be all and end all. In this instance it's our European allies. They're getting a bit nervous about having a gung-ho military junta on their door step. Perhaps it's time to do something about it.

I suppose it has achieved its purpose since, with de Gaulle out of the way, France has become somewhat more compliant.

- Well marginally so, Sir. And there's no guarantee that it was our experiment with Greek democracy, or rather lack of, that did the trick. We'll never know.

No, I suppose not. But at this stage, there's no reason not to let Greece revert back to a democratic system.

- None that I can think of, Sir.

Good.

- Is there anything else, Sir?

Yes there is, Jack. The Watergate situation seems to be getting out of control.

- Yes, I know, Sir. The Senate seems to be taking the bugging allegations seriously.

Well of course they are, after all that was the plan. It's the repercussions I'm worried about. We've handed over the fall guys, but they seem to be out for my blood. There is even talk of impeachment.

- I'm sure it won't come to that, Sir.

Ford

1974

August

- Sir, welcome to the Oval Office.

I have been here before, Jack.

- Yes, Sir, but nevertheless, welcome in your new capacity as President.

Thank you, Jack, but the circumstances could have been better. It's very unfortunate that my predecessor had to leave office under a cloud.

- Yes, Sir.

But what I don't understand is why didn't he simply erase the tapes?

- Ah that would be a good point at which to start my briefing.

One Day Later

But as Vice President, why was I not briefed on STOP?

- Sir, it has always been the case that STOP is known only to those people who need to know.

And the Vice President doesn't need to know?

- Well with due respect, Sir, you did the job of Vice President perfectly well without knowing.

So you're saying that proves I didn't need to know. I suppose I can't argue with you there.

- Whatever you say, Sir.

Well what's the next stage of this debacle?

- That will be where you give a full pardon to your predecessor, Sir. In the circumstances, it's the least you can do.

I suppose I have no choice, but it's not going to look good. After all, he has committed a crime.

- Crimes, Sir, plural. There is more than one offence with his name against it. But remember it's all a smoke screen since he never actually did anything illegal.

I dare say, but it will still look bad for me if I pardon a felon.

- Better that than have him spill the beans on the whole STOP project.

I dare say. OK, issue the pardon.

- Yes, Sir.

October

- Sir, the result of the British general election is in and this time the Labour party has won an overall majority.

So the Conservative party will be ready for a change of leadership.

- I should think so, Sir, although I don't think that Mr Heath has realised that yet. The rest of the party does, but of course they just don't know yet who that new leader will be.

But I dare say we do, don't we, Jack!

- I sincerely hope so, yes, Sir.

November

- Sir, the Indian government has been in touch.

Ah yes. The sterilization programme in India: how's it going?

- Not so good, Sir. The initial success was short lived. Most of the population who were willing to volunteer did so in the first couple of years. And many of them were older people so it hasn't been the success that the Indian government had hoped for.

So what are they going to do?

- They want some money from us. They say that if they had more money they could increase the value of the incentives.

And how much do they want to borrow?

- A billion dollars.

How much!

- A billion dollars, Sir. And I think they want more of a donation than a loan. I don't think we'd be getting the money back any time soon.

What are they going to offer each person, a car?

- No, Sir, without wishing to state the obvious, it's the population of

India that's the problem in that it's very large. It recently passed the six hundred thousand mark and if they don't take any action it will be one billion by the end of the century. They think that if they are going to have any effect on the population they need to get 50 million people to be sterilized. And to do this they think they need to increase the incentive to $100.

But that only amounts to half a billion dollars. What is going to happen to the rest?

- That's what I think they call "shrinkage".

And what's "shrinkage".

- You know, Sir. It's what happens whenever we give money to third world countries. We're lucky if even half of what we donate reaches the end target.

Well "shrinkage" or no "shrinkage", we're not giving them any money. They need to come up with another option.

- OK, I'll relay your response and we'll see what they come up with.

1975

February

Jack, I gather Mrs Thatcher has been elected leader of the Conservative party. That must have been a bit tricky to arrange. How do you get all the Tory party members onside?

- That's not really how it works, Sir. The decision is really made by an inner circle of Tory grandees and then the Tory members of parliament get to vote. The broader membership doesn't have a say.

But I thought that they had a democratic system of government in the UK. This doesn't sound very democratic to me.

- Well obviously the population at large get to vote on which party they want to govern. But I'll concede that the election of the leader is not particularly democratic.

So how does the Labour party do it?

- Ah, there the members do have a vote.

Well that sounds better.

- Not necessarily, Sir. The Trade Unions represent a majority of the membership of the Labour party and their block votes normally decide the leadership contest.

What, you mean Trades Unions like our Teamsters?

- Yes, Sir.

Good grief, Jack. That's the equivalent of the Teamsters deciding who will be the next Democratic presidential candidate.

- Yes, I guess it's very much like that.

So what's the next step?

- Well there won't be another election for four or five years, so we have some breathing space. But in the long term, we need to make sure that the Tories win the next general election.

June

Jack, what's going on in India? There seems to be some unrest.

- There is indeed, Sir. And I think that you can take the credit.

Me! What have I done? I've never been to India!

- Well, Sir, you remember the conversation we had last year about the Indian government's sterilization programme.

You mean the billion dollar loan! I'm not likely to forget.

- As I pointed out at the time, it was a donation, Sir, not a loan.

Well whatever it was supposed to be is irrelevant now. What's going on?

- Well, Sir, the only option the Indian government could come up with was to make sterilization compulsory and the only way to do that is to declare martial law, which is what they've done.

That's a bit drastic isn't it?

- Well under Martial Law I think that there are a few other issues that the Indian government can deal with more easily.

Like what?

- Like clamping down on the opposition.

Martial Law allows you to do that?

- Yes, Sir. But before you even ask, no we can't declare Martial Law in the USA.

Are you sure?

- Yes, Sir.

It would make so many things much easier.

- I'm sure it would, but the answer is still no.

Later That Month

What are the Brits playing at?

- What do you mean, Sir?

They're having a referendum on their membership of the Common Market. And that's after we made so much effort to get them in.

- Well unfortunately, Sir, Mr Wilson made the pledge in his election manifesto and he feels obliged to deliver on the commitment.

Good grief, Jack, we politicians say a lot of things in order to be elected, but we don't have to actually carry them out.

- Apparently not, Sir. But in this case, Wilson feels that it was a significant commitment and as such he must deliver. In any case, he has renegotiated the terms under which the British joined the Common Market and so he thinks he can justify recommending a "yes" vote.

Well let's hope so. And Jack, how's the FAST food project going? I've been seeing a lot of ads on TV for the sort of stuff that we were banking on. I hope we're not picking up the tab.

- Oh no, Sir. The burger and pizza companies are paying for their own adverts and in the main things are going very well.

From your tone of voice can I assume that there are aspects that aren't going well?

- Well, Sir, in some respects things are better than expected. Our plan was that people would augment their diet with FAST food but for some people that's all they eat. Unfortunately it's mainly the poor since it's all that they can afford. For the better off, FAST food is at best an occasional "treat". The rest of the time they are often eating proper meals, some of which are of course JUNC food.

Hang on a minute, Jack. Aren't FAST food and JUNC food the same?

- Well, Sir, in general all FAST food is JUNC food, but it's not necessarily true the other way round, i.e. not all JUNC food is FAST food. For example, if you buy one of our special ready meals from the supermarket it could contain a lot of special ingredients like MSG, Trans Fats and corn syrup. It's therefore JUNC food but there's nothing FAST about it. You still cook it, or should I say reheat it.

- Hang on a minute Jack, what's MSG?

Ah, now that's something we have come up with that's very promising since we can use it instead of salt.

But I thought that we were happy with salt.

- Yes, Sir, but I also said that we would continue to search for alternatives that were even worse than salt and MSG, or to give it its full name, monosodium glutamate, is such a substance. It's made from soy.

Soy? What, like soy sauce?

- Well yes, in that they are both made from the soya bean. We have great hopes for this particular crop and one day we hope that all food will be made from soy.

That's a joke, right, Jack?

- We'll see.

OK, but getting back to the main issue, what are we going to do?

- Well somehow we have to get the people who are better off to embrace FAST food.

1976

January

- Sir, JUNC has been giving some thought to the problem of money.

I've never found money a problem, Jack. It's a lack of money that's normally the problem.

- Not as far as STOP is concerned, where it transpires money is definitely a problem.

How so?

- Well, Sir, we are coming up with ways of killing off the population but people are finding ways of avoiding our traps.

How can that be the case?

- Well, for example, take JUNC food. We have come up with all sorts of stuff that will in the long term shorten people's lives. But those people with enough money can buy good quality food, probably organic and certainly more expensive than our stuff. And the same thing applies to health issues. As fast as we can make them sick, someone will come up with a cure. Those that can afford it will often pay to get better.

Well, what do you suggest?

- We need to make people poorer.

If you think I'm going to raise income tax, you've got another think coming. I've got my re-election to consider.

- No, Sir, taxes are not the answer. For a start, whatever we come up with, it needs to affect the global economy. Although we'd like to do so, we cannot apply taxes to other countries, at least not yet. Also, we need to affect companies, not just individuals. For example, if we can make the drugs companies suffer, they will cut back on research and development.

And that'll mean fewer drugs, and therefore more sick people.

- Exactly, Sir.

Well this is all very well and good, but how do we achieve it?

- We're not sure yet. We need to give it some further thought.

Well don't take too long.

- No, Sir.

A Week Later

Jack, following our conversation the other day about money, I've been thinking.

- In that case, Sir, you'll be needing some aspirin.

What?

- Sorry, Sir, nothing. You were saying?

The banks, Jack, it's the banks. They must hold the key to the money problem. After all, they're central to the financial system. If we can cause some sort of problem with the banks, we'll cause a problem for everyone.

- That's probably true, Sir. But remember, this needs to be a global problem, not just something for the US. We don't want to cripple our own economy whilst the rest of the world thrives.

No, of course not, but we need to come up with something soon. And on a completely different subject, Jack, what's this I hear about something called crop circles.

- I believe that they are circles formed in fields of crops.

Yes, Jack, that I gathered from the name. But why are they appearing? Some reports I read say they are created by aliens and so far they all seem to have appeared in a particular area of England

- Well I doubt that they are anything to do with aliens, Sir. But I'm not sure who exactly is making them, or why. Would you like me to investigate?

Yes, Jack, I would.

- With any particular aim in mind, Sir?

Well first, I think we should make sure they're not alien related, and then we'll figure out what to do. Contact the Brits and see what they know.

- Yes, Sir.

The Next Day

- Sir, the British have come back to me regarding the crop circles.

My, that was quick.

- Well they had in fact already carried out some investigations into these phenomena and as a result they know that they are nothing to do with aliens.

Are they sure?

- Yes, Sir, they are. The Brits have tracked the activity using surveillance aircraft and they're definitely man made. Or rather they're made by two men with a dog, a plank of wood and a rope. We assume that the two men use the rope and plank to flatten the crop. And before you ask, no I don't know what the dog does. We just know he's always there.

And it's always the same two men.

- Until now, yes, Sir, we think so, although the photographs are very blurred. The Brits haven't yet traced the men.

Why's that?

- Mainly because they're not that bothered. Yes, they do a bit of damage to the crop, but this is more than compensated for by the money that comes into the area from the tourists. The farmers don't seem to mind. In fact some of them charge for the pleasure of viewing the circles. Can I ask, Sir, do you have a plan?

Well, it has occurred to me that it does no harm to encourage the public to believe in aliens and flying saucers. After all, for some time we've been using aliens as a cover for our activities at Area 51. Aliens and UFO's are a useful distraction. It helps stop the public thinking too hard about some of the other things that are going on.

- That's true, Sir, but what will we do if we find the perpetrators?

We need to make sure that they carry on with their good work.

- In that case, perhaps for the moment we should just track their activities. We only need to worry if they stop.

Yes, perhaps you're right. But in any case, get onto the Brits and tell them to track down these men, just in case we need to contact them.

- Yes, Sir.

April

- Sir we have a problem with the British.

What is it this time?

- It's to do with the World Cup.

The British play baseball?

- No, not the World Series, it's the World Cup..............

(Conversation continues for some time)

So given that we fixed it for them to win the World Cup in 1966, I suppose they want to do it again.

- No, Sir, it's something much more complicated. Apparently it was England that won the World Cup, not Great Britain.

Great Britain, England. I thought that they were one and the same thing.

- Apparently not, Sir. Great Britain is made up of England, Scotland, Wales and Northern Ireland and they each have their own national soccer team.

But surely when they participate in the Olympics, they are all in the same team.

- Yes, Sir, but not in soccer tournaments.

Why is that? Isn't it a bit confusing?

- I'm not sure why, Sir, but the point is the Scots have found out about the arrangements we made for England to win in 1966.

So I suppose they want to win the next World Cup.

- No, Sir. Even the most patriotic Scotsman knows that their national team will never win the World Cup.

So what do they want?

- They want independence.

You mean they want to have their own team in the Olympics?

- Well ultimately yes, but it goes a bit further than that. They want independence from the rest of the United Kingdom.

Where does the UK come into this? I thought we were talking about Great Britain.

- They are the same thing, Sir, or at least I think they are.

Well let's stick to one name. Let's settle on the UK.

- OK. Well the Scots want to leave the UK and become a country in their own right.

Can they do that?

- Well they can if the UK parliament agrees.

And will they?

- I don't know, Sir, I'll try to find out. But on a different matter, there is some good news concerning the crop circles. The Brits have identified the two men who are creating them, or at least most of them. They're called Doug and Dave and they live in the South of England. So is there anything you want me to do at this stage?

Well there is obviously one thing that we need to know, and that's how it's done. Do the Brits know that yet?

- I don't believe so, Sir. But assuming we can find out, what are we going to do with the information?

Can't you see the problem we have here? The crop circles are appearing in just one area on the world. If it were really aliens doing this, don't you think they would be more wide-spread?

- I guess so, Sir. But the story has always been that the area of England in which they are found has some mystical significance, perhaps something to do with Ley Lines.

That's as may be, but were never going to convince the public at large unless we extend their range. We'll have to train up some of our own men. Now we can either work out how it's done ourselves or we can find out from the people who already know. What do you think, Jack?

- I'll get onto the Brits.

Good.

That Afternoon

- Sir, the Brits have come back to us. They say that they don't know exactly how the crop circles are made.

But I thought The Brits said they used just a few bits of wood and a length of rope.

- The people who make them are always seen carrying a plank of wood and some rope but it seems that the crop circles are always created under the cover of darkness. The Brits don't know the exact technique so the only thing they can do is ask the perpetrators, but of course that risks blowing our cover. They're going to want to know why we're so keen to find out.

Well it can't be that difficult to come up with a cover story. They could just tell them that the government needs to rule out alien space craft. The men will have to show the Brits how it's done in order to prove that they are telling the truth.

- I'm sure that'll work. I'll tell the Brits to get onto it.

The Following Week

- Sir, I have contacted the British about the Scotland independence issue. There seems to be a compromise.

What have they come up with?

- A referendum, Sir.

That's a bit dangerous isn't it?

- In this case, Sir, probably not. The terms of the referendum mean that it is not just a simple majority that will decide the issue. Instead, they came up with a plan such that 40% of the total electorate must vote in favour and we just don't think that will happen.

Why not?

- Because at any moment in time, they reckon that 20% of the population of Scotland is recovering from a hangover and another 20% are still in a bar. So that doesn't leave many people to vote in favour. In any case, the UK government doesn't seem too concerned.

But what about the North Sea oil?

- Well there are two issues there. First, most of the oil is in the sea off the Orkney and Shetland islands. If Scotland gets independence, those islands may then demand independence from Scotland. It will leave the Scots with little oil of their own.

And what's the second?

- Well the Scots get a lot of aid from central government. On a per head basis, it's much more than the rest of the UK, particularly England. So what they lose in oil revenues, they save from social services costs.

Well let's hope that's the last we hear of that matter.

June

- Sir, Doug and Dave have spilled the beans.

Who?

- You know, the men who create crop circles.

Ah yes. So we know how they're made. That's good, let's get on and make some ourselves. Not too far away, I may want to go and see them for myself.

- Yes, Sir.

And Jack, let's make sure that our crop circles are bigger and better than the Brit's.

- Of course, Sir. But on a more serious note, we've given the banking problem some thought, and we keep coming back to the same thing. We've got to make them go bust.

What, all of them?

- Well perhaps not all of them, after all that may be a bit extreme.

Just a bit, Jack, and as an idea it's all well and good but how do we do it? And don't forget we need to affect foreign banks as well.

- Yes, I know, Sir. But we have come up with something. What's the easiest way to make a bank go bust?

Lend money to people who can't repay it.

- Exactly!

But how are we going to do that? The banks are normally careful about who they lend to.

- Yes, Sir, which is why it will take government intervention to make it happen. We'll need to pass a law.

Really, Jack! I just can't imagine the wording of a law that forces a bank to make bad loans.

- Well, we'll need to be subtle.

Too right!

October

- Sir, we've come up with something regarding the banking problem. And hopefully, you'll get some kudos with the voters as well.

That sounds good. What have you come up with?

- Well, as we discussed, we need to get the banks to lend money to people who then can't repay. And who are the people most likely to default on a loan?

Politicians?

- No, it wasn't a trick question, Sir. It's people with the least money, i.e. the poor.

But how do we legislate for this?

- That's where we've been particularly clever. We'll pass a law that instructs banks to lend a proportion of their money back into the communities in which they are located.

But don't they do that already?

- Not really, Sir. Maybe it used to be the case years ago, when each town had its own bank. But now a bank has branches in many states, if not country wide, they tend to take in savings from all branch locations but lend mainly to the more prosperous communities. We'll enact legislation that will force the banks to lend to all communities in which they have branches.

- And that's where the kudos comes in?

Exactly, Sir. You'll be seen to be a champion of the poor.

- And is that good? What'll happen when the banks go bust?

Well, that will take some time, hopefully after you have been re-elected, Sir.

- I'd prefer it if it was definitely after I've been re-elected. And Jack, do you know how I could set up a Swiss bank account?

No, Sir, but I'll find out.

Carter

1977

January

- Sir, welcome to the White House. My name is Jack and there are a few things that we need to cover.

Do we have any nuts?

- I'm sorry, Sir, what do you want?

Peanuts. Do we have any peanuts?

- I'm sure that we can find some, Sir.

That'd be great. I can't concentrate unless I'm chewing on a nut.

- I'll be sure to remember that, Sir. But as I was saying, there are some things we need to go through.

Nuts first, Jack.

- Yes, Sir.

Ten Minutes and a Packet of Nuts Later

Do we have any more nuts, Jack?

Twenty Minutes and Two Packets of Dry Roasted Nuts Later

OK, Jack, thanks for that, now fire away.

Two Days Later

Well, Jack, I'm absolutely amazed at what you've told me but being a farmer, I have to say that I'm not too happy about the way we're manipulating people and food to the extent that we are.

- I know it has come as a shock, but if there was any other way, we'd be onto it. I think we've covered all the options.

It appears so, but I'll give it some thought. In particular, let's do something about this diet committee. I think we need to see some results after a decade of work.

- Yes, Sir.

February

- Sir, regarding the dietary recommendations committee, I think you're right and that now is the time to wind it down. It's had a good run and I don't think that there will be much resistance, apart of course from the committee members themselves.

I agree, Jack, but you will still have the problem of how to get the committee to come up with the right answers. If they don't, a lot of the good work that you have done will have been wasted.

- I still think that they'll deliver the goods, but let's see what they come up with before we start worrying about a problem.

But surely we'd have a problem either way. If they go against our wishes, that's a problem, and if they agree with us, then our ideas on what constitutes good and bad food will be undermined.

- As I said, Sir, let's wait and see.

March

Jack, I see that the dietary recommendations have been published and they appear to be OK.

- Yes, as it turned out we were worrying about nothing. Of course the dairy and meat industries are kicking up a bit of a fuss, but it's nothing we can't handle.

And we owe a debt to the President who set up the whole thing in the first place. It appears that he knew what he was doing after all.

- I'm not sure that's the case, Sir, since if we hadn't moved the goal posts the whole thing could have turned out very differently.

So what do we do now? I can't help thinking that we need to keep this particular idea in the news going forward.

- You're right, Sir, and that also fits in neatly with another thing. The dietary recommendations that the committee has published are OK but they could do with a bit of tweaking. I thought that it would be a good idea to refine them and have them published by a government department. That way we can have more control over the contents.

Right, and I guess you're thinking that we could update them on a regular basis.

191

- Correct.

But how can we make sure that any future recommendations are consistent with STOP.

- I've already thought of that. Of course we'll need to take advice from various people and organisations in order to update the information but if we ask the right people, I'm sure we'll get the right answers.

And who are the right people, Jack?

- That'll be the companies that manufacture the FAST and JUNC foods, Sir.

That'll be convenient.

- Won't it just.

August

- Sir, bad news from India, I'm afraid. Martial Law has been lifted.

What does that mean for the sterilization programme?

- Well the program of compulsory sterilization has had to be terminated, so it's back to the voluntary approach.

And what does that mean?

- A population of one billion by the end of the century, I should think.

Are there no other options to reduce their population growth?

- Only the usual ones; poor food, bad health advice, and so on.

What about war?

- The last one with Pakistan was only a few years ago. It's a bit soon to engineer another one. And in any case, in the scheme of things the body count in wars between India and Pakistan is trivial.

September

- Sir, we've had some good news on the smoking front.

Well it's about time. It's all been so negative recently. What is it?

- Well it's to do with non-smokers.

Are you going to tell me that smoking kills non-smokers? What do they do, trip over a discarded cigarette packet and break their neck!

- No, Sir, it's to do with passive smoking. Have you heard of the term?

Is it when you have a cigarette after sex?

- Er, I'm not sure where you're coming from there, Sir. No, it's where people inhale other people's cigarette smoke. Apparently it does the passive smoker just as much harm as the smoker themselves.

Well that's good isn't it?

- In the short term, yes. But it could give us big problems in the future.

How do you work that out?

- Because it's all very well smokers ignoring health advice when the result is that they kill themselves. However it's quite another matter when it's harming innocent bystanders. It could result in a backlash from non-smokers.

But what can they do?

- They could insist that smoking is banned in public places.

What, all public places, including bars and restaurants?

- Yes, Sir.

Well I hardly think that's likely, do you.

- Not for some time, but it could happen.

Not, I hope, in my lifetime. And there's something else, Jack, have you seen this?

- What is it, Sir?

It's a photograph of a crop circle.

- My, my, Sir, that's very impressive. Where is it?

In England, Jack, but that's not my point. This is a very complex design. It's hardly the sort of thing an alien spacecraft is going to create.

- Oh, I don't know about that, Sir. If the aliens are bright enough to travel all the way across the solar system to our planet, then I'm sure that they can draw a double helix.

Don't get clever, Jack. This is serious. How did this get out of hand?

- Because you said that you wanted our crop circles to be the best.

I certainly didn't say that, it must have been one of my predecessors.

- Well someone did and so that's what we tried to do. But the Brits were not to be out done, so they upped the ante. After all, they invented the modern crop circle phenomenon.

Can't you tell them to stop?

- It's too late for that, Sir. There are now dozens of imitators out there. The genie is well and truly out of the bottle.

That's too bad. We'll have to come up with something else to keep the UFO freaks happy.

- Yes, Sir.

December

Jack, I gather the Community Reinvestment Act has been passed into law, but I'm a bit concerned. How soon will the banks start to go bust?

- Well that isn't going to happen for some time. It'll be at least 5 years by my estimate.

Well, I know you said I'd be safe until after the next presidential election. But even then, if I'm re-elected…

- When your re-elected, Sir.

Well let's not count our chickens. Either way, I wouldn't like to be around the White House when the financial system starts to go into meltdown. Make sure it doesn't happen until I'm long gone.

- Well that will also help with one other issue we have.

What's that?

- Well we haven't yet worked out how this plan is going to affect the global economy. At this time, it only applies to US banks.

Well that isn't good.

- It's not as bad as it seems, Sir. Any significant problem with the US economy is bound to affect the global economy.

I hope you're right. But in the meantime, come up with something a bit more tangible regarding foreign banks.

- I'm sure we can do that, Sir.

1978

February

- Sir, the British seem to have a problem.

What is it this time?

- It's to do with the royal family.

How can they be a problem? I thought they were mainly ceremonial.

- Well yes, Sir, they are, but they can still be very influential.

Which one is causing trouble this time?

- It's Prince Charles, Sir. He wants to take up farming as a hobby and he is starting to promote wholesome food.

And why is that a problem? As a fellow farmer, I can appreciate his enthusiasm.

- His position may be ceremonial but he commands a lot of attention which means that what he does get into the newspapers nearly every day.

Hm, I suppose this sounds serious. The last thing we want is for people to start eating wholesome food, although as a farmer you must understand that I'm not entirely happy with the idea of fake food.

- I realise that, Sir.

What are our options?

- Well, Sir, at this stage our best bet is to make him look a bit foolish. We can try to destroy his credibility.

And what if that doesn't work? Can't we have a word with his wife? See if she can talk some sense into him.

- He's not married, Sir.

He hasn't been eating any of those special communion wafers has he?

- No, Sir, not that I am aware.

Well what's the problem then?

- I believe he has formed a close relationship with a married woman and has not therefore been particularly keen to find a wife.

OK, let's stick with the credibility thing for now. But keep an eye on matters and let me know what happens.

May

Jack, I saw a news item in the paper this morning. It was an article that had something to do with Prince Charles talking to plants. Would this by any chance have anything to do with you, Jack?

- I cannot deny it, Sir, but I'm not sure that ridiculing him isn't being counter-productive. It seems that the British may quite like an eccentric member of the royal family.

So what do you suggest at this stage?

- Nothing yet, Sir, but we need to keep the situation under review.

Is there anything else, Jack?

- Yes, Sir. JUNC has come up with something regarding water.

I hope this is nothing to do with the French.

- No, Sir, at least I don't think so. No, this is to do with its medicinal properties.

I didn't know it had any.

- No, it hasn't, that is if you discount the fact that it is vital to maintain life.

Well there is that.

- In this case, JUNC has been looking into homeopathy. It's an area of alternative medicine which involves putting various special additives into water and using it to cure a variety of ailments.

Like what?

- Like just about everything, Sir.

But the Chinese have been using herbs for medicinal purposes for thousands of years, so I suppose it could work.

- Not really, Sir.

How can we be so sure?

- Because the potion is diluted many times over to the point where no trace of the additive remains.

Not any?

- None, not a single molecule.

Well it all sounds like a con. Shouldn't we put a stop to it?

- Not really, Sir. If people think that it can cure them then they're likely to avoid seeking proper medical attention. Most of them will be worse off, health wise.

Why most? Surely it can't help any of them.

- There's always the placebo effect to consider.

I guess you're right. So what do we do?

- Nothing. We could regulate it as a medical treatment, but since it can have no real effect, we'd have to ban it. No, we'll leave it alone and anyone who wants to use it will be able to. And of course there is one other benefit.

What's that?

- It'll increase the overall consumption of G-Water.

My God, you're right! But hang on a minute, that will only be the case if they're using tap water. If they're using the bottled stuff, it's no help.

- Sir, I can't imagine that they're using the bottled stuff, after all it would eat into their profits. No, I'll wager they're using tap water.

Well you'd better check just in case. But then, either way, I suppose it makes no difference to us.

- No, Sir, not really.

Jack, going back to the basic issue of Homeopathy, aren't we missing a trick here?

- What do you mean, Sir?

Well there must be other alternative therapies around, like for instance acupuncture. They may not be water based but none the less, if they divert sick people from mainstream medicine we can still reap the same reward in that they're unlikely to get better. You remember the motto don't you, Jack.

- "The more they're sick, the sooner they're dead". How could I forget, Sir. But I do see your point. I'll get onto it and see whether there's anything we can do.

Surely the first thing we need to do is pretty obvious.

- And what's that, Sir?

We need to check these alternative remedies and make sure that they don't work.

- Well I think we can safely assume that they don't.

Do you mean we haven't checked yet?

- No, Sir, not really.

No even Homeopathy?

- It's just water, Sir, it can't work.

Let's not make any assumptions here, Jack, let's just do the tests and make sure. It'd be just our luck that we encourage people to use this alternative stuff, only to find out that it actually works.

- I don't think that's likely, Sir.

Jack, just humour me and do the tests.

- Yes, Sir.

October

Jack, I think it would be a good idea if we could review the situation regarding STOP.

- In what respect, Sir.

You know, do a world tour so I can understand what's going on in each part of the world. I don't want to find out that we've been doing our bit to reduce the population whilst the foreigners are still breeding like rabbits.

- OK, where do you want to start?

How about Europe?

- Well, Sir, the experiment with Greek democracy had a limited effect.

You mean "lack of democracy".

- Well in so much as we replaced it with a military dictatorship, yes, Sir. But the effect on other countries has been limited. Although the

European governments seem to be a bit more compliant these days, there are still pockets of resistance.

Like where?

- France, for example.

Well in terms of being difficult, I think we can take France for granted. Is there anyone else?

- They're all much of a muchness these days, mainly due to the Common Market. As a result policies tend to be agreed by consensus.

But as far as STOP is concerned, what are they actually doing?

- In the main they're doing much the same as us although the food thing is a bit of a problem, in particular with the Latin countries. They tend to like the good stuff too much and as a result they don't want our rubbish. But the good news is that the Europeans are less likely to take notice of warnings about smoking. Even more good news is that the northern countries, particularly the UK, are more likely to fall for our JUNC food.

So they smoke more and eat the food that we don't recommend and yet they still live longer than us. Aren't people going to see through this?

- Not if we give them false information, Sir!

And I suppose it's unlikely that there's going to be a significant war in Europe any time soon.

- Well as far as those in the Common Market are concerned, yes, that's right. There's always a chance of something kicking off in the East, but with the Russians keeping a tight grip on things, that's unlikely. And of course, what with their nuclear weapons, we don't want them to get trigger happy. There's no telling what might happen.

And further south?

- Well our best hope was a Greek/Turkish clash over Cyprus, but that petered out after the invasion of Cyprus.

And what about birth control?

- Well there the news is much better and in the short term it seems to be our best bet.

What, even in the countries which are predominantly Catholic?

- There too, Sir. It seems that although the powers that be in the Catholic Church advocate uncontrolled breeding, the followers are a bit more pragmatic. The result is that many of them use birth control; they just feel guilty about it afterwards.

OK, what else have you got? How about Africa?

- More of the usual.

You mean famine and war?

- Yes, Sir.

And further afield? How about China? How's their Cultural Revolution going?

- That's pretty much petered out, Sir. There are only so many intellectuals that can be killed and when the victims include doctors and teachers even the dumbest peasant is going to realise that something's not quite right.

So what are they going to do now?

- Well, Sir, I do believe that they have another plan up their sleeves. They're going to stop people having babies.

And how will they do that?

- By telling them not to.

Oh good one, Jack! No, what are they really going to do?

- No, that's really it, Sir. They are going to tell the population that they can only have one child per couple.

Can they really do that?

- It's a totalitarian communist regime, Sir. They can do what they like.

So it appears, Jack. You know, there are times when I think that there's something in this Communism thing. It seems to make things so much easier.

- Sir, you're not the first President to make that observation. But as I often point out, while it may make it easier for you, it doesn't make the lives of our population any better. In fact, it's bound to have the opposite effect.

So that's why we haven't tried it yet.

- Oh no, Sir. We'd try it if we thought we could get away with it but we haven't come up with a sure fire plan of action yet.

You mean we've actually got people looking at this option?

- We have people covering all eventualities, Sir. I'm sure that's the way you would want it.

So going back to the Chinese, enforced birth control is their main weapon when it comes to population control.

- Yes, Sir, that and of course that fact that the Communist system is still very inefficient when it comes to food and health. The life expectancy of the Chinese is still very low compared to Western nations and that's not something that's likely to change any time soon.

You don't suppose that's deliberate, do you? You know, as part of a plan to control their population growth.

- Well I must admit we used to assume it was just incompetence but we are now wondering whether it is all part of cunning plan. After all, what have they got to lose? It's not as if the problems affect the leaders. None of them appear mal-nourished.

But what about their health care?

- You mean health care for the Chinese leadership?

Yes, Jack.

- I believe it's based in a private clinic in Switzerland, Sir.

I dare say it is. And what about India? How's the sterilization program going?

- Not good, Sir. Since the compulsory element was stopped, it's been far less effective and so far the Indians haven't come up with any else.

What about the war angle? Is there any progress there?

- No, not really. These days the conflicts with Pakistan are mostly to do with political posturing. I think that the war in 1971 had a sobering effect on both countries.

So there's not much good news there then. What about other areas of the globe? How about South America?

- Much the same as Africa. The same can be said for much of Asia. We had thought of trying to start a war or two in South America, but there are a few problems to overcome.

Like what?

- Well money for a start. That's what we normally need in this situation.

You mean to bribe the participants?

- Well not directly, Sir. It's more to do with weapons since they're needed in any war. Without them, there's no prospect of a bloody conflict and most of the potential antagonist haven't got any money.

Well if that's the problem, why can't we just make a donation to the cause?

- Lack of funds, Sir.

That's not normally a problem, Jack. Don't we just hide it in the defence budget?

- That can only happen so often, Sir. Right now, what with STOP, we're stretching things just a bit.

OK, but what about the Middle East?

- Ah, there the news is more promising. Iraq is making aggressive noises regarding Iran and it may well be possible to foster a conflict between the two.

If we do so, make sure it doesn't affect the oil. We don't want our pumps to run dry.

- If there is a conflict, the two parties will need to keep the oil flowing in order to pay for the war. I don't think there will be a problem there.

And which side shall we be on?

- Well I don't think we have a choice there. With the situation in Iran as it is, we'll have to side with Iraq.

OK, see what you can do. There will have to be a legitimate reason for war to break out.

- I'm sure we can come up with something, Sir.

And try to make it a long lasting affair. We don't want it to be over in five minutes. And especially, we don't want any net winner in the end. Let's maintain the status quo in the region, but with a nice big body count.

- Of course, Sir.

And the Iraqis will be paying for the weapons. We won't be giving them away, will we?

- Absolutely not, Sir!

1979

January

Jack, it's been a while since we discussed the subject of alternative medicine. You were supposed to go away and do some tests to see whether they are effective.

- Yes, Sir, that's correct.

And?

- And it appears to be a bit more complicated than we at first thought.

Please don't tell me that they actually do work! That's not something I want to hear right now.

- Well we've not yet completed phase three of the testing and bear in mind there are a lot different treatments to cover.

Phase three? What were phases one and two?

- Sir, when we started we thought that there would only be one phase; that we'd test the treatment and find that it doesn't work.

And?

- And it turned out not to be that simple since a lot of these treatments cover conditions which are not easy to test for. Take pain as an example. It's difficult to measure someone else's pain and therefore it's almost impossible to check whether, after treatment, someone's painful condition has improved or not.

I see your point. So what happened?

- The result was that many patients said that their condition had improved after treatment, so we went on to the next phase of testing. In phase two we compared the real treatment with a placebo.

Should we not have done that to start with?

- We could have done, Sir, but it was all a matter of time and money. If in phase one the remedies did not seem to offer any cure, then there was no need to go any further.

But hang on a minute. How do you test acupuncture against a placebo? Surely a patient knows when a needle is being stuck into their body.

- Good question, Sir. In the case of acupuncture, the traditional treatment is supposed to work because you insert the needles into particular parts of the body depending on the ailment. Our placebo treatment involved inserting needles into random body parts, irrespective of the illness. The results were the same. In fact, we went one step further, just to check whether the needles actually did have some effect on the body. We had dummy needles made up which did not penetrate the skin, but to the patient they felt no different to the real thing.

OK, so what was the result of phase two?

- Well the good news is that, in the main, the placebo was just as effective as the real treatment, so we can be sure that there is no genuine medical effect. This result applies to all the treatments, including acupuncture.

Really? All treatments?

- Well by that I mean all the ones that we tested, but we have specifically excluded herbal remedies. There are just too many of those to cover in the short term and to be fair, some of those are likely to have an effect of some sort.

But in the ones we checked there was some benefit?

- Yes there was, and that's where we are in phase three of the research, and that's to find out why even the placebo has some effect.

And that's where we are now?

- Yes, Sir. I expect to report back on the final conclusions in the next few months.

I look forward to seeing what you come up with, Jack. Don't keep me waiting too long.

- No, Sir, of course not.

February

- Sir, I have a final update on the alternative medicine research that we've been carrying out.

Ah, good, I'm looking forward to hearing what you've come up with. What have you got?

- Well the main conclusion is that when such a treatment works, or at least is seen by the patient as having worked, it's simply because someone, i.e. the person giving the treatment, is paying attention and spending time with them. These practitioners are much more touchy/feely than their traditional counterparts and that seems to have an effect.

But it's nothing that a traditional doctor couldn't achieve if they spent enough time with each patient?

- Broadly speaking, that's correct.

So what are we going to do?

- Our conclusion is that we should encourage these alternative treatments, since there is no evidence that they actually cure real diseases or increase longevity. And there is one particular thing that is very important, particularly for our British friends. Every patient who uses an alternative treatment is one less who's using a traditional doctor and when that doctor's salary is paid for by the government, as it is in the UK, it means less money is being spent out of the central budget.

Fair point, but is there anything else?

- Yes, the British have come up with one other thing. On the basis that the more time you spend with a patient, the better the outcome, they are going to recommend that doctors in the NHS, particularly GPs, cut the amount of time they spend with each patient to a maximum of ten minutes. They expect a significant increase in illness, and in the long term mortality, as a result of this one policy change. Unfortunately, until we adopt a national health scheme in the US, we can't hope to gain the same advantage here.

Perhaps that's something we should look at, Jack.

- We have in the past given it some consideration but the cost of such a system has always been prohibitive.

But just think what we could do if we controlled the access to medical care for most of the population. We could wreak havoc with their health. I think that we should reconsider this option at some stage.

- That would be some stage after you've been re-elected, Sir?

Of course, Jack. We don't want to be too hasty, do we?

- And let's not forget that it would cost an absolute fortune, Sir.

That too, Jack.

March

- Sir, the result of the Scottish referendum is in.

What?

- The Scottish referendum, Sir.

And why should I be interested?

- Well the British are one of our closest allies. If the Scots were to split from the rest of the United Kingdom, it could have significant ramifications.

Like what?

- Well the UK has a permanent seat at the United Nations. If they lose 30% of their land mass and 10% of the population, there may be some countries who will question this.

OK, so what was the result?

- 52% voted in favour and 48% against.

So that's bad news then.

- No, Sir, it means the move for devolution from the UK was defeated.

How come?

- The condition of the referendum was that 40% of the population who could vote had to be in favour. The actual figure was less than 33%.

So the Scots will not be splitting from the UK.

- Not at this stage, Sir. But I suspect that this is not the last we'll hear of this. They're still upset that we helped England win the World Cup.

I didn't realise that the British play baseball.

- No, not the World Series, it's the World Cup………….

(Conversation continues for some time)

- Sir, there's something else. The Prince Charles issue has not gone away. His ambitions are getting more adventurous.

What's he doing?

- Well, he is planning to set up his own farm and sell his produce to the public through all sorts of outlets. It will go by the name of Duchy Originals.

What sort of products are we talking about? And what makes them so special?

- Well for start they will be organic.

As a farmer, Jack, I think I can say with good authority that all food is organic.

- Well yes, Sir, what you say may be true but in this case we mean that it is produced naturally without artificial fertilizers and insecticides.

What, the ones that we are pinning a lot of hopes on?

- Yes, Sir.

That's pretty serious. Perhaps we had better consider the Kennedy solution.

- You mean have him eliminated? Well I think that's a bit drastic and in any case it may not be much use since there's this hereditary issue to consider. Anyone who replaces him in line to the British throne is going to be from the same gene pool which means that we could end up with the same problems. No, the hit man idea is a no go option. We have got to come up with something else.

Well come up with something fast, but in the meantime let's see if we can stop him obtaining any farm land, after all he can't grow food without it.

- Yes, Sir, I'll alert the Brits right away.

Incidentally, Jack, how old is the Queen?

- In her mid-fifties I believe, Sir.

And Charles is first in line to the throne?

- Yes, Sir.

And what's her impression of Charles do you think?

- I'm not sure, Sir. Why do you ask?

Well, Jack, if she sympathises with Charles's ideas, we have an immediate problem. If not, we can take a long term view. It could be years before Charles inherits the British throne.

- I'll try to find out, Sir.

April

- Sir, I have enquired about the Queen's attitude towards her son, Charles. I had a word with someone at the British embassy and apparently she thinks he's a bit of a plonker.

Plonker? What on earth is a plonker?

- I'm not sure, Sir, but from his tone of voice, it didn't sound good. I think we can assume that the Queen does not share Charles's idiosyncrasies, including his passion for wholesome food.

Good, that's what I wanted to hear since it gives us time to hatch a plan. But what about the British government?

- They seem to be very keen on the idea of getting rid of him. Apparently Charles is a bit of a thorn in the side of the politicians.

Can I assume that the Brits vetoed the hit man idea?

- It was a close call, but on balance, yes. So what did you have in mind, Sir?

Well, we'll find him a wife and in due course she'll have children.

- If you think you can keep him busy doing other things away from his work, I'm not certain how that will help us. I'm sure Charles will have loads of hired help around to assist with baby sitting and changing diapers. He'll still have plenty of time to continue developing his food empire.

No, Jack, you've missed the point. This is a long term plan the point of which is to crack the hereditary problem and what's more although I said she'll have children, I didn't say they would be his.

What we need to do is find him a wife who will co-operate with us, someone who fancies the idea of her offspring becoming heir to the throne.

- And how are we going to do that?

I can't think of everything, Jack, so in this instance I think I'll just leave it to you to come up with something.

- And how are we going to persuade Charles to cooperate?

Again, Jack, I can't be expected to think of everything. Just give it some thought and get back to me ASAP.

- Assuming this is feasible, how is it going to help us?

Well, Jack, once the offspring are old enough, the Queen will abdicate in favour of her grandchild, missing Charles out of the line of succession. That way we can hopefully breed out these foodie tendencies, but of course that means that the current Queen has got to survive for a good few years. You had better make sure she gets the very best medical attention.

- No National Health Service for her then!

No, certainly not. And no margarine either.

- Of course not, Sir.

May

Jack, I see Mrs Thatcher has become Prime Minister. I hope she thinks we've fulfilled our end of the bargain, although it seems to have been a bit of a lop-sided arrangement. We get her to stop school milk and she gets to be Prime Minister.

- Well I know it appears that way now, but she knows that she owes everything to us and having a woman in power is sure to make things easier for us. She seems to be a bit of a pussycat, Sir.

I dare say, Jack, and anything that makes my life easier is much appreciated. I am also very impressed at how you managed to make such a mess of the UK economy.

- What do you mean, Sir?

Well the Labour party got ousted because the UK economy is in such a mess, you know "Winter of Discontent". I dare say one of our ad men came up with that one.

- Sir, as much as I would like to take credit, in this case I can honestly say it was nothing to do with me.

Really, Jack?

- Well we took no active part in the problems. But at the same time, we did nothing to help so in the main the situation was all of their own making.

And now they have a woman in charge! I wonder how that will work out.

- I expect it'll be pretty uneventful, Sir. But there is one other thing. We finally have a result concerning Ireland in that the sale of contraceptives has been legalized at last.

So hopefully that'll have an effect on their birth rate.

- Not really, Sir. The Irish have been getting their condoms from Northern Ireland for years so I don't expect much of a change there. But I do expect the priests to have a busy time.

Why's that?

- Because like the Italians, the Irish will all be going to confessional.

But surely if they've already been using contraceptives they'll have been going to confess before now.

- It's one thing breaking the law of the church, but it's another thing to break the law of the land and up until now, that's what they've been doing. For that you can get a criminal record. What's the worst that can happen if you commit a sin?

Isn't that called Eternal Damnation, Jack?

August

Jack, where do we stand with the different food groups? I know we've covered most of them, but, for instance what about vegetables?

- The only groups left are vegetables, fish and some carbohydrates. We are working on those as we speak.

And what have we come up with so far?

- Well, Sir, we dealt with fish pretty quickly. They are generally thought of as being a healthy food and that is correct, at least as far as wild caught fish are concerned.

What other sort are there?

- Farmed fish, Sir.

I know there are salmon farms, but I didn't realise we farmed other sorts of fish.

- Oh yes, Sir, all sorts including prawns.

But why should farmed fish be less healthy?

- There are several reasons. The fish live in crowded conditions and suffer from diseases more often than fish living in the wild. Sometimes, they have to be given medication in order that they survive.

Good grief, what sort of medication?

- Well, for example, antibiotics.

Are you telling me that we give prawns antibiotics?

- Yes, Sir, I'm afraid so.

But how on earth do they get them to swallow those pills? It must be very time consuming.

- Er, I don't think that's how they do it, Sir. I assume the antibiotics are mixed with the feed stuff.

Oh, right, yes of course. And what else?

- Well they can be fed food treated so as to change the colour of the flesh and so make it appear more appetising to the consumer.

It all sounds pretty grim, so what's our plan?

- To do nothing, Sir.

What, nothing at all? What good will that do?

- Hopefully, we'll wipe out most of the fish stocks in the open sea. Then the only fish that will be commercially available will be the farmed stuff.

But how can that happen?

- Well, Sir, the seas are being over fished to the extent that certain stocks are dwindling fast. For example, the cod found in the north Atlantic off Nova Scotia is down to half what it was a decade ago. If we don't do anything, these stocks could disappear within the next decade. However, pressure groups are trying to force the government to put limits on the amount of fish that can be caught in the hope that the remaining stocks can be preserved.

But how can we justify not doing that?

- By saying that we are supporting the fishing industry and the local communities are with us on this.

But surely they must realise that unless we take some sort of action, their industry will disappear within a few years.

- You'd have thought so, Sir, but they don't seem to care. I think it's a case of "we'll worry about that when it happens".

OK, I can see how this will work in certain areas, like North America and Europe. But what about the rest of the planet?

- We are still working on that one, Sir.

October

- Sir, we may have come up with something on the fishing front. It appears that the Spanish are willing to get involved.

About time too. As yet they've done nothing to help our cause.

- Well to be fair, Sir, up until now we haven't actually asked them to do anything. Nothing has come up where they could be of any help to us. Until now, that is.

 And what have we come up with.

- Well, Sir, the Spanish eat a lot of fish. They used to source all of their requirements from the waters around their coast but then, as the stocks dwindled, they moved further afield. The Common Market helped in that respect.

In what way?

- All member states can fish in all the other member states' water. So, for example, the Spanish were given access to the North Sea stocks of fish.

I bet the British weren't happy about that.

- No they weren't. If it hadn't been for the fact that we needed them in the Common Market to keep an eye on things, the fishing issue could have been a show stopper.

OK, so where do the Spanish come into the picture now?

- Well they have agreed to expand their fishing area.

To where?

- To anywhere we tell them to.

What, anywhere in the world?

- Yes, Sir, that's the plan.

But isn't it going to appear a bit odd to find a Spanish fishing boat off the coast of India

- Maybe so, but as I said, that's the plan. They'll build a fleet of long range fishing boats that will be able to reach all the main fishing grounds on the globe. We'll decide which ones to target and they'll go and suck up all living creatures leaving the sea bed barren. After all, we don't want fish stocks to recover.

This all sounds a bit drastic, doesn't it?

- Maybe so, but it's got to be done.

I suppose so. But what about the other food groups?

- I'll come back to you on those when I've got some news.

OK but don't be too long.

- No, Sir.

November

- Sir, we have encountered a problem with our solution to the fish problem.

What, are the Spanish getting cold feet?

- Oh no, that's not something that's likely to happen. No, it's the Japanese who are a bit upset.

Oh, I see. I suppose that they want a bit of the action.

- On the contrary, they think they've already got a bit of the action. In fact, as it turns out it's more than a bit; it's quite a lot but they're not being motivated by same aims as us.

So they're not trying to stop people eating fish.

- Not at all, Sir. On the contrary, they have expanded their fishing fleet in order to satisfy the demand for fish in Japan and as that demand grows, so the areas in which they fish needs to grow.

But surely they must realise that sooner or later, there won't be any fish left.

- They seem to have the same attitude as the people who are decimating the stock of cod in the North Atlantic. They are only concerned with today and they don't much care about the problems that they are creating for tomorrow. They probably figure that a lack of fish will be someone else's headache.

So what do we do?

- As far as we're concerned, it's a case of the more the merrier. It doesn't matter who's wiping out the fish stocks, provided it's happening.

And can the Japanese and Spanish work together?

- Who knows. I don't think that's a situation that's ever cropped up before.

1980

January

- Sir, I've given the Charles situation some thought and I think I've come up with something. What we need to do is find a simple but attractive young girl who fancies the idea of being a princess.

Yes, I realise that, but how do we get her to play ball?

- Well, Sir, we'll try and sell her on the jet set life style. If she's young enough she could be persuaded.

In which case she could also be young enough to be Charles's daughter.

- That's true and being married to Charles wouldn't be everyone's choice but we'll see what we can come up with.

And what about Charles. How are we going to get him to buy into this plan?

- We will tell Charles that if he marries this girl he can continue his relationship with the other woman.

Do you think he'll go for that plan?

- It's highly likely, Sir. He is getting on a bit and he's under constant pressure from his mother to get a wife and settle down.

And what if the girl actually falls for Charles? What will we do then?

- Sir, as soon as she's married, we'll spill the beans to her about the other woman. The hope is that she'll be so upset and angry that she'll play ball. She'll get pregnant and everyone will assume that Charles is the father.

And what if she doesn't play ball?

- Then she'll loose the chance for her offspring to become King.

How will we make sure the real father keeps quiet about the situation? And the child could be a Queen, rather than a King.

- Oh no, Sir, the baby won't be conceived naturally, we'll use IVF. The British have been developing the technology for this very purpose. That way we can chose a father who resembles Charles, but doesn't have any of his organic food tendencies. And of course we'll make sure it's a boy.

Good, make sure we do that. And what about the farm land?

- Ah, there the news is not so good. Charles has obtained a large estate including 900 acres of farm land.

How did he manage to do that? I thought that we were on the look-out for such a move.

- Yes, Sir, we were, but we were looking for land transactions in the name of Charles Windsor or The Prince of Wales. The land was actually bought by the Duchy of Cornwall and Charles is the Duke of Cornwall.

Good grief, Jack, how many aliases does the man have?

- Quite a few, Sir. I believe it may have something to do with tax avoidance.

Even so, we should have spotted it.

- Why do you say that, Sir?

His brand, "Duchy Originals" and the Duchy of Cornwall which purchased the land. I think the clue is in the name, Jack.

- Oh yes, Sir. I see what you mean. Sorry, Sir.

April

Jack, I see that there has been an assassination attempt on the Iraqi Foreign Minister. Is this anything we need to worry about? Or is it all part of the grand plan?

- Very much the latter, Sir. The Iraqis need a pretext to invade Iran and this is the one they'll use.

Well it's as good as any I suppose. And was there in fact any such attempt?

- Not to my knowledge, Sir.

May

- Sir, Monica has been on to me. She has been talking to Rachael.

That's normally good news. What have they come up with this time?

- Well, you know they went to Hollywood to help with the decision on which actor will be president.

How did that go? I thought it had been agreed that Charlton Heston was the man.

- Yes, Sir, that was the plan, but it seems another more powerful position may come up which he would prefer.

What position could possibly be more powerful than President of the United States of America?

- He wants to be President of the National Rifle Association.

I can't argue with that, Jack. So who's in the frame now?

- A chap called Ronald Reagan.

What's he like?

- Well he's seems friendly enough.

And?

- Well that's about it really.

I think you need a bit more than a friendly nature to become President.

- Not necessarily, Sir, you must remember Gerald Ford. Anyway, we agreed that whoever Hollywood chose we would accept. So it looks like it's Reagan.

OK, Reagan it is. Now back to Monica and Rachael.

- Well, Sir, it seems that while they were in Hollywood they caught the acting bug. They want to appear in a film or a TV show.

And why should we help them? Do we still need them?

- Well, Sir, they have developed some of our best ideas. Hollywood seems to think they can come up with something, probably TV rather than film. The main problem they have is their age. They are both getting on a bit and unfortunately TV shows like this normally feature younger people.

Well in this instance they'll have to come up with something different. We all get old eventually.

- Not if we have anything to do with it!

Ho! Ho! Good one, Jack.

- There is one final thing, Sir; they want a part in the show for their friend. Apparently the three of them were at a local bake sale and Monica let slip about the plot to kill off a large part of the population.

How on earth do you let something like that slip out at a bake sale?

- Her friend mentioned the fact that she had used margarine in her cake.

I didn't know you could do that.

- Oh yes, Sir, the scientists have come up with variations on margarine for many different applications, including making cakes. We couldn't just rely on people spreading it on their bread, they wouldn't consume enough. It had to go into other products. Of course, by the time it's been cooked, people can't see it, so we don't have to worry about things like colour, flavour and vitamins.

Why do you need lots of variations?

- Well, Sir, you can't expect any substance to be so versatile that it can be used as a spread, to bake with and to fry in.

Unless it's butter, Jack.

- Yes, Sir, unless it's butter. Anyway, Monica told her friend that she should have used butter and her friend said she was wrong because it is bad for you.

OK, Jack, I can see where this is going. Let them go ahead with the TV show, after all we need to keep them on side. Oh, and just out of curiosity, what's the friends name?

- I'm not sure, Sir. Why do you ask?

I just wondered if it was Phoebe.

- And why would you think that?

No particular reason, Jack.

July

- Sir, I've just come from a meeting of the SCC.

SCC, what's that?

- The Supreme Co-ordination Committee.

No, sorry Jack, I'm still lost.

- I've just had coffee with Monica and Rachel.

Oh, right, why didn't you say so.

- Sorry, Sir, I thought I had. Anyway, we have been discussing the method by which we come up with ideas for STOP.

I wasn't aware that there was a method. It has all seemed a bit hit and miss to me.

- Well I think that's a bit unfair. We have a number of project teams working on the different areas of nutrition, you know, meat, dairy, vegetables....

Yes, Jack, I know what food is.

- Well, Sir, where we are not so well organised is in the area of medicine and general health. I think we could be a lot more pro-active in this area.

But surely the drug companies and health professionals do that.

- Yes, Sir, they do, but they are trying to make people fitter and healthier....

Which is the exact opposite of what we are trying to do, eh, Jack!

- Exactly, Sir!

I dare say that you're right, but if we were to try to cover all the areas of health you'd be talking about a lot of people.

- I don't think that is the approach we would take, Sir. No, what we would do is to gather together a team of people who could review all the latest research being carried out by other people and come up with ways to use the information to our advantage. They would not be specific experts, just people who can think outside the box.

I still don't see how this would work.

- In that case, Sir, why don't we carry out a trial run, say for a month. I'll assemble a small team from the groups we already have working in Area 51. I'll come back to you in four weeks with the results.

OK, Jack, you've got four weeks. And what are we going to call this team?

- Bearing in mind how much time and effort we have put into dreaming up names for the existing teams, I think we should wait until you give the go ahead before we come up with a name.

What do you mean?

- Well some of your predecessors have taken great pleasure in coming up with what they think of as "appropriate" acronyms.

Such as?

- Such as COD for the team looking into fish.

COD?

- The Committee for Oceanic Destruction.

Well it can't have taken long to come up with that.

- No, Sir, but we only came up with COD after I vetoed HALIBUT.

What.....

- Don't ask, Sir.

So what do the other names stand for; for instance TAP?

- The teaming looking at water? That stands for "Team for Aquatic Poisoning".

And SPAM?

- "Special Project Attacking Meat".

Someone has been having fun.

- Either that or someone didn't have enough work to do.

I think that you are being a little disrespectful towards some of my predecessors, Jack.

- No disrespect intended, Sir.

No, of course not.

August

Well, Jack, your four weeks are up. What have you come up with?

- Quite a bit, Sir. We decided to go through all the recent scientific papers covering health and medicines. It was a bit tricky to start with, since the information can be very technical. But we decided to tell the parties involved that, for each such paper, the government needs a simple synopsis, just a few sentences. As a consequence, we have only received a few so far.

Have you found anything useful?

- Yes, Sir, I think we have one that illustrates what we could do.

And which one is that?

- The one that says that more people die of cancer in the northern states of the USA than in the southern states.

And how does that help our cause? I hope you're not suggesting that we move the entire population of the USA to Chicago?

- No, Sir, although that was more or less what one bright spark in the team came up with.

What do you mean, more or less?

- He came up with Seattle, Sir, not Chicago.

Was he serious?

- Well, Sir, at first I thought he was joking. But when he started discussing in detail how his plan would be achieved, I realised he was serious.

I trust he is no longer on the team.

- That's correct, Sir, he's gone back to the fats.

FATS? I assume they're the ones looking at butter and cream. What does FATS stand for?

- Sorry, Sir, fats is not an acronym; it's the nickname we have given a particular group of people working at Area 51. They are all size 20 or bigger and they actually work for PUSS.

PUSS? Ugh, it sounds disgusting!

- Yes, I know, Sir. That's why it hasn't caught on.

What does that stand for?

- "PolyUnSaturated Sub-committee".

Who came up with that one?

- Gerald Ford, Sir.

Hmm, not one of his better ideas.

- Actually, I think it was, Sir.

Jack, are you being disrespectful again?

- Sorry, Sir.

Anyway, getting back to the point, what do you suggest we do with this information?

- Well, Sir, the interesting thing about the research is the reason for the difference.

I assumed it was something to do with the heavy industry which is more often located in the northern states.

- That may account for some of the difference. No, the main cause is sunlight.

Why's that?

- Because sunlight is used by the body to create vitamin D, which is in turn used by the body to ward off cancer. People who are deficient in the vitamin are more likely to get the disease.

But don't you get vitamin D in food?

- Yes, but mainly in oily fish and eggs. There will be many people who do not consume any vitamin D.

So how can we use this for our own benefit?

- What we need to do is persuade people that sunlight is bad.

And how do we do that? It's not going to be easy.

- Perhaps it'll be easier than you think, since sunlight can cause cancer.

Hang on just a minute. I thought you just said sunlight helps prevent cancer.

- Yes, Sir, I did. But if you get sunburnt, you can get a skin cancer, and this is the angle we are going to use. We will advise people to cover up in the sun, including the use of sun screen on exposed skin.

But they'll stop getting skin cancer, so we'll be back to square one.

- Not really, Sir. The skin cancer you get on parts of the body that are usually exposed to the sun is normally non-fatal and often easy to treat. A melanoma is the type of skin cancer that kills you and it's not always caused by sunburn. In fact, melanomas are often found on parts of the body that are covered by clothing. And people with higher levels of vitamin D get fewer melanomas so it's a win/win situation all round.

But isn't this a very long term plan?

- A lot of our projects are long term, Sir. Particularly so in this case, since we will be targeting children as a priority.

What do you mean?

- There's some evidence that the protective effect of vitamin D is most significant with exposure to sunlight at an early age. So we'll persuade parents that they should keep their children covered up. That'll include covering them in sunscreen all day.

What, even at school?

- Especially at school. Just half an hour in the playground at lunchtime on a sunny day could undo all our good work.

But surely someone is going to have to reapply the sunscreen to the children. It won't last all day.

- Well we have already contacted the relevant pharmaceutical companies. They are happy to put some R&D money into coming up with sunscreens that last all day. After all, they are going to sell a lot more of the stuff if our plan is successful.

But in the meantime, I can't see the teachers being happy about rubbing sunscreen onto their pupils.

- I'm sure they won't, but it will only take one litigious parent to sue a school when their child gets cancer for the teachers to fall in line.

But that'll happen only if the parents win their case.

- I'm sure that can be arranged, Sir.

Yes, Jack, I'm sure it can.

September

Jack, I see that Iraq has invaded Iran. I trust things are going smoothly?

- Yes, Sir, things are on track. The initial push has stalled and it looks like it's going to be a long drawn out affair. But on a lighter note, Sir, I think we've found a wife for Charles. She fits the bill; young, simple, attractive and available.

How did you persuade her to co-operate? Was it the jet set life style?

- Of course that helped but the clincher appears to be idea of having her children on the British throne. She seems quite taken with the idea.

And what about the water?

- What do you mean?
Does she drink bottled or tap?
- She drinks tap water, Sir.
Bingo!
- Bingo it is, Sir.

Reagan

1981

January

- Sir, my name is Jack. Welcome to the White House.

Thank you, Jack.

- Do you have any questions before I go through the briefing?

Just the one. I can't find the stables.

- Stables, Sir?

Yes, Jack, stables. In the event that I want to keep a horse on the premises.

Sir, may I suggest that while you are in Washington, you use a car as the main means of transport.

Whatever you say, Jack. I'm the new guy in town.

- Exactly so, Sir. Anything else?

No, not at this stage.

- OK, I'll get on with the briefing.

Several Days Later

So that's why I got elected four years earlier than expected.

- Yes, Sir, as I said, your predecessor was not as keen on STOP as we would have liked him to be so he failed to get a second term.

You really can fix things like that, can you Jack?

- Well, Sir, you got elected didn't you.

Fair point, Jack. Anyway, let's move on. How's the population control thing going at this stage? It sounds very complicated.

- Not too bad, Sir, but our biggest area for concern is the war.

I wasn't aware that there was a war. I hope I didn't fall asleep.

- No, Sir, you didn't fall asleep, at least not for that bit. The problem with war is that there isn't one, at least not a big one. We've been relying on wars to kill off significant numbers of people, but it's difficult to keep finding new countries to fight. Also, with the advance in weapons technology, fewer people are being killed, at least as far as our men are concerned.

Well, what do you suggest?

- I'm not sure yet, Sir.

Can't the British help out.

- The last time we got them involved in a war, it was a shambles.

But I thought that we won.

- Won what, Sir?

The Second World War.

- Oh yes, Sir, we did win that one. No, I'm talking about Suez.

Oh that. Serves us right for trying to get the Brits and the French to work together. It was always going to be problematic. No, this time we should get the British to go it alone. Do you think you can do that?

- Well it shouldn't be too difficult, after all Mrs Thatcher owes us a favour.

So I gather. I always wondered how a woman became Prime Minister of Great Britain. You'd better get in touch with the Brits and see what they can come up with. In the meantime we need to think of something else, since we can't keep starting new wars. Perhaps the answer is that somehow we continue killing people off even after a particular war has ended. See what you can come up with.

- Yes, Sir. Is there anything else at this stage?

Well there is one minor point. It's about the peanut allergies. I'm a bit confused there.

- OK Sir, as I said, as a result of our investigation into vitamin D we've found that we can cause some children to develop an allergy to certain foods, like peanuts. It's a simple process. We tell the mother to avoid certain foods while she's pregnant and not to feed the baby the same foods when they're young. Then there's a fair chance that, because the child hasn't been exposed to the food in question, the body won't be able to tolerate it in later life.

What other foods are involved besides peanuts?

- Well, Sir, you name it and we can make a child allergic to it. There's dairy, wheat, seafood, eggs, the list is endless.

And where does vitamin D come into the story?

- It affects the immune system, Sir. If we can compromise the immune system when a child is young, the more likely it is to develop allergies in later life.

I see.

- Do you have any more questions, Sir?

Well you still haven't answered my main question.

- I think I've covered everything, Sir.

Not quite, Jack. You haven't explained how you presented the little issue of peanut allergy to my predecessor.

Pause

Jack, you've gone very quiet.

- Well, Sir, that's a tricky question. What exactly do you mean by "presented".

Don't beat about the bush, Jack. Did you tell him?

- No, Sir.

Thank you. And have you told me everything?

- Yes, Sir.

And if you hadn't, would you tell me?

- No, Sir.

Well thanks for being honest, Jack.

- No trouble, Sir. Was there anything else?

There are a couple of minor points. Firstly, if you can use almost anything to prompt an allergic reaction, why choose peanuts?

- They seemed to be particularly effective.

Nothing to do with the fact that my predecessor was a peanut farmer and that he didn't seem to be particularly supportive of STOP.

- I'm sure that had nothing to do with it, Sir.

Really, Jack. Well just make sure I don't suddenly become allergic to jelly beans.

- I'm sure that's unlikely to happen, Sir.

Not while I co-operate, eh, Jack.

- Your words, not mine, Sir. And your second point?

Just how would I feed peanuts to a baby?

- You'd use smooth peanut butter, Sir.

Thanks, Jack.

March

- Sir, regarding the issue to do with the war. You know, trying to kill people after the war has ended.

Ah yes, what have you come up with?

- Well, Sir, as for the opposition, we think we've come up with something.

And what's that?

- Land mines.

Go on.

- Well, Sir, normally land mines are laid in order to create problems for the opposing army. But our idea is that they could be laid all over the place during a conflict but not necessarily for the purpose of killing the opposition during the war. The aim will be to continue to kill people after the conflict has finished.

That's all very well, Jack, but that's going to involve a lot of people digging a lot of holes in the ground in order to bury the damn things. It sounds a bit labour intensive.

- The aim will be to design a mine that can be deployed from the air. They will be dropped by the thousand and there won't be the need for any manpower on the ground.

Excellent, I can't see any drawbacks.

- I take it that we can go ahead, Sir?

Absolutely.

- And, Sir, there's some further news on the sunlight project.

Which one's that?

- You know, Sir, the link to cancer, vitamin D. I mentioned it in my initial brief to you.

You mentioned a lot in that briefing, Jack. My head's still spinning. But yes, I do remember now. Don't tell me our assumptions are wrong.

- No, Sir, on the contrary. Things are looking even more promising. We've discovered that vitamin D, and hence sunlight, is good at preventing a number of different conditions, not just cancer.

Like what?

- Well there's heart disease, diabetes, MS...

MS?

- Multiple Sclerosis, Sir.

So this is good news.

- It is, Sir, and it's also helped us with another problem.

Which one is that, Jack?

- The Mediterranean diet problem. This is where people living around the Mediterranean, well at least those in Europe, seem to live healthier lives. I'm not sure it applies to those in North Africa.

And why is that a problem?

- Well, Sir, some people say it's because they eat less saturated fat. Instead, they consume olive oil. So if they were to live longer, that could cast some doubt on our theory about saturated fats.

But surely not all the people who live around the Mediterranean eat the same food.

- That's true, Sir, which means that the Mediterranean Diet is something of a myth. For instance, the French eat more fat, and particularly saturated fat, than we do.

Are you sure?

- We're absolutely sure, Sir. Which particular fat they consume depends on the region. In the north it's butter, the south it's olive oil and in the south west, would you believe, it's duck fat. And do you know what the most common dish is on the menu in a French restaurant?

Frogs' legs?

- No, Sir, if you don't mind me saying, that's a bit of a cliché response.

Well how about snails.

- Ditto, Sir. No, the answer is Steak and French Fries.

That seems a bit unlikely to me, Jack. I wouldn't have thought that the French would eat a lot of French fries. Are you sure?

- Yes, Sir, I think you'll find the clue in the name.

Ah, but I believe, Jack, that you'll find that French Fries were invented in Belgium. I bet you didn't know that.

- Yes, Sir, in fact I did. To be exact they were first cooked in the French speaking part of Belgium near the town of Liège.

OK, you've got the better of me Jack.

- This isn't a competition, Sir.

You and I both know it always is, Jack.

- I'll pass on that one, Sir. But it's still the case that the people who live in Spain, France, Italy and Greece seem to live longer and have lower incidences of conditions such as heart disease.

But surely there are lots of things that could explain that. For instance, they probably have more relaxing lifestyles.

- Exactly, Sir. I would probably have less chance of a heart attack if I could take a three hour lunch break which involved having a four course meal washed down with a glass of red wine.

Jack, that sounds exactly like one of your lunches!

- With due respect, Sir, that's nothing like one of my lunches.

What, you mean that your lunches are two hours, three courses and the wine is white, not red.

- I think we should move on, Sir. Regarding the matter under discussion, at the end of the day there could be a simple explanation.

Which is what?

- Sunlight. People in these countries not only enjoy better weather but they spend more time outdoors, eating, drinking and generally socialising.

So you think sunlight could be the explanation?

- Well, I could give you a dozen different reasons why it could be, but they're irrelevant at this stage. The important thing is that this doesn't undermine our theory about saturated fat.

So what do we do about the fad for the Mediterranean diet?

- Probably nothing, Sir. Of course, if people start eating a lot of oily fish, that will boost their levels of vitamin D and that would not be good news, but the chances of the American population getting a liking for mackerel seems pretty slim.

Not unless McDonalds covers it in tangy sauce, puts it in a sesame seed bun, and sticks it in a Happy Meal, eh Jack!

- I'd better check that they don't have any plans to do so, Sir.

I think you should do just that. We don't want to take any chances. And I guess you've made your point about the usefulness of this type of approach.

- Does this mean that you're happy to keep this group going on a permanent basis?

Yes, Jack, but with one condition.

- You want to come up with their name?

How did you guess.

May

- Sir, something has come up that I think we need to discuss.

Does it have anything to do with margarine, Jack?

- Good lord, Sir. Are you psychic?

Actually I was joking. It just seems that every time you start a conversation with that sentence, margarine is involved.

- Not every time, Sir, surely. Sometimes it's the French.

But I'm guessing that this time it's margarine.

- Well let's not get ahead of ourselves, Sir.

OK, what have you got?

- It has come to our attention that scientists have discovered a new condition that is affecting a small number of people. It's called…

Let me stop you there Jack. I hope you're not going to use a long winded Latin phrase which will mean nothing to me.

- Er…

I'll take that as a "yes".

- Well how about "GRID". That's how the press has started to refer to it.

"GRID" I can cope with. Now what is it?

- It's a condition that has caused the deaths of a number of young men in California.

How many deaths?

- Five, Sir.

Just five! Why should we be so interested?

- We are interested because the cause of death seems to be that in each case the immune system of the man has been compromised. The body's own defence mechanism is not working properly. If we can find out what is going on it could prove to be very useful. After all, it's not the drugs that keep most people alive. It is in fact their immune system.

Oh, I see. If this condition becomes more widespread it could help our cause.

- Exactly, Sir.

Well what have we come up with so far?

- Not a lot I'm afraid. At first it seemed clear that it was connected to the sexuality of the men. They were all homosexuals, hence the term "GRID". It refers to Gay Related Immune Deficiency.

Well that's very interesting. I bet the religious zealots will jump on that when they find out, you know "God's Gay Plague" and all that.

- Hang on, Sir, although that was our first thought, further investigation has revealed that the condition is more widespread than we thought. We've now discovered that it occurs elsewhere, particularly in Africa.

But what's the link between gay men in California and people in Africa.

- Think back to the start of this conversation, Sir.

What do you mean?

- The bit when I said I thought that you may be psychic.

But that's when I referred to margarine. Ah...

- Do I hear the sound of a penny dropping?

This wouldn't have anything to do with our pink stuff would it?

- It's quite possible, Sir, We sent a lot to Africa as part of a food aid program in the early 70's but they didn't take to it so we're still left with a load. It's all in a warehouse in California.

Why there?

- Well. After all the States stopped insisting that margarine contained a pink dye, the only place where there was any demand for the stuff was in the down town area of San Francisco. A lot of the men in the area seemed to buy it.

Why was that?

- I think they liked the colour, Sir. So although we can't be sure just yet, it does seem like a big coincidence.

So what do we do now? Do we start making pink margarine again?

- Oh no, I don't think that's an option, but then it may not be necessary. Whatever happened to cause the problem, the effect is now self-perpetuating.

You mean whatever it is, it's contagious?

- Yes, Sir. We're assuming that it's a virus of some sort although we haven't yet found it. However, you can see what an opportunity we have. This condition could wipe out millions of people, including all the gays.

It sounds like a win-win situation, Jack. Is there a down side?

- Well we don't think that it affects lesbians, which is a bit disappointing, but other than that, no there doesn't appear to be a down side. But whether or not it is a long term opportunity may depend on the drug companies. If this thing gets big then they're bound to start trying to find a cure.

And that could be bad news for us.

- Yes, Sir.

Well let's lean on them and see if we can stop them before the problem arises.

- Yes, Sir.

And Jack, keep me posted on any further news. This sounds like it could be a biggy.

June

- Sir, there is one slight problem with the landmine project.

Oh, and what's that?

- Well, Sir, we had hoped to make the mines undetectable.

Why bother to do that? Surely if we're dropping them in their thousands, it doesn't matter if they can be detected.

- Nevertheless, we had hoped to come up with a non-metal version that could not be detected. That way, we could achieve 100% effectiveness.

Instead of what?

- Instead of about 90%, if you assume that 10% of the mines will be detected before they are detonated.

Well the important thing at this time is to get the mines deployed. In the short term, can't we just drop 10% more mines to make up for those which will be detected? At least until we can perfect the undetectable version. That way the net result will be the same.

- I'll have a word with the military experts at Area 51 and see what we can come up with.

Ok, that's the enemy side covered. What about our own people?

- Ah yes, there I think we've also come up with something. The military have been trying to develop a drug that will protect our troops against possible chemical attack.

Good grief, why are we letting them do that?

- Well there's a big difference between letting them develop something and them being allowed to use it. We can't stifle all such research otherwise people will become suspicious.

So what have you come up with?

- Well, we test all such drugs and we are pretty certain we have come up with something.

You mean a drug that makes healthy people sick?

- Exactly, Sir. It has limited benefits when it comes to protecting our troops from chemical attack.

What do you mean by "limited"?

- I mean that it doesn't seem to have any effect at all. However, in our tests a fair number of people who took the drug had serious long term health problems.

How serious and how long term? I don't want these people going sick while they are still in the military. We'll end up paying their hospital bills.

- That's a good point, Sir. I'll look into it.

And what about the Brits and their war?

- Well they weren't particularly keen, but I managed to persuade them in the end.

How did you do that?

- I promised Mrs Thatcher that, if she starts a war, we'll make sure that she wins the next general election.

That's bit rash isn't it?

- Not really, Sir. The main opposition Labour party is led by a chap called Michael Foot. There's no way Labour will be elected while he's in charge.

Well I hope you know what you're doing. Have they decided on the opposition?

- I think so, Sir. The British want to choose a country which they can goad into a conflict. They don't want to be seen to start a war.

I suppose that makes sense. Who have they come up with?

- Well, they have three options, the first one being Spain. The Spaniards are still unhappy about Gibraltar and the Brits could probably do something bad enough to upset them and start a conflict. But they've decided against Spain.

Why is that?

- Well, it turns out that many people in government own a property in Spain. Also, it's a bit too close to the UK. But those aren't the main reasons.

What is the main reason?

- That they may lose. In terms of manpower and equipment, the British military is not that strong these days. They need to pick a country where they have a good chance of winning, which is why they've chosen Argentina.

Argentina? How on earth are they going to engineer a conflict with Argentina?

- Over the Falkland Islands, Sir.

Falkland Islands? I've never heard of them.

- Not many people have, Sir. They're in the South Atlantic, a few hundred miles off the coast of Argentina, hence the fact that the Argentinians think that the islands should belong to them.

So how did the British end up with them?

- I dare say they're leftover from the days of the British Empire.

But why should the British want to keep them? They're not sitting on vast oil reserves, are they?

- Not as far as I'm aware, Sir. No, I'm sure they'd get shot of them if they could. The problem is that the inhabitants are mostly British and they want to remain so.

And how many inhabitants are there?

- I believe there are around 50,000.

Well that's not that many. They'll need a pretty high hit rate to achieve a worthwhile body count. And how will the British goad the Argentinians into action?

- They don't think that will be difficult. At present, the islands are protected by a Royal Navy ship, HMS Endurance.

You mean a destroyer?

- No, Sir, nothing so impressive. I think it's no more than a fishing boat and a couple of sailors armed with Lee Enfield rifles.

And that's enough to deter the Argentinians?

- Apparently so, Sir. But the Brits think that if they withdraw the ship from protection duties, the Argentinians will take it as a sign of weakness and invade the islands.

And is that likely?

- More than likely, Sir. The government in Argentina is led by a military general who is having a difficult time right now, politically speaking. I'm sure he'll jump at the chance.

Ok, Jack, tell them to go ahead.

- Right away, Sir.

Oh, Jack.

- Yes, Sir.

Just out of curiosity, what was the third British option for a war?

- France, Sir.

July

Jack, come and join me, I'm watching the royal wedding. Don't they make a happy couple?

- Not for long.

Why do you say that?

- Well, we are going to give her the bad news about the other woman later today.

What, today, on her wedding day? That's a bit harsh isn't it?

- We have no choice, Sir. We don't want any accidents on the wedding night.

No, I suppose not.

The next day

Jack, how did things go with Diana?

- As of yesterday, it's Princess Diana, Sir.

Never mind the formalities, how did she take the news?

- As we expected, Sir, she wasn't too happy. I gather Charles spent the night in the spare room.

I bet he was a bit miffed.

- Not really, Sir, he gave Camilla a ring and she came over.

Who is Camilla?

- She's the other woman, Sir.

And how about the pregnancy thing? That needs to happen as soon as possible.

- Well we need to leave it a while, at least until the marriage has been consummated. Otherwise Charles may suspect something.

Well tell her to be careful in the meantime.

- Yes, Sir.

Anything else, Jack?

- There is one thing, Sir. I think we've struck pay dirt on the cholesterol front.

Who's come up trumps this time? Not Monica again, I hope.

- No, Sir, it's the new group who have been checking medical science papers.

Ah, the one without a name. I was going to talk to you about that. But first, your news.

- Well, they have been checking past works, not just the current stuff, and they have come up some interesting information regarding cholesterol and vitamin D. It appears that you need cholesterol as well as sunlight to produce vitamin D.

And why is that so good?

- Well you must remember that we are trying to lower cholesterol levels and stop people being exposed to sunlight. But even if we achieve only one of the two goals, we still get a result.

So even if I get a lot of sunlight, if I don't have enough cholesterol I still won't make enough vitamin D.

- Exactly!

That sounds like good news indeed.

- It is indeed, Sir. But you also had something to tell me, Sir.

What?

- A related issue?

Ah yes. I've come up with a name for this group. They should be called the "Non-Absorption of Nutrition Committee". NANCY for short. What do you think?

- Er, a couple of things come to mind, Sir.

Like what?

- Like the fact that there is no word in the title that begins with a "Y".

Ah, you spotted that.

- It wasn't difficult, Sir.

And your other point?

- That your wife's name is Nancy, Sir.

Ah, you spotted that as well.

- Again, not difficult, Sir.

Well can you do this one thing for me? I'm in a kind of jam with the First Lady?

- What is it this time? Forgot her birthday again?

It's something like that.

- Can't you buy her a bunch of flowers or some chocolates again?

I think it needs to be something different this time, something only a President can fix.

- You mean like naming in her honour a secret committee involved in work on a secret project. You do realise that you won't be able to tell her about the name, don't you.

Ah, I haven't thought this through, have I.

- So is it to be flowers or chocolates?

Chocolates, Jack. Plain, I think.

- But I thought that the First Lady preferred milk.

Just order the chocolates, Jack. If I'm going to be in the dog house, I'm going to need some chocolate to drown my sorrows.

- Yes, Sir. But there is one other thing.

Yes, Jack?

- You do realise don't you that when I said that you must tell no-one about STOP, that includes the First Lady.

Yes, of course, Jack.

September

- Sir, we've approached the pharmaceutical industry and they appear to be willing to play ball on the AIDS cure.

AIDS?

- Yes Sir, AIDS. You know, where there's a problem with the immune system.

You mean GRID.

- Not any more, Sir. Since the condition doesn't seem to be exclusively related to homosexuals it was thought that the term GRID was inappropriate. So it's now referred to as AIDS. It stands for Acquired Immune Deficiency Syndrome.

And do we know what it is that triggers the condition?

- We do, Sir. It's called HIV, which stands for Human Immunodeficiency Virus and it does what we suspected. It suppresses the immune system and as we thought it appears to be associated with pink margarine. It seems that the pink dye used as the colouring triggered a change in an otherwise harmless virus and created HIV.

But how is it passed from one person to another?

- By body fluids, Sir.

That sounds disgusting, Jack. Can you be more specific?

- Sex, breast milk, drug addicts injecting with dirty needles, and blood transfusions. Those are the main culprits.

Well this all sounds very promising but at the same time potentially worrying. I know that we want to reduce the World's population but we don't want to wipe it out completely.

- Well, Sir, if we can keep it confined mainly to gays and Africans then I think we'll be OK.

Let's hope so, Jack.

1982

February

Jack, in all the discussions we've had about cholesterol, fat and heart disease, you've explained to me what you think is wrong with this widely held theory.

- I've certainly tried, Sir. Do you have a question?

Well you haven't come up with an explanation as to what exactly does cause heart disease. Do we have any idea? It strikes me that we are missing something here.

- Well, Sir, I'm not sure that's right since we do think that Trans Fats have something to do with heart disease.

There you go again, Jack. That doesn't sound very definite to me. And also, bear in mind that people had heart attacks before we came up with Trans Fats so there must be something else going on.

- Sir, I know that there were people at Area 51 who were working on this, but I don't think it has priority right now.

Well who exactly is working on it now?

- I'm not sure anyone is, Sir. The committees at Area 51 are organised by food group, for example, fish, vegetables, etc. There aren't any that specialise in the actual illnesses themselves.

But why is that?

- It's to do with the original plan, you know, where we basically kill off the population by poisoning them. It's all based around what they eat and drink.

Well, Jack, I may be wrong but I thought the original plan was to reduce the human population. The main method chosen was through diet.

- I think that's a matter of semantics, Sir.

Whatever it is, Jack, let's see if we can move heart disease up the priority list, or at least get it onto someone's list shall we?

- Yes, Sir. And while we're on the subject of heart disease, we seem to have a bit of a problem with diabetes in that several of our different campaigns are resulting in a steady increase in reported cases.

But surely that's a good thing, Jack.

- Well of course that's right, but we've been so successful that we are now under pressure to do something about it.

Can't we just ignore the problem?

- Not when the numbers are increasing at the rate that they are. If the trend continues it won't be long before everyone is suffering from the condition. We're in danger of being too successful which means we can't ignore it. People are expecting us to do something.

OK, so what do we do? I suppose we're going to have to get the drug companies involved.

- They're already involved, Sir, and not to our advantage. They have come up with treatments which simply manage the condition.

By manage, you mean that the patient has to take the medication every day but it never cures them.

- That's right, which means that big pharma is happy. So we can't go to them in this instance which means that we must come up with something else in order to keep people happy. Of course, it must be something that is neutral at worst but that ideally makes the condition worse.

Well that's a tall order. Do you have anything in mind?

- Not yet, but we're on the case.

March

Jack, how are we doing with the heart disease issue? I assume that we now have someone working on the problem.

- We do indeed, Sir. I believe that we have come up with a few things but it's too early to have a definitive list.

I'm not asking for a definitive list, Jack. Just one thing will do for now. What have you got?

- Well we have stress as a possible trigger.

Stress? That's hardly a new idea, is it?

- No, Sir, but we now have some sound science to back up the theory and an explanation as to how it works. It's all to do with hormones. They…

Jack, I don't need the detail, I just need to know how we can use this information to our advantage.

- I'm not sure we need to do much at all. People are in general leading more stressful lives, partly due to the scare stories we keep coming up with concerning their health.

Ah, is that where the phrase "Scared to death" comes from?

- We all hope so, Sir.

In any case, I'm sure we can do more to get our message across. You know, TV, Radio, newspapers.

- They already report on our information, Sir.

Yes, but it's their choice as to what they report. We need to be a bit more pro-active in this area. See what you can come up with.

- Yes, Sir.

And have you made any progress regarding diabetes? We're still under pressure to address the problem of the rising number of cases.

- Well I'm not sure we'll ever come up with a fix, Sir. To do that, we'd actually have to look for one. That's not something we're going to do, and neither are the drug companies.

OK, perhaps "fix" was the wrong word to use, but we need to take action of some sort.

- Yes, Sir, I realise that and that's why we're going to promote some new dietary recommendations to people already affected by the condition.

Given we are not going to be able to use medication, I suppose that's our only option. What are we going to suggest?

- We think that people suffering from diabetes should cut their intake of fat and increase their consumption of carbohydrates.

I have a couple of issues with that idea, Jack. Firstly, I seem to have heard that message before. "Fat is bad" seems to be our answer to everything. Can't we come up with something different?

- Well at least we're consistent, Sir. What's your other point?

I seem to remember that diabetes is caused by consuming too many carbohydrates all of which, as far as the body is concerned, are treated like sugar.

- That's right, Sir.

So by increasing their intake of carbs, the situation is going to get worse.

- Well it probably won't get worse due to the drugs they're taking. But it certainly won't get better.

I get all that, Jack. My point is; how are we going to persuade people to actually believe this message? Anyone with half a brain will realise that a diabetic should eat fewer carbs, not more.

- I know that, Sir, which is why the actual message will be to eat less fat on the basis that diabetics are more likely to suffer from heart disease. If they reduce fat intake they'll have to eat more carbs but diabetics know that they need to be careful with sugar so they'll go with what we call "good" carbs. These are less problematic for diabetics but they still trigger insulin so they should really be restricted in their diet.

So we'll be seen to be taking some action and you think we can justify the recommendations but on balance, they'll have no effect.

- The worst scenario will be that there is no effect but with any luck it'll make the situation worse. And of course, by reinforcing the anti-fat propaganda, we'll be recruiting more people from the general population into the diabetics fold.

Well it's an unlikely plan. It's like telling a cocaine addict to take more cocaine.

- Yes, Sir, it's exactly like that.

April

- Sir, the plan regarding the Falkland Islands is going smoothly, with one slight exception.

And what is that?

- Well, Sir, the British withdrew the protection vessel and the Argentinians have occupied the islands as expected, but the number of casualties is not as great as anticipated.

And why is that, Jack?

- Well there are two main reasons, Sir. The first is that the British troops on the island did not put up a fight.

That's a bit surprising, isn't it?

- Not really, Sir, there were only a dozen or so of them.

Well what about the 50,000 inhabitants? Didn't they put up any resistance?

- Ah well, Sir, there we come to the other reason. When I said there were 50,000 inhabitants on the islands, strictly speaking that's true, but unfortunately that number includes the sheep.

What!

- It was a simple mistake by one of the statistical assistants at Area 51.

Well how many inhabitants are there, excluding sheep?

- Around 2000, Sir.

2000! Is that all! It hardly seems worth the effort. So how many casualties have there been.

- Including or excluding sheep?

Excluding.

- None, Sir.

And if we include the sheep?

- Three, Sir.

But this is terrible. At this rate, there will have been no point starting the war. You'd better tell the British to pull their finger out. Make it clear to Mrs Thatcher that, unless she achieves a decent body count, she can kiss goodbye to a second term in office.

- With Michael Foot still leader of the opposition, she may regard that as an empty threat.

Well get her on the phone now, I'll speak to her directly.

- Yes, Sir.

Ten Minutes Later

Jack, I've spoken to Margaret and...

- Margaret, Sir?

Mrs Thatcher, Jack.

- I think using her first name is being a bit familiar.

Well she didn't seem to have a problem, in fact she sounds very charming.

- Well try not to find her too charming, Sir, at least not until the body count is considerably higher.

I think she now understands where we're coming from, Jack. But as well as discussing the war, I spoke to her about the stress issue. It turns out that the Brits seem to be ahead of us in this area.

- What do you mean?

Well they have already instigated a plan to raise the stress levels of the UK population in a controlled and managed way.

- How are they doing that?

They've signed up a national newspaper to do it on their behalf. It's the Daily Mail.

- Well that's good planning on their part, but it's hardly radical. How does "controlled and managed" come into it?

Ah, that's where the Brits are being particularly cunning. They get the Daily Mail to print a health story one week, and then contradict it a few weeks later. The readers become really confused about what they can and cannot eat and drink. Their stress levels must be sky high.

- Give me an example.

Well, perhaps contradict isn't the right word. Take red wine as an example. In the first article, they say that it's good for your heart. But a few weeks later, they'll print another one that says it causes cancer. In fact, both stories may be correct, but by printing them separately a few weeks apart, they confuse the reader. They don't know whether red wine is good or bad.

- And hopefully they get more stressed.

If I were a Daily Mail reader, I'm sure that I would be extremely stressed!

- But at the end of the day, they're only doing what we do. They concentrate on a particular thing, like red wine, and a particular disease, whereas what is important is the overall effect on the quality and quantity of life. If you drink red wine, are you going to lead a longer and healthier life, that's what we want to know.

And?

- And what, Sir?

If I drink red wine, will I lead a longer and healthier life?

- Now that depends, Sir.

I thought it might.

Later That Month

Jack, I see the body count in the Falklands war is creeping up, but it's mainly the British who are suffering.

- Yes, Sir, and that's partly due to the French.

Why is that?

- Well, Sir, they are supplying Excocet missiles to the Argentinian army and these are being used to good effect against the British navy.

Why are the French helping the Argentinians?

- I believe they found out that they were on the list of British targets for a possible military conflict.

Oh, I can see why being on such a list would upset the French.

- Oh, it wasn't the fact that they were on the list that upset them. It was the fact that they were third, behind Spain and Argentina.

Well that's all academic, Jack, the Brits need to hit back and boost the numbers. Hasn't Argentina got a navy?

- Yes, Sir, they have.

Well why don't the British sink some boats? They've got a bloody nuclear submarine in the area haven't they?

- They have, Sir.

Well tell them to use it.

- I have spoken to them on the matter and apparently there's only one ship worth bothering with and that's the Belgrano. It's a cruiser with more than one thousand men on board.

Well why don't they go for that?

- Because the British feel that it's bad form to sink a ship that's facing the wrong way, Sir.

Facing the wrong way! What's that got to do with anything?

- They think it may be heading back to port.

Jack, tell them the clue is in the name; it's a warship, not a cruise ship. It doesn't matter what way the Belgrano is facing, it's a legitimate target.

- I think that such reasoning would be best coming from you, Sir. I know how well you get on with the Prime Minister. Perhaps you could use your charm.

This doesn't have anything to do with the fact that you find Mrs Thatcher rather formidable is it, Jack?

- Sir, she reminds me of my mother, and not in a good way.

OK, Jack, I'll do the dirty work.

- Thank you, Sir.

May

- Sir, your personal intervention seems to have done the trick.

You're referring to the Belgrano?

- Yes, Sir. Apparently, there are between 300 and 400 casualties. The total on both sides in the conflict is about 700.

Well we still need more.

- That may be a bit tricky, Sir.

Why is that?

- Because the Argentinians have surrendered.

Oh no, that's not good news. I suppose there's not much chance of upping the body count now.

- No, Sir.

What a waste of effort. When it comes to a war, remind me never to let the British go it alone again.

- I will, Sir.

Jack, one other thing. I see Princess Diana is pregnant. Is everything going according to plan?

- Yes, everything is on track. Anything else, Sir?

Yes, there is. I've been thinking about all the aspects of STOP that you explained to me in my initial briefing and there are a few things that concern me in particular.

- Which ones are they, Sir?

The Moon landing and G-Water, those are the ones I'd like to start on.

- OK, let's take the Moon landing. What's your concern?

My concern is the prestige and credibility of the USA for future generations.

- In what respect, Sir?

In respect of the fact that sooner or later we're going to be rumbled and it's not going to look good.

- Well it will be a long time before anyone goes to the Moon again.

Maybe so, but they will eventually. And they don't have to go and land there to prove that we didn't. They just need a powerful telescope. They'll be able to see all the rubbish we left there. Or rather they won't.

- It would have to be a lot more powerful that any currently available.

Not if it's in a space craft that's orbiting the Moon.

- No, Sir, I guess not.

I suspect that other nations, especially the Russians, would love to prove that we never got there at all. It's a pity we didn't adopt a more "green" approach to the whole thing.

- What do you mean, Sir?

You know, bring our rubbish home with us. There'd be no stuff for people to look for.

- I think it was difficult enough just to take the stuff there without bring it all back again.

Jack, it was a hoax, remember.

- Well it was eventually, but in the planning stage it was for real, and clearing up after ourselves would have made it a whole lot more difficult.

Well that's by the by now. I want to take action so that we avoid a big problem in the future.

- Well do you have anything in mind, Sir?

Yes. I want to launch a space craft on a mission to the Moon.

- The purpose of which will be what, Sir?

To drop a whole load of crap on the surface. Stuff that looks like it was left there by the original Apollo missions.

- Well that could take an awful lot of effort.

By effort, I guess you mean money, Jack.

- Yes, Sir, it will need a lot of money, but I meant effort as well in that we will have to build replicas of the things we left there, like the Moon buggies.

I was thinking that we would just do mock-ups in cardboard or something.

- That may fool people looking through a telescope, by not someone who lands on the Moon.

Yes, you're right there, but the timescales involved are a whole lot different. Someone could take a peek at the surface tomorrow but they're unlikely to actually get up close for years to come. And when they do, the chances are it'll be an American, so we'll solve that particular problem at a later date. But just in case, come up with two cost figures; one for the cardboard mock-ups and one for the real thing.

- Yes, Sir. And there was something else?

What?

- You have a concern about G-Water, Sir.

Ah yes. It's just that we seem to be putting a lot of our eggs in one basket. The growing trend of drinking bottled mineral water is giving us problems of coverage.

- That's certainly true. But what else can we do?

I haven't got as far as to come up with an answer, Jack. I thought that finding a solution to this problem is something you could do.

- I'll certainly look into it, Sir.

June

- Sir, I have some budgetary figures for your "Dump Crap on the Moon" project.

Ah, that was quick. What have you come up with?

- Well, for the first option, it's about three hundred million dollars.

Hm. That's a bit less than I thought.

- That's probably because it turns out that sending a spacecraft to the Moon and just dumping something on the surface is relatively easy.

Compared to what?

- Well compared to bringing something back or sending something back, even if it's just a picture. And they expect to do it in one hit.

Can they do that?

- They can if the objects are made of polystyrene.

They didn't like my idea of using cardboard then.

- Not if it's supposed to be a three dimensional object, and in any case cardboard would be heavier. So although the physical size of the craft would need to be large, the weight would be low and that's what counts. Even then, we won't be sending copies of all the stuff we left on the Moon, just a few token examples like moon buggies and landers.

OK. But what about the second option, you know, we send up the real replicas.

- Sir, I'm not sure that the phrase "real replicas" isn't some sort contradiction in terms.

But you know what I mean, Jack, so don't be so picky. What have you got?

- Sorry, Sir, but I don't have a figure. The experts just don't think it's possible.

Jack, everything's possible if you throw enough money at it.

- That may be true, Sir, provided you don't want to keep it under wraps. The problem with sending the replicas is that it would take many missions and we can't keep them all secret.

Well if we can do it for one, why not more than one?

254

- The single mission won't be a secret in that we will launch a space craft for everyone to see, it's just that the real purpose of the mission will be a secret. We'll say that we're sending it to Mars and then pretend to lose contact for some technical reason. In the meantime, it will really be heading for the Moon and once there it'll dump its cargo. But you can only do that once. We can't have a succession of failures, it'll look suspicious.

OK I take your point. Let's go ahead with the polystyrene option.

- Yes, Sir.

What about the other issue I raised, you know, the G-Water problem?

- We're still thinking about that one, Sir.

Don't think for too long Jack, we need to come up with something sometime soon.

- Yes, Sir.

October

Jack, give me an update on the G-Water problem.

- We haven't come up with an answer yet, Sir.

Give me an update anyway.

- OK, Sir. The first thing that we considered was whether we need to do anything.

Why would you think that?

- Because since tap water is already used in food production, we thought that there would be traces of fluoride in many types of processed food.

And was there?

- No, at least not at the levels that would be of help.

OK, what next.

- We considered whether we could persuade manufacturers to add it to their products but we decided that is also a no go.

Because?

- Because, Sir, the public won't wear it. They'd get suspicious and that's the last thing we want. There's already a lot of resistance to adding fluoride to drinking water. Adding it to food could be the last straw.

OK I can see that. So where does that leave us?

- We have to go back to square one. Why does fluoride have the effect it does? If we can discover that, we can then decide what the next step is.

OK, Jack. Keep up the good work.

1983

January

- Sir, we have come up with an idea to increase sales of margarine. We're going to put more water into the mix.

And what good will that do?

- Well, we've promoted the idea that fat is bad, but of course we have to remember that there's also fat in margarine.

Yes, but it's not the same fat is it?

- No, Sir, it's not, but the public don't seem to be able to differentiate. They think all fat is bad.

Whereas we know that it's only the Trans Fats in margarine that'll kill you!

- Exactly. So we've come up with the idea of adding more water to the margarine and advertising it as "Low Fat". It will also make it easier to spread so that's another selling point.

Won't the fact that we're putting less fat into the margarine make it less harmful?

- No, Sir, we've covered that point. If you add more water you have to add more emulsifier, which isn't exactly healthy. Add there's one other big plus point. Remember, we're adding more water.

So what?

- We will be using G-Water.

Brilliant! Well done, Jack. So this solves our gullibility problem as well.

Er no, Sir, probably not since the levels of fluoride in the margarine will not be that great. We are still working on that particular issue but I hope to have something for you soon.

OK, but there's something else I need to have a word with you about. What's the situation regarding smoking? I gather the number of people giving up has tailed off. Why is that?

- Well, Sir, it's to do with the advertising.

But I thought that we'd stopped advertising.

- Only on TV and radio. Advertising is still allowed elsewhere, like in magazines and newspapers. And the number of people giving up hasn't tailed off; it's just that they are being replaced by new smokers.

You mean the youngsters?

- Yes, it's an easier sell to the teenagers. They want to look cool and there's a lot of peer pressure. Also, they don't much care about the health issue; they figure that any problems that arise are too far away to worry about. It's not difficult for the tobacco companies to get youngsters to smoke.

But I can see a situation when all tobacco advertising will be banned. What will the companies do then?

- They've already thought of that one, Sir. They are going to bring out a range of non-tobacco products.

Like what?

- Designer clothes, watches, that sort of thing.

Well I can't see them making up the loss in tobacco revenue by selling watches.

- No, Sir, that's not the aim. The goods will be marketed under the brand name of the cigarette, logo and all. The companies will then be able to advertise the goods, but the public will associate them with the cigarettes.

That's neat!

- Well it's not bad, but it will only work for a while. Sooner or later, we will have to legislate to stop it.

But not for a while, Eh!

- No, Sir, not for a while.

March

Jack, I'm still a bit concerned about cigarette smoking. I know we are doing our best to delay any further legislation, but it's only a matter of time.

- Yes, Sir, I know. So far it's just TV and radio but in due course I dare say all advertising will be banned, as will smoking in public. I suspect Hollywood will eventually have to toe the line, although they may get away with playing the "artistic license" card.

So what are we going to do about it? Smoking has been one of our best options when it comes to killing off a significant number of Americans.

- Yes, Sir, I realise that, but let's face it; people in general are not going to simply stop smoking. However, there is likely to be a gradual decline, which is why the tobacco companies have been formulating a plan. They want to actively promote smoking in other countries, particularly in the Third World. There will be a couple of important advantages to this option. First, the body count from smoking will be maintained, if not increased. And secondly, there will be no loss of revenue to the US companies. They will just divert some of their production to exports.

But these other countries are going to want their own companies to get a bit of the action.

- Yes, but the plan is to buy up as many overseas tobacco companies as possible, thus keeping the ultimate control in our hands.

And the revenue?

- Well yes, of course they'll get the income. But on a more cheerful note, Sir, we think that we have finally come up with something on the issue of G-Water.

I hope so; we could do with some help after the tobacco setbacks. What have you got?

- We have discovered the secret of how fluoride makes people gullible. We think that we can do the same for food.

But I thought that we had ruled out adding anything to food.

- That's the beauty of the solution we have come up with. We don't add anything, at least not in the way you mean. What we do is to modify the genetic structure of the food at the molecular level. We add a sort of gullibility molecule.

Good grief Jack, that sounds a bit of a Frankenstein approach.

- Whatever you want to call it, it's a great solution in many respects. For instance, take corn. Once we have added the G-Molecule to the seed, it will be automatically reproduced in all the seed that it grows. Once it's there, it will always be there. And that's not all. If we distribute that stuff abroad, we will be affecting people who don't have access to any sort of tap water, let alone the stuff that's had fluoride added.

And apart from corn, what else can we add this GM to?

- As I understand it, almost anything, but we don't need to cover all the bases, we just need to select a few key ones. They'll probably be some of the main crops. It'll be much easier to distribute the stuff around the globe via seeds than it would be if we chose, say, pigs.

I can see that. So where do we stand?

- Well we have to get some of the big players involved and the whole thing is still at the experimental stage, but in a few years we should have something. Hopefully, in time, GM crops will become the norm.

May

- Sir, we have a couple of worrying situations regarding AIDS. Things are not turning out as we'd hoped.

Well I know that it seems to have gotten into the heterosexual community, so it's not just the gays that will be affected.

- Well that's one of the issues. The other one is that the drug companies seem intent on trying to find a cure.

But I thought that they'd agreed to hold back on such research.

- They had but two things have changed. The first is that with the spread of the disease into the wider community they can see that there is a much larger market out there.

Well can't we twist their arm? Surely the government can put a lot of pressure on these companies.

- We can, Sir, but not as much pressure as another particular group.

Like who?

- The gays, Sir. It appears that the drug companies are more afraid of the gay pressure groups than they are of the government. They can be quite scary when roused.

I can see that, Jack. Have you seen the sorts of outfits they wear?

- Well, Sir, I wasn't quite referring to their fashion sense.

No, I dare say that you weren't, but where does this leave us?

- I'm not sure yet, Sir. We've got our people onto it and I'm hoping they'll come up with something soon.

Let's hope so, Jack.

August

- Sir, we think we've come up with something on the subject of vegetables.

It's about time, Jack. Why has it taken so long?

- Well, Sir, we can't tell the population to stop eating everything.

Everything except margarine!

- I'm trying to be serious, Sir.

Sorry, Jack. You were saying.

- We had to come up with a strategy which involved telling people that vegetables are good and that they should eat them.

But isn't that right?

- Yes, Sir, but as with all foods, in moderation, as part of balanced diet. What we want to do is convince people that they can live on vegetables alone.

What, no meat or fruit?

- Sorry, Sir, I should have included fruit when I referred to vegetables.

And is it possible to live on fruit and vegetables alone?

- Well that's a very complex question.

No, Jack, the question is simple, but I suspect the answer you're going to give me is complex.

- Sorry, Sir, your right. There are many aspects to the answer. As far as adults are concerned, they could exist on only fruit and vegetables for some time before showing any ill effects. But eventually, they will suffer from vitamin deficiencies and that will cause health problems.

Also, they will have less body mass which.....

You mean they'll be thinner?

- Yes, Sir.

Which means that their life expectancy will be shorter?

- That's the plan.

Well it doesn't seem much.

- In fact, Sir, there are quite a few other points. One is the fact that the farmers are using a lot more chemicals on their crops these days. Some of the stuff is pretty nasty and anyone who confines their diet to just fruit and vegetables will be consuming a lot of the chemicals. It won't be good for them.

And what else have you got?

- Two things. The first is regarding children. Whereas adults can survive on a vegetarian diet for some time, it could cause serious problems for youngsters, particularly infants. They need a balanced diet to develop and a vegetarian diet could cause serious problems.

Like what?

- Well their diet is going to lack vital vitamins and minerals like B12, iron and calcium. And of course you don't get much in the way of saturated fat in fruit and veg. These things are all important for a body that is developing.

But why would a child be a vegetarian?

- Because of its parents. A vegetarian parent is unlikely to feed meat to a child. If the parent allows them to eat dairy products, i.e. milk, cheese and eggs, they'll probably be OK. But a child of a vegan is going to have real problems.

When you put it that way, I guess you must be right. Is there anything else?

- One last thing. A vegetarian or vegan diet is going to be pretty boring. No sausages, no burgers, no hot dogs.

It all sounds pretty grim.

- Exactly, so it will make things easier for vegetarians if we can come up with something that looks and tastes like meat, but is made from vegetable matter.

And have you come up with anything yet?

- Not yet, Sir. It's proving to be a very tricky problem.

I bet it is. And what about fruit? Should we be encouraging people to eat the stuff?

- The same thing applies. Chemicals are used on them just like vegetables. The one additional thing in our favour is that most fruit contains sugar, and it's not good to consume too much of that.

But I thought that the sugar that is bad for you is the sort of sugar you put in your coffee.

- It's a different type of sugar, fructose, but it's still sugar so it's still going to be bad news to consume too much.

It sounds like we've got most things covered.

- I certainly hope so, Sir.

September

- Sir, I've had some feedback from the agrichemical companies. They seem keen on the idea of modifying the genetics of certain plants, particularly the soya bean. However, they want to take the process a bit further than we intended.

Well as long as they add our gullibility molecule, I don't see that it matters what they do. What do they have in mind? I suppose they want to increase yields.

- Good grief no, Sir, at least not directly. No, they have a couple of other things in mind. The first is to modify the genetics of a crop to make it resistant to the chemicals that are used to control the weeds. That way the farmers will be able to spray a lot more of the stuff onto the crops. And of course that's of benefit to us since the weed killers concerned will include organophosphates.

I like the sound of that, Jack. And I dare say the company that makes the weed killer is going to be pretty happy.

- Er, it's the same company, Sir.

Wow, that's pretty lucky.

- I'm not sure luck has anything to do with it, Sir. It was all part of a co-ordinated approach and what's more, they've come up with another clever wheeze. The seeds that come from the crop are going to be infertile.

In practice, what does that mean?

- It means that the farmer will not be able to use the seeds from one crop to create the next. They will always have to buy new seed.

Can you be sure that the farmers will buy our GM stuff? After all, if the yields don't increase and they can't use the crops for seeds, what's the benefit?

- Well it's not true to say that overall the yields do not increase. The GM crops currently under development don't have increased yields. In fact in some cases the yield is actually lower.

How can that be?

- We believe it's to do with the fact that the GM plants don't absorb the nutrients as well as the standard crop. However, the fact that they will not be competing with weeds means that for some crops the yield could increase. And for other crops we'll have to come up with something to get the farmers to buy the stuff and that is going to be increased yield.

But surely that's a good thing, Jack. In fact, doesn't this put our whole plan into question? I mean if GM crops can increase yields significantly, then surely we won't have a problem with a shortage of food.

- Sir, when it comes to population control, there are more issues involved than just food. There's energy, land, water. GM crops aren't the answer to every problem caused by the population explosion. In any case, even with GM crops, all that you are doing is postponing the inevitable. If for example they were to increase yields by 20% across the board, in a few years the population of the planet will have increased by 20%. We'll be back to square one.

So project STOP continues.

- There was never any danger that it wouldn't, Sir.

1984

February

- Sir, we have a problem with the TV show idea.

Don't tell me. Hollywood can't come up with a show featuring old people. It must be years since we first suggested the idea.

- It is, Sir, and the girls are getting impatient. No, Sir, that wasn't the problem, but the writers seem to think that they have come up with something. Apparently, they are of the opinion that subjects like incontinence can be funny.

When you get to my age, Jack, you'll realise that there's nothing funny about incontinence.

- No, Sir. Anyway, as I said, that's not the problem.

Well what is the problem?

- They can't act.

What, none of them?

- That's right, Sir.

What are we going to do?

- Well, luckily they all realised that they are not cut out for the stage. They've gone away to think about it. In the meantime, Hollywood has already produced the scripts so they will go ahead with the show.

OK, but no incontinence jokes.

- No, Sir, understood.

What's the show going to be called?

- The Golden Girls, Sir.

I'll be sure to watch it.

- Is there anything else, Sir?

Yes, Jack, I see Diana is pregnant again. I didn't realise that we were planning on a backup for William.

- We weren't, Sir, she's done this without our help.

Good grief, I hope Charles was not involved.

- No, Sir, he wasn't, and from what I gather that's part of the problem. They do not have relations these days, so she has found some other male companion. It's really hardly surprising at her age.

She's a bit frisky is she?

- You could say that. Anyway, whatever the reason, the damage is done.

What's Charles going to do when he finds out?

- Oh, he already knows. Of course he's not best pleased but he'll just have to play along, otherwise he's going to look a bit foolish. Let's just hope the child looks like him, and not like the boyfriend.

April

- Sir, we have a bit of a problem with margarine.

I thought we had that covered with the "Low Fat" idea.

- No, Sir, that particular project is going very well. In fact we aim to bring out a whole range of "Low Fat" products.

Will they all be as unhealthy as margarine?

- We hope so, Sir. When we take out the fat we normally have to replace it with something else, otherwise no matter what it was when it started out, it'll end up having the wrong consistency.

So what do we use instead of fat?

- Well that will depend on what type of food you are dealing with. It could be sugar or some sort of thickening agent like gum. But you can be assured that whatever it is, it won't be good.

So what's the problem?

- We have a lot of the old stock of margarine that we can't get rid of piled up in warehouse. Some of it is quite old.

How old?

- 20 years or more.

Good grief! Is it still edible?

- It's probably as edible now as it was when it was manufactured but as yet we haven't found anyone who will try it in order to find out.

But that's not all. I'm afraid that some of it is dyed pink.

I thought that problem was resolved some time ago.

- Yes, it was, Sir. The last state changed the law in 1967. But we still have some old stock.

Well just get rid of it. I don't care how.

- Yes, Sir.

Sometime Later

- Sir, we have a situation in the UK.

Don't tell me they want to win the World Cup again.

- No, Sir, it's more serious than that.

How can it be more serious than that? It cost us a small fortune to bribe that Russian linesman.

- It wasn't the money, Sir, it's the free vodka for the rest of his life that really hurts. Especially as it turned out he wasn't Russian. He was from Azerbaijan, so the transportation costs have been somewhat higher than expected.

He's still alive then?

- Yes, Sir.

Well didn't he accept the offer of free margarine to go with his free vodka? That should have killed him off by now.

- Yes, Sir, he did accept the offer, but he doesn't eat it himself. He feeds it to his donkey and uses it to grease the axles on the cart.

But that's terrible.

- Well it is for the donkey, since he's dead.

Ho, ho, good joke Jack.

- No seriously, the donkey ate too much margarine and died. We had to supply a replacement donkey and stop the supply of the free margarine.

Haven't we persuaded the Russians to put fluoride in the drinking water yet?

- Yes we have, Sir, and the Azerbaijanis, but with all that vodka he doesn't drink much water.

Well, going back to your first point, what's the problem then?

- Someone has noticed that people in Africa are starving and he wants to do something about it.

Like what?

- He's going to get a few friends together to make a pop record.

And what good will that do?

- Well, he's had a bit of a lean time career-wise so he could probably do with a bit of publicity.

No, I mean in terms of feeding people in Africa.

- Hopefully, not a lot.

What's his name?

- Bob Geldof. He's Irish.

May

- Sir, I think we've come up with something regarding a meat substitute.

I'd completely forgotten that we were still looking for such a thing.

- We weren't, it was the Brits who came up with it. We gave them the challenge in the mid-sixties when we were still looking into the possibility of such a substance.

What, and it's taken them 20 years to come up with something?

- Not quite, Sir. They found it within a few years but it has taken them time to go through an evaluation process to prove that it's safe for human consumption.

What on earth did they do that for!

- Well exactly, Sir. But they gave the challenge to a commercial company who, not surprisingly, thought that it should be safe to eat.

And is it?

- Unfortunately, it may well be. But of course, it won't be as nutritious as the real thing.

Well what's it made of?

- Mycroprotein, Sir.

And what's that?

- It's a fungus, Sir.

You mean a mushroom?

- Unfortunately not, Sir. It's more towards the athlete's foot end of the fungus spectrum.

It sounds pretty grim, Jack. What does it taste like?

- I've brought a sample for you to taste. It's in the style of a burger.

This isn't going to be like the yokeless omelette is it?

- What do you mean?

You know, I taste it and say it's awful and you say no one else has been brave enough to try it.

- But that wasn't you, Sir. That was a different President.

But word gets around, Jack.

- Apparently so, Sir. If you like, I'll try it first.

Pause for chewing

- Now you try it, Sir.

Pause for more chewing

Hm, that's not bad. I think I'll have another bite.

- I wouldn't do that if I were you, Sir.

Why not?

- Because we haven't yet decided what is a safe dose.

Dose? You make it sound like a drug.

- Well you could look at it that way. The industrial process which turned the fungus into this stuff is very complex. We're not sure how dangerous the result will be to health.

I thought you said it was safe.

- Tests in the lab haven't shown up any serious problems, at least not as far as hamsters are concerned.

But I guess you need to test it on some human guinea pigs. Do you have anyone in mind?

- We thought we would just market it to vegetarians. After all, as far as they are concerned we're more limited in how we can kill them off. They eat fewer food groups.

I guess you could. What's the worst that could happen?

- That it does them no harm what so ever, Sir.

After all this effort, let's hope that's not the result. But to be on the safe side, we'd better test it on a few people, just in case it's so toxic that they keel over within days. It would look pretty bad if that happened and it turned out we never tested it on humans before putting it on the market.

- Yes, Sir, you're right. I'll get the tests underway.

You'll try it on the usual test dummies?

- You mean the diners in the press corps restaurant?

I do.

- Yes, Sir.

The Next Day

How did the test go?

- You mean with the meat substitute? Good and bad news there, Sir. None of the diners suffered any ill effects.

Is that the good or the bad news?

- That's the good news. The bad news is that they weren't particularly keen on the fake meat loaf. But then, it's not designed for meat eaters.

No, I guess not. The real test will be the vegetarian community. Is it on the market yet?

- It is, Sir, in the UK. We'll see how it goes there before we introduce it into the US.

Let me know how it goes.

- Yes, Sir.

October

Jack, I'm getting a lot of stick about the fact that we still haven't come up with a fix for this AIDS thing. I know it's a tricky problem but we need to do something.

- I know that, Sir and I think we've come up with a solution which has several advantages.

OK, fire away.

- Well the drug companies had two opportunities. The first one was to find something to stop people contracting HIV in the first place, probably a vaccine. As you can imagine I wasn't too keen on that one.

No, and I can see why. But what's the alternative?

- They can come up with something that helps those people who have already contracted the disease. It won't cure them but it will increase their life expectancy.

I'm not sure that I like that idea, Jack. We're trying to kill people off, not keep them alive longer.

- Well bear in mind that we don't have any choice here. The gays won't let this one go and for them it's the ideal solution. Those of them that already have the disease will be able to get help. And if they live longer what do you think will happen? Bear in mind that it's not just the gays we're talking about here but anyone with HIV.

I'm not sure what you mean, Jack.

- Sir, what do you think will happen to the incidence of HIV, given that the people who are infected are going to live longer?

Ah, I see where you're coming from. The longer they live the more likely it is that they will pass on the virus to other people.

- Exactly, Sir.

But if we have a cure...

- Remember it won't be a cure, Sir. It will stabilise the condition but the patient will still have the virus in their body.

Well whatever it is, where's the long term advantage?

- Well, Sir, we're hoping that the treatment for HIV will go the same way as antibiotics.

You mean that the virus will become immune to the treatment.

- Yes, Sir.

And is that likely?

- I'm sure it can be arranged, at which point there will be far more people infected with HIV and they'll start dropping like flies.

Well if you think that's the route we have to take, so be it. But I still think it's a missed opportunity.

- Not necessarily, Sir. Remember there are far more people with HIV in Africa than there are in the USA.

But won't they be able to benefit from the new treatments.

- Not at the sort of prices we intend to charge for the drugs. After all the pharmaceutical industry has to get a reasonable return on its investment.

I dare say it does, Jack. In the meantime we need to be seen to be doing something to stop the spread of the virus otherwise we're going to get some bad press.

- I've already got my people onto it, Sir.

I don't mean that we actually want to stop the spread, just that it must appear that we are doing something.

- That goes without saying, Sir.

1985

February

- You remember the chap who wanted to make a pop record to feed Africa.

Yes.

- Well he did and he is.

He is what?

- Feeding Africa.

What? All of them?

- Not quite all, Sir, but a fair number.

How did that happen?

- Well the record went on to become the biggest selling single in history. The money he raised has been used to buy food.

Do we need to worry? I thought that we were going to leave the Africans to their own devices.

- Yes, Sir, that's right, Sir, and if he had stopped there it would not make much difference to STOP. But now he wants to hold a pop concert.

Well I still can't see what the problem is.

- How about the fact that it's going to be broadcast live to the entire globe.

Holy shit!

- Exactly, this could be serious.

Have we made contact with him to see if we can head him off?

- Yes, Sir, but in return for abandoning the concert idea, he's asking for the impossible.

You mean money?

- If only it were that simple, Sir.

Don't tell me he wants Ireland to win the soccer World Cup.

- No, even worse.

What?

- He wants to have a number one hit record in his own right.

And what's wrong with that?

- Well the experts say there's no way Bob Geldof will ever have another number one hit.

So what are we going to do?

- Nothing for the moment. I've arranged for one of our agents to keep a close watch on him.

Which one?

- Bono, Sir.

March

Jack, I see that the Iran/Iraq war seems to be going well.

- I'm not sure that you're correct there, Sir.

Why not? The conflict seems to be a stalemate at the moment but the body count is continuing to rise. It sounds like the ideal situation to me.

- Yes, but for how much longer. Thanks to our help, the Iraqis are better equipped and are likely to gain the upper hand eventually.

Why do you say that? They haven't done so yet.

- That's mainly due to the fact that Iranians have been throwing bodies at the conflict, but they can only do that for so long before they run out of manpower. And if that happens, Saddam will overrun Iran and the conflict will end.

And so will the killing.

- Exactly, Sir! And it will also make Iraq a significant power in the region, which is the last thing we want.

So what can we do? We can hardly change sides at this stage of the game.

- No, Sir, of course we can't. Or at least we can't be seen to be changing sides.

So do you have something in mind?

- Not yet, but we have a lot of people working on the problem. It shouldn't be long before they come up with something.

Good. Keep me posted.

June

- Sir, we may have come up with something on the war issue.

Which one, Iraq/Iran or South America?

- In fact it's both, Sir.

I don't see how they're connected, Jack, unless you've persuaded Jordan to attack Peru.

- At this moment in time, they're not connected, but if we have our way, they will be.

And how will we do that?

- Well first we'll sell arms to Iran. That'll even up the score with Saddam and keep the war going longer.

But surely the Iraqis aren't going to be happy when they find out that we've changed sides?

- They won't know, Sir. This will be a secret operation.

But where will the money go? I trust we're not going to just give the weapons to Iran?

- That's where South America comes in. We'll give the money that we receive from Iran to one of the opposition groups in South America and then they can buy the arms from US companies in the normal way. That way, everyone is happy.

Not quite everyone, I suspect, but it sounds promising if we can swing it.

- So I have your authority to go ahead, Sir?

Jack, as far as I am concerned, I know nothing about this. If the shit hits the fan, I don't want to be involved.

- So we'll need to find a fall guy.

I think so, don't you?

July

- Sir, the first shipment of arms has been sent to Iran. The funds have been passed on to the Contra rebels in Nicaragua.

So we can expect to see some fireworks in Central America some time soon.

- I certainly hope so, Sir.

And the fall guy?

- There's a colonel in the US army who is facilitating the overall plan. He'll be sacrificed if needs be, along with a few minor helpers.

And my name won't figure in the frame?

- Of course not, Sir.

September

- Sir, Monica has come up with something that we need to consider. She says it's all very well trying to kill people off, but as fast as we make them ill, the medical profession, that is the doctors and the pharmaceutical companies, is making them better.

But I thought that our plan to break the banking system was supposed to address this issue.

- That's certainly true but Monica feels that we should attack this problem on more than one front, just in case the first plan fails.

Good point, Jack, but what can we do about it?

- I'm not sure yet. But there is a bigger issue at stake here. By definition, STOP needs to be kept secret from all but the essential few who need to know.

What, you mean me, you, Monica and Rachael. And of course most of Hollywood.

- Well Hollywood only knows about the fake moon landing, not the rest of STOP. But there are several thousand scientists based at Area 51.

Several thousand! I assumed there would be just a few dozen.

- Well no, Sir, if you think about all the different things going on, it takes a lot of people to cover all the different areas of expertise.

Yes I suppose it does. Even so, several thousand! I think it may be a good idea to go through a summary of the on-going projects, just so I know where we stand.

- Yes, Sir.

Anyway, you said there is a bigger issue.

- Yes, Sir. As highlighted by Monica's thoughts on the medical profession, we need to be careful that certain areas of government and industry aren't working against our long term aim.

Yes, that's perhaps true, in which case what do you suggest?

- We need to set up a committee to check where such conflicts occur. We can then decide what, if anything, we need to do.

Well that's all very well, but these people on the committee need to be recruited from the group that is already privy to the information on STOP. Otherwise, we are just adding to the total number of people in the know.

- Yes, Sir, in which case the names are obvious.

You're thinking what I'm thinking?

- Yes, Sir. I'll notify Rachael and Monica right away.

Going back to the problem of the medical profession, do we have any ideas yet?

- No, Sir, but I'll get onto it as soon as I can.

October

- Sir, we've given some thought to the problem that we have with the medical profession.

You mean where the doctors keep curing the people that we are trying to kill.

- Well luckily for us, the doctors manage to kill off a fair number of people each year. Bear in mind that you are more likely to be killed by your doctor than by your spouse.

Really? But that's terrible. How do they get away with it?

- By saving the lives of many others so that on balance they end up ahead. But in this instance we're not talking about doctors, we're talking about the medical profession in general.

And what have you come up with?

- We've decided to concentrate on the things that save the most lives which we think are vaccinations and antibiotics. In the first case, you are stopping people contracting a lot of diseases, some of which could be fatal. In the second case, you have medication that can cure a lot of different illnesses once a person has caught them. Either way, they are bad news.

Well someone has got a lot to answer for. Who is to blame this time?

- Well normally I'd refer to my dictionary of things to blame.

And what on earth is that, Jack?

- Oh, it's just a list of likely targets that we can point the finger at when we need to; things like saturated fat, sunlight and the French. In practice it's normally the French but in this case it's not really a question of blame so they're not in the frame. Instead it's the British, Sir, since they both discovered penicillin and invented vaccinations.

So what do you suggest?

- Well, there's no point in dealing with the medicines currently on sale if someone then brings out new ones. So for a start we need to have a word with the pharmaceutical companies. We've got to stop the companies developing new drugs.

We already tried that once with HIV but the Gays got the better of us.

- Well in this instance things aren't quite so focused. If we come up with something, I can't see who is going to outgun us.

OK, then what?

- Well, we haven't come up with anything yet for vaccinations, although we're pretty sure that there's nothing we can do for people who have already been vaccinated. There, the damage is done.

Well, why don't you give the problem of vaccinations to the British? After all, they got us into this mess.

- I'm sure they invented vaccinations with the best of intentions at the time, Sir.

I'm sure they did, but that doesn't matter now. And while you're at it, mention the antibiotic problem as well.

- Yes, Sir.

November

- Sir, our people at Area 51 have come up with something that makes our work on antibiotics even more urgent.

And what might that be, Jack?

- It's called Methicillin-resistant Staphylococcus aureus.

OK, Jack, let's try one syllable at a time shall we.

- Perhaps if I use the alternative name, Sir.

Which is?

- That would be multidrug-resistant staphylococcus aureus, Sir.

And you think that helps?

- Let's call it MRSA.

Let's do that, Jack. Now why are we interested?

- The clue is in the name, Sir.

Not much of a clue there, Jack.

- There is if you concentrate on the phrase "multi-drug resistant". MRSA is an infection that is resistant to most antibiotics. It was originally discovered by the British in the early sixties and now it has made its way to the USA.

That was a stroke of luck wasn't it?

- Not really, Sir. We brought it over in a briefcase. We got tired of waiting for it to come over the Atlantic of its own accord so we had to intervene.

But why? What's so important about this little bug?

- Well, Sir, you remember our conversation about medical treatment. We have a big problem because so many medical conditions can now be cured, either by using drugs or surgery. It's not at all easy to stop such treatments, particularly where surgery is concerned. Surgeons can be a pretty gung-ho bunch, always trying to outdo one another but luckily all surgery, even the most basic operations, involves the same basic stage. You have to cut the patient open and that's where our new friend MRSA will come in. If we can get this bug widely circulated then even the simplest operation could become life threatening.

This sounds promising, Jack, but surely the drug companies will come up with a drug that will see off this MRSA.

- Exactly, which is why we need to do something fast. We need to encourage them to put all their efforts into something else.

Well even if we can persuade them to do that, surely the public at large will start to get suspicious. After all, in the past the drug companies have always come up with a new antibiotic to fight the latest infection.

- I suspect that you are right, Sir. We'll have to come up with a strategy to overcome that little problem. I'll see what our people can come up with.

December

Jack, what's the situation regarding antibiotics?

- Sir, the news isn't good. Understandably, the pharmaceutical companies seem to think that if they stop making drugs that cure sick people, then they'll go out of business.

Yes, I can see that. It's a pity they can't come up with something that makes healthy people ill!

- Sorry, Sir?

Well, if we want the pharmaceutical companies to stay in business but we don't want them to cure sick people, that's the only option.

- Hm, you may have an idea there, Sir.

I do?

- Well, as you say, it's the only option.

Even so, assuming you can come up with a "sick pill", how are you going to get healthy people to actually take the medicine?

- That's something I'm not sure about. But first we have to find ourselves a "sick pill".

Well I'm not sure about that option, Jack. I think perhaps we need to come up with something regarding antibiotics.

- I'll give it some thought, Sir.

1986

February

- Sir, Bono has come up with an idea. He thinks that we should let Geldof continue with his aim to feed Africa.

That doesn't sound like a good idea to me.

- Well he says it would be if we were to supply the food.

That sounds even worse.

- Not if the food is margarine, Sir!

Sometimes, Jack, your brilliance is just breath-taking.

- Thank you, Sir, but the bad news is that I don't think we'll be able to palm them off with any more of the pink stuff.

You mean we've sent them some before.

- Yes, Sir.

Well see what you can do. Surely there must be some other "Special" food stuffs that we may want to donate to Geldof?

- I'm sure that we can find something, Sir. It will look a bit suspicious if the only thing we donate is a hundred thousand tons of margarine.

A hundred thousand tons!

- They are big warehouses, Sir. It will only be a small part of our stockpile and that doesn't even include the pink stuff.

But why do we have stocks of normal margarine.

- Because it's considered a strategic commodity, just like oil. After all, we don't want to run out of the stuff, do we?

No, I suppose not.

March

- Sir, we may have come up with something regarding the pill for healthy people. It's called a Statin.

What does it do?

- It helps people with heart disease.

Helps them do what?

- Helps them get better, Sir.

What good is that? We want to make people ill, not healthy.

- I realise that, Sir, which is why we haven't yet approved them for use. However, when we were testing them, we found that they lowered cholesterol levels.

Good grief, I hope that's not the reason why they're effective at treating heart disease. 'Cos if so, we've really shot ourselves in the foot.

- No, Sir, we're pretty sure that's not how they work.

Pretty sure? Shouldn't you be certain?

- I'm not sure that anything in this world is absolutely certain.

You mean that we could be wrong about margarine?

- Well alright, there are some things that are cast iron certainties. But as far as Statins are concerned, we tested them on patients with high and low cholesterol levels and they were just as effective. So we're pretty sure they work by some other mechanism.

Like what?

- Well, amongst other things they're anti-inflammatories and anti-oxidants. Either could be the reason.

Ok, let's assume that it's not their effect on cholesterol. Where does that get us?

- Well, Sir, it gives us our "sick pill". What we'll do is persuade people with high cholesterol levels, who are otherwise healthy, that they should take Statins.

And what will that achieve?

- If you remember, Sir, cholesterol is good for you; amongst other things, it's good for your immune system.

Yes, I do remember that. What I mean is what good will it do in the long term? Surely once someone finishes their course of Statins, their cholesterol levels will go back to normal.

- Oh, they don't stop, Sir. Once they're on Statins, they'll take them for the rest of their lives.

Brief pause

- Sir, are you OK?

Yes, Jack, I'm fine.

- Sorry, Sir, I thought that you were having some sort of seizure.

No, I was just in a state of shock, since I'm trying to get my head round this idea. Are you telling me that you expect to get perfectly healthy people to take a pill every day for the rest of their lives?

- Yes, Sir.

And that for some of them, it will actually hasten their death?

- Yes, Sir, that's the expectation, although of course we won't tell them that. But as well as lowering their cholesterol we're hoping that there will be unhealthy side effects. Of course, if there are, the fact that a person will be taking these drugs forever will mean that, however slight the side effect, it's bound to build up over a period of time. With any luck they'll be life threatening.

Well, Jack, if you manage to pull this one off, I'll be amazed.

- Thank you, Sir.

When do you expect to start?

- Well the first step is to set the level of cholesterol which we will regard as "normal". The level hasn't been determined yet.

Can't we set it low enough so that everyone thinks that their cholesterol level is too high?

- No, not yet, after all people may smell a rat if we do that.

Well let me know when we have settled on a level.

- Yes, Sir.

Is there anything else?

- There is one thing, Sir. We seem to have a problem with margarine.

That's not the first time you've come in here and said that. I hope it's not the pink stuff again.

- No, Sir, not the pink stuff. It's a problem with its popularity. Sales have levelled out. We could do with doing something to increase consumption.

Well what do you have in mind? Have you spoken to Monica?

- Yes and she's suggested we use a publicity campaign to target children.

I can see where you're coming from, Jack. If we get them young they'll be ours for ever. I think you'll find that we've used this ruse before.

- Well I think that's a rather crude way of putting it, but yes, Sir.

So what do you have in mind? Some sort of TV program I would imagine. Say a cartoon?

- How perceptive of you. Yes, Sir, a cartoon. We've already been on to Hollywood. They seem keen but they have a couple of conditions.

Oh really. What are they?

- Well they want a guarantee that the program will be sold around the world.

Well I can't see we'd have a problem with that.

- No, Sir, it suits our purpose.

What's the other condition?

- They want one of their number to be President again.

You mean like me?

- Yes, Sir.

Well I haven't got a problem with that either, since it won't affect me. Whoever it is will have to get into politics and be elected a governor of a state before they can consider standing for the big one. It'll all take time. Who have they got in mind?

- Arnold Schwarzenegger.

And do we have a problem with that?

- Not as far as I can see.

OK, let's go ahead. Let's take the same route as I did.

- You mean get him elected governor of California.

Exactly! It worked for me so why shouldn't it work again.

Later That Week

- Sir, we have come up with the recommended maximum cholesterol level. It's 200.

How did you arrive at that?

- It was Monica's idea.

I didn't know she was a doctor.

- She isn't, Sir, and she didn't come up with the actual number. But she said that since for most people, their cholesterol level goes up in middle age, we should set it at whatever level brings most older people into the net, while leaving out the younger people.

And you think that level is 200?

- Yes, Sir. What's more we have reason to believe that the people who live the longest have a cholesterol level of between 240 and 250. As soon as you deviate from this figure, up or down, your risk of dying increases. And the link to heart disease makes sense since it affects mainly older people.

But does that mean we can say that cholesterol causes heart disease?

- We'll go with that to start with but if anyone starts to look closely at the evidence we'll have to amend it to "cholesterol is a risk factor for heart disease".

And is that true?

- Remember the example we discussed some time ago. Or perhaps that was before your time, Sir.

Was this to do with baldness? If so, you mentioned it in your initial briefing.

- OK, so you understand the principal. Cholesterol tends to go up with age, certainly from middle age. Heart attacks also increase in number with age. Therefore we can say that cholesterol is a risk factor for heart disease, even though there is no direct connection. You could equally say that grey hair is a risk factor. Luckily reducing your cholesterol will have the same effect on heart disease as dyeing your grey hair black.

What, you mean none?

- Dyeing your hair certainly wouldn't have any effect. However, if anything, lowering your cholesterol would likely increase your chances of a heart attack.

And you say we're going to concentrate on older people.

- Exactly, Sir. It will give the plan credibility. We estimate that 80% of people over the age of 50 will end up on Statins.

Wow, that's a lot of "sick pills". And have you spoken to the pharmaceutical companies about this plan?

- Yes, Sir.

And what was their reaction?

- As you expected, Sir, they were pretty keen.

I imagine that's an understatement.

- Put it this way, Sir. The boss of one such company left the meeting and went off to order a new yacht.

What, just the one?

- Well, one for each day of the week.

May

Jack, I've just seen some rather disturbing video of what appears to be a drunken cow. The poor thing was staggering all over the place. Do you know what's going on?

- What did the cow look like, Sir?

It was white with black patches but I don't know what difference that makes. How many drunken cattle are there?

- Unfortunately, Sir, quite a few, mostly in the UK.

Well what's going on?

- We are looking into the situation and if you can bear with me I should have something to report in a few days.

OK, Jack, but make sure it includes a solution.

- Sorry, Sir? I don't follow you.

Well I'm assuming that this cow is going to be part of some sort of problem, so when you come back to me I'd the explanation to include a solution.

- In that case let's make it a few weeks, Sir.

June

- Sir, we've completed our investigation into the drunken cow and we think that we've come up with an explanation.

And a solution, Jack?

- Of course, Sir, and a solution. We've identified the cause of the problem as being.....

Hang on a minute, Jack. Give me the solution first and let's see if I can guess what the problem is.

- I'm sorry, Sir?

Bear with me, Jack. It's just a little game to give us both some light relief so give me the solution and let's see how I get on.

- OK, Sir, if you insist. The solution to the problem that we have come up with is that we are going to blame the sheep.

Blame the sheep! Hm, this could be a toughie. It can't be anything to do with the dictionary again can it?

- Dictionary, Sir?

Yes, Jack, the dictionary of things to blame. You mentioned it to me once before.

- Er, no, Sir. This solution is not dictionary based.

I thought not. I couldn't see how we got from "French" to "sheep" without me noticing.

- Sir, can I just make the point that we don't use that particular dictionary in sequence. It's bad enough trying to come up with scapegoats without doing it alphabetical order.

OK, and I assume that the sheep haven't been distilling illicit liquor, have they?

- I think that we can safely assume that the sheep haven't been distilling any sort of liquor, illicit or not.

OK, so the cow wasn't drunk, in which case I give up. What's going on?

- The cow is infected by something called bovine spongiform encephalopathy.

Jack, you know what my rules are concerning big words don't you.

- You don't like them, Sir.

Exactly! Three syllables maximum and then only when absolutely necessary. So let's try again.

- For those of us that are syllable-phobic, Sir, the cow has BSE. It's a disease that affects the brain of the animal which in turn causes the symptoms that you saw in the clip.

So why are we blaming the sheep?

- Sir, can I continue with the problem before going on to the solution?

If you think it will help.

- I do, Sir. We believe that the cows are staggering around because they are suffering from the side effects of organophosphates, or for your benefit, Sir, OPs.

I seem to remember that you've mentioned them somewhere before.

- Ah, I'm surprised that you remember that. Yes, it was during our initial briefing when we discussed DDT. As I said at the time, we weren't so bothered about the ban since we had a few other tricks up our sleeve. But following the ban on DDT, other organochlorine based products have also been banned and now the cupboard is getting a bit bare when it comes to insecticides.

So what if we stop using the OPs? What would happen?

- Well we couldn't stop using them until we'd found a suitable alternative.

No, Jack. I mean what if we don't use insecticides at all.

- You mean go organic! I don't think so, Sir.

Sorry, Jack, I was just trying to wind you up. Let's get back to the subject. You still haven't explained where the sheep come in to this.

- We need the sheep to deflect attention from the OPs. We have to have an alternative theory as to how the cows managed to get BSE and someone at Area 51 has come up with the fact that sheep also get a BSE like condition called scrapie. The theory is that the cattle can catch BSE from the sheep. That doesn't really hold water since many cattle don't come into contact with sheep so we then came up with the idea of blaming the feed stuff.

Surely you're not telling me that we feed lamb to cows?

- Not directly, Sir, but a lot of leftover food stuffs are combined to make the cattle feed. The brains from lambs are sometimes included.

But there can't be that many sheep's brains, Jack.

- Well I do believe that there is on average one brain per sheep, Sir.

That seems a bit high to me, Jack. Have you seen how sheep behave?

- Well let's assume that the brains are spread pretty thinly in the feed, but people don't need to know that. What they do need to know is that the feed causes BSE and that they could also catch the disease if they eat infected meat.

And is that true?

- We've no idea, Sir, but it sounds convincing and for our purposes we need it to be true. People need to think BSE is somehow contagious.

But isn't this whole thing going to put people off eating meat? Surely we want them to continue. That's why we add the little extras like growth hormone and antibiotics.

- No, Sir, that's not it at all. In the ideal world we would stop people eating meat at all since it's a very important source of vitamins and minerals. However, that's not likely to happen so we resort to contaminating the meat. Also, if people can be put off eating real meat they may be more inclined to try our substitute stuff, either the soya based products or one of the other varieties.

Good grief, Jack, do you mean the one made from athlete's foot? Is that still around?

- Sir, as I've pointed out before, it isn't actually made from the athlete's foot fungus, just something that's related, chemically speaking. Anyway, whichever one it is, it's in our interest that more people try it. And there's also one other thing. If we can blame the sheep then there's a better chance that we can do away with them altogether.

And why would we want to do that?

- Because food wise they're too safe for our purposes. With beef and pork we have much more control over the animals. With sheep they are often left to their own devices where they can eat what they want.

You mean real natural food?

- Exactly. In the UK, when the weather is bad the farmers have to feed the sheep so that gives us some opportunities. But in New

Zealand the sheep spend most of the time grazing on the natural grassland. It's our worst nightmare.

So the sheep have to go.

- I'm sorry, Sir, but yes, the sheep have to go.

One last thing, Jack. The word "syllable-phobic". Is that a real word? I only ask because it seems a bit strange that the word used to describe some who doesn't like long words should itself have five syllables.

- I think you'll find it's hyphenated. It's in fact two words each having less than four syllables.

Thanks, Jack. That makes me feel so much better.

August

- Sir, I have some good and bad news regarding the TV program for children.

You mean that one that's going to advertise margarine.

- Well the word advertise is a bit strong since it's not an advert as such; I think we need to be a bit more subtle than that.

These are kids we're aiming at here. I wouldn't have thought that subtle comes into it.

- It does if the parents are going to be watching, and I think they will. The producers have come up with a cartoon that they hope will work on two levels. It will appeal to both young and old. It's going to be called the Simpsons.

What's it about.

- It's an everyday story of a dysfunctional American family.

And where does the margarine come into it.

- It's the name of the mother. She's one of the main characters.

Well that doesn't sound particularly subtle to me. How many people do you know that are called Margarine.

- Not many, Sir.

No, me neither. No, Jack, I'm not happy with this. Go back to the drawing board and see what you can come up with.

- Yes, Sir.

October

- Sir, the British have reported back on a couple of matters regarding BSE. The first involves the sheep. Apparently there's some considerable resistance to the idea of culling the whole herd.

You mean resistance from the sheep?

- Not the sheep themselves, although if they could make their feelings known I'm not sure that they'd be in favour. No, I mean in general. The idea seems not to have gone down well.

What about in the USA?

- I thought that it would be best to try out the plan in the UK first before risking it here.

Is that because they've had far more problems with BSE? Why is that?

- Well there are a couple of reasons. Apart from the feed stuff, there is another way that the cattle can be exposed to OPs and that is the treatment for the warble fly. This is compulsory in the UK but here it's optional. The other point in our favour is that we have a much more industrialised cattle industry in the USA. It's much easier to manage a situation like BSE.

By manage I assume you mean cover-up.

- I prefer the word "manage", Sir.

And what about other countries? How are they fairing?

- As we would expect. Switzerland has a compulsory warble fly treatment regime and they are suffering, but nothing like the UK.

But why is that?

- We're not sure yet but the Brits are on the case.

And what about France?

- There the warble fly treatment is optional but the French maintain that they don't have any BSE.

And is that true?

- No, Sir, or at least it's very unlikely. But then you can't expect the French to own up, especially as they've banned the import of British beef. It suits their purpose and what's more there's something else very worrying. Some chap in the UK has come up with the idea that OPs are responsible for BSE, rather than the sheep.

And he could well be right, Jack!

- Could well be is an understatement, Sir. Of course he's right.

So we need to discredit him.

- Yes, Sir. We'll use the usual method.

What, you mean appoint a committee to look at the problem?

- Yes, Sir. I'll get onto the chemical companies and get them to nominate the right sort of people for such a task. But although we know what their conclusion will be we do have a bit of a problem stored up for the future.

And what's that.

- Well now that we have stopped adding animal bits to the feed the incidence of BSE should dry up.

But it won't?

- No it won't, not until the warble fly treatment stops.

Well you'd better get onto the Brits and find out why they are suffering so much more that the rest of us. It may throw some light on the situation.

- Yes, Sir.

November

I've caught what appears to be some public service announcements concerning AIDS. They all sound pretty convincing. I hope we're not doing too much, Jack.

- Well as we discussed some time ago, there are various ways in which the virus can be spread. Do you have any particular concerns?

Well what about sex? You seem to be advocating the use of condoms to stop the spread of the infection. How effective will that be?

- Well for people that use them properly, we're assuming that they'll be as effective as they are in preventing conception, say 90%.

But should we be pushing this sort of thing so strongly? I thought that we wanted the virus to spread as quickly as possible.

- Well, Sir, the operative word was "properly". In practice we don't see there being much of a problem. People who have always used condoms will continue to use them. Of those that didn't, some will use them properly but many will not or won't use them at all. In the heat of the moment we think that passion will score over common sense. And the same applies to drug users. We advocate using clean needles but if someone is desperate for a "fix", they'll use whatever needle is available, clean or not.

And what about blood transfusions?

- Ah there we had to do something. Drug users are just the sort of people to first, be infected and second, to donate blood to help fund their addiction. So we're now screening all blood for HIV. No choice I'm afraid.

So you're reasonably comfortable with our efforts.

- Yes, Sir, it's enough to make it seem that we're doing something but not so much that we'll stop the spread of the virus.

Fine, Jack. Carry on the good work.

- Yes, Sir.

1987

January

- Sir, we've come up with a revised plan for the kids cartoon, you know, The Simpsons.

Good, what have you got?

- Two things, Sir. First of all it's not going to start off as a programme in its own right. It will be shown as part of The Tracey Ullman Show.

But isn't that a late night show?

- Yes, Sir, but remember we said that it needed to appeal to grownups as well as children so we've agreed with the producers that they have a three month shot at it. If it does well it'll become a program in its own right.

OK, that sounds fine. What about the other problem.

- We think we've cracked that one as well. The mother will be called Marge.

Marge?

- Short for margarine, but also short for Margery.

You don't think that's a bit too subtle?

- The TV people think not. They say that if the program runs for long enough, the audience will get the message, albeit subconsciously.

Let's hope they're right.

- Yes, Sir. However, there is one other slight problem. It's to do with Arnold Schwarzenegger.

What's the problem?

- Well you know you promised that he could become President.

I believe that we promised, Jack. It was a joint decision. Anyway, regardless who made the promise, what's the problem? I'm sure it isn't anything I can't fix.

- He's not an American, Sir.

What!

- He was born in Austria.

(No Response)

- Shall I leave you to give that some thought.

(Still No Response)

February

Jack, I've been reading in the newspapers that there is an issue with the ozone layer.

- Yes, Sir, I believe there's a problem over Antarctica and that the ozone layer has been depleted.

Well I think we need to get the scientists involved. This could be a very serious matter.

- I don't think that'll be necessary, Sir.

And why is that Jack?

- Because I already know what caused the hole in the ozone layer.

You already know?

- Yes, Sir. It's all to do with something you said some time ago.

Are you suggesting I am responsible for the hole in the Ozone Layer?

- Well, only indirectly, Sir.

Indirectly? Until this morning, I'd never heard of the Ozone Layer and now you're telling me that I've destroyed it.

- Well not permanently, Sir, at least we hope not. It's all to do with the margarine again I'm afraid.

How can it possibly be to do with the margarine, Jack?

- If you recall, you said that we had to dispose of the stockpiled Pink Margarine in California. Well, one of the few places where we could dump the stuff was in Antarctica. Unfortunately, there were some unexpected ramifications. Apparently the margarine reacted with the penguin droppings.

Good grief, how did that happen?

- Well, Sir, it wasn't actually the margarine itself that caused the reaction. It was the pink dye.

Not that stuff again. That pink dye will be the death of us.

- Well, Sir, hopefully not us specifically, but probably a lot of other people.

Well, what are we going to do about it?

- Sir, there is nothing that we can do. The effect will gradually wear off although it may take a few years.

And how are we going to explain the problem in the meantime. We need to say something.

- I know, Sir. I have passed the problem over to some of our people at Area 51. I am waiting for their response.

Well, let me know what they come up with. And are there any other piles of the pink stuff that I need to worry about?

- No, Sir, all the Pink Margarine was dumped in Antarctica. I know we said that we would try to offload some of it on Geldof but as we suspected, the Africans would not touch it. However, we did manage to get rid of several thousand tons of the standard margarine. The stock pile is now down to manageable levels.

Well at least that's some good news.

- Well it is for us, but not for the unsuspecting Africans.

Later That Month

- Sir, we've come up with something regarding the ozone layer.

What, you mean you've found a way to repair the hole?

- No, Sir, it's not quite that good. In any case, the hole in the ozone layer lets through dangerous rays from the sun. There are bound to be casualties.

That's a good point. Do you have an estimated body count? Are we talking tens of thousands?

- Unfortunately not, Sir, there aren't that many people living in Antarctica. No, we've found a scapegoat to deflect attention from the Pink Margarine. We're going to blame it on fridges.

Fridges? On my list of possible scapegoats, fridges would have been pretty low down. Top of the list would have been the French.

- Sir, we can't blame the French for everything. No, fridges are it.

Why's that?

- Well, initially it was because "Fridge" follows "French" in our "Dictionary of Things to Blame". So when we decided we could not use the French again, the next option on the dictionary was "Fridge". And once we started looking into the issue we discovered that fridges were a good target.

Why's that?

- Well, Sir, the coolant in a fridge contains CFC's.

I've never heard of them. What are they?

- CFC stands for chlorofluorocarbon. It's used in fridges and air conditioners. It does react with ozone, although not enough to cause the hole over the Antarctic. Of course very few people would know that.

Very few people would have heard of CFC's in the first place, which is presumably another good reason to choose them.

- That's right, Sir.

So what are we going to do?

- We are going to get the manufacturers to phase out the use of CFC's and replace them with something else.

Have we come up with a replacement yet?

- Oh no, Sir, we're not looking for a replacement. We only needed to come up with a scapegoat. The industry will have to come up with an alternative.

That's a bit hard on the refrigeration industry.

- Yes, Sir, it is. So do you want me to use our resources at Area 51 to come up with an alternative?

Good grief no, they've got many better things to do.

- Absolutely, Sir.

But if and when they do come up with a replacement for CFC's you could ask them to make sure that, whatever it is, it's dangerous to humans

- Good idea, Sir.

And Jack, there is one other thing. Could I please have a copy of that list? It could come in useful.

- Which list, Sir?

The dictionary of things to blame.

- Of course, Sir.

October

- Sir, we've had some good news from NANCY regarding antibiotics.

What are you doing talking to my wife about these sorts of things? I thought she was off limits.

- No, Sir, not your wife Nancy, I mean the group at Area 51 that you christened "NANCY".

Oh right. OK, what have they come up with?

- Well it ties in with something we already know, that is that farmed fish and animals are regularly given doses of antibiotics.

Ah yes, I remember you mentioning prawns. I must admit, it beats me how they get the hypodermic needle into the little buggers.

- Sir, I think that you are confusing antibiotics with vaccines. And no, before you ask, they don't give them pills either. I believe it's included in the feed stuff.

Now that makes a bit more sense.

- I think you'll find that it makes a whole lot more sense, Sir, since injecting each individual prawn would have taken rather a long time. But that's by the by. The thing we've come up with is that the widespread use of antibiotics in animals is helping to make some bacteria antibiotic resistant. It's not just the drugs that are taken directly by people that are causing the problem. It all helps us get to the stage when there are infections in humans that cannot be treated using the current antibiotics. MRSA is just the start.

And now that we have the "Sick Pill", the drug companies aren't going to be falling over themselves to develop any new ones.

- Exactly, Sir.

Jack, are there any other things that are routinely fed to animals?

- Like what, Sir.

Well, I don't know, do I. But if there were, we would need to check whether it is working to our advantage, wouldn't we?

- Yes, Sir, your right. I'll get NANCY to investigate.

And ask her to start getting my tea ready. I'm starving.

- Sir, when I said "NANCY", I meant.....

Yes, Jack, I'm only joking.

- Oh, right. Only sometimes it's difficult to tell, Sir.

That's the way I like it, Jack. It keeps you on your toes.

- It does indeed, Sir.

The Following Week

- Sir, I've followed up your idea about the additives fed to animals and fish. NANCY has done some digging and come up with something.

Nancy? I didn't know.....

- Sir, before you start making jokes about your wife, can I suggest that we move on.

OK, Jack. Sorry. Anyway, what have you got? Is it good news?

- Well, Sir, at first glance, it doesn't look good. What we've found is that farmers inject their cattle with growth hormones.

I suppose I don't need to ask why, the name is a give-away. But why is it a bad thing?

- Well, it's good in that it can have a bad effect on the human body. The side effects can cause cancer, amongst other things. But we also think it could have the same effect on humans that it does on the cows, in other words the practice could make us fatter.

Ah, that doesn't sound so good, not if our "Fat People Live Longer" theory is correct.

- Exactly, Sir, and there is an associated issue here. Now that we have convinced the population at large that eating fat makes you fat and is bad for you, we have discovered something alarming. The people who are taking our advice by cutting the fats and eating more carbohydrates, they are the ones getting fat.

How on earth can that be happening?

- We're not sure yet, but NANCY is working on it. And please don't mention anything about her getting your tea ready.

March

- Sir, I've been in discussions with Diana. She's getting a bit restless tagging around behind Charles. She wants to do something in her own right.

Well I don't see that there's any harm in that. What sort of thing does she have in mind? What about cooking? She could always do her own cookery book.

- Er, Sir, I think that she's looking to something a bit more rewarding than that.

Well from what I hear, cookery books can be very rewarding. In fact I believe that some of them become best sellers. All she needs is a nice photo of herself for the cover in one of those skimpy little numbers.

- Sir, you've gotten completely the wrong idea. When I said rewarding, I didn't mean financially, I meant in a self-fulfilling sense.

Well what sort of thing does she have in mind? If she's talking about some sort of charity work or support for a good cause then I can't see the harm in that.

- That depends on the cause involved.

Well whether it's cats, dogs or orphans, I can't see that it makes any difference.

- How about if it's to do with people suffering from Aids?

Now if that's the case, it needs some thought.

- I'll give it some consideration, Sir.

April

- Sir, regarding Diana and the Aids thing, we've decided that, on balance, it's something she can go ahead and promote. On the one hand, it may encourage sexual partners to be more careful, but on the other hand, if people are more prepared to mix with Aids sufferers, the more likely it is that the disease will spread.

So the two things may balance out.

- Yes, Sir.

September

- Sir, I think we've cracked the fat people problem.

When you say "we", do you mean Nancy?

- I'm not playing that game anymore, Sir.

OK, Jack. So what have "we" found? Is it good news?

- Generally speaking, yes, Sir. Our basic premise that fat people live longer is true up to a point.

And what point is that, Jack?

- Well, being fat, as determined by the BMI...

BMI?

- Body Mass Index, Sir. It's where you divide your height by your weight to get some idea of how fat you are.

OK, so what have we come up with?

- Well according to the index, the ideal BMI value is between around 18 and 25. Between 25 and 30 is regarded as overweight, or fat. Over 30 is regarded as obese. However, our own statistics show that those between 25 and 30, i.e. the fatties, are the ones who live the longest. In fact by our reckoning the best BMI is 27. The more you deviate from this value, the worse your life expectancy. So as far as we are concerned, our theory is OK, but we need to make sure people are either thin to average weight, or huge. We don't want them to be just a bit overweight.

So we need to keep up the health propaganda.

- Absolutely, Sir.

November

- Sir, following on from our discussion about carbohydrates, one of our researchers has mentioned something that could be very relevant.

Relevant to what?

- Relevant to our efforts to make people very fat. Luckily, it confirms that the strategy we are following is bang on target.

You sound very positive, Jack, what on earth has he come up with?

- Well I'm not quite sure you can say that he came up with this point, since he didn't actually make the discovery, but he does know the research. He says that, in order to put on weight, you need carbohydrates.

I think that you need to fill in the details, Jack. I'm not sure that I understand what you mean.

- Well apparently the mechanism that enables the body to store fat is triggered by insulin. That in turn is produced in the body by the pancreas, mainly to cope with sugar in the body, which is in turn mainly created by the consumption of carbohydrates. It therefore follows that if you reduce your consumption of carbohydrates, you will reduce insulin levels and therefore limit the ability of the body to store fat and hence to put on weight.

But this is very important news, which begs the question, why did we not know about this before? Just imagine if the opposite had been true.

- I agree, Sir. The person in question says that he didn't think to mention it because, and I quote, "I thought that everyone knew how the body works".

So this means that the more carbohydrates we get into the diet of the average American, the better it will be.

- The better for us, Sir, but needless to say, not for them.

Well that goes without saying, Jack. But getting back to the basic point, we'd better keep this information under wraps. The last thing we want is for this sort of information to get out to the public at large, although if it hasn't done so up until now I guess we may be safe.

- Let's hope so, Sir.

December

- Sir, I think we may have gotten to the bottom of the BSE puzzle in the UK. The problem may have been caused by a change in the regulations regarding the treatment of the feed stuff. The temperature at which the food needs to be heated was lowered in the UK some time ago. We think that the heat treatment eliminates or at least reduces the effect that the OPs can have on the cattle. This would explain why the UK has suffered so much more than other countries.

But why did they change the system?

- It was done in order to save money. The lower the temperature the less energy is used.

How much money did they think they would save?

- The change would save the feed companies several hundred thousand dollars over a five year period.

And how much is it going to cost the UK government to sort out the whole sorry mess.

- Several billion dollars, Sir.

So where does that leave us?

- Well now we've explained the whole situation I think we're OK. The warble fly treatment campaign is coming to an end as the incidences diminish. So that means that BSE numbers should drop, just as they would if the sheep were to blame. Also we can continue to use OPs on crops since the committee has rubbished the warble fly connection.

So we're out of the woods.

- Yes, Sir, but as yet we've had no net gain. Initially there were predictions that there would be tens of thousands of people who would contract the human version of BSE but of course we know that is unlikely.

We can keep our fingers crossed that we're wrong.

- If only, Sir, if only.

1988

January

Jack, I see The Simpsons has been a success, even better than we expected. When is it going to become a show in its own right? I thought the initial plan was for a three month trial.

- Yes, Sir, it was.

So what's happened?

- The network is being difficult. Apparently they want something in return for the show continuing.

But surely a successful TV show is the ideal result here. What could be better than that?

- It's to do with the TV rights to screen football.

Well there's nothing we can do to help them get the contract. That's down to good old American market forces.

- No, Sir, not in the USA, in the UK.

I didn't know they played football.

- No, not American football. It's what we call soccer.

(Conversation continues for some time)

So what does the network want us to do?

- They want us to fix it with the Brits so that they win the contract to show live soccer on TV in the UK.

And do we have a problem with that? What's the contract worth?

- Well it's just been sold for £44 million pounds.

Well that doesn't sound much for a year's TV rights.

- No, Sir, that's not for one year. It's for four years. 11 million pounds a year.

That's less than 20 million dollars a year!

- Yes, Sir.

Then why are we even having this conversation. Get on to the Brits and see what they can do.

- Is there anything else, Sir?

Yes, Jack, there is. I think we need to come up with something new on the food front. I think things are getting a bit stale.

- What did you have in mind, Sir? I think we've got just about every food group covered.

Yes I know, but we need to come up with something. Get onto some of your people at Area 51 and see what they can come up with.

- Yes, Sir.

March

- Sir, you know you mentioned the need to come up with something new on food. Well JUNC may already have something. It's all to do with eggs.

What about them?

- We've uncovered recent research that suggests that some of them contain salmonella.

Good Grief, that sounds serious. What are the ramifications?

- Well, Sir, it doesn't happen that often and if the eggs are cooked properly, then there's normally no danger. But it can be a problem if they are used raw.

How many people eat raw eggs?

- Not many, but they are used as an ingredient in things like mayonnaise and chocolate mousse.

And when you say 'not often', how often is 'not often'?

- Perhaps one egg in ten million.

Oh right, so we'll have to exaggerate the problem to make it news worthy. Where did this story crop up?

- In the UK, Sir.

Well in that case, let the Brits break the news. Get onto Thatcher and see what she can come up with. And tell her to get someone she can trust to do the dirty deed.

- Yes, Sir.

August

- Sir, regarding organic food, I'm sorry to report that it seems to be making a bit of headway in the market place.

Is this anything to do with Prince Charles? I thought that we had that situation covered.

- I'm not sure that he has much influence over here, but the Brits are certainly concerned about him.

So is there anything we can do?

- What, about Charles?

No, Jack, about organic food.

- Hopefully there is, and with your permission, I'd like to instigate a plan to provide the public with a variety of useful information in order that they may make an informed choice when buying their food.

So you're going to bad mouth organic produce.

- Yes, Sir.

And how are you going to do that?

- We've come up with several lines of attack and the first one is yield. We're going to suggest that organic crops produce less food per acre.

But Jack, surely that's true.

- That depends, Sir. Lucky for us, it's certainly true when a farmer first starts growing the organic stuff, but as time goes on the yields end up pretty much the same. That's with good growing conditions. Unfortunately, if things turn bad, for instance in drought conditions, then the organic crop comes into its own and the yields will be better than the conventional stuff.

Why's that?

- It's mostly to do with the ability of the soil to retain moisture. The stuff that the organic farmer puts on the soil not only helps to control the weeds and fertilise the soil, it also helps to stop the water evaporating.

So when it comes to yield, conventional crops don't have any advantage over organic, and indeed the reverse could be true.

- Well it does vary from crop to crop, but as a general rule, that's correct. And then there are the nutrients. The organic produce tends to contain more vitamins and minerals than the conventional stuff, although, again, that's not always the case. And of course, just because a food has more goodness in it doesn't mean that it benefits the person eating it. Whilst organic foods have a price premium it's only the wealthier members of the public that can afford to buy it and they are probably the ones which will benefit the least from the extra goodness. That's one good reason why we need to maintain the higher prices. If the public at large start eating organic, they are likely to benefit far more and that's not something that we want to happen.

No, of course not, Jack. Is that all?

- No, Sir, there's just one more point. When the conventional stuff has higher levels of a particular nutrient, that's often caused by the chemicals that are used on the crop. For example, conventional apples may have more zinc because the fruit has been treated with a chemical that contains zinc.

What's your point, Jack?

- My point, Sir, is that the biggest problem we have with organic produce is the fact that it's treated with fewer chemicals than the standard stuff and that's a difficult problem to counter. One avenue will be to emphasise the fact that even organic food is treated with some chemicals and that's going to be one line of attack. The other will be to emphasise the fact that the chemicals used on conventional food have been tested and approved as being safe.

And we both know that's not true don't we Jack.

- Well let's just say that it's an incomplete truth, Sir. We have tested the chemicals and we don't know for definite that they are dangerous if used as recommended, but that doesn't mean that they are safe. The farmer could use more than the required dose, the residue could still be present when consumed and of course we only test each compound in isolation. There's no telling what effect the various chemicals will have when combined with one another. Lastly of course, there's time. We can't possibly tell what the long term effects will be for people consuming these compounds. We will only test them over a relatively short period but in some cases people will be consuming these chemicals for their entire life. Anyone with any sense would realise that the only way to be safe is to avoid as many of these chemicals as possible.

By eating organic produce.

- Yes, Sir.

So all in all it's not good news.

- At this point in time, it's not bad news, but we need to keep this organic stuff in check. If it goes mainstream, we could have a major problem.

November

- Sir, the Brits have given the FAST food thing a bit more thought and they've come up with something that we appear to have overlooked, and that's school meals.

What about them?

- Well, we plan to deal with the meals that people consume at work but we've completely ignored what children are eating at school.

You're right, it never crossed my mind.

- And it didn't occur to the FAST team either, but luckily the Brits have it covered.

What are they going to do? Close school canteens I suppose.

- No, Sir, I don't think they could get away with that. No, they've come up with a plan to privatise the school meals service. They'll get private contractors to come in and provide the food.

And are we sure that'll do the trick?

- Well they seem confident, Sir. I did query this with them but as they pointed out, whenever they privatise something standards go down and costs to the consumer go up. Why should school meals be any different? Apparently one of the companies has already developed what they are calling a "turkey twizzler". As far as school meals are concerned, it's their secret weapon.

And I suppose it's like a doner kebab in that nobody knows what's in it.

- I don't know, Sir. After the mushy peas experience, I decided it's best not to ask.

But if the costs go up that'll have to be passed on to the kids. Won't that mean that some of them will stop eating school meals altogether?

- The Brits have thought of that too, Sir. They are going to make sure that there's a readily accessible supply of FAST food available within easy reach of every school.

And that'll include doner kebabs?

- I'll check, Sir, but I'm sure it will.

Good. And one other thing, Jack. Find out a bit more about this turkey twizzler. I'd like to think that we can come up with our own special version.

- Of course, Sir. And by special, I assume you mean bigger, cheaper and more deadly.

Why not, Jack.

December

I see the eggs story has broken in the UK.

- It certainly has, Sir. It made the front page of the Daily Mail, which is no surprise. The sale of eggs is very much in decline, but the egg industry is already fighting back. They are saying that the story has been greatly exaggerated, which of course is correct. The Minister in the UK who broke the news is having a tough time. She may need to resign.

That must be where the phrase "having egg on your face" comes from!

- I'm not sure it's a laughing matter, Sir.

Why's that?

- Well Mrs Thatcher delegated the egg problem to one of her trusted colleagues, Mr Major. But now he's not too happy since he was never told that the research was a bit suspect. He gave the task of breaking the news to a close friend, Edwina Currie.

How close a friend is she?

- Very close, Sir.

Oh, that close!

- Exactly, and she thinks that he set her up so she's broken off relationships with him in retaliation.

So he's not getting any.

- No, Sir, at least not from Edwina.

Oh dear!

- And I've been onto the Brits. I've told them that we don't want any stories in the Daily Mail in the next few weeks about how eggs are good for you.

But they are, aren't they, Jack?

- Exactly, Sir!

Bush

1989

January

- Good Morning, Sir. My name is Jack and there are a few things I need to explain to you as a matter of urgency.

Well there is one thing you could explain.

- Well I'll certainly try, Sir. What's the question?

How on earth did someone like Ronald Reagan get to be President?

- Ah well, that's a long story.

Try me.

The Next Day

Well that explains a lot but there seems to be a just a few loose ends. Where do you suggest we start?

- Sir, we need to revisit the problem of money.

In what respect, Jack?

- Well you remember the Community Reinvestment Act.

Ah yes, the one which was supposed to bankrupt the banks. That plan didn't go too well did it?

- No, Sir.

Why was that?

- Well, although the banks did as they were told and lent money to poorer communities, they still checked the creditworthiness of the applicants. The result was that the loans were in the main repaid. The rate of defaults was no worse, and in some cases better, than those on loans to more affluent people.

So what can we do about the situation?

- Well, Sir, we have two problems. The first is to get the banks lending to less trustworthy people. That shouldn't be too difficult; we'll just relax some of the regulations.

And what's the second problem.

312

- Well, Sir, if you remember, we never solved the problem of how to affect the rest of the world. And we still haven't come up with an idea for that problem.

Have you spoken to Monica and Rachael?

- No, Sir, not this time. They're getting a bit long in the tooth and they're not as bright as they used to be.

How old are they?

- I believe that they're both in their late 60's.

Then why are they still around? Shouldn't they have both retired by now?

- Yes, Sir, but they refuse to retire.

What do you mean, they refuse. Surely it's not up to them to decide, is it?

- Well in this case, it probably is, Sir. They know too much about STOP for us to force them out.

And what about you, Jack?

- What about me, Sir?

Aren't you approaching retirement age?

- I believe that I'm in the same situation as the two ladies.

What, you mean you'll retire when you're ready.

- Yes, Sir, I believe that's the case.

Well we can't afford to implement a plan to let the US banks go bust without having the foreign banks covered as well.

- I'll see what I can do.

June

- Sir, we seem to have a bit of a problem with the drug companies.

Don't tell me they are going to renege on our deal over MRSA!

- No, Sir, on the contrary. It appears that they have no intention of developing drugs to treat any of the most recently discovered infections.

That must be a good thing surely.

- It depends on what these companies are doing instead.

Well whatever they're doing surely it involves trying to cure people doesn't it?

- Well, Sir, by using the word "cure", you've rather hit the nail on the head. These days the drug companies aren't that interested in curing people.

That's nonsense, Jack, what do they do if they don't cure people?

- They manage conditions, Sir, some of which may not, strictly speaking, have anything to do with health. And it's all our fault, since we're the ones who came up with Statins. They've taken the idea of long term drug treatment and run with it.

Well what's the difference, Jack? Whatever they do it results in selling drugs.

- The difference involves maybe a hundred fold increase in sales, and therefore profits. Let's take MRSA. If a drug company were to come up with a cure it would probably involve an antibiotic that someone would take for say seven to ten days. If instead they come up with a blood pressure drug, the patient would have to take it every day for the rest of their lives. In that example the idea that there's a hundred fold difference is a gross underestimate. The difference could be a thousand fold.

Yes, well I see what you mean.

- Wait, there's one other bonus. Someone who is on a drug long term is more likely to suffer from side effects. After all, if you take a course of antibiotics and you have problems you can stop and the side effects will normally go away. With the blood pressure treatment you can't do that. Instead, what the doctor will do is give you another drug to counter-act the side effects of the first one. And of course that one will also have to be taken for ever. It's a never ending cycle. It's reckoned that if everyone who's on a series of drugs long term would stop all medication, most of their health problems would disappear. Unfortunately the one that's left could kill them.

But that's what we want isn't it?

- Yes, Sir, but due to the litigious nature of our legal system, doctors won't countenance that option. And of course the drug companies aren't interested.

That's a pity. Perhaps we should have thought of this sooner. In any case, surely a cure for MRSA would make a company some money, even if the pills are only taken for a short time.

- Yes, Sir, they could make a profit if it weren't for one thing. We've made sure that the regulations the drug companies have to adhere to are very onerous. It's virtually impossible to bring a drug to market in less than ten years. That means that a new antibiotic would never make money unless each pill cost ten dollars and at that price nobody would use the drug. Certainly the medical insurance companies would not authorise its use. And to be doubly sure we've refused to increase the patent period.

What effect does that have?

- It means that the drug company has less time to recoup their investment before the patent runs out and other companies can start producing competitive products.

It sounds like at some stage the drug companies could stop developing drugs completely. And that would be a good thing, yes?

- Well in the ideal world, yes, but in practice we can't let that happen since people would eventually notice if no new drugs were to be produced. They would start asking questions about the policies that we have been adopting over the years and that would certainly not be in our interests. No, Sir, what we need to do is to wait and see. If some of the main players start getting cold feet we'll have to relax things a little just to keep them in the game.

But in the meantime there won't be a cure for MRSA any time soon.

- No, Sir, not MRSA nor any of the other so called super-bugs. But we need to worry about these long term treatments. On the one hand some of them are making people sick who would otherwise be well. On the other hand people who may well have died are still alive. It's a difficult call as to which one gives us the higher body count.

Well how important is it to decide which is which? After all, what's the absolute worse that could happen, Jack?

- The absolute worse, Sir? That'd probably be when we discover that neither gives us the body count we hoped for and the costs of medical treatment for old people cripple the economy.

315

But isn't that what we're trying to do with our plan for the banks?

- We're trying to break the banks, Sir, not the US treasury.

December

Jack, I see that the Simpsons show has got its own slot on TV. I assume everything has been sorted out with the network.

- Yes, Sir, they will be getting the UK TV soccer contract when it comes up for renewal in 1992.

How can we be so sure?

- Because they are going to bid a vastly inflated sum for the rights. The other companies will be blown out of the water.

Well provided they are happy, that's fine with me. Let's hope that it's a success.

- And while we're talking about success, Sir, I think we've come up with something regarding the banks.

It's about time. When did we first try to crack this particular nut?

- In 1977, Sir.

Hm, so let's see what you've come up with this time.

- Well you know I said there were two problems. Well we've come up with a solution for both, and they're closely connected. First, we need to expand the rate of lending. Concentrating on small loans to poor people was never going to get us the momentum we needed. We are going to encourage all manner of banks to start lending money, not necessarily directly to poor people but instead for building projects in poorer areas, so called "affordable housing".

And how does that link to the second problem.

- Well some of the investment bankers have come up with an interesting idea. What they want to do is package up these loans and sell them on to other banks, mainly those located overseas.

But surely the foreign bankers will see these packages for what they are.

- You mean "suspect".

Yes, Jack.

- Well our guys think they can make the products so complicated that no-one will understand them. All they will see is the rate of return and they'll look no further.

You really think that's going to happen?

- Yes, Sir, and even if anyone realises what's happening they'll still probably go for them. The rates of return in the short term will give them the performance they need to get their bonuses. By the time the shit hits the fan, they'll be long gone.

There is one other thing, Jack. I think that we'd better keep quiet about this particular plan.

- With regards to what, Sir?

With regards to our allies, particularly the British. London is the centre of the world's financial system. If it all goes pear shaped, there will be a lot of fallout in the UK.

- But won't they be a bit miffed when they find out?

We'll cross that bridge when we get to it.

- When you say we, Sir, you mean your successor.

Exactly, Jack. Perhaps you'd better give some thought to your retirement plan.

- I might just do that, Sir, after all it could get very nasty.

And you should remember, Jack. We need to make sure that there are a few secure banks left. We don't want them all to go down the tubes.

- And I guess you'll want to know their names?

I think that would be wise, don't you?

- I do, Sir.

1990

January

- Sir, the French still won't drink tap water. I'm not sure what more we can do.

Can't we try to put them off the bottled stuff?

- I'm not sure how, Sir, but I'll give some thought.

February

Jack, I saw a report in the newspaper yesterday and I thought of you.

- Why's that, Sir?

It was about a problem with Perrier mineral water. I believe it's the most popular brand in France.

- Is that so? And what made you think of me?

As I understand it, someone has found traces of benzene in a few bottles of Perrier.

- I still don't see what the connection is, Sir.

The connection is a laboratory in North Carolina. I believe that's where the contamination was discovered.

- Ah, you know about that.

It's in the newspaper, Jack, of course I know about it. What I don't understand is why you didn't tell me and how you got the stuff into the bottle. I assume that there actually was benzene in the water.

- Oh yes, Sir, it was there and what's more we didn't add it.

Well, that's a bit of luck that you discovered it.

- Not really, Sir, we've been testing Perrier for years hoping to find something and at last we've been successful.

Why didn't you tell me? And there's something else. Where's my decanter of water? It's normally on the side table.

- We haven't got any bottled water at this moment. It's been returned to the supplier. Apparently it's contaminated, that's why I didn't mention anything.

You mean we've been serving Perrier in the White House?

- Well until now the lab reports have said how good it is and we can hardly drink the tap water can we.

No, I suppose not.

June

- Sir, the British have come up with a novel idea to get people to drink more water. They're going to tell them that it's good for them.

That's very imaginative of them, Jack.

- Thank you, Sir.

No, Jack, I was being ironic.

- Sorry, Sir, I didn't understand. It's probably because I'm an American.

I dare say. Anyway, back to the subject in hand. There must be more to it than just telling people that water is good for them.

- Yes, Sir, there is. The British are going to say that everyone should drink 5 glasses of water a day in order to detoxify their system.

What does that mean in plain English?

- It means that they will flush the bad things, in other words the poisons and the toxins, out of the body.

You mean the ones that we have put there due to them eating our JUNC food?

- Yes, Sir, those things.

But surely we don't want those poisons flushed out of the system. They're there for a purpose, and that is to kill people off.

- I know that, Sir, but there's no evidence that this sort of thing will actually work. But it sounds logical at first glance so there's a fair chance that people will fall for it.

Well I can't see it working, but if the Brits want to try it, I can't see any problem with that.

Later That Month

- Sir, there are signs of a problem brewing in the Middle East.

It's not Iraq and Iran again is it?

- Well you're half right, Sir. Of course it's Iraq, it always is, but now their target is Kuwait.

And what's their problem this time?

- Apparently the Iraqis think that Kuwait belongs to them.

And does it?

- It did used to be part of Iraq, that is if you go back far enough in time, but these days it's recognised as an independent country. There's no justification for Iraq's stance.

So what do we do? I suppose we'll need to send in some troops. That should scare off the Iraqis.

- I think that before we do anything, Sir, we need to think about what we want to achieve in the long term.

You're thinking in terms of the body count?

- Sir, when Saddam's involved there are always opportunities to increase the body count. It's just a question of by how much.

So what do you have in mind?

- I've got some of our experts giving it some thought right now. They'll report back in a couple of days.

OK, keep me posted.

- Yes, Sir.

July

Jack, is there any news on the situation in the Gulf? It's just that things seem to be hotting up and the Iraqis are threatening an invasion. The Kuwaitis are getting a bit jumpy

- I realise that, Sir, but I think we've come up with a plan which, as far as I can see, doesn't have any downside.

Sounds good, Jack. What have you got?

- We do nothing, Sir, at least not in the short term.

What, nothing at all?

- To all intents and purposes we'll do nothing, but of course we will try diplomacy to resolve the situation.

As far as Saddam is concerned, has that ever worked?

- No, Sir, and it won't work this time either, in which case Iraq will mount an invasion

And I guess at that point we'll join in?

- No, Sir, on the contrary. We want the invasion to succeed so we'll leave the locals to defend themselves. In fact, if we make it look like the diplomatic route is likely to succeed, the Arab countries will have their guard down and that way the Iraqis will probably be able to mount a surprise attack.

Well the Kuwaitis won't be happy about that, will they? Aren't they going to be a bit put out?

- Not for long. If the invasion is successful they'll be only too grateful for any help they can get in order to drive the Iraqis out of their country.

So what happens then?

- Well the first good thing about this plan is that we think we'll be able to get Arab countries in the region to rally round and join a coalition against Saddam.

Are you sure about this? I can't see the Arabs standing shoulder to shoulder with our troops if we invade Iraq.

- There you're right, Sir, but the plan won't be to depose Saddam. Once we've driven him out of Kuwait, we'll make sure that we destroy most of his forces, then we'll leave him to fester. He's bound to create more trouble in the future and it also gives all the other countries in the region a common foe that isn't Israel.

And are the Israelis happy with this plan? After all, if this thing kicks off, Saddam is bound to start lobbing a few grenades in their direction.

- Of course he will, but the Israelis will not retaliate since if they do, it'll be difficult to keep the Arabs onside.

OK, it all seems feasible, but who's going to pick up the tab? This whole thing sounds like a costly exercise.

- I'm thinking that the Saudis are good for most of the costs. After all, if the invasion is a success they'll have Saddam breathing down their necks and that won't be a comfortable feeling.

Well it sounds like you've got all the angles covered, Jack. Let's keep our fingers crossed that it all works out as planned.

August

- Sir, I believe the Iraqi invasion of Kuwait has started. So far things are going according to plan.

So I hear. I gather that the Kuwaiti forces were somewhat taken by surprise.

- Yes, Sir, as I said, things are going to plan. Once Kuwait is under Saddam's control, we'll get the Arab countries to rally round and join our coalition.

And don't forget to ask the Saudis to open their cheque book.

- That's already in hand, Sir.

September

- Sir, we have some good news and bad news regarding water.

Give me the good news first. I need cheering up.

- Well, Sir, the British plan to get people to drink more water is having some limited success, partly due to a bit of a mix up at the time they first publicised the advice.

Why, what happened?

- Well, Sir, you remember how the advice was to drink five glasses of water a day. Due to a misunderstanding, the published advice is to drink five pints of water per day, which is nearly twice the volume intended.

Good grief, five pints? That's quite a lot.

- I know, and it excludes other liquids. It's supposed to be just plain water. And it gets even better. When the advice was taken up by the Europeans in general, they forgot to convert pints to litres. So the French are being advised to drink five litres of water per day.

I'm sorry, Jack, but how many pints are there in a litre?

- Five litres equates to almost nine pints.

Is it actually possible to drink that much water in a single day?

- It is if you are determined. But the good news is that you are likely to end up in a coma.

So that's the good news. What's the bad?

- The bad news is that most of the extra water that people are drinking is the bottled stuff. Obviously, the Brits hadn't quite thought things through. Basically, if people really are going to drink a lot more water they can only do so if they carry a supply around with them at all times. They can't rely on finding a supply of tap water whenever they fancy a drink.

Well it's not difficult to see how that could happen but the result is that we need to put people off the bottled stuff. Have the Brits come up with an idea for that yet?

- Not yet, Sir.

November

- Sir, Mrs Thatcher has called. She needs a bit of help with something. Like what?

- Like staying in office. It appears that there is some discontent within the Tory ranks and there are moves afoot to get rid of Thatcher and elect a new leader.

What? And she wants us to fix it for her? Is that possible? And would we want to? She's been a right pain in the bum at times.

- Well in answer to your first question, at this short notice we probably can't do anything even if we wanted to. And to answer the second point, no we probably don't, so the first question is irrelevant.

And who would we get in her place?

- A chap called Heseltine. He's a pretty dynamic guy from what I can make out.

And acceptable to us?

- I think so, Sir.

OK, so tell Thatcher there's nothing we can do, but try to let her down gently.

- Yes, Sir.

Later

Jack, I thought that a chap called Heseltine was going to be the next British Prime Minister. Now I hear that someone called Major is in charge. What's going on?

- Ah yes. Mr Major. I believe he's a little going away present from Mrs Thatcher.

What do you mean?

- Well I believe she was more than a bit miffed that we didn't do more to keep her in office so she sabotaged Heseltine's leadership ambitions and supported this chap Major instead.

And what's he like.

- We have no idea, Sir. Until yesterday, the only time we have come across him is during the "salmonella in eggs" promotion.

This doesn't sound good.

- No, indeed it doesn't, Sir. He may still be a bit peeved.

1991

January

Jack, I have been thinking about STOP. As time goes on, more and more people are getting involved and the secret is bound to get out.

- I know, Sir, but I'm not sure what we can do. With due respect, Sir, one of the main problems is the Presidential election every 4 years. With a change of leader, there is a change of personnel at the centre of government.

All except for you, Jack!

- Well, Sir, there needs to be some continuity.

Yes, Jack, and I think we could take things a stage further.

- What did you have in mind?

Well instead of elections every 4 years, we could change the constitution to make it every, say, 20 years.

- Starting when, Sir? Now?

No time like the present, eh Jack.

- I don't see how we could get such a change implemented, Sir.

Remember G-Water, Jack.

- G-Water makes people gullible, Sir, not completely stupid.

So you don't think we could get away with it.

- No, Sir. But I will give it a bit of thought.

The Following Week

- Sir, I've given more thought to your idea about presidential elections.

Good, I fancy the idea of being president for another 16 years.

- No, Sir, I still don't think your idea is an option. But I have come up with an alternative option. It's been tried before but without success. However, it was the British who gave me the idea of resurrecting the plan.

How did they do that? I hope you didn't spill the beans on my idea.

- No, Sir, it's to do with their monarchy. It's hereditary.

What, like a disease?

- Not exactly. What I mean is that when a king or queen dies, they pass the position of head of state to their next of kin.

What, you mean they keep it in the family? A sort of "Dynasty"

- Yes, Sir. So it occurred to me, why not adopt the same principle here.

I like it. Can you imagine, Jack; the Bush family would be in charge of the USA for all time.

- Er, I'm afraid it cannot work like that since the Democrats will surely want their share of the action.

I thought it was too good to be true.

- Well, we are going to need their buy-in for this to work.

I guess you're right but I'm surprised no-one has thought of this before.

- Well, as I said, Sir, it has been tried before, in the Sixties.

What do you mean?

- The Kennedys tried it. That's why we had to stop it in its tracks.

Wasn't it a bit of bad luck that it didn't succeed? You know; the failed transmission "get The President"; Lee Harvey Oswald.

- Er, Sir, that was just the excuse, not the actual reason. We had to get rid of him, it was no accident.

But why? Surely with the Kennedy clan you could have implemented the "Dynasty" idea years ago.

- Except that it wasn't our idea. Kennedy was planted by the "religious sect" based in Rome. By that of course I mean the Catholics. They had found out about our attempts to doctor the holy water and they were determined to infiltrate central government.

Yes, not one of our best ideas.

- No, Sir. Anyway, once we found out what they were planning, we had no alternative but to eliminate him. What we didn't know at the time was the plan for his family to continue what he had started.

So Robert Kennedy went the same way?

- Yes, Sir.

And I suppose Edward Kennedy, Chappaquiddick, that was us too, to destroy his credibility.

- No, that was entirely down to him. We knew he'd screw up at some stage; it was just a question of waiting, but at the end of the day it did serve our purpose.

It's hard to believe that Johnson believed the story about the failed transmission. He must have been a pretty gullible President.

- Yes, Sir, he was.

Nothing to do with the water he was drinking, I suppose.

- What do you mean, Sir?

I assume he was on the bottled stuff.

- Oh yes, Sir, all Presidents are on the bottled stuff.

If you say so, Jack. However, in future, just make sure all the bottles of water are unopened when I get them.

- Of course, Sir.

February

Jack, I see that Saddam's troops are beating a hasty retreat. Are you sure we don't want to pursue them all the way to Baghdad? I can't help but think that we're missing an opportunity here.

- I think we need to concentrate on the long term plan, Sir. I'm sure that one day we'll get a second bite of that particular cherry.

So it's game over for now.

- Not quite. One of our advisers has come up with a little plan that may prove productive.

What does it involve?

- We'll let it be known that we want to go for Saddam's head and depose him.

But you said that we should leave him be for now.

- Yes, we will, but we believe that there's some mileage in getting local people to think otherwise.

Like who?

- Like the various ethnic groups in Iraq who want to overthrow Saddam and gain some degree of independence. These include the Kurds in the north of the country and the Marsh Arabs in the south. If we encourage them to act against Saddam there's bound to be a bloody outcome.

But suppose they succeed in getting rid of him. What will that do for our long term strategy?

- Well it's an unlikely event since, even after we've finished with him, Saddam will have a lot more fire power than the various ethnic groups. That is unless we supply them with weapons.

And that's not something that we are likely to do.

- No, Sir, it isn't. But of course, they don't know that yet.

Well it looks like you've got everything covered. Let's hope it all works out as planned.

March

- Sir, the Scots are still insisting that we owe them one for the fact that we helped England win the World Cup.

I didn't realise that the British play baseball.

- No, not the World Series, it's the World Cup.............

(Conversation continues for some time)

So what do they want us to do?

- They're not clear on that, Sir. They just keep going on about the fact that they want to have some degree of power. But without their own parliament, they can't.

Well tell them to come up with a concrete plan that we stand some chance of helping them achieve.

- Yes, Sir.

May

- Sir, the Scots have come up with an idea. They want to take over the UK.

What! You mean invade? Do they have their own army?

- No, I don't mean by military means. They think that they can take over the government of the UK.

You mean a coup?

- No, I think they intend to use democratic means.

How are they going to do that?

- They think they can infiltrate one of the main UK political parties. Their likely candidate is the Labour party. They have been out of power for some time and with their current leader they stand little chance of winning the next general election. That will give the Scots their chance to get one of their own elected as leader of the Labour party with the aim of winning the next election in or around 1997.

Well I can't see that it makes any difference to us. If they think they can get away with it, let them go ahead. After all, if they succeed they owe us a big favour.

- More than one I suspect, Sir.

August

- Sir, there's been an unexpected bonus as a result of the fall of Communism.

Well there have been plenty of those, so another one shouldn't come as a surprise. What is it this time?

- It's to do with smoking.

Well we need all the help we can get in that area, but I'm not sure I can see a connection. What is it?

- It's to do with the sell-off of nationalised industries. One thing that the ex-communist countries have in common is that they all have a tobacco industry and it's one of the few areas where the businesses are actually worth something.

But why does that affect us?

- Well if you remember, since the tobacco industry is facing difficulties in the USA, one option is to promote smoking in other countries. The best way to do that is to set up manufacturing operations abroad. Normally, that means starting from scratch, but now there are countless opportunities to buy up existing companies in the Eastern bloc.

And I assume that our manufacturers are doing that.

- Yes, Sir. The Brits are getting some of the action, but that's only to be expected. And of course, they are very much on our side when it comes to promoting smoking in other countries, so the net effect won't be much different.

Except that the US companies won't be making the profit from the ones that go to the Brits.

- No, Sir, which is why we won't let them get their hands on too many of them.

Too right, Jack.

- Anything else, Sir?

Yes, Jack, I see the crop circle thing is finally dead and buried.

- You mean the newspaper article in the UK?

Yes. I believe that one of the originators has come clean and sold his story to the press. I suppose it was for the money.

- No, Sir, I don't believe it was. Instead, it seems his wife was to blame.

You mean he's married? How on earth did he get away with it for so long?

- Well that's more or less the problem. He was out most nights and she became suspicious. She thought he was having an affair and as a result he had to confess.

But this has been going on 15 years. What took her so long?

- I don't know, Sir.

So it's bad news.

- Well not entirely, Sir. Apparently, some people think that the UK government has persuaded Doug to admit to creating the crop circles just to hide their contact with alien space craft.

It's good to know that there are still true believers out there, Jack.

- It certainly is, Sir.

October

- Sir, there's something that's cropped up that I think you need to know about. It's known as the World Wide Web.

Well what's it about and is it something I need to worry about?

- To answer the second question first, quite probably. It's a system for linking various computers together so that people can access documents on one another's systems. In fact the physical links between various systems have been around for some time. That's called the Internet. What they've done now is to come up with a framework of software that makes it much more useable. As of now it's in its infancy but it's something we've been aware of for some time. Our initial reaction was that we should not encourage it.

Why not?

- Because we think it has the potential to be a considerable problem for STOP. One of the things we rely on is that people do not have access to the information that will lead them to doubt our propaganda.

So why is the thing not dead and buried?

- We thought it would be once we turned down the request for funding and assistance with the development. But it's gone ahead anyway.

But who's responsible?

- Some British chap working for CERN.

What? One man! Surely he must have had some help.

- I believe that there was one other chap who chipped in but that essentially it was a solo effort, which is why we are a bit taken by surprise. We assumed that it would take a lot more effort.

So what do we do now?

- Well in the short term it may be of use to us, since we also need access to a lot of documentation and the Web will give us that. The trouble is that other people will have the same access, but provided the system remains a tool for academics we should be able to keep it under control.

So, this World Wide Web, I guess there's no chance that the public at large will have access to it.

- None at all, Sir.

1992

February

- Sir, I'm afraid we still have a problem with bottled water. It's not just the French that are drinking the stuff and as a result it's becoming very popular in other countries, including here in the USA.

But, Jack, this is serious. We need people to drink G-Water otherwise the whole Project could be at risk. Can't we persuade the companies which produce bottled water that they should add fluoride?

- I could, Sir, but there are many of them and their main selling point is that the bottled water is pure straight from a natural spring.

Well unless we get someone to sell bottled tap water, I'm not sure what else we can do.

- Sir, perhaps that's the answer. We'll put the tap water into bottles.

Well to do that you'll need a big company with experience of bottling and a very powerful marketing organisation.

- Yes, Sir, I agree. I'll get on to them right away.

April

- Sir, the result of the UK general election is in. As expected, the Conservatives have won again.

Even with John Major in charge? That Neil Kinnock must really be a hopeless case.

- I believe so, Sir. Anyway, it leaves the door open for the Scots to take control of the Labour party as part of their long term plan. It's a safe bet that Kinnock will resign as leader.

And the Scots have a ready-made replacement?

- Yes, Sir, John Smith.

And we've checked him out?

- Yes, Sir, he's a safe bet.

OK, keep me posted.

- Oh, and one other thing, Sir. Diana says she's had enough. She wants to divorce Charles.

Do we have a problem with that?

- Not that I can think of, Sir. Once she is no longer part of the Royal Family, she'll probably fade into obscurity. Meanwhile, our two "cuckoos in the nest" can continue to thrive.

OK, but keep an eye on her and let me know what she gets up to.

- Yes, Sir.

And, Jack, where do we stand with the "Dynasty" project?

- Well, Sir, we have come up with someone in the Democrat party who's willing to play ball over the dynasty idea.

And who's that?

- Bill Clinton, Sir.

That sounds fine to me. Draw up an agreement.

- Well before we can do that, the Clintons have a couple of issues they want to raise.

Oh yes, what do they want?

- Well the first point is to do with how the idea of succession will work. The Clintons don't want to use the same principal as the British Royal family. There, the heir is always the eldest son.

And what's wrong with that?

- Well, that may well suit you, Sir, but it may not suit everyone. For a start, the Clintons don't have an eldest son. In fact they don't have any sons and the daughter is too young.

So who would be the heir?

- Bill's wife, Hillary.

What, a female President! I'm not sure I like the idea of that.

- Well, the British didn't do too badly under Margaret Thatcher and you have to remember that this won't happen until 2009. Anything could happen before then.

You mean I'll probably be dead by then, so why should I worry.

- I wasn't going to be that indelicate, Sir.

Ok, the succession thing is fine by me. What's the other point?

- Ah, that's a bit trickier. Bill Clinton wants to start his term as President at the next Presidential election. He wants you to stand down.

You mean I only get one term! That's not what I had in mind when I first came up with this idea.

- I know, Sir. But if it's any consolation, it will guarantee that George W Bush will become President in due course. I can't see any other way for that to happen.

Careful, Jack, that's my son you're talking about.

- Sorry, Sir, I didn't mean any offense.

No, I'm sure you didn't. Anyway, you'll have to let me think this over.

- Well the Clintons are waiting for a response, Sir.

I bet they are. I'll get back to you before the end of the week.

- Thank you, Sir.

July

Jack, I've given the dynasty thing some thought and I've decided to go ahead with the deal. Tell the Clintons and draw up the paperwork.

- Yes, Sir. Thank you. I realise that it must have been a painful decision.

Not half as painful as it will be for you, Jack, if Hillary Clinton becomes President!

- Thank you for that thought, Sir.

No trouble, Jack. And on a more positive front, I see the first GM crops have been sown, and not a moment too soon. There are a growing number of sceptics out there.

- Yes, Sir, I realise that, but there is a bit of a problem on the horizon.

What's that?

- The French, Sir, or at least they're the ring leaders.

Jack, why is it that the French always seem to be so difficult? It seems that any time we come up with something, they try to block our way.

- Well I'm not sure that's quite true, Sir. What in fact happens is that they agree in principle to the plan but then they find some reason why it's difficult for them to implement. It has to be said that it's also sometimes true of other Latin nations in Europe.

But this has been going on for a long time. I'm not sure that they have bought into to the whole STOP plan at all. Get on to the British and see if they can throw some light on the matter.

- Yes, Sir. But in fact in this instance it's the European Union as a whole that's going to give us a problem.

Why's that?

- They don't like the idea of our GM foods.

But don't they realise what we're trying to do?

- Well, of course the powers that be understand, but the public at large don't.

But why do they need to know anything?

- They don't know about the grand plan but the companies had to come up with something to persuade the farmers to buy their seed, so they did things like improve the yield and make them more resistant to disease. Those are their selling points, but the public at large aren't convinced. Unfortunately their reaction is very much the same as your predecessor's.

Which was what?

- That it's something to do with Frankenstein.

Ah, that's not helpful. What can we do?

- Well at this moment, our only strategy is to get the WTO involved. Unless the EU can prove that our GM crops are harmful, they may have to accept our exports, but it will take a long time. In the meantime, at least we are back on track with the American public. There's only one thing on the horizon that could cause a small problem.

What's that?

- Organic food. I don't think that farmers who produce the stuff are going to accept GM seeds on principle, so there may be an issue with that in the future. But for the time being, we're safe.

Good.

August

- Sir, I have spoken to the Brits regarding your misgivings about the French. They say that their attitude to STOP is not dissimilar to their conduct regarding the European Union. Apparently the French often agree to changes in the regulations and they do so readily, knowing full well that they have no intention of abiding by the new laws. The British seemed a bit peeved about this since they often fight hard over particular points in the legislation because they have every intention of implementing the changes once they are agreed. Because of this they are sometimes characterized as being difficult and anti-European.

Well we need to keep an eye on the French, Jack. We need to look for confirmation that they are, at least in principle, supportive of STOP.

- Yes, Sir.

September

Jack, what's this I hear about something called the Atkins Diet? The first Lady seems quite keen on it but from what she's told me about how it works, I must say I don't like the sound of it at all.

- Well you're right to be concerned, since we've spent a lot of time and effort trying to persuade the public that saturated fat is bad and here we have this Atkins chap telling them to eat it in order to lose weight. So far it's been very successful and it's not looking good for us right now. Eat fat and lose weight is not a message that we want people to hear. However, this Atkins guy is of course spot on, based on what we know about insulin and carbohydrate consumption.

So what can we do?

- In the short term we'll just try to rubbish his theories using our usual team of experts. We'll get them on all the right TV programmes and in all the right newspapers. That should have some effect in the short term. However, this is not the first time that this particular diet has been popular. It was first promoted in the early 70's but, like all diets, it eventually faded away and was replaced by the next

337

fashionable method of losing weight. We can only hope that the same thing will happen this time and that in the long term the Atkins Diet turns out to be a passing fad. That's what normally happens with these things.

Well let's hope so. Although rather than leaving it to chance, perhaps we should look at starting our own diet fad.

- I'll certainly look into it, Sir. In the meantime, how's the first lady getting on?

You mean on Atkins?

- Yes, Sir.

Well she's lost 20 pounds and she says that she's feeling fitter than ever.

- I was afraid that you'd say that.

November

Jack, I see that the Canadian government has put a stop to fishing for cod in the North Atlantic. Is this anything we should worry about?

- No, Sir, I don't think so.

But surely the stocks will recover which means that people can start fishing and eating fresh wild fish instead of the farmed stuff.

- As far as the stocks are concerned I don't think there's any chance of a recovery in the foreseeable future. As we predicted years ago, there was no action until the stocks of cod had all but disappeared, and that's what's happened. It will take years for the stocks to recover, assuming that they ever do.

Well I hope you're right. You'll need to keep an eye on the situation.

- Yes, Sir, and by the way, I'm sorry about the election.

Well it hardly came as a surprise, we knew what the result was going to be some time ago. I'm just a bit pissed off at how much time I had to put into campaigning for a lost cause.

- No doubt it will all seem worthwhile when your son takes over in eight years' time.

I hope so, Jack.

December

Jack, have we made any progress with the Atkins diet?

- Not really, Sir. We've floated a number of alternative diets but none of them have caught on. I'm afraid that the Atkins diet is still very popular.

But with all our efforts to counter it, why is it still around?

- Well it has something that is very difficult to defend.

You mean the fact that it works.

- To put it bluntly, yes. We've tried all sorts of things to put people off but none of them has been particularly effective. Not only that, there's also a danger that our message on cholesterol and saturated fat is being undermined and if that happens we really will be stuffed. Various tests have been made checking the cardio-vascular health of people on the Atkins diet and, if what we say is true, their health should deteriorate, but of course it doesn't. In fact, by any measure of heart health that you can choose, they were normally better off.

But we shouldn't be surprised should we? After all, it's what we'd expect.

- I realise that, Sir, but what we don't want is for this information to get out into the population in general.

So what do we do?

- We carry on doing what we're doing and hope it all goes away. But just now, things are not looking good.

Clinton

1993

January

- Sir, my name is Jack. Welcome to the White House.

Thank you, Jack, although of course the result was no surprise. What I don't understand is why Bush offered the deal in the first place. Surely he can't have been so keen to see his son as President that he was willing to sacrifice a second term to achieve it.

- And two terms of a Democratic President, Sir.

Exactly, so I suspect that there is more to this than meets the eye.

- There is indeed, Sir.

Two Days Later

Wow, I never realised there was so much going on.

- And you can see the attraction of the dynasty option. The fewer people know about STOP, the better.

But surely there are thousands of people involved.

- Yes, Sir, but only on small parts of the whole thing. Very few people see the entire picture.

Well I'm going to have to give this whole thing some thought, especially my planned health care reforms.

- I'm sure you are, Sir, but let's not be too hasty. And bear in mind that you must not mention any of this to anyone else.

That includes my wife?

- Yes, Sir, I'm afraid it does.

Now that could give me a bit of a problem.

- I wouldn't be at all surprised, Sir.

March

- Sir, I think it would be useful to have a discussion about you're healthcare reform proposal.

After what you told me at our initial meeting, I assumed that any proposals in that area would be dead in the water.

- Not necessarily, Sir, although I wouldn't get too excited since any such reform may not work out exactly as you originally planned.

Why, what do you have in mind?

- It's something that I've discussed any number of times in the past but so far no one has been brave enough to address the issue.

By brave, I assume you mean foolhardy, Jack.

- Whatever you call it, so far we haven't made any progress.

Well let's see what you have in mind.

- It's all to do with controlling the healthcare of the people in the US. As you know, the British have a national health service and in this respect we've learnt a few things from them.

Like what?

- Like the fact that when treatment is free that's what people tend to use even if the service is not necessarily that good. They're not likely to pay for treatment. Therefore the British authorities have much more control over the sorts of treatments and drugs that are available and how long it takes to get to see a doctor or consultant. Of course there will always be some people who will pay for the treatment that they want but that is very much the exception. If we were to have the same sort of thing here it would be so much easier to implement our policies regarding healthcare.

But it sounds like a bit of a minefield to me. Who would I get to promote such a policy?

- Ah, that's where I've had an idea. Your wife seems to be very interested in policy matters across a broad spectrum of issues.

You mean she's a bit interfering, Jack. Let's call spade a spade.

- In that case she appears to be a very large shovel, Sir, and I thought it could be a good idea to give her something meaty to keep her occupied.

And keep her out of your hair, Jack.

- That would of course be a bonus, Sir. But just think about it, if the healthcare reform succeeds then everyone's a winner and I feel confident that you would win some kudos with the good lady for letting her get involved.

And if it all goes pear-shaped?

- In that case you'll be far enough from the action that it won't reflect on you.

Are you suggesting that I put my wife in the front line as a potential fall guy?

- Well it's merely an option, Sir. I suggest you give it some thought.

I don't need to, Jack. Let's go with it.

The Following Week

Jack, I've been giving STOP some thought and there are a couple of things I would like to discuss.

- Certainly, Sir. What are your concerns?

Well firstly I think we need to have a back-up plan.

- What do you mean, Sir?

Well supposing the plan doesn't work. What if we can't stabilise or reduce the population of the planet? What are our other options?

- Well I'm not sure whether there are any other options. It all depends on what happens.

I assumed that when this project was started, we kind of knew what would happen if we did nothing and the population just got bigger and bigger. Are you telling me that is not the case?

- I'm not sure we postulated exactly what would happen. We just assumed it wouldn't be good.

Well if we're going to have a contingency plan, perhaps we should give it more attention. We need to know what we're planning for. Give it some thought.

- Well, Sir, we're not going to know exactly what will occur.

I know that, but I'm sure we can come up with some intelligent guesses. Then we can discuss what we can do in such an eventuality.

- OK, Sir, we'll get onto it right away.

Good.

- What's the second point, Sir?

I've been thinking about the whole cholesterol thing and I'm a bit concerned about some of the questions that are being asked in certain quarters. It seems that some people are questioning the connection between cholesterol, saturated fat and heart disease.

- Well that's hardly surprising is it, after all the whole thing's a fabrication.

Exactly. I guess we've had a good run for our money but perhaps it's time to come clean.

- Come clean? Good grief, Sir, we can't do that; there's too much riding on it. No, we can't do that but you're right, we need to review the situation. Perhaps we need to come up with something new that continues along the same line, i.e. cholesterol and saturated fat are bad.

And how do you suppose we are going to do that?

- By making the situation more complicated. At the outset we relied on the fact that most people had no idea what cholesterol is. Now, thanks to our publicity campaign, everyone has heard of it.

Even though they still don't know what it is or what it does.

- That's right, Sir, and that's where I think we may be able to take this whole thing forward. We'll look at the options and I hope to be able to report back soon.

April

- Sir, we've given your problem some thought and we think we've come up with a likely scenario.

Which problem is that, Jack?

- You know, the "what if it doesn't work" problem.

Ah right, that one. What have you come up with?

- Well we think that we can safely predict what will happen if we don't control population growth, it's the timescales which are difficult to predict.

OK, give me what you've got.

- The problem with over-population is that we will run out of resources, the key ones being food, water and energy. Of course it won't happen suddenly, it'll happen gradually to start with. Prices will increase making it difficult for people, particularly the poor, to buy the basics. Civil unrest will result and that's where we have an issue with timescales.

Why's that, Jack?

- It's because supply and demand of food and energy is an organised international affair these days. It wouldn't take much to upset the system and we think that the effects could be very rapid. For example, a country such as the UK imports 50% of its food, so if the international supply chain stopped, they would have a big problem. Civil unrest is likely and a breakdown in law and order would occur very quickly. And it's then going to spread across international borders. There are bound to be wars and with some of the protagonists possessing nuclear weapons, it'll be very nasty.

So if we want a contingency plan, it's got to be something that we can implement very quickly.

- I'd say so, Sir. But then what sort of plan do you have in mind?

Well we need to decide what we are trying to achieve, Jack. If nuclear weapons are involved, then we're probably talking about the survival of the human race. That's going to be a problem if the planet is contaminated by radioactive fallout. We'll have to move off the planet.

- Well that's not going to be easy.

I didn't say it would be, Jack, but give it some thought and see what the options are.

- Yes, Sir. But on a more positive note we think we've cracked the cholesterol problem.

And how have you done that?

- We've come up with the idea that some cholesterol is good for you and some not so good. Up until now it's all been lumped together so that when we say that people should have a cholesterol level of 190, that's a value for total cholesterol.

190? I thought the recommended level was 200.

- Yes, it was but the drug companies thought it would be a good idea to set a lower level in order to get more people on Statins. It was hard to say no.

OK, but where does that leave us now with these two types of cholesterol?

- Well it's not quite the case that there are two types, it's more like two stages. Cholesterol is produced by the liver and is sent to the parts of the body that need it.

And what's it used for once it gets there?

- Mainly to repair any damage and to create new cells. It's an important part of the body's survival system. When it's been used it goes back to the liver to be reprocessed.

Right, so the stuff that the liver produces is good cholesterol and the stuff that comes back is the bad stuff.

- In practice, there's no such thing as good and bad, it's all part of the cycle of cholesterol production and use. But for our purpose, yes, there will be good and bad cholesterol but not the way you think. We're going to say that the stuff that the liver produces is the bad stuff.

But that's ridiculous. How on earth are we going to suggest that cholesterol which the body produces in order to repair cell damage can possibly be bad. I think that you've lost the plot here, Jack.

- We'll see, Sir. We think we can carry it off on the basis that, given we have said that lower levels of cholesterol are beneficial, any process that increases the levels in the body must be bad and conversely, anything that reduces the level must be good.

But surely the actual overall level in the body isn't changing, the cholesterol is just being moved around.

- That's right. Let's hope that the average member of the public isn't as bright as you, Sir.

May

- Sir, we've given the survival of the human race some thought and the options aren't good. In fact, there aren't many options at all.

OK, let's see what you've got.

- Well the first option would be a space station, but in the long term, that's no use. If the Earth is uninhabitable, there's no point in staying around. We need to move on.

You mean the Moon?

- No, that's not an option either, since it's barren and anything we need for survival would have to come from here. But I suppose it could be used as a staging post and that's what the guys at Area 51 are looking at now.

You mean go somewhere further afield?

- It looks like that's our only option. I'll let you know if they come up with anything concrete. In the meantime, there's better news on the TV issue, Sir. Monica and her friends have come up with an alternative plan. Instead of a TV show about three old women, they want one featuring three young ones.

I don't see how that will work. If they can't act as old women, they'll never pull it off as young ones. And they're ten years older than they were when they first came up with the idea.

- More like 15 years I think. No, Sir, they don't want to act in the show, they just want their names to be used for the three main characters.

Is that all?

- No, Sir, there's one other thing. They want the show to be shown on TV every day for the next 100 years.

But that's a ridiculous idea.

- So it seems, Sir. We'll just have to wait and see.

And, Jack, I see that there is a new bottled water on the market.

- Yes, Sir, it's proving very popular.

I trust it is being produced using tap water.

- Yes. It's been purified and has had a few minerals added to it.

That doesn't sound like a good idea. Why didn't they leave it alone?

- Well they had to have some sort of selling point and that's what the company came up with.

But when you say "purified", you don't mean that they removed the fluoride?

- Oh no, Sir, they haven't touched the fluoride.

Thank goodness for that.

June

- Sir, the guys have been looking at the problem of travelling to another planet. They've decided that using the moon is probably a waste of time.

You mean they think we should just launch a rocket and head straight for another world?

- No, Sir, that's not an option since the journey time means that we will need a lot of supplies. The space craft will need to be pretty big.

So what do they propose? Surely the only other option is to build something on the Moon?

- Your right in that we need to build something large outside of the Earth's orbit, but why take all the stuff to the Moon. The experts suggest that we construct a space station in orbit around the Earth. When it's complete and fully equipped, the rocket motors will launch it on its way to another planet.

But what sort of engine could be used?

- That's the main issue that we have since as yet there is no such technology. But the space industry reckons that if we throw enough money at the problem, they can come up with something.

And do we have that sort of money?

- Well there, Sir, I thought we may need to bring in some other countries to help with the costs and technology. The Russians will need to be in on it, and the Europeans.

I don't think we should do that, Jack, we need to keep this thing under wraps as far as possible.

- We needn't tell them the real reason for the space station. They'll think it's just to be used for research.

Well if you think it'll work, let's go ahead. Ask the Japanese if they'd be interested, they've got plenty of money. And do we have a timescale?

- No, Sir, just as soon as possible. It will take many years to come up with the propulsion technology, let alone anything else. But as a back-up plan, it's the best we have.

August

Jack, I'm afraid that it looks like the healthcare reform is dead in the water. It has proved to be just too difficult to come up with something that's workable and affordable.

- No surprise there, Sir. When it comes to healthcare it appears that you can have workable or affordable, but not both. But we have got a few things from the whole exercise.

You mean that my good wife has been kept busy for a year and a half.

- Well there is that, Sir, but no, that's not what I have in mind. Instead, it's the fact that we've learnt a lot from the whole process and that if we try again, we'll probably stand a better chance of success.

Well good luck with that. I guess it's not something you'll try again for a while.

- Not for at least 15 years, Sir.

That's a very precise number, Jack. How do you work that out?

- Well I think it's fair to say that you won't be trying it again.

Too true!

- And then we'll get eight years of Bush and there's no chance of healthcare reform under a Republican, so that takes us up to 2009. Perhaps the First Lady would like another shot at it.

Right, I see where you're coming from. And do you think that you'll still be around at that time?

- I think so, Sir, after all, the health care that's available to me is second to none.

You mean you get to enjoy the same excellent health care that I do as President.

- It's actually the other way round, but you get the general idea, Sir.

November

Jack, do we have news about the possible side effects of taking Statins? I haven't heard anything for quite a while.

- Well the good news is that there definitely are some side effects with perhaps one in five people suffering some sort of adverse condition. The bad news is that they don't at this stage appear to be fatal, at least in the short term.

Well what things are we talking about?

- Quite a few, as it happens. Statins can affect the nervous system and there can be some adverse effects on the liver and kidneys. We have also noticed that a significant number of patients have developed Rhabdomyolysis, and that's a disorder which results in muscle degeneration. Lastly, there seems to be some effect on the brain which results in short term memory loss.

Wow, that's a lot of problems. Surely people are going to start putting two and two together and they're going to realise that Statins are making them ill.

- Not necessarily, Sir. For a start, the number of people who suffer really serious side effects are fairly small, say less than two percent, and they are unlikely to associate the symptoms to their Statins. With the kidney and liver issues, they probably won't notice that there's anything wrong and with the muscle ache and memory loss, they'll probably put it down to old age. The only people who may notice a trend are the doctors and we'll try to keep any feedback from them under wraps.

Can we do that?

- I think so, Sir. Just imagine that you are a doctor. You have a perfectly healthy patient who comes to you for a routine check-up. You tell them that their cholesterol level is a bit high and you put them on Statins. A few months later they come back suffering from the side effects. They can't walk due to muscle waste and they can't see.

What do you mean they can't see!

- They've developed cataracts as a result of taking Statins. Did I not mention that one? Of course it's likely to be a few years later rather than just a few months. It's just another situation where it's a good job that we restricted Statins to older people since they won't necessarily put these side effects down to the drug. If younger people were to start suffering from loss of memory or going blind they'd likely start asking questions. But going back to the point about the doctors, if you are that doctor who made a healthy person sick are you really going to own-up? I think not, which means it won't be too difficult to keep the extent of the side-effects away from public view.

And if you forgot to mention blindness, are there any other side effects that I should know about?

- Nothing that's really serious, Sir.

Well let me be the judge of that, Jack.

- Yes, Sir, of course. Well, the list includes insomnia, constipation, diarrhoea, headaches, loss of appetite and loss of sensation in the hands and feet. But one of the other more promising effects of Statins is to reduce levels of a substance called CoQ10 in the body.

And is that a bad thing?

- We believe so, Sir, since this will in turn lead to heart problems; at least that's what we expect.

But hang on a minute here, Jack. I thought that these Statins were supposed to prevent heart problems.

- No, Sir, they're supposed to help reduce the chance of a heart attack, but there are several other problems that can occur with the cardio-vascular system including heart failure and strokes. Both of these conditions are more likely to occur if you are taking Statins. Whether that's a direct result of the drug or a side effect of the reduction in cholesterol we're not sure, but then, do we care? Either way it's a win for us.

Well that all sounds promising but in terms of our long term aims, are Statins going to help us to reduce the life expectancy of the population as a whole?

- Well the jury is still out on that one, Sir, although things are looking good. However, all we know for definite just now is that they don't extend the life expectancy of those people taking them regularly. Any benefits there are regarding heart attacks are cancelled out by an increase in the other medical issues that I've just listed. But bear in mind that one of the other points about Statins is that they distract the drug companies from developing other more useful drugs and in that respect we've been very successful.

So on balance it's looking positive.

- Very much so, Sir.

1994

March

Jack, you know you were told by my predecessor to keep an eye on Princess Diana and to keep me up to date.

- Yes, Sir.

Well as you may have realised, that isn't necessary. She seems to be on the front page of the newspapers every day. I know more about what she is up to than I do my own wife.

- If you want me to give you regular updates on the First Lady's whereabouts, I can, Sir.

No, I think you miss the point, Jack. You said she would probably disappear from view, and yet the opposite has happened.

- Yes, Sir, I realise that. But so far, she hasn't done anything which will seriously jeopardize our long term plans. I think we need to wait and see how things pan out.

OK, Jack. At this point I'd normally say "keep me informed", but in this case, that won't be necessary.

- No, Sir, I guess not.

And Jack, there's one other thing. I think I'll take you up on your offer.

- I thought you would, Sir. Do you want the reports on The First Lady's movements daily or weekly?

Make it daily.

- Certainly, Sir.

May

- Sir, there's bad news from the UK. The Labour leader, John Smith, is dead.

How did that happen? I hope he hasn't been bumped off by the English.

- No, Sir, at least I don't think so.

Well I think you'd better check, just in case.

- Well even if they did it won't make much difference.

So you don't think that it affects the plan for the Scots to take over the UK?

- No, because the Scots have already managed to get a lot of their people into positions of power within the Labour party. John Smith wasn't the only one.

Hasn't anyone noticed that all the senior people in the Labour party are Scottish?

- If they have they certainly haven't said anything.

So who's likely to take over?

- Well it seems to be between Tony Blair and Gordon Brown. Needless to say they're both Scottish.

I'd better take this seriously if one of them is going to be Prime Minister in a few years' time, so let me know what happens.

- Yes, Sir.

Later That Month

- Sir, we have a bit of a problem.

Not the French again?

- No, it's the Scots.

That figures, in fact they would have been my second guess.

What, ahead of margarine?

OK, third guess. But tell me, what have they been up to?

- Well they are having a bit of a problem electing a new leader.

Why's that?

- The Scots cannot agree which of the two possibilities, Blair or Brown, should be leader.

Well can't they just let the party decide? Surely there's an election process.

- Yes, there is. But if they both stand the Scots vote would be split and one of the other candidates could win. No, that's not an option. One of them needs to concede to the other.

Well who's going to decide?

- They want you to make the decision.

What! How am I going to do that? I don't know the two men.

- Well, from a policy point of view, I'm not sure it makes any difference. But remember you will have to deal with the man if they win the next general election.

So, of the two, who do you recommend?

- I think that it would be easier to deal with Blair. He's the more personable of the two and probably easier to manipulate. Brown's a bit dour.

OK, Blair it is. But what if Brown asks why I chose Blair.

- You could say it's alphabetical order, "Bl" comes before "Br".

OK, we'll go with that.

- Yes, Sir.

Even Later Still

- Sir, just one minor issue with the Scots.

I thought that problem had been put to bed.

- In the main yes, Sir, but there is just one point though. You were correct; Brown did want to know why we chose Blair. When I explained the reason, you know, alphabetical order, he seemed to get the idea that it means he will get a turn at some stage.

And is that a problem?

- Not for you, Sir, since it won't happen for some time. However Blair has had to agree to hand over the reins at some stage.

Good grief! Why did Blair do that?

- Well apparently Brown took Blair out for a meal to some fancy restaurant and got him pissed. Blair was in such a state that he would have agreed to anything.

Well I'm sure Blair can deny all knowledge of the conversation.

- Not so, Sir. Brown's got it all on tape.

Ah, that's not good. I think you'd better remember this and warn my successors to be careful of Brown. He sounds a bit untrustworthy.

- Not so much untrustworthy as clever, Sir.

Whatever you say, Jack.

July

Jack, there is just one thing about the Scots that we need to consider.

- I'm glad you mentioned that because I've discovered something that I need to discuss with you. But you go first, Sir.

Well, I spoke to Mr Blair today. I thought I'd better phone him to congratulate him on being elected leader of the Labour party.

- Good idea, Sir. You're likely to have to deal with him a lot at some stage in the future. What's your point?

Are you sure he's Scottish? He sounded mainstream English to me. It occurred to me that this could be a double cross and that the English could have infiltrated the Scottish ranks.

- Well I'm pretty sure he's Scottish. He was born in Edinburgh, or at least I believe he was. But where his allegiance is today I don't know. But does it matter?

No, probably not. What was your point?

- It's a bit more serious, Sir. It's come to my notice that the Labour party have something in their constitution called "Clause Four" which commits the party, and I quote "to the common ownership of the means of production and exchange".

What on earth does that mean?

- It means Nationalisation, Sir.

Good grief, they're communists!

- Not quite, Sir, but it's certainly an alarming discovery.

It certainly is. How long has this been the case?

- I believe it has always been the case. But with mainstream communist countries around, like the USSR, this aspect of the Labour party policy was overlooked. Now that the Communist governments have in the main disappeared, Clause Four is a bit more significant. It would be ironic if we were to defeat Communism in the eastern bloc only to have the UK fall under the shadow of the hammer and sickle.

What are we going to do about it? We cannot allow the Labour party to gain power and risk that sort of thing happening.

357

- Well the Labour party are not going to gain power without our support. We'll have to make it a condition that they change their constitution and get rid of this commitment.

Will they do that?

- The Scots will do anything to gain power.

Let's hope so.

September

- Sir, just to let you know that Monica's TV show has been completed. It's on tonight.

What's it called?

- It's called Friends, Sir.

How original. And when is it on?

- It's on at 8pm, Sir, and again at 9:30, then 11:00pm and midnight.

Well at that rate, Jack, people are going to get sick and tired of it pretty quickly. But onto weightier matters, I hear on the grapevine that the World Wide Web is still around. What's the latest?

- Not good I'm afraid. It looks like it's gaining in popularity. Indeed CERN have released the software into the public domain so that anyone can use and enhance it. It's not going to be limited to the professionals for much longer. It seems that the cat is well and truly out of the bag.

Oh dear. It's a shame that it wasn't invented by an American.

- Well I still don't think we could have kept a lid on it, Sir.

No, I realise that, Jack. I mean that we darn well wouldn't have given it away. We'd have charged for it.

- Good point, Sir. At one cent per message, we'd have made a fortune.

One Cent! Jack, you're aiming too low. I was thinking of one dollar per message.

- Sir, in ten years' time there are likely to be hundreds if not thousands of messages every hour on the Web. I think one cent would be enough. But that's academic now since CERN has given it away.

And this CERN, where are they based?

- Near Geneva, Sir. On the border with France.

And have the French got anything to do with this?

- With what, Sir?

With putting the system in the public domain. I'm just wondering whether it's all part of a French plan to undermine STOP. What language do they speak in Geneva?

- I believe it's French, Sir.

And the British guy who came up with the system, does he speak French?

- Well he's British so it's unlikely that he'll speak a foreign language.

But he works at CERN so you can't rule it out. And this man who helped the Brit. What nationality is he?

- He's from Belgium.

So he may speak French as well?

- It's a distinct possibility, but I'm not sure where you're going with this, Sir. Are you having a "Blame the French" day again?

Jack, if I had my way, every day would be a "Blame the French" day.

1995

February

- Sir, we've come across some interesting research regarding cholesterol. Apparently people who have lower levels of cholesterol are more likely to die a violent death or to commit suicide.

Well there is an obvious question here Jack, isn't there. What's going on? I assume that the two things are linked in some way.

- Well we're not sure what the cause is yet but although at first glance it looks like the two could be linked. But if you think about it, although in each case the deaths may be bloody, the causes are probably different. On the one hand such people are more aggressive and in the other instance they may be more depressed. So I expect there are two different things going on here.

And are we sure about the science?

- Well when we first heard about this we thought it might be a statistical aberration. But we now have several independent pieces of research all pointing to the same conclusion.

But none have identified a cause?

- Not as yet, Sir.

On the same subject, I must admit your plan concerning cholesterol seems to have paid off. These days, whenever I hear about the stuff, the word is always preceded by "good" or "bad". Well done.

- Thank you, Sir. Things do seem to be going well.

Of course, in a few years' time when people realise that things still don't stack up, we'll have the same problem again.

- Possibly so, but when that happens we'll be ready.

You already have something planned?

- We do, Sir. It involves LDL particle size, but you don't need to worry just yet.

That's just as well since I didn't understand any of that.

March

Jack, where are we at with the plan to break the banks?

- Well, Sir, we weren't planning to break all the banks, just some of them.

And how many have we broken so far?

- Do you want the number including overseas banks?

No, just the US ones for now.

- Then the answer is none.

And what if we do include overseas ones?

- Well that then depends on how exact you want the number to be.

How about very exact.

- Then that number is also none.

And if the number isn't so exact.

- One, Sir. There was a bank in the Cayman Islands which went bust last year, but I'm not sure that we can take the credit for that.

So what's gone wrong?

- I think it's to do with our timing, Sir. Unfortunately we chose the start of a small recession to push our latest attempt to undermine the financial markets.

But I thought that our plan is to lend money to poor people who then can't make the repayments.

- That's right, Sir.

So surely a recession would be the ideal time for the plan to work.

- Only if you can persuade these people to borrow the money in the first place. Most people will borrow money with the intention of paying back and they have to think that it will be possible to do so. Unless they think they can, they won't take out the loan in the first place.

Well surely some of them will.

- Oh yes, a small number of people will take out loans with perhaps no intention of repaying, but there are not enough of them to kick start our scheme. I'm afraid that we'll have to wait until we've had a sustained period of economic growth and stability.

Perhaps we need two terms of a Republican President!

- Quite possibly, Sir.

I was joking, Jack!

- Yes of course you were.

But you seemed to take me seriously.

- I was just playing along with your little joke.

I dare say. But you still think there's time for the plan to work?

- Oh yes, but not during your Presidency, Sir.

I'm sure you'll understand when I say that I'm not sorry about that. It'll be one almighty mess.

- Let's hope so. However, there is one slight problem with our plan for the banks and that concerns the French. They don't appear to be willing to play ball.

And why is that, I mean apart for the fact that they're French?

- Well the basic reason is very simple. They are much more cautious than our banks and in fact this applies to a lot of the European banks.

But not the British ones?

- Oh no, Sir, certainly not them.

So what can we do? I'm assuming that we can't persuade all these banks to change their tune.

- Not in the timescales that we are talking about, if at all. No, we'll have to come up with something else.

Well we'd better had. We don't want to cripple our own banking system only to have the French survive unscathed.

- Don't worry, Sir. I dare say we'll come up with something.

May

- Sir, we have some news on the cholesterol/suicide link, and guess what. You were correct. There is apparently a common link between the suicides and the violent deaths. It's all to do with serotonin. We believe that if you have lower levels of cholesterol in the body then that in turn leads to lower levels of serotonin. It's a chemical that controls mood and therefore it can affect a person in a violent way or it could cause depression. In the first instance the person is likely to cause damage to a third party and in the second, to themselves.

So either way it's a result.

- Yes, Sir.

And what are the long term implications for our cholesterol campaign?

- No change, Sir, since it largely confirms that we are on the right track. It just means that if our campaign to lower cholesterol levels across the population succeeds, the streets are going to get a whole more dangerous.

You mean from muggers?

- Well yes of course, but also from bodies dropping from tall buildings. There are all sorts of possibilities.

And are there any military implications, Jack?

- In what respect, Sir.

Well if we could make our soldiers more aggressive, wouldn't that give us an advantage on the battle field?

- It would, Sir, but only if it isn't balanced out by those committing suicide.

Unless they're kamikaze pilots, Jack.

- I think we'd have a bit of a problem setting up such a squadron in the US air force, Sir.

OK, fair point, Jack. But do you suppose that's how they did it?

- Who did what, Sir?

The Japs. Did they put their soldiers on Statins in order to get them to become kamikaze pilots?

- Sir, there's so much wrong with that question it's difficult to know where to start.

Then let's just assume that I'm joking, eh Jack.

- Yes let's do that, Sir.

August

OK, Jack, it's obvious that the Web is going to be the next big thing, so do we have a plan? What options do we have to limit its spread? The way things are going every household will have a computer giving them access to the system.

- Well I don't think I'd go that far, Sir. But nevertheless I agree that we need to plan for the worse scenario.

And have you come up with anything?

- Yes, Sir. It's pornography.

Pornography? What, you plan to send out so many porno magazines that they will be too busy tossing off to use the Web?

- No, Sir. The plan is to transmit the pornography via the Web, but otherwise you're right. The plan is to keep people too occupied with matters of the flesh to worry about our stuff.

I can see how that would work for men, but what about the ladies? I can't imagine that they will be preoccupied by the porn.

- We don't think that there will be many ladies using the system, Sir. Bear in mind that it's computer based so we anticipate that, for the average female, the system will be far too complicated to use. And before you ask, yes, we will be charging for the porn. We don't intend to make the same mistake as CERN.

Damn right.

- Is there anything else, Sir?

Yes, I think I need to be up to speed on this Web thing. Make sure that I have a system installed as soon as possible.

- In the Oval Office, Sir?

No, in my private quarters. And make sure that I have access to the porn. I need to check the system out personally.

- I'm sure you do, Sir.

And that's free access, Jack. I don't want any unpleasant surprises on my credit card statement.

- I'm sure you don't, Sir.

And there is one last thing, Jack. I've been giving some more thought to the whole cholesterol/suicide/violence thing. I think it might be a good idea if we get on to the NRA. Now would be a good time to start a recruitment campaign. Whether people are going to be more inclined to kill themselves or someone else doesn't matter. Either way they'll need the means to do it and that means guns.

- Good idea, Sir. I'll get in touch with them right away.

No need, Jack. I'll do it myself. I have Mr Heston on speed dial.

October

- Sir, I'm getting some interesting feedback from Asia on the subject of GM crops.

This had better be good news Jack. I hope they're not going down the European route by rejecting the technology.

- Oh no, nothing like that. No this is an unexpected side effect of the whole GM crop project. It turns out that in India farmers are dying at an increased rate in areas that grow GM crops.

Well that's hardly surprising, what with the increased use of chemicals.

- In this instance it's not exposure to the chemicals that is causing the problem.

No? If not, what are they doing? Don't tell me that the GM crops are poisonous. Now that would be a bonus.

- Actually, Sir, that would not be anything like a bonus. We're trying hard to convince people that GM crops are safe so the last thing we want is to find out that they are killing people, at least not directly due to the genetic modification. In any case the farmers don't eat this particular crop. It's cotton.

OK, so what is the cause and how do we know it's linked to our GM crops.

- The cause is suicide, Sir. The farmers are killing themselves and we know that it's connected to our crops because the suicide rate is far higher in those areas that grow GM crops.

Well, Jack, I can't see how this can be relevant. A few dead farmers are hardly going to contribute to our overall body count are they?

- Well how many bodies would you consider to be a useful contribution?

What do you mean, Jack?

- Put a number on it. How many dead farmers would you consider to be a result, Sir?

Well that's a bit of a distasteful way of putting it.

- Sir, we're trying to kill off large numbers of the world's population. Distasteful is hardly the right description.

Yes, yes, I know, but I'm not going to put a number on it. Just tell me. If you're making this much fuss it must be a big number, well into the hundreds I guess.

- How about a thousand?

Per year?

- No, per month, Sir.

A thousand suicides per month! But that's incredible. Are you sure, only I haven't heard anything about this on the news?

- Well if they all died in the same place at the same time it would be noticeable but, since it's just one by one and spread over a large area, it takes a while for the pattern to be established.

But I still don't understand. What's the cause? There must be a common thread here.

We're looking into it. I'm sure we'll come up with something soon, Sir.

November

- Sir, you called.

Yes, Jack. I think I've come up with a solution to your conundrum concerning the Indian farmers and their suicide rate.

- Well we have in fact discovered what's causing the problem, Sir.

I bet it's Statins. I'm right aren't I?

- Statins, Sir?

Yes. I bet the farmers are all on Statins. Their cholesterol has gone down and they've got depressed so they've been topping themselves

366

by the score.

- Well that's close, Sir.

How close?

- The sort of close that's a million miles away. No, Sir, it's not Statins. Instead it's depression, which is hardly surprising. The farmers are having a tough time and as a result they are committing suicide.

But surely all Indian farmers can have tough times at some stage. What's so special now?

- It's the GM crops, Sir. Previously all the farmers had a more or less level playing field but now those who can afford to grow the GM crops have a distinct advantage.

Well can't they all grow GM stuff?

- Only if they can afford it, Sir. GM seed costs many times more than the standard seed. And if you are going to take advantage of the tolerance to weed killers you have to buy a lot of chemicals. Initially the farmers could try to borrow money in order to pay for the stuff but that just gets them into more and more debt. In the end it appears that there's only one way out and that's suicide.

Well we'd better roll out this business model to other parts of the globe. Let's see if we can't get rid of a few more poor farmers.

- Such a scheme is already underway, Sir.

Let's stick to Asia and South America. I don't think it would be good publicity if we had American farmers topping themselves at the rate of one an hour.

- No, Sir. That would certainly be bad news. And by the way, in India the rate is now one every 30 minutes.

Incredible! Surely at some stage they are going to run out of farmers.

- It is rather hard to believe, but if there's one thing that India is not going to run out of it's people.

No, I suppose not. Is there anything else, Jack?

- There is one last thing, Sir. It's to do with Statins. I'd like to make it clear that their use is restricted to the developed countries like the USA and Europe. They're not used to kill people in the Third World.

Well what do we use instead?

- Poverty, Sir.

1996

February

- Sir, we've come up with a solution to the problem of the French Banks, albeit in a small way.

Well whatever you've got, let me hear it.

- We considered all the options and we decided that it was pointless trying to influence the banks at the top level. Let's face it, the French senior executives are hardly likely to take any notice of us. So instead we think we can place someone at a much lower level in one of the banks but in such a position that he can take risks with the banks money.

Can one person have so much influence over a bank's assets?

- Indeed they can, Sir. Remember Nick Leeson, the chap who brought down Barings Bank? He gave us the idea since he didn't even work at head office; such is the inter-connectivity of the banking system these days. We see no reason why we can't achieve the same thing so we're going to place a number of people in various European banks and hope that one or more of them gets the opportunity to create a bit of trouble.

And how long will it take before they strike.

- We don't want to do anything before the financial meltdown takes place here. Things need to coincide so in the meantime our people will remain as sleepers await our instructions.

Good work, Jack.

August

Jack, following our conversation about the French banks, I've been giving our plan some thought and I'm a bit concerned about the fall-out there is going to be.

- In which particular respect, Sir, given that when the shit hits the fan it's literally going to end up all over the place.

I'm thinking of our relationship with the British government.

- Well we have to remember that we're not going to go public on the background as to why the financial meltdown occurred. The Brits will be none the wiser.

Even so, I think that we need to deflect some of the damage from them onto someone else.

- Did you have anyone in particular in mind? You're not thinking of the French are you, since we already have that situation covered.

I'm not sure what I'm thinking yet, Jack, but I do feel that we need to perhaps have a fall guy lined up to take a lot of the pain. Can you go away and think about it?

- Yes, Sir.

The Next Week

- Sir, we've given some thought to your idea concerning the need for a fall guy, you know, when the banks go belly-up.

That was quick. So what's your plan?

- Well we thought about several different options including individuals and companies who could fill the role but none of these are going to be big enough for what we have in mind. So the only option we have is a country.

That figures. Do you have any targets lines up?

- We've narrowed the choice down to one, Iceland.

Iceland! How did you come up with that gem?

- By a process of elimination, Sir. It's got to be a country which has a modern, sophisticated banking system, which excludes most of the third world. However, it also needs to be a relatively small country, preferably an island, but with ambition and we think the current situation in Iceland fits the bill.

Why an island?

- So that if things get really bad, the population can be more easily contained.

Well what's the plan? How are we going to break the banks in Iceland? Surely we can't use the normal tactic.

- You mean property? No, I don't think that there's any chance of a significant property boom in Iceland, there just aren't enough people. Instead we're going to suck money into the Icelandic banks by offering attractive interest rates.

But surely we'll have the same problem.

- Not really, Sir. Overseas investors may be reluctant to buy a property in Iceland but with the internet there's nothing to stop them putting their money into an Icelandic bank. And in order to keep the savings rates high the banks will need to lend the money out and that means that, when the crunch comes, they'll have serious liquidity problems.

And you think that Iceland is the ideal target for this little ruse?

- We think it's the best option, Sir.

November

Jack, I've been thinking about the issue of sunlight and cancer. You gave me a brief overview some time ago and we've taken your advice on board, particularly where the children are concerned.

- Good, I'm glad to hear it, Sir. Lots of long vacations in Florida for you then to boost the vitamin D, eh.

No, Jack, you know I don't spend much time on vacation. No, I decided to cut out the middleman by taking vitamin supplements. And that's why I need to speak to you.

- Sorry, Sir. By "middleman", I assume that, in the case of vitamin D, you mean sunlight.

Well yes, but we're not the only ones taking the stuff and I'm a bit concerned that people may be circumventing our plan to undermine their nutrition by using vitamin supplements.

- Oh, I'm sorry that you didn't consult me on this matter. I could have saved you time and money.

Really, Jack. What haven't you told me?

- I know that I should have mentioned it, Sir, it must have been an oversight, but we have been looking at the whole question of vitamin supplements for some time. I should perhaps have discussed it with you sooner.

Well the damage is done now, Jack. You'd better give me the low down.

- The bottom line is that for most people most of the time, vitamin supplements do them no particular good at all and in some cases, may actually do them harm. For example, many of the cheaper supplements come in a pill form that results in the ingredients being destroyed in the stomach and consequently flushed down the toilets.

Ah, I am aware of that, Jack! We've been buying the more expensive "coated" pills. Rather than passing straight through, they get absorbed into the blood stream.

- In terms of not being trashed by the stomach, that may well be the case, but that's only the first stage. In order to be correctly absorbed by the body you may well need other vitamins, minerals and nutrients. For example, for Vitamin D to be absorbed you will need dietary fat.

Well that's OK, Jack since we're all consuming plenty of butter and full fat milk.

- All of you, Sir?

Absolutely!

- Then why is there a carton of soy milk in your fridge?

Er, I believe that belongs to Chelsea.

- So that's all of you except your daughter.

Well she's going through an animal welfare and veggie stage and I can hardly reason with her without giving the whole game away. We're hoping she'll grow out of it.

- Let's hope so, although if she doesn't we may of course be able to study the health effects of soy and vegetarianism first hand!

I'd rather not joke about this, Jack.

- Sorry, Sir, but do bear in mind that you can speak to her in general terms without mentioning STOP. However, getting back to the main subject, even if you absorb the vitamins, there's no guarantee that they will be handled by the body in the same way as the naturally occurring ones. At best there may be limited beneficial effect for some vitamins, for others it may be downright dangerous. It's really more luck than judgement and of course, for certain vitamins, you can take too many. The ones that occur naturally will tend to be consumed in the right proportions, assuming that they're consumed at all. It's all a question of balance. On the other hand, those vitamins taken in pill form can be taken in any sort of quantity. That's not good, especially when some people think that "more is better".

When you say not good, Jack, I assume you mean for them, not for our grand plan.

- Of course, Sir.

So we're not concerned about the growth of the vitamin supplement market.

- No, Sir, not right now. But I am concerned about Chelsea's carton of soy milk. However I think we'll save that for another day.

Is it anything I need to worry about?

- Well put this way, if you see another one, let me know right away.

So that's a "Yes" then.

- Yes

December

Jack, I think I need to talk to you about soy.

- Ah, so you haven't managed to talk your daughter out of drinking the soy milk then.

To be honest, Jack, I haven't spoken to her about it yet. I don't want to tackle her until I have all the facts at my fingertips. At this stage I can extol the virtues of milk and butter but if I need to dish the dirt on soy, I'll start to struggle. So what have you got?

- Well like most of these things, there's good and bad news. In this case, it's good news for us and unfortunately, bad news for your daughter. Soy is one of the food stuffs in what we call our "Magic Triangle" of dangerous substances.

And what's that?

- It's a list of the main suspects that we have been promoting in the food industry. They are the ones that JUNC pins most hopes on

373

when it comes to undermining the health of the nation.

Well what are the other ones?

- They're Hydrogenated Vegetable Fats, Monosodium Glutamate and High Fructose Corn Syrup.

In total that's four, Jack!

- Yes, Sir, I know. We coined the term "Magic Triangle" when there were only three, before HFCS was added. The phrase "Magic Square" didn't have such a ring to it, so triangle stayed.

OK, but what's so special about these four foods.

- Well for start, I don't think we should be calling them "foods". If there was anything food-like about them, they wouldn't be in the Magic Triangle. No, they're either food additives or food substitutes.

Whatever they are, why these four?

- Hopefully, Sir, you remember that early on in the project, JUNC came up with the idea that we should promote processed food. This was based on the premise that it is far easier to contaminate food when it's all mixed up with other stuff than when it is in its raw state. Take vegetables for instance. We can poison them with pesticides and insecticides but there's not a lot else we can do.

Good grief, Jack, isn't that enough?

- Well we thought not and with the growth of organic foods, that turned out to be a good decision. We are able to produce rubbish stuff for people to eat no matter how good the original ingredients are.

OK, so far so good, but back to the Magic Triangle.

- Ah yes, Sir. Well after JUNC came up with the idea of promoting unhealthy food, they quickly realised that they needed a reason to put our rogue ingredients into processed food. It wasn't going to be good enough just to add them without good reason, so the plan of action was to find substances that could be used as alternatives for four main items; fat, sugar, salt and protein. And that's why we've come up the four things in our Magic Triangle.

Well I do have one question.

- And what's that, Sir?

Well if you always knew that there were four, I still don't see why you used the term "Triangle".

- Sir! Please let's forget "Triangle". Let's concentrate on the core issues. At this rate, Chelsea will be middle aged before we wean her off soy.

OK, Jack. Sorry. You carry on.

- Well in general terms, there's not much more to say about the plan. As I said, over a period of time we've come up with the stuff we needed. Of course, at the start we already had Trans Fats from our early margarine days so the issue with fat was sorted. It was just a question of concentrating on the other three areas of opportunity.

OK, but let's get back to soy. That's what I need to worry about just now.

- Right, Sir. Well soy is one of hundreds of different basic food stuffs that we have looked at since STOP started.

I notice that you just referred to it as a food, Jack.

- Well before we've waved our magic wand over it, it is a food, albeit in its mature form a toxic one. It comes from the soya bean and has been consumed for hundreds of years in the Far East. However, the Orientals don't consume a great deal of the stuff and what they do consume has been prepared using fermentation to remove the toxins.

But I thought that the Chinese had been consuming soy for many centuries.

- They may have been growing soy for centuries, but not in order to eat it. The young immature beans were occasionally eaten but when mature the main use was for industrial purpose like lubrication and candle making. What was left over after extracting the oil was used by the farmers as a fertiliser. It was only when they tried fermenting it that they started eating it.

So I'm assuming that the soy that we use has not been fermented.

- Oh no, Sir, certainly not, but we were interested in the fact that we can use the basic raw material to produce both a liquid, hence soy milk, and a solid protein.

And what are we going to do with the solid stuff?

- We're going to use it to make all sorts of things like burgers and other meat products. In fact anything that contains protein.

I thought that we were already doing that, you know the fungus based stuff.

- We are, Sir, but you can never have too many such options and the soy based one is more acceptable to the public. At least soy is something that grows in fields.

As opposed to a Petri dish, eh Jack!

- Exactly, Sir.

And why do we think that people will buy these products? They don't sound very appealing.

- Well Chelsea is one example. The vegetarians will want to avoid dairy products and meat in general. Our soy products give them that option while at the same time avoiding a diet that mainly involves gnawing on raw carrots. But we also needed to attract the non-veggie crowd and that's where our old friend cholesterol comes into the frame.

Oh dear. What have you come up with now, Jack?

- Only that we have discovered a couple of bits of research. The first report suggests that soy consumption reduces cholesterol levels in the body.

Well that's a bit of luck, Jack. Although on second thoughts, I guess it wasn't luck, was it?

- Not entirely, Sir, since the report was funded by a company that produces soy and the result gives a triple bonus; more soy consumption, more people buying the stuff because they think it'll lower their cholesterol, which will in turn result in more unhealthy people. And that takes me to the second bit of research and that says that soy reduces the sperm count in men. Of course as far as we are concerned, this is great news.

This all sounds too good to be true, Jack.

- With any luck, Sir, it will get even better. There are reports that soy interferes with a woman's cycle and that in some cases it stops completely. So it won't matter whether the Veggie is male or female, we'll have them covered.

Well that all sounds good, Jack, but what do I do about Chelsea?

- You can start by trying to talk her out of drinking soy milk and try to persuade her to eat natural products instead. And there is one tactic you could use that could be persuasive.

And what's that?

- It's the fact that soy milk has a somewhat bitter taste so most of it is sweetened. You could play the fat card and suggest that she'll put on weight if she consumes soy milk.

I can certainly try that, but if I fail, how much of a problem do we have?

- Whether you, or more importantly she, will have a long term problem is going to depend on whether she's a vegan. If she is, it could be serious. But if she's a veggie and she consumes fish, eggs and even possibly chicken, she'll probably be OK. One consolation is that she didn't start drinking soy milk as a baby.

Goodness me, Jack, why would she do that? Or rather, why would we do that, since as an infant I don't remember her expressing a preference regarding milk?

- Well no, I realise that, but soy formula milk is regularly fed to young babies.

These veggie parents are going to be in for a shock.

- It's not necessarily because the parents have a problem with real milk. It's because the babies have an intolerance for the stuff. In fact they will normally have a problem with all dairy products.

Well that's a bit of luck, Jack!

Short Pause

Can I assume from the look on your face, Jack, that it's got nothing to do with luck?

- Actually, Sir, in this instance I suppose there is a bit of luck involved. It's to do with the fact that we have been pretty successful in getting people to give up dairy products. And even when they do consume them, it will often be the adulterated version, e.g. low fat milk.

Yes, I know that, Jack. Where does the poor baby come into the picture?

- They come into it because they have an allergy to cow's milk and we think that it's due to the fact that the mother consumed fewer dairy products when she was pregnant, especially milk. The baby did not develop a tolerance to milk in the womb and therefore has a problem with it as a baby. And that's lucky because it wasn't something we planned.

Yes, I remember now that in the early days you explained about allergies, I just didn't realise where soy fitted into the picture.

- Now, Sir, you need to be careful not to confuse a food allergy with food intolerance. They're two different things.

But they both mean that you can't eat certain foods because if you do they both make you ill. Have I got that right, Jack?

- Yes, Sir.

Then I don't really care whether there is a difference between the two, do I?

- I guess not, Sir.

1997

January

- Sir, you called?

You're damned right I did.

- What seems to be the problem, Sir?

You know very well what the problem is. You've seen the front pages.

- Ah, you're referring to the pictures of Diana.

Of course I am. What is she playing at?

- I think she's concerned about land mines, Sir.

I can see that. She's wandering through a minefield wearing a Red Cross outfit. She looks like a latter day Florence Nightingale!

- I'm well aware of that, Sir.

Well why did you let this happen? Surely we must have some influence with the Red Cross.

- I was in fact aware of the plan from the start. In fact, I arranged it.

You arranged it! To what end? Land mines are one of our long term plans to kill off as many people as possible. If my memory serves me right, using landmines, we've eliminated more than 3,000 people in the last 10 years. Not our highest body count by far, but they all add up.

- 3,807, Sir, to be exact. And the aim was to get rid of the Diana problem once and for all.

And how did you plan to do that, by blowing her up? From what I understand, the mine field had been cleared. Isn't that true?

- Well, Sir, the mines that were detectable by conventional means had been cleared. There may have been some mines remaining that were not so easy to detect.

Jack, can you just get to the point.

- Well, Sir, following Diana and the AIDS debacle, we agreed that she was getting to be a bit of a loose cannon.

Well the AIDS thing didn't turn out so bad, did it?

- As it happens, no, but that was more luck than judgement. It was only a matter of time before Diana turned her attention to another worthy cause and as I see it the only way to stop her is to eliminate her.

By blowing her up! That's a bit crude isn't it?

- Well it's academic now, Sir, since the plan didn't work.

And why is that?

- We're not sure yet, Sir. It's possible that she avoided treading on any of the mines, although it's unlikely.

Why's that? How many did we lay?

- 200, Sir.

200! Good grief! That's enough to destroy a small army.

- Not quite, Sir, but it should have been enough to do the job, or at least so we thought.

So either she was very lucky or the mines malfunctioned. Have you got the results of the tests yet?

- You mean the tests on the malfunctioning mines?

Of course!

- Not yet, Sir.

Why not?

- Because we haven't carried out any tests yet.

And why is that?

- Because we can't find the mines.

Don't tell me. It's because they're undetectable!

- I'm afraid so, Sir.

But how did that happen? You said they couldn't be detected by conventional means. I assumed that meant we had some unconventional means at our disposal.

- We should have had a means of detecting these mines. It was in the original plan, but that part was dropped from STOP due to cuts in the military budget.

Good grief, which idiot did that?

- Er, you did, Sir.

Well I must have had a good reason at the time.

- You did, Sir. It was to do with getting re-elected.

I knew there would be a good reason, however at this stage there's no point in looking back at past mistakes. The important thing to consider now is where do we go from here?

- Well, we have considered poisoning her, or employing an assassin.

No, no, Jack, I don't mean doing away with her. In any case, those options are too obvious.

- So the landmine option is a no-go then, Sir.

The whole killing off option is a no-go, at least for the time being. No, we need to be more subtle. Can't we have a quiet word with her? You know, appeal to her better nature.

- I think that it's her better nature that gets us into these fixes.

That's as may be, but I want you to give it some thought. See what you can come up with.

- Yes, Sir.

February

Jack, I have spoken to Chelsea but she's not very receptive on the issue of soy. Is there anything you can come up with to help me here?

- Well that could be a bit difficult, Sir, although I do have a lot of information that is very compelling.

Like what?

- Well like eating vegetables and fruit is good for you, but only if eaten in conjunction with dairy foods and of course this is what we would expect. You need the two together in order for the body to be able to absorb the nutrients. Unfortunately soy doesn't count as dairy.

OK, can I have the details so that I can show Chelsea?

- Not really, Sir. This information comes from one of our groups in Area 51 which means that it's not in the public domain.

Well what have you got that is in the public domain?

- I've got a study that proves that margarine causes heart disease but butter doesn't. Will that do?

What! You mean to tell me that sort of thing is readily available to the public? Why is that?

- Yes, Sir, it is, and that's because the study is being done in public. In fact it's a study involving the public so inevitably the results are in the public domain.

So how come everyone still thinks that butter is the enemy.

- That's because we use a couple of techniques, the first of which we call headlining.

I seem to remember something about this in your introduction to STOP some years ago. Just refresh my memory.

- Well, Sir, when a scientific study is published, the detail contains the actual results of the work but it's worded in such a way that very few people will be able to decipher it. So in order to be helpful, we include a synopsis which will be worded in a way that the average person can understand. That way we can get our message across.

What, even if it goes against the science?

- Let's just say that, as far as the synopsis is concerned, we often have to be economical with the truth. If something really goes against us we'll stop the research being published, after all there's no law that says that all test results have to be published.

It's all coming back to me now. If I recall, when that doesn't work, we get the scientists to add the caveat that "more research is required".

- Yes, Sir, but that's only as a last resort.

So in the case of this study that proves that margarine causes heart disease, what did the synopsis say?

- It says that the investigators feel that more research must be done to establish whether butter causes heart disease. The reporter from the newspaper sees that phrase "butter causes heart disease" and that's what he remembers. Job done!

But surely the reporter will read the detail and realise that he's been misled.

- Sir, the reporter hasn't got time to do that sort of thing and even if he did, he wouldn't understand it.

But surely the reporter is qualified enough to understand the science?

- Sir, you have to bear in mind that there aren't many qualified science reporters working in the media. The previous day this same person was probably reporting on the latest baseball game.

OK, but how do we get the scientists to play ball. They must realise that the results have been misreported.

- Now that's where funding comes in. Most research is funded by either the government or the food and drug companies. Either way, the research will tend to confirm whatever the sponsor wishes.

And what if it doesn't?

- Then two things happen. The researchers find it difficult to get further funding and the report fails to get published. Sometimes, if the results seem to be going the wrong way, we'll pull the plug before the research is complete.

And you said that headlining was the first option we use. What's the other one?

- That's where we decide what the answer is and then frame the question in order to get a result.

I'm sorry, Jack, I don't understand how that will work.

- Well, Sir, let's imagine that we want to target meat, particularly red meat. We could commission a piece of research which will come to the conclusion that it's bad for you.

What do we do, bribe the scientists?

- Oh, no, nothing like that. Our strategy involves something much simpler and that concerns the remit that we give to the scientists.

I don't get you.

- Well we could ask the scientists to check whether people who eat red meat are more likely to suffer from cancer. But in the detail we will say that we want to include all meat, including the processed stuff. Anything that includes any significant amount of meat would be included, even stuff which contains less than 50% meat.

But why is that sort of meat going to be bad whereas whole fresh meat is good?

- Well it's all to do with the non-meat portion which can contain all sorts of goodies. And smoked meat is the worst offender. The smoking process alone can conjure up some pretty unpleasant side effects.

Like what?

- Like cancer, colon cancer in particular. And it's not just the smoking process that's to blame. The modern method of smoking fish is, needless to say, quicker and more industrial than the old fashioned way of doing things. This means that the fish comes out looking a bit anaemic so the producers use chemicals to dye the fish and luckily these can often be harmful in their own right.

So that explains why we don't ever have kippers on the breakfast menu.

- Er, no, Sir. The reason for the lack of kippers is that this is Washington, not London.

That wasn't a serious statement, Jack, but never mind. Let's get back to the subject. In the example of red meat, you're saying that our carefully crafted wording gives researchers carte-blanche to include all sorts of crap in their research including hot dogs, salami, and doner kebabs.

- Exactly, and of course in this example we would always make sure that the survey is carried out in the US. That's because the meat being consumed here contains some of our special additives, including growth hormones and organophosphates, and the cattle here are more likely to be fed grain rather than grass. That alone will produce less nutritious meat but if that grain contains some of our GM stuff then it's like a turkey shoot. The scientists can't fail but to find something that's not good. Of course when they do hit the target they won't differentiate between whole meat and the processed stuff, the headline will just read "meat is bad".

And you're saying that this technique can be repeated across any number of different food stuffs.

- Pretty much. We've already used it very successfully on fats. We know that Trans Fats are bad so in the past, whenever researchers wanted funding to look at fats, we always made sure that they lumped the Trans Fats in with the saturated fats. That way any bad health effects can be blamed on the saturated fat. Of course, since Trans Fats have become headline news we can't use that ruse any more but we had a good run and nobody can go through the old literature to see what stuff is still relevant since figures for the Trans Fats were never kept separate.

So I don't have to worry about any budgetary implications concerning bribes for scientists.

- I didn't say that it never happens but if it does it's not often enough to worry about, Sir.

Amazing! All this is going on and I don't know about it.

- Well it should be obvious, Sir. How do you think we get all this bum information out there?

But there must be some genuine unbiased research going on out there.

- Unfortunately for us, there's quite a lot, hence the report which is damning about margarine. We can't keep tabs on all research, especially the stuff being carried out overseas. We just have to try and keep it under wraps.

But this still isn't helping me regarding my daughter. Do you have any other ideas?

- If she's a vegan, then I'm sorry but there's nothing we can do. If not, and if you can't convince her of the error of her ways, we'll have to keep her under observation medically speaking.

What do I need to be on the lookout for?

- You need to keep a look out for signs of the following: diabetes, vitamin deficiency, osteoporosis, cancer, thyroid problems, kidney problems, anything unusual with regard to the nervous system or brain function...

Steady on, Jack. That's a long list of problems for vegetarians. Can't we just stick to the issues regarding soy?

- Those are the list for soy, Sir. And in addition, for goodness sake don't let her get pregnant! Although, of course, if she's consuming a lot of soy, that's not likely to happen.

Well that's something I suppose, but I'm not in a position to watch out for all this stuff. It sounds like we need to have her take a medical, perhaps as often as every six months, Jack.

- If you can't get her off the soy then I think that a medical examination every six days would be preferable, Sir.

I'll bear that in mind, but your mentioning of diabetes has reminded me of something. I have some concerns about the current situation.

- Sir, it's taken a while but our policy seems to be bearing fruit. The number of people suffering from diabetes is climbing steadily and shows no sign of levelling off.

That may well be the case Jack, but my concerns aren't with the effectiveness of the policy but with the cost of treatment which is becoming unsustainable. As with a lot of our policies, we've been successful in making people ill but less capable when it comes to killing them off.

- Well to be fair, Sir, diabetes is now number seven in the top ten causes of death in the USA and it's climbing up the list each year.

It's not a pop chart, Jack. It's just as well our reforms didn't get adopted. The budget for healthcare is beginning to take a big hit from treating diabetes.

- That's unfortunate, Sir, but luckily the health budget isn't my responsibility.

No, but it is mine. In future let's see if we can come up with strategies which are more cost effective. The motto should be "Kill 'em or Cure 'em". Don't leave them in expensive limbo, healthcare wise.

- Yes, Sir, I'll try to bear that in mind.

May

- Sir, I think I may have come up with something on the Diana problem.

I hope it doesn't include the word "landmine".

- No, Sir, in that respect I've heeded your advice. Instead I've tried to come up with a way to persuade Diana to co-operate, at least as far as things that affect STOP are concerned. And I've come to the conclusion that there is only one thing that we can use to make her see sense.

Or at least our version of sense, eh Jack?

- Yes, Sir, exactly. Anyway, the only leverage we have is with the two sons, William and Harry.

You're not suggesting that we threaten to assassinate the two of them, are you?

- No, Sir, not at all, at least not at this stage. But we can threaten to do something which for Diana would be almost as bad.

What an earth could that be?

- We would threaten to expose the two boys as impostors.

And why would that be so bad for Diana? And surely it would ruin our grand plan.

- Well as far as we are concerned, we have already achieved our aim. Charles is not going to have any off-spring now, at least not real ones. He has hitched up with Camilla and she's well past child bearing age.

But he could ditch her and go for someone younger.

- If he tried that, he'd be lynched, if not by Camilla, then by his mother. No, he's not going to produce any true heirs.

OK, I see why we could afford to go public, but why should Diana play ball?

- Well there are two very good reasons why she won't want to rock the boat. The first is the one she has had all along. She wants the eldest to be heir to the throne.

She must be talking long term there. The Queen is still alive and then it'll be Charles's turn.

- She doesn't care about that. She just wants to pay them all back for the treatment they gave her, especially her father-in-law. Also, she's hoping that they'll skip Charles and go straight to William.

That's not likely is it?

- It's not beyond the realms of possibility. But even if Charles does inherit the throne, it'll go to William eventually.

OK, what's the second reason she'll play ball?

- Well the two boys believe that Charles is their true father. It would be a devastating blow to them to find out that he isn't. Also, they wouldn't be too impressed with their mother's behaviour. In William's case she doesn't even know who the father is.

How can that be?

- IVF treatment, remember?

Oh, yes, that's right. And the boyfriend fathered the younger one.

- Correct.

Yes, I see what you mean. If the truth comes out, it wouldn't look good for Diana would it.

- No, it wouldn't, which is why I think we've got a pretty strong hand.

OK, have a word with her and see what she says. If she wants to take up any more good causes, she needs to clear it with us first.

- Yes, Sir.

June

- Sir, I've spoken to Diana.

Really, and what was her reaction? Did she play ball?

- Well, Sir, it's difficult to say.

How can that be? She either agreed to tone down her public utterances and keep a lower profile, or she didn't.

- Well, Sir, it wasn't quite as simple as that. She saw the wisdom of keeping secret the situation regarding her two sons but now she wants more than that in return.

I wouldn't have thought that she is in a position to bargain, Jack.

- She might be if it suits our purpose.

Why, what does she want?

- She wants to drop out of sight completely.

Why would she want to do that?

- She's had enough of the publicity and now it's getting to her. She can't do anything without the press following her and pointing a camera lens in her face.

Yes, I can appreciate the problem, but in the circumstances that was always going to happen. I don't see how it could have been avoided.

- Neither do I, Sir. I haven't come up with a solution yet.

Well I don't see why we need to worry about it too much. If she has agreed to clear things with us first, that's all we need to worry about.

- Provided she keeps her word, Sir.

Yes, provided she keeps her word. See if you can come up with something to solve her problem, but don't spend too much time thinking about it.

- Yes, Sir.

August

- Sir, I've come up with a plan for...... Oh, I'm sorry, Sir, I didn't realise you had someone with you.

Er, Jack, This is Miss Lewinski. She's helping me with a little project.

- Why is she on her knees?

Er, she's lost a contact lens, Jack.

- But she's wearing glasses.

Alright, Jack, never mind that. What do you want? Is it important?

- It's about you know who. You know, the one who wants to drop out of the public eye. I've come up with a plan.

Oh, yes, I see. Well I can't discuss it now, Jack, I'm far too busy. If she's happy with it, go ahead.

- Yes, Sir.

August 31st

Good Grief, Jack, have you seen the news.

- You mean Diana?

Of course I mean Diana. There isn't any other news. What a shock!

- Well not entirely, Sir.

What do you mean "not entirely"? Did you have something to do with this?

- You mean did we have something to do with this.

What do you mean "we"? I don't know anything about this.

- Not in detail, Sir, I'll grant you. But it is the part of STOP that you gave the go ahead for a couple of weeks ago.

I did?

- Yes, in a brief conversation. I think Miss Lewinsky can confirm the conversation.

Ah, that conversation. Well what on earth have you done?

- You mean, what have we done?

Yes, alright Jack. I get the picture. Just tell me what has happened.

- Well, Sir, as you know Diana wanted to disappear from public view.

Not, presumably, by getting killed in a car crash.

- No, Sir, not that.

So what then?

- Well, Sir, as you can imagine, someone like Diana cannot simply disappear from view. There would always be someone looking for her, to get the photo which could earn them a fortune.

Yes I realise all this. Cut to the chase, Jack, what was the plan?

- Body doubles, Sir. We planned to swap Diana and Dodi with look-alikes and then the two of them could disappear into obscurity.

But they would always be recognised.

- Not after we had finished with them, Sir. They were going to be taken to Area 51 where they would undergo extensive plastic surgery. By the time we had finished with them, their own mothers would not recognise them.

And why would Dodi agree to this? I can't imagine he's so fond of Diana to accept such a plan.

- You might do if you had Mr Al Fayed as a father.

Fair point, Jack. But what about the body doubles? It wouldn't take long for them to be rumbled, would it?

- No, Sir, which is why they had to be quickly killed off.

I think you'd better explain the whole plan.

- Well, Sir, once we had agreed the plan with the happy couple, we searched for two willing body doubles. In Diana's case, it wasn't difficult since there are plenty of women around who earn a good living impersonating Diana. With Dodi it was more difficult, but then we figured he wasn't so important since nobody was going to pay much attention to him.

But surely these body doubles weren't happy about being bumped off.

- No, Sir, of course not, but they weren't in on that part of the plan. They were told that the subterfuge would last only 24 hours, enough time to give the real couple some respite.

And when was the swap-over due to take place?

- Last night, Sir. The plan was that it would happen in the underpass. The doubles were waiting in a white Fiat Uno.

But why in an underpass? It's a bit odd isn't it?

- At first glance, yes, but we wanted the pair to be seen in public at the hotel and clearly identified as the real thing. The swap was to be made in the underpass because it's completely hidden from view. Anywhere else and anybody could have seen what was going on. We were particularly concerned about satellites, after all you never know who's looking down.

Well I think we do, Jack. It's us!

- Mostly, Sir, but not exclusively.

So what happened?

- Well, as far as I am aware, things went according to plan until the car reached the underpass. Then, from what I can gather, the driver lost control of the car. Whether he misunderstood the plan or was simply drunk I don't know, but he entered the underpass at high speed and swerved to avoid the Fiat. He crashed into the barrier with the result that Diana and Dodi were killed.

But weren't they wearing seat belts.

- No, Sir, they weren't. I can only assume that they had already undone them in order to make a quick exit from the car.

So the swap was never made.

- No, Sir.

And the body doubles?

- They and the Fiat have been disposed of, Sir.

Well this is a right mess. What are we going to do?

- I'm not sure that there is anything we need to do. Diana will no longer be a problem and we just need to make sure that nothing can be traced back to us.

Too true, Jack. If this got out, I cannot imagine what it would do to Anglo-American relations.

- I'll make sure there is no come back, Sir.

Make sure you do. And just in case there's any suspicion of foul play, you had better line up a suspect.

- I have already spoken to the Brits about that and they have suggested the father-in-law as the most likely candidate.

1998

April

- Sir, the British have come back with an idea to solve the vaccination problem.

Good Grief, I'd forgotten all about that. When did we first ask for their help?

- 1985, Sir.

They must have a pretty small team of people looking at problems like this.

- I don't know how many people they have, Sir, but their equivalent of Area 51 is something called "The Shed".

Well judging by how much they've come up with and how long it takes them, this Shed must be pretty small.

- I guess so, Sir. Anyway, the British have realised that we need to get people to stop being vaccinated.

It's taken them 13 years to come up with that? Hell, even I worked that one out. Did they come up with anything else?

- Yes, Sir. The problem is that most vaccinations are given to children, because their parents think it is the best thing to do. They say that what we need to do is make the parents think that it is dangerous to get their children vaccinated.

And how do we do that?

- Well, you know we have identified a number of diseases that may be attributed to STOP.

Yes. It was an impressively long list.

- Thank you, Sir. Anyway, on that list there were a couple of things that can particularly affect young children, Autism and Asthma. The British have suggested that we pick one of these and blame it on vaccinations.

What, all vaccinations?

- I'm not sure that's possible, after all each vaccination attacks a different disease. No, the suggestion is the MMR vaccine. It is designed to protect against three diseases, Mumps, Measles and Rubella.

So we get "Three for the price of one".

- Yes, Sir.

OK, let's go with that idea. Which disease shall we choose?

- I suggest Autism, Sir, since it's the most difficult to diagnose.

OK, Autism it is. And how do we start the rumour?

- I think we'll let the British come up with an idea for that, Sir.

What, and wait another thirteen years.

- I'll ask them to give it some priority, Sir.

July

- Sir, we have a bit of a situation regarding the plan for the banks in Iceland.

Is this a good situation or a bad one?

- I have to say that I'm not sure yet, but if I can just explain perhaps you can be the judge. I'm not sure exactly when it happened, but at some stage the reference to "Iceland" in the paperwork was changed to "Ireland". So the current plan being worked on is to break the Irish banks.

How on earth did that happen?

- Well, Sir, we're assuming that it was done by someone creating a document and they used a spellchecker without paying enough attention. They somehow misspelt Iceland, say as "Iveland", and the system corrected it to read "Ireland".

Well what can we do? Is it too late to correct the error?

- No, Sir, it's not too late, although if we change our minds now, a lot of time and work will have been wasted. So the question is; what do we do?

Is there a down side to going with the Irish option?

- Sir, whenever Ireland is mentioned to any President their first

394

reaction is to consider the Irish vote.

And is there an Irish vote angle to this situation?

- Well there will be if the Irish ever find out what we've done.

Jack, if word gets out about our plan to break the banks, the Irish vote will be the least of our problems.

- So we stick with the Irish option?

I see no reason why not.

- Of course, as far as Ireland is concerned, we can use a property boom as the catalyst for the financial meltdown and there is the added bonus that, if things go according to plan, the Irish will be in the Euro zone. That means that we could end up causing a lot of problems for the French and Germans.

I like the sound of that.

- I thought that would appeal to you, Sir. But what do you want to do about Iceland?

Well is there any reason not to go down that route as well?

- Not really, Sir, and in fact of course some preparatory work has already been done.

Well it would be a shame to waste all that effort, in which case let's go for both targets.

- Yes, Sir.

November

Jack, I see that Charlton Heston has finally made it as President.

- Yes, it has taken a while but I'm sure he's pleased.

And does he realise that the fact that he succeeded is down to us?

- Well we can't take all the credit but he was certainly grateful for the heads-up we gave him on the fact that the number of suicides was likely to increase.

Did he never enquire as to why we thought it was likely to happen?

- Well he did mention that he thought it had something to do with the fact that George Bush may become President. That's a depressing thought for many people and what's more he's assuming that if it actually happens there will be another surge in suicides. I believe that the NRA is stock piling recruitment posters so that they are ready for just such an eventuality.

And to think that he could have been President of the USA instead, and it could all have happened a long time ago.

- Sir, I'm sure he's happy with his decision.

No, I don't mean sad for him, I mean sad for us. We had eight years of Reagan!

- Hm, yes, I see your point. But while I'm here, is there anything else, Sir?

Yes, Jack, I think we need to revisit the problems that the Web is giving us. I understand that the pornography plan has been a limited success.

- It has, Sir. We estimate that 60% of the traffic on the Web is porn.

But that means that 40% isn't and that worries me.

- Me too, Sir.

So what do we do? I'm assuming that we can't close it down.

- I think that you're right there, Sir.

So can we put limitations on the system? You know; restrict what people can see?

- No, Sir, I don't think that's really feasible either.

So what's the answer?

- I'm not sure yet, but be assured, we are working on it.

And there's one other thing, Jack, regarding the revenue from the pornography. Where is it going?

- Into the defence budget, Sir.

So it's helping to fund STOP.

- That's the plan, Sir.

Good.

December

- Sir, regarding the World Wide Web, we think that we've come up with something.

I hope it's good.

- I think it is, Sir.

So what have you got?

- Well, Sir, the great thing about the Web is that it gives you access to a massive amount of data.

Yes I know that. I thought that was the problem.

- But it can also be the solution. We could add a whole lot of information of our own to the pool.

I don't think we want to do that Jack! We don't want people to know what we're up to.

- This won't be the real stuff; it'll be our version of the truth; margarine is better than butter; saturated fat is bad. You know, the usual bumf. We'll put a whole lot of duff information out there and then if anyone searches for anything related to STOP, they'll get our version.

But they'll get the other stuff as well, you know, the genuine research?

- Yes, we can't stop that, but if we put enough of our misinformation on the Web, it'll swamp the real stuff.

I hope that you're right.

- So do I, Sir.

And while we're on the subject, there is one other thing, Jack. Can I assume that Area 51 is connected to the Web?

- Yes, Sir.

So what is there to stop someone actually accessing our systems?

- Good question, Sir, and one that we have already thought of. The big problem with the Web is that everyone who uses it is by definition connected to it.

So anyone could access our STOP files?

- In theory yes, but not in practice. We have built a series of software defences that limit access to the system.

But what if someone breaches the defence?

- Then they'll have full access to the database.

But that sounds like a nightmare.

- Not really, Sir. The database in question is ALF which stands for Alien Life Found.

ALF? That sounds familiar.

- Yes, that's possible. It was the name of a TV program in the eighties.

Oh yes, I remember now. Wasn't it also about aliens? That's a bit of a co-incidence, isn't it? Which ALF came first, ours or theirs?

- Ours, Sir. We've had our database since 1975.

But why? The Web wasn't around then.

- We developed it in order to keep track of all the misinformation regarding UFOs that we have generated over time, after all if we are going to be credible we need to be consistent. In fact, that turned out to have been a handy decision to make since, when we needed a bogus front to our computer system, ALF came in useful. And of course its contents confirm the misinformation that we have made public.

So how come the TV program has the same name?

- We're pretty sure it's just a co-incidence, although it did give us a bit of a fright when we first heard about it. But then we thought that in order to come up with the name the program makers had just gone through the same process as we did. The acronym needs to start with "A", for alien. It then needs to be preferably three letters and it needs to be a cuddly name. ALF is the only one to fit the bill.

Well apart from the cuddly name bit, I guess it all sounds logical. So you're pretty sure that we're covered when it comes to protecting our systems at Area 51.

- Yes, Sir.

1999

January

Jack, I keep hearing about this Global Warming issue. Do we have a take on the situation?

- We have a team looking at that very subject as we speak. It seems like it's a hot topic right now.

Is that your first climate joke, Jack? In which case let's hope the rest are a bit better.

- I'll see what I can come up with, Sir.

But what are your team doing exactly? It looks like I'm going to need to make a policy statement on the matter in the near future, so there is some urgency here.

- We'll have something by the end of the month, Sir.

February

Jack, I'm receiving a lot of queries regarding Global Warming. Do you have anything I can use?

- Yes, Sir, we've completed our investigation and the first point I should make is to say that we need to refer to the issue as Climate Change.

But overall are things getting warmer or not?

- Yes, Sir, but that doesn't mean that everywhere on the globe will get warmer. Take the UK as an example. Currently they enjoy a relatively mild climate, certainly when compared to other places at the same latitude like Newfoundland, and this is thanks to the Gulf Stream. But climate change could result in the slowing down or even the disappearance of the Gulf Stream and if that happens the Brits could find themselves feeling very chilly indeed.

But why is that?

- Do you really want me to explain the scientific justification, Sir?

399

On second thoughts, no. Let's just assume that you're right; we're talking here about climate change, not global warming. So what's the deal?

- Well, Sir, at the start of our investigation we decided that there were four questions we needed to address, these being: Is climate change occurring? If so, is it man-made? And if so, is it a bad thing? And again, if so, is there anything we can do about it?

Well they seem to be very relevant questions, Jack. Shall we deal with the last one first? That way we could save ourselves a lot of time.

- How do you make that out, Sir?

Well because if the answer is that we can't do anything about it, the rest of the stuff is somewhat irrelevant.

- Well there probably isn't anything we can do about it, certainly not in the short term, but I hardly think that's the point, Sir. If someone at the next press conference stands up and asks you for your thoughts on Climate Change, you can hardly say that there's no point in worrying since there's nothing we can do about it.

But you just said there isn't!

- Yes, but you can't say that.

Well I suppose you're right. You'd better get me up to speed on the whole thing. Let's start with the first question; is Climate change taking place?

- Well that one was a bit of a no brainer since climate change is always taking place. It has done since the Earth was created. So let's say that the answer to number one is "probably". It's that second question that's a bit trickier.

You mean whether the change is man-made?

- Yes, Sir. But it's a difficult question to answer since we can't turn back the clock and compare the current situation with what would have happened if mankind had not developed as it has. So we can only look at the likelihood that the carbon dioxide that we are pumping into the atmosphere is having an effect.

And what's the answer?

- Probably, Sir. One significant clue is the rate of change. Things are warming up pretty quickly and it's unlikely that this is due solely to natural causes.

But it's not impossible.

- No, Sir, it's not impossible. It could be that climate change is a bit like a seesaw. Once you get past the tipping point the change could take place very quickly.

OK, now we get to the question that I'm not quite sure about. Given that we are possibly responsible for Climate Change, how can that not be a bad thing?

- Well that takes us back to the last question. Without the ability to rerun history we'll never know but it is possible that without our intervention the climate could have gotten a lot colder. Ice ages have occurred before and there's no reason why they shouldn't crop up again. By warming the planet we may have been doing ourselves a favour.

Well that could be the case if we were maintaining the equilibrium, by that I mean if temperatures were remaining stable, but they're not.

- But it's still the case, Sir, that it could have been worse.

OK, so that takes us to the last question, can we do anything about it? You say we can't, but surely there's something we can do.

- There may be some effect from the extra carbon dioxide but it can't account for all the change, we think that there's something else going on. It could just be part of the natural cycle of climate change or there could be something, as yet unidentified, that's affecting the situation.

But what if we were to reduce our output of carbon dioxide, wouldn't that help?

- For that to happen we'd need a degree of co-operation between nations that's just not going to happen, at least not for some time. And even if it does, unless we achieve our objectives regarding STOP, it's going to prove a waste of time.

Why do you say that?

- OK, let's imagine that we reduce overall carbon dioxide emissions by 30%. It would be a tall order but let's assume we can and it'll take

15-20 years. But when governments talk about what that would mean to the average person, they omit to mention that the population of the planet is still growing. Even by conservative estimates it will increase by 15-20 per cent over the same period, so individuals would have to reduce their carbon footprint by say 50-60 per cent. And that assumes that everyone on the planet continues with the same or lower standards of living but that's hardly likely to be the case in the Third World. Just look at the changes taking place in China.

So it all sounds pretty grim.

- Well, Sir, as far as STOP is concerned, the current situation may serve a purpose. The guys at Area 51 are suggesting that we hold back on any international agreement that does not address the need to reduce the population of the planet.

Well we're hardly likely to get any agreement on that matter any time soon.

- We realise that, Sir. We think that it'll take some major disasters caused by climate change to bring the various parties to the table. At that stage we'll stand some chance of agreement.

But in the meantime you say we're going to have to refuse to sign up for any international agreement on reducing CO_2.

- Yes, Sir.

And what excuse do we use?

- Well, Sir, you'll just have to say that you don't believe the science.

Suddenly "we" has changed to "me".

- I think if we're going to plead ignorance, Sir, then you'd be the person most likely to carry it off.

Thank you, Jack.

March

Jack, I see the MMR vaccine thing has been a success.

- Yes, Sir, the take up rates have fallen sharply. We only need them to drop a bit further and we'll have a big explosion in the number of cases of Mumps, Measles and Rubella. But there is another bonus.

What's that?

- Well, I said that we couldn't smear all vaccines with the same rumour, because they are all different.

Yes, I do remember that.

- Well I was wrong, Sir.

That's not something that happens very often. In fact I can't remember the last time.

- No, Sir, neither can I. But it turns out that there are some common ingredients in vaccines, something to do with how they are preserved. One of them is mercury.

Good grief, Jack, I thought mercury was supposed to be a pretty dangerous substance. Are we sure that vaccines are actually safe, after all I'd hate to think we've stopped people being vaccinated when in fact the jabs could have killed them.

- No, Sir, I don't think there is anything to worry about since it's not the same sort of mercury. But it does mean that we can start to cast doubts about other vaccines.

Ok, that's good news.

- By the way, Sir, I forgot to ask. How is your daughter?

In what respect, Jack.

- You know the veggie fad.

Oh that. Well it turned out to be more than a fad unfortunately. She's still off the red meat I'm afraid.

- Is that all?

No, not really. She's not quite a vegan, but it's not good. We're having to resort to the regular medical check-ups I'm afraid, although I have done one useful thing. I've persuaded her to change to a different brand of margarine.

- But why would you do that, Sir? They're all pretty bad.

Ah, but I've come across one that is high in omega-3. I bet you're impressed, Jack.

- Oh dear!

Now come on, Jack, I may not remember every little detail of STOP but I do remember that omega-3 is good for us. You explained that to me as part of your briefing on fish stocks. I seem to remember tuna featuring quite prominently.

- Well, Sir, that part you remember correctly.

So where have I gone wrong this time? Surely omega-3 is good for you.

- Well that depends, Sir.

Good grief, Jack. I can imagine that phrase being carved on your headstone.

- What phrase?

"It all depends…"

- But in this case, it does depend, Sir.

On what, Jack?

- On what sort of omega-3 you're talking about.

You've never before mentioned that there's more than one type.

- You never asked, Sir.

I shouldn't have to ask. You need to volunteer that sort of information in future.

- I'm sorry, Sir, I'll try to keep you better informed, but in the meantime let me explain. There are in fact ten omega-3 fatty acids.

Ten!

- I'm afraid so, Sir. The first one is alpha-linolenic acid.

What's the common name for this substance?

- That is the common name, Sir. The chemical name is "all-cis-9,12,15-octadecatrienoic acid". But if it makes it easier we'll refer to it as ALA. Then there's eicosapentaenoic acid or EPA, and docosahexaenoic acid, that's DHA. Do you want to know what their chemical names are, Sir?

I believe you're getting a bit cheeky here, Jack. Let's just cut to the nitty gritty.

- So you don't want the names of the other seven?

Jack!

- OK, Sir. As it happens, these three are the main ones we need to concern ourselves with. The first one, ALA, is the one that we've used in the margarine.

We've used?

- Why of course, Sir. Nothing happens to margarine that I don't know about.

No, I don't suppose there is, but let's just recap here. What is the stuff found in fish?

- That's EPA and DHA omega-3. These are made by algae which are in turn eaten by the fish and we're pretty sure that they are good at preventing heart disease.

Just heart disease? I thought that they were also good for a whole host of other things like brain function, cancer, immune system…

- Sir, let me stop you there. You really need to ignore any health advice you get off the TV or from the newspapers.

So you're saying that this list isn't real?

- I don't know, Sir, although it sounds convincing and that's why we spread such information. It gives people all the more reason to buy our super-improved margarine.

But the heart disease bit, that's real.

- As far as we are aware, yes, Sir.

And going back to the main issue, what's the omega-3 in margarine?

- That's the ALA version. It comes from plants which makes it much cheaper for manufacturers to produce. In fact in the main we haven't had to lean on the food manufactures to use ALA for that very reason.

So ALA is of no use.

- Not quite, Sir. The body can convert ALA to DHA but it's not a particularly efficient process.

So is the margarine with omega-3 better than margarine without?

- By a small margin, Sir, but you'd still be better off trying to get your daughter onto butter.

Yes, I know that Jack but that's proving difficult. Apparently people keep telling her how butter is bad.

- I wonder who that could be, Sir!

August

- Sir, I had a communication from the Indian government. It's about the farmers. Apparently the news has gotten out about the number of suicides. It seems that, even in a country as large as India, it's difficult to keep this sort of thing under wraps indefinitely.

So what's the problem?

- Well people are expecting the government to do something about it.

I hope they're not looking to ban our GM crops. That would be bad news indeed, although I was going to ask you about something that occurred to me after our previous discussion.

- And what was that, Sir?

Well presumably the Indians don't eat cotton.

- Not yet, Sir.

What do you mean, not yet?

- Well I believe that there is one company who is trying to genetically modify cotton so as to make it edible.

What, you mean that in the future, when I get fed up with my old t-shirt, instead of throwing it out I could just eat it?

- I'm not sure exactly how it will work, but that's by the by. What was your point, Sir?

My point, Jack, is that since the Indians aren't eating the cotton, why does it have our GM modification?

- Well, Sir, GM these days means genetically modified, not Gullibility Molecule. We had to make the change otherwise it would have been a bit of a give-away, wouldn't it?

I did wonder, Jack. I always assumed that to be effective you had to eat the crop. It suddenly occurred to me that perhaps it worked if you just wore it.

- Oh no, Sir. You can wear your t-shirt safe in the knowledge that it won't make you any more gullible than you already are. But if you do attempt to eat it, can I suggest that you wash it first.

Thank you, Jack. I feel very reassured. But regarding the Indians, if the government is not going to ban the GM stuff, what are they going to do?

- Well they aim to increase the value of the grants that the farmers can get to help them, plus there's going to be counselling for those that need it.

And overall, what effect will this have?

- I have it on good authority from the Indian government that these measures will have no effect on the rate of suicides of farmers.

Keep me informed if the situation changes.

- Yes, Sir.

2000

February

- Sir, our bottled tap water has been so successful that it's going to be introduced into the Canadian market.

That's good news, but we do need to spread the sales area to include Europe. The Brits are concerned that their population is becoming less gullible and they believe that it's something to do with the internet. People are becoming better informed.

- Well I think it may take a while to get production going in Europe. The British will have to come up with something in the short term.

And get onto them again about the GM stuff. I see that in the US there are plenty of GM foods around now, but what's the situation in Europe. They don't seem to be making any progress.

- It's still a stalemate, Sir. I'm not sure what else we can do.

Have you contacted Blair?

- Yes, Sir, he's very much onside, but his credibility with the British public is not too good. It's a bit of a vicious circle. We need the GM stuff to make them more gullible but until they start consuming it, they won't believe what the government tells them. But one consolation we have is that there is so much GM stuff in processed foods these days that it is virtually impossible that some of it doesn't get into the food chain in Europe. Unfortunately, it probably won't be enough for our purposes.

And Jack, I've been hearing some bits and pieces about the AIDS problem? Do you have anything to report?

- As far as the US is concerned there's not much happening that's new but regarding the situation in Africa, there are a couple of things that you should be aware of.

Good news I hope. I could do with some.

- Well it's certainly not bad news. The first concerns South Africa in particular. Apparently the President there has decided that HIV does not cause AIDS.

Really? So what does he think is the real cause?

- Poverty, Sir.

Which would explain why it's so common in Africa.

- Apparently so, Sir.

And how exactly did he come to this conclusion, Jack.

- I believe he is being advised by a number of experts.

And where did these experts come from, Jack? Do you know any of them?

- Well, Sir, I don't know all of them.

But you know some of them.

- Yes, Sir.

Why am I not surprised? And so what's the second thing?

- It's the fact that the Catholic Church does not condone the use of condoms to prevent the spread of AIDS. Of course this will be less significant if the President's opinions gain credence, but in the meantime anything that deters the use of condoms in Africa is to be welcomed.

And I suppose you had something to do with this as well, Jack.

- No, Sir, not at all, it was nothing to do with me. In view of our history concerning the Catholic Church I hardly think that they are likely to take any notice of me.

But this doesn't make sense. To some extent I can understand it when the Church says that they don't want people to use condoms for contraception. They think that they are saving lives, at least in the most basic form. But surely they must realise that using condoms to stop the spread of AIDS is also a way of saving lives?

- You'd think so but apparently that's not how their thought processes work.

You're assuming that they have actually gone through some sort of logical thought process but I can't see how that can be the case. I think it's pure dogma.

- You may well be right, Sir, but they have come up with a rationale.

They say that condoms don't work because the virus is smaller than the holes in the condom.

They think that there are holes in a condom? That can't be right.

- Well they're not visible to the naked eye. They are I believe referring to the space between the molecules.

And can this possibly be true?

- No, Sir, not as far as I am aware, but whatever the reasoning it's obviously good news for us.

I suppose so.

May

- Sir, I think we need to have a discussion about ALF.

You mean the alien contact database at Area 51?

- Yes, Sir.

What about it? Don't tell me someone has gained access to it.

- Yes, Sir, they have.

I thought you said originally that it was so secure that it was unlikely anyone would ever get through to it.

- I believe that I may have said that, but I wasn't 100 per cent sure, hence the second line of defence.

So do we know who it is?

- It's more like who they are, Sir.

There's been more than one person?

- Yes, Sir, there have been twenty three successful attempts.

Twenty Three! For goodness sake, Jack! How many unsuccessful attempts have there been.

- I'm not sure, Sir.

What? You don't monitor unsuccessful attempts?

- Oh no, Sir, of course we monitor them, it's just that there have been so many, we've sort of lost interest in counting them. However, if you need to know a precise figure I could always get one for you.

I don't need an exact figure, Jack, but can I assume that it's in the hundreds?

- You can, Sir, if you mean hundreds of thousands.

But how can that be? Surely there can't be that many people out there who know of the existence of our system?

- They don't know that it exists exactly; they're just trawling the Web looking for secure sites and then they attempt to access them just to find out what's behind the security.

But you're sure that no-one has got any further yet, you know, into the real stuff.

- Yes, Sir, at least for now, but I have to admit that we can't be certain that we will never have a successful breach of our system. What we need to do is to decide what procedures we have to put in place now so that when it happens, we're ready.

What have you got in mind?

- Well the most important thing would be to interrogate the hacker and find out what they know, that is what exactly did they see and do they understand it.

Well that shouldn't be too difficult, should it?

- It could be if the culprit lives outside the USA.

So these twenty three people who have got through the first line of defence, where do they come from.

- There are several from the USA and a couple from Russia, but mostly they're from the UK.

Why's that?

- I'm not sure. Overall we get attempts to access the system from all over the globe but those from the UK have a very high success rate. I suppose that since they invented the Web, they stand a better chance of understanding its intricacies.

Well it was only one man who came up with the Web in the first place. You don't suppose he slipped a little security loophole into the system, do you?

- There's no chance of that, Sir. The system is in the public domain so someone would have noticed by now.

Well although I don't like the sound of the Ruskies, I assume that there's not much we can do about them but as for the Brits, I don't see much of a problem there. The British authorities can question on our behalf anyone who gets through to the real stuff, can't they?

- Well that assumes that the Brits know all there is to know about STOP.

And they don't?

- Not by a long way, Sir. For instance, they don't know about the plan to break the banks so if we want to know what the hacker discovered we would have to personally get our hands on the guy.

Well we have an extradition treaty with the Brits. Surely we can use that, can't we?

- I believe so, but I'll check to make sure.

October

- Sir, we have a bit of a situation at Area 51. It appears that some of the inmates have escaped again.

What do you mean "escaped"?

- I mean exactly what I say.

Are they all held captive?

- Well of course. How else do you think we keep them working there?

But I thought that the staff had days off and vacations like everyone else.

- In the early days they did, Sir. But then we had a bit of shrinkage in terms of staff numbers.

What do you mean shrinkage?

- Some of those who went off on vacation never came back.

Well what happened to them?

- We tracked most of them down.

And?

- And they were either returned to Area 51 or not as the case may be.

The case may be what, Jack?

- Well put it this way, they won't be posing us any problems.

God, it's like getting blood from a stone. Do you mean that they are dead?

- In the main yes, Sir. Or they have disappeared, presumed dead.

And what about those who returned to work?

- Well they didn't exactly return to work. That would not have been appropriate. No, instead they have been used in some of our experimental projects.

You mean as guinea pigs?

- Yes, Sir.

So what happened in this instance?

- I'm not sure yet, but it was obviously an organised escape. It has happened before, for example the first time was in 1974. But in that instance, it was an opportunistic escape. This time I believe that it was a much more organised affair.

How many people were involved?

- About a dozen, as far as I can ascertain. They were all male.

Well, apart from the obvious, what was their motive? Is it anything to do with the fact that someone hacked into the ALF database?

- That we're not sure about but at this stage we can't rule it out. That's where things may get a bit tricky. These guys seem to be against the whole aim of STOP and I'm afraid they could cause some trouble.

How do we know that?

- We've found some material in their quarters that leads us to that conclusion.

How much do they know?

- Not a lot. Nobody at the site knows about the entire project. But they do know enough to realise that we don't have the best interests of the general public at heart, except of course in the broadest sense.

You mean the survival of the planet, or at least of mankind.

- Of course, Sir. They can only see the short term issues; they cannot see the bigger picture. And of course, we don't want them to.

Perhaps that's where we're going wrong.

- What do you mean, Sir?

Well perhaps we should go public with the whole STOP project. It would solve a lot of our problems.

- And give us a whole lot more. For instance, the religious groups wouldn't see the sense of what we are doing. Just look at the Catholics. Even though it's obvious to anyone with half a brain that the planet is over-populated, the Pope is still against contraception.

Is that his attitude just for Catholics or everybody?

- Good question, Sir, I'm not sure. But like all religions, they need a good supply of young recruits to keep the faith going. You don't see many non-Catholics taking up the faith, just like you don't see many people converting to the Muslim faith. In the main the big religions have to breed their recruits and while that's the case they'll never agree to population control. But we're getting off the point. We have a number of escapees at large and they could cause us a problem if we don't track them down.

Well you can use whatever resources you need to do so.

- Thank you, Sir.

November

What's the latest on the escapees from Area 51?

- No more news yet, Sir, but we've found some disturbing stuff on the computer of one of the men. As we thought, they're not planning to lie low; instead they're going to try something to disrupt the STOP project.

And can they do that?

- It depends on what they have in mind. I don't think they can stop us completely but they could cause us significant problems.

Why don't they just go public?

- Probably because they don't have the whole picture. In any case their main gripe seems to be that they have been locked up at AREA 51 for reasons that they don't understand.

Well what were they working on?

- Misinformation mainly.

Jack, the whole STOP project deals with misinformation. Try to be

414

more specific.

- UFOs, crop circles, that sort of thing. They were mainly tasked with protecting the Area 51 site itself. But a couple of them come from the group looking at vitamin D, sunlight and cancer, so they know that there are bigger issues at stake.

Well let's throw as much resource as we can at the problem. If we don't catch up with them soon, I suspect we'll regret it.

December

Jack, have we heard any more about the escapees from Area 51?

- No, Sir, we haven't. They seem to have disappeared without trace.

Isn't that a bit worrying?

- Well we've tried very hard to locate them. Our thinking is that they may have perished in the desert around Area 51.

But why do you assume that?

- Simply because we haven't come across any sign of them, not a whisper.

Well that could mean that they're just that bit smarter than us.

- That's always a possibility, Sir. In which case we could be in for a whole lot of trouble.

G W Bush

2001

January

- Sir, my name is Jack. Welcome to the White House.

Thank you, Jack. It's good to be back.

- Of course, Sir, you have been here before.

Just a few times, Jack! But now I'm here in my own right and as a result of my own endeavours!

- Er, not quite, Sir.

What do you mean?

- Let me brief you on STOP and I think all will become clear.

30 Minutes Later

Hold on, Jack, this is a lot to take in. Can we continue tomorrow?

- Well you need to know the full history of STOP. There are some issues outstanding that need your attention.

Tomorrow, Jack.

- Yes, Sir.

3 Months Later

So that's all there is to it, Jack?

- That's everything, Sir, broken down into 30 minutes chunks.

A bit like a soap opera!

- Exactly so, Sir.

Although it's a bit disappointing to discover that my success was not entirely down to my own efforts. In fact, it appears that I have you to thank. If it wasn't for the way you fixed things in Florida, things could have been a whole lot different.

- Well, the fact that your brother is governor of the state was also a factor. Things would have been a whole lot trickier in, say, Vermont. And in fact, this takes me onto one of the most important decisions you need to make.

What's that?

- Your successor, Sir. As part of the agreement with the Clintons, you need to nominate your successor during your first year in office. Have you given it any thought?

Hardly, Jack, I've only just found out about this dynasty business.

- Of course, Sir, but if you can give it some consideration over the next few weeks, I'd be grateful.

Of course, Jack.

Next Day

Jack, I've thought about a successor and there's really only one option.

- You mean your brother Jeb.

Yes. How did you know?

- Well you're not spoilt for choice, Sir, and after he fixed things in Florida it would be hard to choose someone else.

You don't sound too keen, Jack. Do you have a problem with my choice of Jeb?

- It's not for me to have a problem, Sir, but I think it could be an issue with some Democrats. They are pretty sore about what happened during the election.

But they must have realised it was my turn.

- Sir, it's not the whole Democratic Party that's in on this arrangement, just a select few. Just like it's not the whole Republican Party who knows. For instance, you didn't know about it until you had been elected.

That's true, Jack. Which begs the question, how is it done?

- You don't need to know that, Sir. You just need to know that it can be done, but it still needs some co-operation from within the respective parties. And that's where we may have a problem, but then I'm only guessing at this stage. I'll tell the Democrats about Jeb and we'll take it from there.

Let me know what they say.

- Yes, Sir.

Later

- Sir, as expected, the Democrats are not happy about Jeb. They intend to end the agreement.

Can they do that, Jack?

- Of course, Sir.

When?

- They are committed to letting you have a second term, so for you the news is good; for your brother, not so good.

And there's no chance we can get them to change their mind?

- I don't think so, Sir. They appear to want change.

What sort of change?

- Well they think that there have been too many middle class, middle aged, white, male presidents. They want someone different.

Well Hilary Clinton would have broken the mould. After all, she's a woman.

- But she's still middle class, middle aged and white.

So what could be better than her?

- Apparently, that would be someone who's young and black, Sir.

!!!!!

September

- Sir, there seems to be trouble brewing between England and Germany.

Thank goodness, Jack, it's about time we had another big war.

- Er, although it's serious, it's not quite that serious. It involves football.

I didn't realise that the Germans played football.

(And so on)

So the agreement was that Germany should win all future matches between the teams.

- That's right, however the English team are getting a bit fed up with this arrangement so in the most recent match they decided to ambush the Germans. They let them score a soft early goal and the

Germans thought that everything was going to plan. As a result England caught the Germans unaware and the result was a 5-1 victory. The Germans are livid and they want to know what we are going to do about it.

Well what can we do? The World Cup final was played more than 40 years ago. Surely the Germans realise that they've had a good run for their money.

- That's my reaction too, Sir.

Good, get onto the Germans and tell them that in future they'll have to win their games against England on merit.

- Wouldn't you prefer to do that yourself, Sir?

Not really, Jack.

September 11th

Ah, Jack. Thank goodness I've got through to you. I gather a plane has hit the World Trade Centre. What's the latest?

- Not good, Sir. The plane hit the north tower of the World Trade Centre about 45 minutes ago and now a second one has hit the south tower. These obviously aren't accidents, the place is under attack.

What sort of planes are they?

- Commercial airlines, Sir. Boeing passenger jets. I don't know exactly what type but we know that they were both hijacked sometime after take-off. And news is coming through of two others so there's more to come.

Has the Air Force been alerted?

- Yes but it will take time for them to get airborne. It's doubtful whether they will catch up with the planes.

Where are the hijacked planes right now?

- We're not sure, Sir. The hijackers have switched off the transponders so we're having trouble tracking them.

Well we need to find them fast before they do any more damage.

- I realise that, Sir. I'll call you if I get any further information.

Minutes Later

- Sir, they've hit another building.

Which one this time?

- The Pentagon.

Good grief, have they done much damage?

- We're not sure yet. From the TV pictures, it may not be too bad. Most of the building seems to be intact.

And what about the fourth plane? Any news of that yet?

- Not yet, Sir.

How about the hijackers? Do we know who they are yet?

- No, Sir, but I can probably guess.

You mean our escapees from Area 51?

- That'd be my guess, in which case we have a bit of a problem.

That must be the understatement of the century. If this gets out the whole STOP project will be down the drain.

- I realise that, Sir, which is why we need to come up with a cover story pretty damned quick.

We need someone to blame, but I don't suppose that's going to be too difficult to arrange.

- Shall we choose the usual suspects?

Well it can't be the Libyans again, can it? They took the rap for Pan Am 103. So it'll have to be another bunch of Arabs.

- I'll set the wheels in motion, Sir.

Good. I'll make my way back to Washington. I'll meet you back at the White House.

- If there's anything left of it, Sir.

What do you mean, Jack?

- Well there's still one plane unaccounted for and if you were going to fly a plane into another building, which one would you choose?

I'd choose the United Nations, Jack.

- OK, I can see where you're coming from, Sir, but let's imagine you're a hijacker and you're a bit pissed off with the US government. Now which one would you choose?

OK, Jack. I get the picture. I'll wait until the fourth plane is accounted for.

- I think that would be best, Sir.

A Bit Later

- Sir, the twin towers have collapsed.

I know, Jack. I've been watching the TV pictures. What's the situation regarding our staff in Area 52?

- I'm not sure yet, Sir. As you can imagine, things are pretty chaotic. But at least the south tower was the second one to be hit. I gather that, after the first plane hit the north tower, instructions were given to evacuate the south tower. I'm hoping that many of our people got out before the second plane hit, or at least they got down below the impact point.

And are you assuming that the World Trade Centre was targeted deliberately due to Area 52?

- Well we can't be certain at this stage but if the perpetrators are indeed our escapees, then it would be too much of a coincidence.

In which case I think we have a security issue. How would these people have known about the location of Area 52? Was its existence widely known at Area 51?

- Well, Sir, when we asked for volunteers to move to a new location, I believe that New York was mentioned, but not the specific location.

In which case these guys have either obtained more detailed information from somewhere or it's a lucky guess.

- Bear in mind they also went for the Pentagon. Was that just an obvious target or did they know that some of the STOP staff are also based there?

Well before we start making any guesses let's establish that these hijackers really are our guys.

- Yes, Sir.

Later

- Sir, the fourth plane has come down.

Has it hit the White House?

- No, Sir. It came down in a field in Pennsylvania.

Did the Air Force bring it down?

- No, apparently not, Sir. We think it may have been the passengers who resisted the hijackers and caused the plane to crash.

Well whatever it was, I assume it's safe to return to Washington.

- Yes, Sir.

And do we have any more information about the hijackers?

- Not yet, Sir. The crash sites at the World Trade Centre and the Pentagon are just one big mess so in the short term it'll be difficult to find anything conclusive. We'll stand a better chance at the other site in Pennsylvania.

But then we already know who's responsible, don't we?

- Well we're 99% sure, but it pays to be certain. In any case, we've got to start planting evidence. We thought we'd choose Al-Qaeda as the fall guys since that way it'll give us more flexibility when we choose a target for retaliation. We could choose any one of the Arab countries.

Good idea. It won't be too difficult to convince the American people of the need to go to war this time.

- We'll see, Sir. But there is one other issue you need to be aware of. We appear to have a problem with some of our military computer systems. Someone has hacked into the systems and made them inoperable.

By someone, do you mean one of our escapees?

- We're not sure yet, but it has made it more difficult to track and deal with them.

Well you'd better find out who this person is, and quick.

- Yes, Sir.

The Following Day

- Sir, we've found evidence at the crash site in Pennsylvania that definitely points to the escapees from Area 51.

Well that comes as no surprise, but I see from the news that Al-Qaeda is being blamed so I assume that so far our plan has been successful.

- So far, Sir, yes.

424

So we'd better start planning for the retaliation. What are the likely targets?

- Afghanistan is the obvious one. That's where Al-Qaeda has been training their men, with of course the support of the Taliban.

Yes, but that's not a good place to send our troops. Look what happened to the Russians when they invaded Afghanistan. They had to leave with their tails between their legs.

- Sir, I'm confident that with our superior military strength and financial muscle, we won't suffer the same fate. I reckon we can be in and out in 6 months.

Well I hope you're right.

- I've every confidence, Sir.

But what about other targets? How about Iraq?

- There aren't any particularly strong Al-Qaeda links to Iraq. There are plenty of other states in that region who are more justifiable targets.

Like who.

- Saudi Arabia.

Oh yes, right. I can just imagine attacking the Saudis. The oil tap would be switched off before you could say "Fill her up with unleaded". No, they're out of the question. I favour the Iraqis.

- This wouldn't have anything to do with unfinished business, would it, Sir?

What do you mean?

- I seem to remember that your father had a spot of bother with Saddam Hussein during his tenure.

What do you mean "seem to remember". From what he tells me, you were responsible for advising him not to chase the retreating Iraqis after they invaded Kuwait. If we had followed them, I don't think that Saddam would be in a position to taunt us now.

- I'm not sure that I can remember the exact details, Sir, but I think it was something to do with the fact that we wanted to leave him weakened but still active in the region. In any case, we didn't have an exit strategy.

Again, what do you mean?

- It would have been the same then as it is now. Let's assume that we crush the Iraqi army and enter Bagdad. What then?

We'll give the Iraqis their freedom and they can enjoy all the benefits of a democratic system.

- Really!

Well, whatever you think, Saddam must be the favourite now. Iraq is the only country in the region which we could attack without fearing a backlash from the other countries in the region. They all either fear him or hate him.

- Or both.

Yes, or both.

- But we still need a solid reason to attack Iraq.

Yes Jack, I realise that.

- And, Sir?

And, Jack, I think that you should go and find one.

- Yes, Sir.

In the meantime, let's get moving on Afghanistan.

- Right away, Sir.

And bear in mind that we need to decide what to do with the survivors from Area 52. How many were there?

- Almost all the staff got out, Sir. Of course they got the warning to evacuate the building before any of the other occupants. As for what we are going to do with them, that doesn't seem to be a problem.

What do you mean? Where are they?

- Most of them are now at Area 51.

How did you manage to persuade them to go there?

- It wasn't difficult, Sir. After 9/11, most of them reckon that Area 51 is the safest place to be.

And when you say "most" are at Area 51?

- There was a bit of wastage on the way, Sir. And we have some sort of good news regarding the hacker. It appears that the culprit resides in the UK, so it's unlikely to have anything to do with our guys from

Area 51.

Even so, his actions may have helped their cause. Is there any way we can stop him doing further damage, just in case? Speak to the Brits about it.

- Yes, Sir.

October

- Sir, it appears that we may have a problem regarding our hacker. You know, the one who caused all the computer problems on 9/11. In fact, we have two problems. The first and most significant one is that he may have gained some sort of access to the core system at Area 51.

Good grief, Jack, I thought you said we had a secure system.

- We do, Sir, but this guy is good. He didn't gain access direct from the outside; we think he came in through one of our own systems, like a sort of back door. We need to talk to him urgently, in which case we need to sort out a little issue that we appear to have with the extradition treaty. That's the second problem. I've taken legal advice and it seems that we are going to have a bit of a job extraditing our hacker.

How much of a job?

- Well we're not going to be able to get our hands on him.

Why is that?

- It's because we have to prove to the British courts that we have prima facie evidence against the person in question. In fact of course, we don't want him in order to prosecute him. We just need to question him, but we can't tell the British about that.

So what do we do?

- We'll have to get them to change the treaty so that the criteria for extradition are less onerous.

Will they do that?

- Well they should, since the treaty is already one-sided in their favour. We have a bigger burden of proof than they do if they want one of our guys.

OK, get in touch and see what they say.

- Yes, Sir.

November

I see the Afghan war is going well.

- If you mean that our troops have taken Kabul without much resistance, then you're right, Sir. But this sort of easy victory could spell trouble in the longer term. And of course the body count isn't too good.

Yes, I know what you mean. The Taliban are just retreating to the hills so that they can regroup and fight another day.

- I'm afraid so, Sir.

And where do we stand on Iraq?

- That's going to be a bit trickier, Sir. We need a good reason to invade, otherwise the other countries in the area are going to be more than a bit upset. And the same applies to other countries around the world. Unfortunately, we're going to have to go through the motions as far as diplomacy is concerned.

Oh no, you don't mean the United Nations!

- I'm afraid so. We need to come up with a convincing argument.

And what will that entail?

- I'm not sure yet, Sir.

2002

March

Jack, how's the introduction of the meat substitute product going in the US?

- Do you mean the one based on fungus or the soy based product?

Let's start with the fungus.

- Well in that case, not so good, Sir. We've had a bit of a problem with the marketing strategy.

Why's that?

- We've been advertising it as being "mushroom based".

Ah, that, Jack, was perhaps a step too far.

- Indeed, Sir. The American Mushroom Institute has complained to the trading standards watch-dogs in both the US and in Europe. Not only that, some vegetarians are against the product since it's made using eggs.

Why is that?

- As a binding agent, Sir, I believe. But whatever the reason, the vegetarians weren't happy.

So what's happened?

- The mushroom link has been dropped, and the veggies have agreed to a compromise. The eggs can be used, so long as they're free range.

So the hens are happy, the veggies are happy. Everyone's happy, Jack.

- Not quite, Sir. Apparently, nearly 5% of the people who eat the product report an adverse reaction. So presumably they're not happy.

But that was the whole point of the exercise, wasn't it.

- Yes, it was, Sir.

Which means that we're particularly happy!

- I guess it does, Sir, although I dare say we'd be happier if the figure was 10%.

And the soy based product? Where do we stand there?

- As far as soy is concerned, we're forging ahead on all fronts.

That's great news, Jack.

April

Jack, I've been thinking about our efforts regarding the banks. Presumably, if things go according to plan, the stock market is going to take a bit of a hit.

- I think it's fair to say that it's not going to be a good time to be in stocks and shares. I assume that you've taken the necessary precautions, Sir.

As far as I am aware, yes I have. But there's one area that I'm particularly concerned about and that relates to my pension.

- What's your concern, Sir?

Well, Jack, my concern is that, if everything goes belly up, will I still have one?

- I think you should be OK, but I could check up for you if you wish.

I think I'm looking for reassurance that amounts to a bit more than "I think you should be OK".

- I'll get back to you as soon as I can.

So that'll be this afternoon, Jack.

- Absolutely, Sir.

Later That Day

- Sir, I've checked your pension arrangements and I can confirm that you are on a final salary scheme.

Which means what?

- It means that the pension you will receive is guaranteed and therefore not subject to the vagaries of the stock market.

Thank goodness, although I should perhaps have thought about this before, when I first became aware of the plan. And what about you, Jack?

- What about me, Sir?

Are your pension arrangements secure?

- Yes, Sir, I believe so. I took the precaution of checking before we launched the plan to break the banks. I thought it wise.

And you didn't think to mention it to me?

- Well I knew that you had a lot on your mind at the time. I didn't want to worry you.

Well thanks for that Jack. It's good to know that you are always looking after my best interests.

- It's no trouble, Sir.

June

Jack, I can't help but think that project STOP is running out of steam. Where do we stand with the main aims of the plan?

- Like what, Sir?

Well let's start with the population of the world. When did the STOP project start?

- Well it really got under way in 1950, Sir. Before that the only weapon in our armoury, so as to speak, was to instigate World Wars at a regular frequency.

OK, so what was the population at that time?

- I'm not sure, Sir, but I can find out. Can I ask, what is the reason for you wanting to know?

Well if the aim of the project is to stabilise and ultimately reduce the population of the planet it may be useful to know how well we are doing. I think that with any large project like this we should set objectives at the start and periodically measure our progress.

- Sir, is this going to be some sort of personal performance review?

Well I wouldn't call it that exactly Jack. Let's just say I'm curious to see how we're doing.

- I'll have the information for you by tomorrow, Sir.

Thank you, Jack.

Two Weeks Later

Jack, do you remember a few weeks ago I asked you for some data on population. I expected a response before now.

- Sir, I have that information, it's just taken a bit longer than expected to gather all the facts.

Jack, when I asked you come up with a figure for the world's population, I didn't expect you to go round and count them all personally, one by one. What took you so long?

- Well it was all the additional information that took a while to determine.

But I didn't ask for any additional info.

- Not at the time, Sir, but I think you will. There are bound to be supplementary questions.

Why's that?

- Well let's start with the figures you asked for. In 1950 at the start of project STOP the total population of the World was around 2.5 billion. The latest figures we have which are for the year 2000 when it was estimated that the population had grown to more than 6 billion.

So let's see if I can summarise. The world's population has more than doubled since the project started.

- Yes, Sir.

Why is that, Jack?

- And there's the first supplementary request for information. Of course that one involves an answer that's at bit more complicated than the first.

Well let's try to keep it simple shall we.

- Well, Sir, put simply, some countries haven't been pulling their weight.

Can you be more specific?

- I certainly can. In fact it comes down to areas really. The main culprits are Africa, Asia and to some extent South America.

And is there a common factor between these areas?

- There is one main thing that links them all and that's poverty.

And whose fault is that, Jack.

- Well I don't think this is the time to start pointing the finger, Sir.

Oh go on, Jack. We must be able to point the finger at someone.

- Well if you insist, there's always Bob Geldof.

The name rings a bell. Remind me who he is.

- He's the Irish guy who wanted to feed the world in the 80's.

And did he succeed?

- Unfortunately he kept them alive long enough to cause a problem. I recall a TV program recently where a chap in Ethiopia was being interviewed. He was a youngster when Band Aid was raising all that money. It was the food aid that kept him alive.

And what has he been doing in the meantime?

- Well what would you do if you were living in a scorching hot desert and you have no job?

Well I'd probably watch a bit of TV.

- They don't have TV's, Sir.

Well then I'd perhaps surf the Web.

- Sir, they have neither TV's nor computers.

Are you sure?

- Well whether I'm sure or not is pretty academic since they don't have electricity.

Well how do they run their air conditioning if they don't have electricity?

- They don't have air con, Sir.

Well alright, how do they power their ceiling fans?

- Sir, your idea of what constitutes poverty seems to be a bit off the mark. Apart from the fact that they don't have electricity, the reason why they don't have ceiling fans is partly because in fact most of them don't have ceilings. So in that situation, with no job, no electricity and no money, what would you do to pass the time?

Jack, I have a feeling that the answer isn't Sudoku is it?

- No, Sir, that would require a copy of a book or a daily newspaper, and a pen. No, it's something that everyone is equipped to do at all times without any special equipment.

I-Spy?

- Oh for goodness sake. It's sex, Sir! That's what they have been doing! Having sex! That chap who survived due to Geldof's largesse has now sired ten children. The situation is untenable.

Well should we prosecute him?

- What? You mean the chap with the ten kids? I hardly think that will help.

No, I mean this Geldof chap. It seems to me that he's got a lot to answer for. This plan of his to feed the World, he obviously never thought it all through.

- Well I think that we all need to accept some responsibility for the mess that we find ourselves in, although I agree that Geldof should probably be at the front of the queue. But there are a number of things that have contributed to this situation. As far as STOP is concerned we didn't take much notice of the Third World. We thought that poverty and a regular supply of guns would take care of the situation. The trouble is that it didn't take care of them quick enough, hence their numbers have increased. Instead of keeping them poor perhaps we need to make them more prosperous.

What, so that they have better things to do than have sex?

- Well put crudely, Sir, yes. But it's not just the fact that they have nothing better to do. From their point of view it's also an investment. There's no social security system in most of these places so the only way you are going to survive as you get older is if you have children who can look after you. However, since child mortality rates are so high you can't just have two kids and know that you're covered, you have to have a lot more and hope that enough of them survive.

So even if we gave them all a pen, a Sudoku book and a comfy armchair we're still not covering all the bases.

- No, Sir.

So what are we going to do?

- We do need a bit more time to come up with a detailed plan, Sir.

Well get back to me when you have something. How long is it likely to take?

- That depends on what you want, Sir. We have been working for some time on a complete appraisal of STOP, you know, what works and what doesn't. It may be a good idea to wait until that work is completed before we review the situation.

OK, Jack, but don't leave it too long. In the meantime can't we find anything that can keep these people in Africa entertained?

- Without electricity I'm not sure what we can do, Sir.

December

Jack, what's this I hear about the Iraqis and Weapons of Mass Destruction. It all sounds pretty serious.

- I'm glad to hear you say that, Sir.

What do you mean you're glad? It sounds like a very dangerous situation.

- It would be if it were true, Sir.

Are you saying it's not true? But I've seen the dossier and there are photos of military installations where biological weapons are being stored. Is there something you need to tell me?

- These dossiers are part of the plan to get the UN on-side for a war against Iraq.

But what about the pictures?

- Which ones in particular?

Well for instance this one here. It's a nuclear weapon storage facility outside Bagdad.

- Er, no, Sir. That's in fact a hen house on a farm near Decatur in Alabama. But I can see why you would be confused. One tin roofed building looks much like another.

Why wasn't I informed about this sooner?

- I thought it best to keep quiet until the plan was well under way. You know, just in case things got a bit tricky. It would be beneficial if you could say that it was all done without your knowledge. You'd be in the clear.

I like the sound of that.

- I thought you would, Sir.

So there's nothing for me to worry about?

- Not as far as these dossiers are concerned, since they seem to have been credible enough so far. If things go to plan, we should be able to start the military action within a couple of months.

And what will happen when people find out it's all a con, that there are no such weapons? We'll need a fall guy.

- I think Mr Blair is lined up for that role, Sir.

Good, it looks like you've got all the bases covered.

- Yes, Sir, I hope so.

2003

January

- Sir, I think we may have an issue regarding the Olympic Games.

Oh no, don't tell me the Scots want to win the most medals!

- No, for once it's not the Scots.

Then it must be the French.

- You're correct, Sir.

So what is it? Do they want to come top of the medals table?

- Well if they do, they'd hardly come to us for help. No, it's even worse. They want to host the 2012 event.

And do we have a problem with that?

- Well I think we do. Just remember how insufferable they were after they got Disney World. We thought it would shut them up for a while and bring them over to our side. But oh no, they're even worse now. If they did somehow manage to get the Olympics, it would be a nightmare.

So what can we do to stop it? I assume that we'll have to put up a city of our own.

- I believe that New York is already planning to do that, Sir, but I have two main issues. The first is that, having hosted the event twice in recent years, I can't imagine that we'll get it again. But secondly, and more importantly, the planned financial meltdown is due to hit at about the time that someone is going to have to lay out a lot of money on this event. I don't think that we want to be involved just as the banks go belly up.

So what do we do?

- Well the next best option would be the British. We could encourage London to get into the bidding.

But they'll have the same attitude as us. They won't want to risk such a high cost event around the time the banks go belly up.

- But they don't know about that little project, do they? Or at least I assume that they don't. I hope you haven't forgotten and spilled the beans, Sir.

No, I haven't done anything like that, Jack, there's no need to worry on that score. I'd just forgotten for the moment. But even assuming that the Brits bid for the games, how can we make sure that they win, or at least beat off the French challenge?

- I think that can be arranged, Sir.

Really?

- How do you think we got the Olympics twice in twelve years? No, Sir, you needn't worry, we should be able to get the matter sorted.

OK, get in touch with the British and see what their reaction is.

- Yes, Sir.

And make sure that you get their buy in before New York declares its hand. We don't want them frightened off.

- Yes, Sir.

I don't suppose we can persuade New York to drop the idea, can we?

- Not at this stage. I think the Governor has his sights on re-election.

February

- Sir, the allies are mostly onside regarding the invasion of Iraq, except of course the French.

We need to do something to try and bring them into line. Do you have any ideas, Jack?

- Well short of invading I'm not sure what we can do.

And would the Brits be on board with that?

- I'll ask them, Sir.

Next Day

- Sir, I've spoken to the British regarding a potential invasion of France and they are not keen on the idea, at least not at this stage. They say they would prefer to continue with their current plan.

Which is what?

- To take over France bit by bit, property by property.

You mean that they're operating some sort of guerrilla war?

- Oh no, Sir, nothing like that. The Brits are just buying up properties.

Buying up properties? How many?

- To date they reckon about half a million.

Half a million! Well what's going to happen when the French find out? They're not going to be best pleased.

- The French already know and are more than happy. In fact they encourage it since the Brits are restoring rural France at their own expense, something the French themselves have neither the inclination nor the money to do.

Well what's going to happen when the Brits finish the job?

- Sir, have you seen the state of rural France? I don't think it's anything we need to worry about for a very long time.

And what do the Brits get out of it? It seems like a bit of an expensive one way street.

- Well in fact there seems to be a significant exchange of people going on. The Brits send their old people to France to renovate the place and die and in return France sends its young people to England to work.

OK, so if an invasion is out, we need to come up with something else that'll put the French in their place.

- I'll see what we can come up with, Sir.

March

I see the Iraqi war is going well, except for one thing.

- Bodies, Sir?

Exactly, Jack. There's not much point in waging a war if the enemy just gives up and runs away. Where are the bodies going to come from? I look back on the wars like Korea and Vietnam with a certain fondness in that respect.

- I know, Sir. It seems to be more difficult these days but if the enemy won't stand up and fight there's not a lot we can do, is there.

And I suppose carpet bombing of civilian areas is out of the question?

- I think so, Sir, don't you? In the old days, those sorts of things could be kept quiet, but with live TV being beamed by satellite into the homes of US citizens, we have to be a lot more devious these days.

It seems the war option is not much use to us these days. In terms of body count, it's a good job that we have other things up our sleeve.

- Like margarine?

Yes, Jack, like margarine!

- Also, Sir, I've spoken to Blair and he seems very receptive to the idea of London bidding for the Olympics.

Good. I trust that he made no mention of Scotland winning the most medals?

- No, Sir, but bear in mind that the British enter a single team for the Olympics. It's the World Cup where they have separate teams.

World Cup? I didn't realise that the Brits played baseball........

April

Jack, I just received the news that the man who came up with the Atkins diet has passed away.

- Yes, I believe that's the case.

Well what are we going to do?

- Do you mean that you want to send a wreath, Sir?

No, Jack, that's not what I mean at all. I'm suggesting that we use the event to our advantage.

- Did you have anything particular in mind?

Not specifically, but can't we somehow blame the Atkins Diet for his demise?

- He fell over in the snow and hit his head. Are you suggesting that we blame the fall on the diet?

I'm sure that you could come up with something, Jack. For example, we could suggest that he was so overweight that he just toppled over. Or maybe he had a heart attack and just keeled over.

- Well whatever we say, the doctors who treated him will know what really happened, Sir.

Well the truth has never stopped you before, Jack. Are you by any chance getting soft in your old age?

- Not at all, Sir. I'll get onto it right away.

Thank you, Jack.

May

Freedom Fries! Is that the best you can come up with, Jack! Freedom Fries! That's certainly going to get the French quaking in their boots!

- Don't forget the toast, Sir.

Toast? What's toast got to do with it?

- Freedom Fries and Freedom Toast. They're already on the menu in government run restaurants.

Jack, it's pathetic and don't try to suggest otherwise. When I asked you to put the French in their place, I was expecting a bit more than this.

- I know, Sir, but we have a lot of people off on vacation and of those that are left most are involved in the Iraq war. And then there's the bout of Summer Flu that's gone through the workers at Area 51.

Summer Flu? I've never heard of Summer Flu. In any case it's spring not summer.

- Sir, in Nevada it can be whatever season we want it to be. And you may not have heard of Summer Flu as yet but you will, Sir, in due course. Anyway, the point is that we were a bit stretched when it came to resources.

Well I guess someone needs to provide support for our troops.

- Er, they're not exactly doing that, Sir. They're busy inventing the background to support our dossier on the weapons of mass destruction. If it's going to be convincing it's going to take a lot of man power.

Even so, Jack. Freedom Fries! When I spoke to the French Ambassador he seemed to think the whole thing was a bit sad and I have to say, I tend to agree with him.

- Sorry, Sir.

I should think so. However, on a more positive front Jack, I see you've been at work on the Atkins diet man. I've read a couple of different accounts of why he died, one suggesting some sort of heart problem and the other the fact that he was significantly overweight.

- Well I thought that we'd try a two pronged attack on the basis that it's better to be safe than sorry.

Too true, Jack. At least it looks like you got that one right.

Later That Month

Jack, what's this I hear about the BBC suggesting that there may be some doubt about the existence of Weapons of Mass Destruction in Iraq.

- Luckily for us, Sir, that's not quite what they said.

Really? What did they in fact say?

- They said the suggestion that such weapons could be deployed within 45 minutes was somewhat dubious.

And is it?

- Well strictly speaking it is dubious since, if you remember, Sir, there are no Weapons of Mass Destruction. It would have been much more serious if they'd made that allegation.

None the less, how did they have the nerve to make such a statement?

- The Brit's can't be certain, Sir, but they think that the journalist was briefed by someone at the Ministry of Defence.

Well wherever the information came from, they'd better make sure that it doesn't happen again. And while they're at it, can't they do something about the BBC? The last thing we need right now is someone broadcasting the truth about the Iraq war.

- I understand, Sir.

July

- Sir, I've spoken to the Brits about the extradition treaty and they say that, if we want their co-operation, then they want something in return.

Oh dear, what is it?

- They want us to fix it so that they host the 2012 Olympics.

But we already have plans for them to do that, don't we?

- Yes, Sir, you know that and I know that, but they don't. Since New York has also put in a bid they could reasonably assume that we are in competition with them.

And is that all they want?

- I believe so, Sir. After all, they were a bit peeved that, having agreed to put in a bid to beat the French, we also entered the fray. They assume that if we give them the games, it'll be a big deal for us.

In that case let's get a little something extra out of the deal. Why not make sure that the extradition treaty isn't just equitable, but a little bit slanted in our favour.

- I think we can manage that, Sir.

Anything else?

- Just one thing. I believe that the Brits have taken care of the situation regarding the leak of information concerning Weapons of Mass Destruction.

Really? What did they do?

- They didn't reveal all the details but they assured me that it won't happen again, at least not from the same source.

And the BBC?

- It appears that the British government is only too willing to bring them down a peg or two. It's the sort of thing that you can do when the broadcaster is state funded.

So we couldn't use the same tactics with Fox News?

- If only, Sir.

August

- Sir, the European committee on chocolate has reported back. There seems to be some agreement at last.

Good grief, is that matter still unresolved?

- It was, Sir, but not anymore.

And what have they come up with?

- The main proposal is that milk chocolate that contains a lot of milk will in future be called "Family Milk Chocolate".

That sounds like radical stuff. What about the vegetable fat?

- The manufactures are going to have to print a message on the packaging of chocolate that contains vegetable fat.

What will the message say?

- The message will read "Contains Vegetable Fat".

And it took them how long to come up with that?

- 27 years, Sir.

Sometimes, Jack, the wheels of progress can move very slowly. Let's hope that's the last we've heard of the chocolate problem.

- What about a chocolate opportunity, Sir?

Is it Hershey bar time already?

- No, Sir, not quite. Instead we've had a request from the main players in the business. They want to put our Trans Fats into chocolate.

What, instead of the vegetable fat?

- No, instead of chocolate, or should I say instead of some of the chocolate. Unfortunately I feel that we are going to have to leave a trace of the real stuff in the mix.

Otherwise we couldn't call it chocolate?

- Exactly, Sir.

OK, go ahead, but make sure that we get in a stock of Hershey bars before they mess with it.

- Yes, Sir.

October

- Sir, we may have come up with an idea regarding the body count in Iraq.

You mean our need to increase it?

- Yes, Sir.

OK how much do you want?

- With respect to what, Sir?

Money, Jack. Whatever this plan is it's bound to involve an increase in defence spending.

- Well not in this case, Sir, since the plan is to get the Iraqis to kill one another.

Ah, so it'll be an increase in health costs.

- Health costs, Sir?

Well I assume that we're going to put all the Iraqis on Statins. That way, when their cholesterol goes down, they'll start killing either themselves or one another.

- Sir, I think we need to put this low cholesterol/suicide business into context. It doesn't affect people in the numbers that we would require in this instance. Just forget the idea that Statins are always the answer.

OK, Jack, in which case what have you come up with?

- Well we don't think we're going to have to do too much at all. We'll rely on the religious conflict within the country to do the job for us.

Well that's not going to be much of a contest. The Christians will be wiped out in no time.

- No, this won't involve the Christians.

Well I hope it's not the Jews. Come election time I may need their votes.

- No, Sir, the Jewish vote is safe although I'm not sure that there are that many Jews in Iraq. In any case this plan involves only the Muslims in Iraq and if everything goes according to plan they'll be killing one another by the bucket load.

I can't see why they'd do that. Are you sure about this?

- Pretty sure, Sir. There are two groups of Muslims in Iraq, the Sunni and the Shia. The Sunnis are the smaller group but they are the ones that have been ruling the country under Saddam Hussein for many years.

Even though they were in the minority?

- Yes, Sir. We're not talking democracy here, at least not as we know it.

So now that Saddam has gone, there could be some scores to settle.

- I believe so, Sir.

Well I hope so, after all we're getting pretty low on the body count. Perhaps we need to come up with a new strategy.

- I'll get onto it, Sir.

2004

January

Jack, I've been thinking about the fact that my first term of office will soon be drawing to a close. I feel that we really need to do something special to mark the occasion.

- Well, Sir, I'm sure that the White House budget can stretch to a few balloons and party hats.

No, that's not what I have in mind at all. I'm talking about some sort of strategic initiative.

- Really? That sounds like a very bold gesture, Sir.

Exactly, Jack, the bolder the better.

- Well if you are set on such a plan I'll get my guys to give it some thought and see what they can come up with.

Oh no, Jack, that won't be necessary. I already know what I'm going to do. I'm going to announce to the nation that we are going to send a man back to the Moon!

- Will it be just the one man, Sir?

Do I detect a certain sarcastic tone in your voice, Jack? I seem to remember that when JFK made a similar announcement it had quite an effect.

- Well, Sir, that may have something to do with the novelty value.

So do you see any problems with this idea?

- Well, Sir, there is perhaps one big problem. I don't know if you can recall the briefing I gave you at the start of your first term.

Was that the one where you mentioned that we hadn't in fact landed a man on the Moon?

- Ah, so you do remember.

Of course I remember, Jack. I may be simple but I'm not stupid.

- Well in that case I'm not sure what you have in mind, Sir.

You're a bit slow on the uptake today, Jack. We're not actually going to go to the Moon.

- If you're suggesting that we do another fake Moon landing then I think that I would have to advise against it, Sir. It was a close call the first time and I'm not sure that we could get away with it again.

You're not on my wave length at all are you, Jack. Let me help you. What do you need in order to put a man on the Moon?

- Well, Sir, you need a rocket and a lunar landing craft of some sort.

And what do you need in order to make a rocket?

- Rocket scientists and engineers, Sir?

It's money, Jack, that's what I'm talking about. You need money, and if our strategy regarding the banking system goes according to plan, what is going to be in short supply?

- Money, Sir?

Exactly!

- But that means that we won't be able to afford the cost of sending a man back to the Moon. We'll have to cancel the project.

Not 'we', Jack, 'you'. And by 'you' I mean you and my successor. So now do you see where I'm coming from?

- Yes, Sir, and I can't help thinking that the old Jack would have caught on a lot sooner.

I have a feeling that the old Jack would have come up with the whole idea in the first place. I don't suppose that you have reconsidered the issue of retirement, have you?

- Not at this stage, Sir.

No, I thought not. And there's one other thing, Jack. This Moon landing thing. That's as well as the balloons and party hats, not instead of.

- Of course, Sir.

February

- Sir, we've had a bit of a set back on the water front.

In what respect?

- Well, it's all to do with the launch of our bottled water in Europe.

Oh dear, what's happened?

- Well, two things have occurred that have really stopped this particular project in its tracks. First, apparently the idea of bottling tap water and selling it is not new. A British TV comedy programme had the same idea some years ago. At the time it was treated very much as a joke and therefore the British are not taking our bottled water seriously. But the final straw was the fact that bromate was discovered in the water.

What's that?

- It's a substance that can cause cancer.

Well shouldn't the company have taken it out of the tap water?

- Oh no, Sir, it was never in the tap water.

So how did it get there?

- We suspect the French, Sir.

Have you been looking in your "Who to Blame" dictionary again? The page with "French" on must be wearing a bit thin.

- In this case, we didn't use the dictionary. We think it actually was the French and it was retaliation for the Perrier contamination.

I thought that the Perrier issue was nothing to do with us.

- It wasn't, but we were never able to convince the French of that. They still think that we were responsible and this was their chance to get their own back.

So where does that leave us?

- Well as far as Europe is concerned, the project is dead. The UK operation has been closed down and the plan to expand into Europe has been abandoned.

Is there nothing we can do?

- No, Sir, not in the short term.

So do you have any good news for me?

- In fact I do, Sir. The new extradition treaty has become law in the UK.

Well that's obviously good news but I know you'll understand me when I say I hope that it's all been a waste of time.

- You mean that if he'd found anything, he'd have made it public by now.

Exactly, and because he hasn't we can probably assume that he didn't find anything of interest. Even so, I still think that we need to have a word with this chap, just to be on the safe side.

- Of course, Sir.

May

- Sir, London has made it into the last five in the bidding for the 2012 Olympics.

I hope that I'm not supposed to sound surprised, Jack. After all you're aiming to get them to win the bidding process.

- I know, Sir, but I thought that I should just keep you updated.

August

- Sir, I'm pleased to say that we've completed our assessment of the STOP project and I can go through a summary of the findings if you want me to. I can break it down into manageable chunks if that helps.

Thanks, Jack, I'd appreciate that. Where shall we start?

- Perhaps at the beginning, Sir. The first option we implemented was war and this is still used today. But our analysis shows that these days it's next to useless when it comes to controlling population growth. Unfortunately the days of the Big War are over and the relatively insignificant skirmishes which occur today are very much small beer. To give you some idea, more people were killed in one day during World War One than in the entire duration of most wars these days. The Falklands War was a prime example where even though we aimed for a high body count we failed miserably.

But why is this, Jack? Is it to do with technology?

- It is, Sir, but in two very different respects. In the old days it was very much man against man and therefore we could rely on a high number of casualties. These days it's more like machine against machine, hence fewer casualties. This is less true of course when you get a guerrilla type conflict but even then the body count is low. And of course the other issue to do with technology is news reporting and specifically the Internet. Although it's low key now, we anticipate that in the not too distant future people will be exchanging information about all sorts of things as they happen and this will include armed conflicts. It will almost certainly mean some bad publicity coming our way.

So wars have been a failure as far as STOP is concerned.

- Yes, Sir, which is why we suggest that we scale back the defence budget.

Er, I don't think that will be necessary, Jack. The defence industry is a very important part of our national economy.

- Not to mention a big contributor to campaign funds, Sir.

That's by the by, Jack. Let's move on. What's next?

- Well some better news is that our JUNC food project has been pretty successful. More and more people are eating the stuff and so far they seem to have an almost unlimited appetite for just about everything we can come up with.

Is there a "but" coming, Jack?

- There is, Sir. But, we're still not getting the demographic penetration that we need.

Put simply, Jack?

- The poor are signed up but well off people are less co-operative. However the plan to break the banks is coming to a climax and then we hope to see some results.

That's when we expect that the well-off members of the community will no longer be able to afford the good stuff?

- Exactly, Sir, and when the JUNC food takes hold and makes them sick they won't be able to afford the medical care to put things right either. But you're still talking about long term effects and the bodies are not mounting up yet, at least not in the quantity we need. However the latest figures do indicate about 365,000 deaths due to bad diet and lack of exercise in 2000 in the US alone, so not insignificant.

So wars have failed and so has JUNC food.

- Well I wouldn't use the word "failed", Sir. I prefer the phrase "less productive than anticipated". However there is one bright spot. The figures for the number of deaths from smoking have held up better than expected. It was 435,000 in 2000 so it trumps the JUNC food figure. It was thought that all the bad publicity, the ban on advertising and the deaths threats being printed on the cartons would have had a significant effect but things are still looking good. And our attempts to spread the habit to all parts of the globe have proved successful. In fact worldwide the number of deaths from smoking exceeds five million per year. The figure for China alone is two thousand per day. The trouble is that even these number are not good enough, which just goes to show the size of the problem.

But Jack, can you put this all into context. How many people die each year, worldwide?

- It's about 57 million, Sir.

So smoking accounts for about ten per cent of all deaths.

- Worldwide, that appears to be the case.

So can't we just try to recruit many more smokers? If we increased the consumption tenfold, we'd get ten times as many deaths.

- Sir, I think you would find that the only way we could get a tenfold increase in the consumption is if people smoke multiple cigarettes at the same time. I any case we'd need to grow an awful lot of tobacco to meet the demand. So no, cigarettes are not the answer.

OK, I thought I'd at least ask. So if JUNC food and cigarettes are covered, what else is there?

- Well unfortunately, as far as the US is concerned, if you look at all the causes of death, these two are by far the most effective. All others are way down the list.

Well let's leave the deaths for a moment. What about births?

- Well, there we have had some success. Worldwide there are about 140 million births each year, but this figure is down from the peak of over 160 million just a few years ago. Our efforts regarding birth control seem to be far more effective than our attempts to kill people off.

At some point the births and deaths figures are going to coincide and so when will the total population level off?

- At the current rate, not until the middle of this century, Of course something will have to give before then since the population will have reached nine billion by that time. According to our figures, that's more than the planet can support.

Well then we need to do something now. We have to try and come up with a plan that's not covered by any of our current projects. And it needs to be big.

- I know, Sir. I'll get our best people onto it right away.

2005

February

Jack, do we have anything yet concerning the "Big One".

- Well we have made some limited progress, Sir. We've come to the conclusion that it's going to have to be another pandemic. There's no other way to get rid of the required number of people in a short period of time.

When you say "another", what's the other one?

- AIDS, Sir. At the last count, we reckon that there were 2.5 million Aids related deaths, although since a lot of these cases are in Third World countries this figure can only be an approximation.

Oh yes, of course. But do you have something else lined up as a possible option?

- We do, Sir. It's influenza.

Don't we want something a bit stronger than that?

- You mean like a plague of some sort?

Exactly.

- Not really, Sir. We just want to reduce the human population of the planet to manageable numbers. We don't want to wipe it out completely.

Well yes, I guess you're right, but when you referred earlier to the "required number", how many are we talking about?

- Well the last really big one was Spanish Flu which accounted for anything up to one hundred million deaths.

Wow, that sounds promising. When was that?

- 1918, Sir. And since then we've had a few less lethal versions like Asian Flu in the late fifties and Hong Kong Flu in the late sixties.

So it sounds like we're due another one.

- I'd say we're overdue, Sir.

So how soon can we go ahead?

- Not yet, Sir. We're still working on the overall strategy.

What's to work on? Surely we just come up with a particularly nasty version of the flu virus and unleash it on an unsuspecting population.

- You would have thought so, but unfortunately it's not that easy.

Why not?

- Well for a start, what's the first thing that's going to happen when a new strain of flu appears?

People start dying?

- Well, Sir, to some extent that's a given. No, I'm talking about vaccination. Each winter the drug companies come up with a new vaccine against the latest version of the virus. Luckily for us, there's no such thing as a generic vaccine which guards against all versions of influenza, otherwise we'd be scuppered.

Well can't we just tell the drug companies not to make a vaccine for our version of the virus?

- I don't think that's an option, Sir. The population at large may start to ask questions.

So what's the answer?

- At this stage, we're not sure.

March

- Sir, our worries about the French have proved well founded. It turns out that they are not really with us on the whole population control issue. Actually, no, let me correct that statement. They're happy about population control except when it applies to France.

Well what have they done?

- They've announced a series of initiatives which will encourage French couples to have more children.

Like what?

- Like free child care, keeping jobs open while women are on maternity leave, paying people extra money to have a third child, all that sort of thing. Of course there may be a very valid reason why the French need to increase the birth rate. At some stage someone is going to have to pay a lot of tax in order to finance the care of all the old British people in France.

Well we need to do something. They can't be allowed to get away with this.

- Let's hold fire for now since there may be something coming up which will stop this plan in its tracks.

What do you mean?

- Well what's your first reaction to these plans?

My first reaction is that we can never trust those Frenchies.

- OK, what's your second reaction?

Er, well I guess that would be that this plan of theirs is going to cost an awful lot of money.

- Exactly! And what do we suspect is just around the corner, finance wise?

A banking crisis?

- Precisely, Sir. When that hits, it's hard to believe that the French will be able to afford to keep this thing going, so I suggest that we wait and see.

OK, but we need to keep a close eye on the French.

- As always, Sir.

April

Jack, I've come across some disturbing news. Apparently, fat people live longer than thin people.

- Sir, yes, we know that.

Do we?

- Yes, Sir.

(Jack spends some time recapping)

OK, so I now understand. We are telling people that being slim is better than being fat because we want to kill them off. But how come this report in the JAMA got out? Can't we put a stop to this sort of thing?

- It's difficult, Sir. We can't control every scientist or academic. This research was carried out as a joint effort between two separate organisations. Sometimes they do research that confirms what we already know and it gets out. What amazes me is that it makes no difference. The public still believes what we tell them.

Surely that's to do with the G-Water.

- Well that certainly helps. And the GM crops of course. But I'm not sure they account for everything, so there must be something else going on.

Well whatever it is, it had better continue.

- I certainly hope so, Sir.

Well I think we need to do more than just hope, Jack. This is a crucial part of our overall plan. Let's see if we can't get a handle on what's happening.

- Yes, Sir

July

Jack, I see that London has won the bid for the Olympics, but it looks like it was a close shave.

- Indeed it was. We had to get Blair to go out to Singapore personally to help seal the deal.

And did it involve a lot of grease?

- I beg your pardon?

You know, to grease the palms of the delegates.

- I'm not sure what you mean, Sir. The voting process was completely fair and above board.

I'm sure it was, Jack. But well done anyway.

- Thank you, Sir.

November

Ah, Jack, any news on the Big One? I'm only asking because I've had a thought about a matter that we didn't cover last time.

- Well we have made some progress, but you go first. What's on your mind?

Well one thing we need to do is come up with a name for the new flu. And so far we've had Spanish Flu, Asian Flu and Hong Kong Flu. So I've had an idea. Let's call it French Flu.

- And how long did it take you to come up with that idea, Sir?

Not as long as you'd think, Jack.

- Well I'd be surprised there, Sir. I reckon it took you all of a nanosecond.

How long is a nanosecond, Jack?

- Sir, you just need to know it's a very short period of time. And no, we can't call it French Flu.

But why not?

- Because the name has to relate to reality. Typically it's to do with where the initial outbreak occurs.

Well that's even better. We'll release the infection in France and those Frenchies won't know what's hit them.

- Well attractive as that option is, Sir, we've already ruled out France.

So you thought of the same idea?

- No, not exactly, but we don't want to start the thing off in a country that has an efficient and sophisticated health care system. They could put a lid on the outbreak before it takes hold. Unfortunately, France has one of the best health care systems in the world.

Well what about the UK?

- We're going to have to get their co-operation on this plan so I don't think that's an option.

So you didn't rule them out due to their efficient and sophisticated National Health Service.

- No, Sir.

OK, so where does that leave us on names?

- Well we're probably going to go down the alternative naming route and use the name of an animal. Avian Flu is an example where it's been done before. This has the advantage of not alienating one of our allies but also gives us the option of choosing a name which itself makes the virus sound nasty.

You mean like Cockroach Flu?

- Yes, something like that, Sir.

Do you want me to give it some more thought?

- No, Sir, that won't be necessary. Believe me, it's all under control.

I hope so, Jack. So tell me, what's your news?

- We've made some progress on the vaccine front. As I said, we can't stop the drug companies developing a flu vaccine, since it's what they always do when a new strain of flu comes around.

Ah, actually on the subject of vaccines, that's also something I've been mulling over. But you go first. Give me your ideas and let's see if great minds think alike.

- OK, Sir. Well we've already sown the seeds of a couple of things. The MMR scare is still having some effect and as a result we reckon that 5-10 per cent of people will refuse to be vaccinated. Then there are the side effects. For the flu vaccine there are normally very few, apart from some occasional mild flu like symptoms. We need to come up with another, preferably scary, side effect but it needs to have some credibility. Which one we chose will probably depend on the strain of flu that we use.

So how many people are likely to be put off by possible side effects?

- Again, around 5-10 per cent, and that means that we're still left with 80-90 per cent of people who will go for the vaccine. For them we think we'll use complacency as our secret weapon.

I'm not sure that I'm with you here, Jack. Exactly how is that going to work?

- Well let's start with the fact that for a number of reasons we think that we need to have a trial run.

Meaning what exactly?

- We'll create a flu virus which is not particularly virulent and we'll give it a sinister name. The working title is Pig Flu.

Not bad. Not as good as Cockroach Flu, of course, but not bad. And is there any particular reason for choosing pigs as the culprits?

- Well they're assumed to be dirty animals and of course there are a number of radical groups who already have a problem with the idea of eating pork. This will just reinforce the message.

You mean vegetarians?

- Well them too, but I was thinking more of the Jews and Muslims.

I hardly think that you can label the Jews as radical, after all I rely on them for many of my votes.

- My case rests, Sir. But anyway, the point is that if we can get people to think that the virus originates in pigs then it will put them off eating the stuff, and in certain cases put them off all meats. It's a minor thing but useful nevertheless.

Will you be able to catch the virus by eating pork?

- No, Sir, but as always, the public don't need to know that. Even if we were to tell them you can't, they wouldn't believe us.

But if putting people off eating a particular food is a consideration, why not choose something more significant?

- Like what?

Like say eggs. I seem to remember you saying once that they are one of the most nutritious foods around.

- That's correct, Sir.

So if we could put people off eating eggs, wouldn't that be better than pork?

- Somehow I don't think that Egg Flu has quite the right ring to it.

I was thinking more of Omelette Flu, Jack.

- And you think that's sounds better, Sir?

Well it sounds pretty scary to me, Jack.

- I think we'll stick with Pig Flu, Sir. Apart from anything else we've already had all the posters printed warning people of the dangers.

OK, so that's the name done with, what about the idea of a trial run? What's that about?

- Well the main reason for a trial run is that we are going to promote the Pig Flu big time as a serious pandemic. We'll get millions of doses of vaccine produced and vast numbers of people will be inoculated.

Then what?

- Then, at least as far as deaths are concerned, not a lot. There will be a lot of scaremongering and hopefully this will cause some level of panic in the population. I believe the Brits have already put the Daily Mail on stand-by which means that we'll have saturation coverage. But then, when it's all over, people will start asking questions, mainly because they'll feel that they have been misled by the powers that be. The plan is that a few years later we'll have another go. This time it'll be the real thing but we're banking on the fact that the vast number of people will have been lulled into a false sense of security and opt not to be vaccinated. And of course vaccination will only be an option in the richer countries. In the Third World most people won't have the choice. They'll be dropping like flies.

Well it sounds promising but I'm a bit worried about the timescales here. If we have a trial run, when is that likely to take place?

- It'll take a while to get things ready but we assume either the summer of 2008 or 2009.

Summer? But I thought that flu was a winter thing.

- Not our one, Sir. That's one of the things that will make it seem like it's something special and give the whole plan a bit more credibility. If we were to make it a normal winter flu it would not have the same impact.

Very clever, Jack. And so where is the epidemic going to start?

- We thought Mexico, Sir. It's close to our borders but outside our jurisdiction and of course their health care system isn't going to pose a problem. But of course it won't take long to spread to the US.

OK, let's go ahead with the plan. Anything else?

- Well you did say that you had an idea to do with the vaccines. What was it?

Ah, perhaps we'll leave that for now.

- No, go on, Sir, what was your idea?

OK, but if I tell you the plan, let's see if you can work out where I'm coming from.

- Agreed. What's the plan?

We kill all the chickens, Jack!

461

- Well, Sir, I have to say that nothing immediately springs to mind. If there is some logic behind this idea then it eludes me.

Go away and sleep on it.

- Sir, I shall probably have nightmares about it.

2006

March

- Sir, the British have come to me with some news about school meals. Apparently, they believe that someone is going to expose the fact that they're not as nutritious as they should be.

Well we all know that, Jack. How did the Brits get to hear about this?

- They've got wind of it from an insider at a television production company. Apparently one of their celebrity chefs is going to do a program about the subject.

Are they sure it's about school meals?

- I think the clue is in the title.

Which is?

- The working title is "School Dinners Are Killing Your Children", Sir.

Good grief, it sounds like a headline from the Daily Mail.

- If it hasn't been already, Sir, it soon will be.

This must all be a bit worrying for the Brits. What do they intend to do?

- They're already in touch with the company and I'm waiting for a progress report back.

Let me know as soon as you hear something.

- Yes, Sir.

April

- Sir, I've heard back from the British regarding the TV program.

Have they stopped it being shown?

- No, Sir, but they have managed to get the title changed. It's now going to be broadcast with the title Jamie's School Dinners.

Well that sounds a bit better, but what else are they going to do?

- In the short term nothing. They reckon that if they have done their job over the years, the kids are not going to be particularly receptive to proper food. They predict that after the program has been aired there will be even more children consuming FAST food, especially when the schools start serving salads.

So there's nothing else they plan to do.

- No, Sir. Except of course they plan to increase the number of kebab vans to cope with the increased demand.

They think that they'll have more customers.

- They hope that they'll have more customers and they want to be ready. And incidentally, there is one other issue; it's regarding vaccines, Sir. The guy who came up with the dodgy research which maligned the MMR vaccine now says that he is unemployable in the UK.

Well that's hardly surprising. What does he expect us to do about it?

- Well he thinks we have a moral responsibility to help him.

And do we?

- Well, Sir, that depends on how you define "moral responsibility ".

Let's not get too clever here, Jack. Do we owe him a favour or not?

- On balance, I'd say that we do, Sir. We planted the rogue research that started him off on his mission.

Well OK, let's see what we can do for him.

- Yes, Sir.

May

- Sir, there's just one minor thing regarding Swine Flu.

Swine Flu?

- Yes, it's not Pig Flu any more, it's Swine Flu. Just like Bird Flu became Avian Flu. We think it sounds even more convincing; at least that's what the ad men are saying.

Ad men? We have ad men working on this project?

- We have ad men working on just about all aspects of STOP, Sir. How else do we get our message out there?

By using a blog, Jack!

- A blog, Sir?

Yes, a blog, it's a web site….

- Sir, I know what a blog is. I just wondered how it would be used for our purposes. For example, we've come up with a side effect for our flu vaccine. It's called Guillain-Barre Syndrome.

What? That sounds a bit foreign. Couldn't we have come up with something a bit catchier?

- Sir, this isn't something we invented, it is in fact a genuine disease and the name is French.

Well I do like the sound of that. It makes up for the fact that you wouldn't use the term French Flu.

- Well that may be a bonus but I can't take the credit. We're using Guillain-Barre Syndrome as the scary side effect because it was associated with the vaccine for a similar version of the flu virus in the 1970's. It results in paralysis and if untreated, death.

And is it a real risk?

- It's unlikely but even if it is, there were tens of millions of people vaccinated in 1976 and only 25 people contracted the disease. The risks of getting the disease from being vaccinated are minute and bear in mind that tens of thousands die from flu each year. It's a no brainer. So going back to your point, in this particular situation how would a blog help?

Well I could…….

- Oh, I see, Sir. This is a Presidential blog, is it?

Well never mind whose blog it is. All I'm saying is that we could use it to tell people that the vaccine is dangerous.

- Sir, if this information is going to come from an official source, you would have to say that it's not dangerous. For a start, that's the reality of the situation, and secondly the conspiracy theory freaks out there will assume that you're lying.

OK, let's go with that.

- We could, Sir. Or we could leave it to the ad men, who would in turn get onto the Daily Mail. We'd end up with a headline that reads something like "Swine Flu Jab link to Killer Nerve Disease". It would be read by millions of readers at their breakfast table. It would scare them witless.

But only in the UK, Jack.

- Well as far as newspapers are concerned, I'm sure the National Enquirer would be an option on our side of the pond.

Not the New York Times?

- Not yet, I'm afraid, Sir. But I'm sure they'll come round. We've got our man Murdoch on the case.

So who do we use? Who's our equivalent of the Daily Mail?

- Fox News, Sir.

Now there's a surprise. Anything else, Jack?

- No, Sir, I think that's it.

So you're not going to come back to me about my vaccine idea?

- What, your "kill all the chickens" moment. I was rather hoping that was a joke, Sir.

Not at all, Jack. It was a serious suggestion. I can guarantee that if you were to kill all the chickens you would not have a problem with the flu vaccine.

- And why is that, Sir?

Because you need hen's eggs to make the vaccine, Jack. No eggs, no vaccine. Did you not know that?

- No, Sir, I wasn't aware of that.

So if you were to kill all.....

- Yes, Sir, I get the picture. I just have a couple of questions.

Just two?

- Well let's start with two. How do you propose we kill all the chickens? And even if you managed to do that, how do we explain to people why there are no eggs in the shops?

Well the second one's easy. We can explain that there are no eggs in the shops because there are no chickens.

- OK, Sir, let's just stick with the first question.

Jack, I'm supposed to be the ideas man. You're the one who looks after the details.

- Well if it's OK with you, I'll pass on this one, Sir.

As you wish, Jack.

November

- Just one other thing, Sir. It's about school meals. Apparently in the UK the schools have been fighting back regarding FAST food. They've started locking the school gates, so preventing the pupils from reaching the kebab vans.

And what have the authorities done to stop them.

- They haven't done anything, Sir. They didn't need to, since the British public has come to our rescue. They are buying FAST food for the pupils and they're shoving it through the bars at the school gates. It's like feeding time at the zoo. It makes you proud to be British.

But, Jack, we're not British, are we?

- No, Sir, but if we were, we'd be proud.

2007

January

- Sir, at last we've come up with a reason why people should stop using bottled water in water coolers.

How long has it taken?

- 37 years, Sir.

Why did it take so long? Why didn't we come up with it 37 years ago?

- Well, as I said at the time….

Not to me you didn't.

- Well no, Sir, not you personally, but certainly to one of your predecessors. I said we might have to wait until circumstances changed and I now believe that they have.

So what have you come up with?

- We'll suggest that using bottled water is not eco-friendly. It costs a lot to transport it and with global warming, that's not good when there's a perfectly adequate alternative.

That's true. And presumably this principle will apply to all bottled water, not just the stuff used in the water coolers.

- Yes, Sir. You're absolutely right.

March

Jack, I hear that Hilary Clinton is running for President.

- I believe so, Sir.

So how did that happen? I thought that the agreement had ended.

- So it has, Sir, but that doesn't stop her running. In any case, I think she's on a promise.

What do you mean?

- Well she was told about the agreement and expected to be the first woman president.

Who told her?

- Her husband, Sir.

But I thought it was supposed to be a secret. How come she got to know?

- I believe it was something to do with the incident over the intern.

You mean Miss Lewinsky?

- Yes, Sir. Clinton had to make amends for that little episode, so he told his wife about the agreement. She kept quiet about the whole thing on the promise of being able to run for President.

Wow, I bet she's gutted to find out that the deal's off.

- She still thinks she can win.

And what if she does win?

- What do you mean?

If she wins, does that mean that the dynasty agreement is still on?

- No, Sir, it doesn't. If she wins, it will be on merit.

From your tone, Jack, I assume you think that I didn't win on merit. For all you know, I could have won without your help.

- I think we both know that would have been unlikely, Sir.

June

- Sir, you may remember that we had a discussion a while ago about gullibility and the fact that it may not be all down to fluoride in the water and our GM foods. At the time we speculated that there may well be something else going on.

So what, you think you've found something?

- Well before we discuss the possibilities I think we need to stop referring to gullibility and start talking about stupidity. What we've discovered is more than a question of people being gullible.

OK, stupidity it is. What have you come up with?

- Well, Sir, for some time we have been looking at a number of possibilities including Darwin's theory of Evolution.

What! I'm not sure I like the sound of that. Who authorised expenditure on such work?

- You did, Sir, when you signed off the defence budget for the year.

You used part of the defence budget to study the Theory of Evolution?

- Of course, Sir. Everything concerning STOP comes out of the defence budget, you know that.

Well yes, but perhaps I didn't appreciate the ramifications.

- Well regardless of any budgetary issues, let me explain what we found. You've heard of the principle of natural selection, or as we prefer it "Survival of the Fittest", otherwise known as SOFT.

Shouldn't that be SOTF?

- Yes but the guy who came up with the acronym is dyslexic.

Well OK then, SOFT it is. But I assume that you are aware of my thoughts on the whole matter of evolution aren't you, Jack.

- Well let's leave religion out of this for now. Let's just go through what we've found. Until recently it seemed pretty clear that the SOFT principle did indeed operate in nature but recently humans have been intervening in such a way as to upset this process.

In what way?

- Well in nature the sick and weak normally go by the wayside. It's only the fittest that survive, hence the name. But with modern medicine and changes in society as a whole that principle no longer applies. The sick and weak can indeed survive. Not only that but they can reproduce. In the past, someone with a serious disease would die off pretty quickly but now they can have offspring which in turn may well inherit the same condition. Previously the disease could well have died out by the process of natural selection. Now it could be propagated through the generations.

Well this all sounds logical but why does it help our cause now?

- Because we think that nature may be coming to our assistance. We had a feeling that somehow things were happening to people that made them stupid, or at least more stupid than the norm. Once we realised this, things started to make sense since it helped to explain a situation that was somewhat puzzling.

And what was that, Jack?

- It's the fact that if people's stupidity, or rather gullibility, was partly due to our efforts with the fluoride and GM food then there would be some sort of pattern. We'd expect to see more stupid people in the areas that receive the most input from our stuff. But this isn't true, at least not any more. There is a pretty uniform spread of stupid people around the globe, once religion is taken into account.

Religion? Where does that come into things?

- Well there are a lot of stupid things done in the name of religion so we have to factor that into our calculations. Let's leave that for the moment, I just mentioned it for completeness. Going back to the main point, let's take Statins. If our stuff was having an effect the take up rate would be higher in those areas where the water contains fluoride when compared to those that don't, but there's no such effect. But we know that there used to be an effect, or at least we think we do, so the question is, what's going on?

Well perhaps stupidity, or at least our version of it, is contagious.

- We did look at that option but we couldn't find anything to suggest that something like an infection is involved. But we have come up with one explanation that fits the bill and that's the possibility that our fluoride or GM stuff has triggered some sort of genetic change in people. That would explain how it works. It's not then too far-fetched to imagine that nature intervenes and that this genetic mutation starts to occur spontaneously, without our help.

But this is pure guess work, Jack.

- Well in scientific terms we'd call it a theory.

A bit like the Theory of Evolution.

- No, Sir. I believe that Evolution has progressed from theory to scientific fact, Sir.

Whatever you say, Jack. So where do we go from here?

- Well we have a team of people at Area 51 who are searching for DSG.

DSG, Jack?

- Darwin's Stupid Gene, Sir, named in honour of the great man.

Can't we have GSG?

- Don't tell me. It's God's Stupid Gene isn't it, Sir.

Maybe.

July

- Sir, our proposal concerning Trans Fats and chocolate doesn't seem to have exactly gone to plan. It looks like we're going to have to drop the idea.

Why on earth would we do that?

- Due to public pressure, Sir. It seems that the good old USA citizens don't want us messing with their chocolate.

Well I can hardly blame them, Jack. Perhaps it was a step too far.

- Perhaps it was, Sir, but it's difficult to see how we could have foreseen it. After all, we've messed with just about every food stuff known to man and got away with it. It's strange that Joe Public draws the line at chocolate.

It's not just the fact that it's chocolate that's involved, Jack. These Trans Fats are getting a pretty bad press right now. If we'd tried to do this 10 or 20 years ago we'd probably have gotten away with it.

- You may well be right there, Sir. The Brits are having a difficult time with their Trans Fats. For example, some manufacturers are taking them out of their processed foods.

That's bad news for us. I hope there's still a lot of other crap being used.

- Well of course that's true and you also need to bear in mind that it will take a long time before all Trans Fats can be replaced. There just aren't enough alternatives around to replace them.

I'm glad to hear it, Jack.

August

- Sir, we have some more information regarding DSG.

Ah you mean the Stupid Gene, Jack.

- Actually, Sir, it's not called the Stupid Gene any more. It's now referred to as the Darwin's Sensible Gene. Of course it's still DSG.

Why the change?

- Well it's because we realised that the problem was not directly connected to intelligence or should I say stupidity. It was more to do with a lack of logical, sensible thinking, which is not the same thing at all. In any case, rather than someone having a stupid gene it's the lack of a sensible gene that causes the problem. We had it the wrong way round. So most normal people have this gene but if you don't then you start to do things that lack common sense.

Like what?

- Well it could be not getting your child vaccinated, not wearing a seat belt in the car, smoking cigarettes when the packet shows a clear warning that doing so will eventually kill you.

Ah, but surely the latter is more to do with addiction.

- Yes, there is something in that idea, but where you get a parent smoking while holding a baby and blowing the smoke in the child's face, that's not addiction, that's....

Stupidity, Jack. We're back where we started.

- Ok so that was a bad example. But our new theory covers people who are in other respects intelligent. They just have a bit of a blind spot when it comes to common sense things.

But you're still referring to it as a theory.

- Well with something like this it's difficult to come up with a definitive proof but we have tested a lot of people and it all seems to fit. Time will tell if we're right.

OK but where does it leave us?

- In the sort of timescales we're talking about it makes no difference. It will take nature, in the shape of natural selection, too long to achieve our aim. We're still going to have to continue with our plan. In the meantime, if you want to see some of the stuff we have come across during our research, just have a look at the Darwin Awards web site. It was put together by some of the guys at Area 51. It'll give you some idea of stuff people get up to.

September

Jack, I took a look at that Darwin Awards web site and two things struck me. The first is that alcohol seemed to feature quite a lot.

- Well that's a fair comment, although these were extreme examples. And I could argue that consuming an excess of alcohol is not in itself a sensible thing.

I think you're clutching at straws here Jack.

- Maybe, Sir. What's the other point?

Well you said that we should be thinking of this condition as being a lack of common sense rather than outright stupidity.

- Yes, Sir.

Well what about the guy who tried to weld a hand grenade with a blow torch and blew himself up. That seems to be more than a lack of common sense. That was downright stupid.

- I'll give you that one, Sir.

October

- Sir, I've given the go ahead for our people in the French Banks to start the irregular trading. We should see some results very soon.

And how many of them are there?

- We started out with more than a dozen but some of them fell by the wayside. It turned out that they were no good at the job and as a result they did not progress to the required level within the bank.

So how many are we left with?

- Just five, Sir.

November

- Sir, we have received some bad news regarding our plan for the French banks. Some of the remaining five sleepers have decided not to co-operate.

How many?

- Four, Sir.

Four! Are you saying that we only have one person ready to take action?

- I'm afraid so, Sir.

What an earth happened?

- Basically it's that they are all too good at the job, which means that they are earning so much money, the last thing they want is to damage the bank. There's just one person who is still willing to play ball.

Well one is still better than none I suppose, but it's not much of a result is it.

- If things work out there's still one thing in our favour and that's the fact that the French banking system will be drawn into the dirt with the rest of us. In the short term it won't matter that the underlying reason is different.

2008

January

- Sir, it looks as though the plan concerning the banks will come to fruition this year. All the bits of the jigsaw are falling into place.

Like what, Jack?

- Well there's been a period of sustained economic growth. Consumer confidence is strong, particularly with house prices going up as they are and that of course is another big part of the plan. It means that people have been keen to borrow money to buy their own property.

And where do you suggest I put my money right now? I don't want to be caught out.

- Well, Sir, Collateralized Debt Obligations are the key to all this, CDO's for short, which are based on sub-prime mortgages.

OK, keep it simple, Jack. I don't want to be confused by these highfalutin words. Remind me in simple terms, how are we going to break these banks and why do some of them survive?

- Right, Sir. Let's imagine that Bank A lends money to Joe Bloggs so that he can buy a house. He isn't particularly credit worthy but Bank A doesn't mind because it won't have the loan on the books for very long. And because he is a risk, the interest rate they will charge him will be above the norm. They'll then package it up with a number of other dodgy loans and sell them on to Bank B. That's what's called a CDO.

OK, but why would Bank B buy them?

- Because the overall rate of interest on the package of loans will be attractive.

But Bank B must know that the loans are suspect.

- Oh yes, they know, but they have to take a view on what percentage of them will become toxic. If a small enough number default, the overall package will still pay dividends.

But how will they work out whether a particular bunch of loans is good or bad.

- Bank A will tell them.

What, and Bank B will accept that! I find that hard to believe.

- They'll believe them because there will be computer models which will confirm the predictions.

What sort of computer models, Jack?

- I believe the most popular formula is based on a Gaussian Copula, Sir.

And how does that work?

- Er…

You don't know, do you Jack.

- No, Sir. Sorry.

Don't apologise, Jack. You passed the test.

- And what test was that, Sir?

Well if you don't know how it works, then I'm pretty sure the bankers won't!

- We're banking on it, Sir.

That's perhaps a joke too far, Jack.

- Sorry, Sir.

But you still think this whole plan will fly?

- It is flying, Sir, and up to now it's been a win/win situation for everyone.

But not for long.

- No, Sir, not for long.

So I need to put my money into Bank A.

- Oh no, Sir. You mustn't put all you hard earned cash into Bank A.

But surely Bank A has got rid of its dodgy loans. I hope you're not suggesting I put it into Bank B? 'Cos if you are, then I really have lost the plot.

- Oh no, of course not. But at any point in time, Bank A will still have a lot of sub-prime mortgages on its books waiting to be packaged, so it's not a good bet either. Use Bank C instead.

Sorry, I don't see where Bank C comes into the equation?

- Bank C bets Bank D that.....

Bank D!

- Bear with me, Sir. Bank C bets Bank D that the value of these sub-prime derivatives will fall. Of course it needn't be Bank D. It could be any one who is willing to take the bet.

What, you can really do that can you?

- These days you can bet on almost anything on the financial markets.

But I thought that these financial markets involved people investing in companies who in turn make things or provide services that people want to buy. In return for the investment, these people get back a share of the profits.

- With all due respect, Sir, I don't know what version of capitalism you think we have these days, but in the main that one certainly isn't it.

Apparently not, Jack. But OK, let's assume I accept that Bank C can bet on the situation. Why should I put my money with them?

- Because they will win the bet. Far from losing money, Sir, they will actually make a profit out of the whole debacle.

And does Bank C have a name?

- Well I suspect there will be more than one "Bank C".

Just give me one name, Jack.

- Then that'll be Goldman Sachs, Sir.

Thank you, Jack.

Later

Jack, I see that one of the French banks has a bit of a problem. Or should I say a rather large problem. The figure that I've seen mentioned is 50 billion Euros worth of losses.

- Well unfortunately that figure is their exposure in the market. Once they have unwound their positions the actual losses will be somewhat less than that.

How much less?

- About 45 billion Euros less.

45 billion! You mean that they are only going to lose around 5 billion?

- Well 5 billion is still a large figure for a bank to lose.

That may have been the case a few years ago but, Jack, as you and I both know, in comparison with our current problems 5 billion is a drop in the ocean.

- I can't disagree there, Sir, but remember; the bigger issue here is that the French banking system is under suspicion and anything that can deflect a bit of flak from us is to be welcomed.

I suppose so, but it's still a big disappointment.

- Yes, Sir, it is.

August

- Sir, the Democrats have a bit of a problem, in that they think they may not win the Presidential election.

How can that be the case, after all we did nominate John McCain as our candidate, in which case what else can we do?

- The problem they have is that Obama is young and black.

Didn't the Democrats notice that when they elected him?

- Well of course they did, but there is still some voter resistance.

And what do they expect me to do? Surely it's not my problem.

- Well it is in a way. It's their turn to win and if they don't, there could be all sorts of trouble.

Who for?

- Anyone who has a secret or two that they would prefer to keep quiet about. Can you think of anyone that might include, Sir?

OK, Jack, I get the picture. What are our options?

- Well, as far as I can see, there is only one thing we can do. You have to choose a running mate for McCain that will seal his fate.

Do you have anyone in mind?

- Yes, Sir, I do. It's Sarah Palin.

I've never heard of her. Who is she?

- She's the governor of Alaska, Sir

And what's she like?

- Oh you'll find out soon enough, Sir.

September

Jack, things seem to be getting a bit serious regarding the world's finance system. I thought the plan was to take out a few banks in order to get consumers to tighten their belts. I think we're beyond that point now.

- Things do seem to have gone a bit further than we expected, Sir.

That's somewhat of an understatement, Jack. What's going on?

- Well it turned out that these derivatives are so complicated that no one can understand them. The markets can't work out just how much trouble any particular bank is in. And the banks themselves certainly don't know.

Well what is it going to take to stabilise the situation. I assume we're talking money here.

- Yes, Sir. 700-800 should do it.

800 million dollars is a lot of money. We won't be able to hide that in the defence budget.

- Er, that's 800 billion dollars, Sir, not 800 million.

!!!!!

- And that's not the end of the bad news. Some of that money is going to have to go to the insurance company AIG.

And what are they going to do with the money?

- They're going to pay it over to the banks in order to stop them going bust.

I hope this is a joke, Jack.

- Unfortunately, no, Sir, it's not a joke. Apparently, some banks insured themselves against the chance that some of these sub-prime loans would go bad and they did that through AIG.

But we still caught the foreign banks.

- Unfortunately they also used AIG.

So the whole thing is a very expensive mess, Jack, and if I remember rightly the whole point of this exercise was to try and stop the middle classes buying organic chickens.

- Well it wasn't just the chickens, Sir.

I bloody well know that, Jack. I was being sarcastic.

- To be fair, Sir, it wasn't just food either. We also wanted to stop them being able to get medical treatment to the extent that they currently do.

Well I think we can safely say that they won't be buying organic food any time soon. In fact, if the recession gets any worse, many people won't be able afford any food at all.

- Well we could look on that as a bonus, Sir.

Well all I can say is that I'm glad I won't be around to clear up this mess. But I take some consolation in the fact that you will be, Jack.

- Thank you, Sir.

November

Jack, I gather that the Palin woman did the trick.

- Yes, Sir, Mr Obama has been elected by some margin.

Well I think it's pretty unbelievable.

- What, just because he's black, Sir?

No, I don't mean Obama. I mean Palin and the fact that we were able to get away with nominating her as a running mate. Did you hear some of the things she came up with? Even I wouldn't have said some of that stuff and it makes you wonder how on earth we got away with it.

- Well, Sir, I did take the precaution of increasing the supply of G-Water.

That can only mean one thing.

- That's right, Sir. The dental health of our nation has never been better.

Obama

2009

January

- Mr President, Sir. Welcome to the White House. My name is Jack, and there are a few things I need to go through.

I dare say. This global financial meltdown is a disaster and what I cannot understand is why someone didn't see it coming?

- Ah, yes. Perhaps we'd better start there.

Ten Minutes Later

So this banking problem, it's all part of some grand plan!

- Yes, Sir.

That makes it worse than I thought.

- In what respect, Sir?

Well, Jack, I assumed that Bush was an incompetent idiot and that it would not be that difficult to do a better job. But now you're telling me he was screwing up on purpose.

- Well, Sir, not all his screw ups were deliberate. But as far as the banks are concerned, and now the wider economy, yes it was a deliberate screw up.

Shit.

- Shit indeed, Sir.

February

- Sir, I've been giving some thought to the briefing I gave to you on your first day.

Do you have a problem, Jack?

- Well, Sir, it does appear on reflection that you caught on very quickly to a lot of the areas covered by STOP.

I'm very quick on the uptake, Jack, especially when compared to my predecessor.

- Well there is that, Sir, but even so….

Is there some point you're trying to make, Jack.

- No, Sir.

I hope not, Jack. And while we're on the subject of your briefing, I've given all the information some thought and there is one particular issue that I'd like to revisit and that's space exploration. If I remember rightly we're committed to going back to the Moon.

- If you mean that you're predecessor announced a project to send a man back to the Moon then you are correct. If you mean that we're actually planning to do it, then no we're not; we won't be going back.

I hope that you're not suggesting that we fake it again.

- Oh no, Sir. But in one respect it may be even worse.

What do you mean?

- Well, Sir, with the apparent success of the plan to create a financial meltdown there's no way that we can afford such a project.

So why did we make the commitment? Surely my predecessor knew that the original moon landing never actually happened and he was also aware of our plan for the banks.

- Yes, Sir, of course he knew.

What, so he just forgot?

- No, he knew when he made the announcement that it could never go ahead.

Oh, I get it. He got the credit and now some poor sap is going to have to cancel it.

- Yes, Sir. And when you refer to "some poor sap", you do know who you're referring to don't you, Sir?

You mean that I am that person?

- I'm afraid so, Sir.

Well I think we'll wait a while until we make that announcement. Just make sure we don't spend too much money on the project in the meantime.

- Oh I don't think there's any chance of that, Sir. There's no money in the budget for it.

Surely that doesn't stop people spending money.

- It does when there literally isn't any actual money, Sir.

March

- Sir, there is one minor issue with the Swine Flu plan and it's regarding the World Health Organisation. They seem to have a problem with our version of the flu virus. They are thinking of changing the definition of a pandemic in which case our flu bug won't qualify. Currently a pandemic must just be capable of spreading quickly around the world. The new definition means that it must also be dangerous. They say that under the new classification, Swine Flu would not be deadly enough to be declared a pandemic and of course for our plan to work, we need that seal of approval. People need to think that it's seriously life threatening.

Well can't we have a word with someone in the organisation?

- I think that we may need your influence, Sir, top man to top man, so to speak.

OK, get whoever it is on the phone. I'll have a word. What sort of leverage shall I use?

- I find that money normally works, Sir and remember, all you need to do is to get them to postpone the decision until after Swine Flu has run its course. It goes without saying that, if everything goes according to plan, our next effort will certainly be a pandemic. It won't matter what definition they use.

OK, Jack, consider it done. And do we have a date for the second hit?

- 2012, Sir. And since we're talking about health issues, I feel it may be time to revisit the idea of a national healthcare scheme here in the US.

Don't you think that particular idea has passed it's sell by date, Jack?

- Maybe, Sir, but there's no harm to be done in trying to go forward with such a plan at this time. After all, what have we got to lose?

How about a second term?

- If we go ahead now, any fallout will be a distant memory by the time we get to the next election and in any case, if our current big plans don't work out, we're going to need something to fall back on. In any case, you can always give the responsibility for implementing the plan to someone else. That way you can avoid most of the flak if it doesn't all work out as planned.

If you think I'm going to get the wife to take the rap, you can think again, Jack. That plan may have worked once but not again.

- You mean she's too smart to fall for such a ruse.

Your words not mine, Jack. But I'll give your idea some consideration and I'll let you know by the end of the month.

- Thank you, Sir.

April

- Sir, there seems to be an issue with your birth certificate.

Ah, really.

- You don't seem surprised.

You're talking about the rumour that I wasn't born in the USA.

- Yes, Sir. Why do you ask? Is there another problem I don't know about?

I think you'd better sit down, Jack.

- I hope you're not going to tell me that you weren't born here, Sir. I can cover up most things, but that may be a problem too far.

Well the good news is that I was born in the USA.

- So that means that the birth certificate is genuine.

Er yes, Jack.

- I sense some hesitation in your voice, Sir, What's the bad news.

It's not exactly my birth certificate, Jack.

- What! How can it not be yours?

As I said, it's not mine.

- I think you'd better explain, Sir.

I still think you'd better sit down, Jack.

- Yes, Sir. Go on.

Well, Jack, the birth certificate belongs to my "parents" real son. He died shortly after birth. My "parents" were devastated but they had the chance to get over their grief quickly when they were offered the chance to adopt a baby boy. That child was me.

- But I don't understand. Why did you not have your own birth certificate?

Well when I said "adopt", what I should have said is "obtain". The process wasn't exactly legal.

- You mean they bought the child?

Oh no, no money changed hands. But the child was born out of wedlock to a young mother who wanted to keep the baby's existence a secret from her family. But they found out and arranged for the baby's secret adoption. You see, my mother was white but my father was black which made things even trickier than they would otherwise be.

- Well, Sir, it's all irregular, but if you were born in the USA I don't see what the problem is. It's not your fault that your adoptive parents falsified your birth certificate, is it, Sir? Is there something you're not telling me?

It's to do with my mother, Jack.

- Oh yes, I forgot to ask. Do you know who she is?

Yes, I do.

- And are you in contact with her?

Yes.

- What? On a regular basis?

Yes.

- How regular?

I talk to her most days.

- Daily contact! How do you manage that?

It's not difficult when she's the Secretary of State.

- But Hilary Clinton is…. Oh no!

Oh Yes, Jack…. Jack…. Jack, are you OK? Do you need a glass of water? Or something stronger?

- I don't think any drink would be strong enough at this moment, Sir. Let me just try to digest your little bombshell.

A Few Moments Later

Jack, you're looking a bit better and the colour is coming back to your cheeks.

- I'm OK, Sir. It was just a bit of a shock.

Yes, I can see that.

- But there are some things that are now making a bit more sense.

Like what?

- Like why you gave Mrs Clinton a position in your administration.

Well, she was the best person for the job.

- With all due respect to your "mother".....

Jack, are you OK.

- Sorry, Sir, the whole thing is still a bit too much to comprehend.

Perhaps it will help if you refer to her as Mrs Clinton rather than "mother". I find that it helps me.

- Yes, Sir, I think it would.

Well that's fine with me; that's what I call her. I don't think it would be a good idea if I start referring to her as "Mom".

- No, Sir, I can see that. So where do we go from here?

In what respect, Jack?

- In respect of the rumour about your birth certificate.

Luckily, Jack, that's not my problem anymore.

- Ah, I see where you're coming from here, Sir. Now that I know, it's become my problem.

Glad to see you're on the right track, Jack. But I don't see why we don't just keep on the same path.

- Which one is that, Sir?

The one where we give the conspiracy theory people enough to chew on without them getting anything concrete to pin on us.

- And in the meantime, they fail to see the main target.

Exactly, Jack.

- I'll keep an eye on the situation for you, Sir.

Thanks, Jack.

Pause

Is there anything else Jack?

- Well there is the whole issue of how you became President. How did you connect up with your mother....

Steady, Jack.

- Sorry, Sir. How did you get in touch with Mrs Clinton?

It was the Clintons who found me. It was to do with the whole "dynasty" project.

- Ah, I see. And Bill was in on this?

Exactly! It was his idea. The Clintons realised that the dynasty thing would fall apart after Bush. There was no way Jeb would ever be President. Not even you could fix that.

- Oh I don't know, Sir. But it would have been a challenge.

It wasn't a risk worth taking. In any case, the country was going to be ready for change after 8 years of Bush.

- But where did you come into the frame, Sir.

Well the Clintons wanted to continue the dynasty thing but without the need for Republican help. Hilary was the only option, but she was by no means a cert. The country may not be ready for a woman President. By having a Clinton as both the Democrat candidates they covered all the bases.

- But the country would be ready for a black President, Sir?

Apparently so, Jack. The country had a choice and they chose me.

- But they could have chosen McCain.

Not after Palin got involved and I believe I have you to thank for that, Jack.

- But how did you make it a choice between just the two of you? What about the rest of the potential Democrat candidates?

You're not the only one who can fix these sorts of things, Jack.

- Obviously not, Sir. And during the election contest, what about the antagonism between the two of you?

Oh, that was genuine. There were no holds barred. So is there anything else, Jack?

- One last thing. The briefing I gave you on your first day.

Ah, yes.

- I said you seemed to cotton on to everything very quickly and you said it was because you are a quick learner.

Yes.

- That is presumably not the case.

Are you suggesting that I'm not a quick learner, Jack?

- No, Sir, I'm suggesting that you caught on quickly because you'd already been given the heads up on STOP.

OK, I confess, you've caught me red handed. Are you OK with that?

- But you didn't know about the banks.

Bill Clinton briefed me on the main points when I was recruited to the cause.

- So you did know!

I knew about all the stuff up to the point where Bill Clinton left office.

- Judging by your reaction, Sir, you must be a good actor.

I'm a politician, Jack. You of all people should know that being a good actor is part and parcel of the job. So are you OK with all this?

- Yes, Sir, I'm OK. It's just good to know that my basic instincts are still in good order. I knew that there was something that was not quite right.

That may be, but I can't help thinking that the old Jack would have worked it all out a bit sooner. Perhaps you're slipping in your old age.

- I trust we're not going to be raising the issue of retirement again, Sir.

I wouldn't dream of it, Jack.

- Thank you, Sir.

And Jack, one other thing. I've decided that we can go ahead with the healthcare proposals.

- Thank you, Sir. I'll push ahead with the plans without delay.

August

Jack, I've come across something that suggests we may have a leak from Area 51. It concerns the proposed flu pandemic.

- What makes you think that we have a problem, Sir?

Well you said that our target is to launch the plan in 2012 and I've just seen some publicity about a film by the same name. My understanding is that it predicts some sort of cataclysmic event that year. Do you think that the two things are connected?

- Ah, now I see where you're coming from. I had the same thought when I saw the press release but on inspection it appears that there's no need to worry. The basis of the film is the Mayan calendar which counts down rather than up.

As calendars go, isn't there some sort of design fault in that version?

- It certainly appears that way. It will reach zero at the end of 2012 and some people see this as predicting some sort of apocalypse.

What's supposed to happen?

- There's nothing specific, Sir, it's all conjecture and it doesn't affect our plans.

Well it could do. It would be a shame to spend a lot of time and effort on the flu pandemic if, in any case, the world is going to come to an end.

- You're right, Sir, that would be a shame.

September

Jack, this climate change conference in Copenhagen.

- What about it, Sir?

Well it's getting pretty difficult to go against the science. Unlike my predecessor I feel that I have a certain reputation, intellectually speaking, and I don't want to jeopardise it by denying something that is bloody obvious to everyone else. So what can we do?

- We could cast doubt on the scientific reasoning, Sir, but it needs to be short term. In the long run the science is sound and we are going to need to go along with it if we are going to fulfil our ultimate aim regarding STOP.

You mean tie it all in with population control.

- Yes, Sir.

So what are our options?

- Let me give it some thought and I'll get back to you as soon as I can.

Well make it quick, the conference is only ten weeks away.

- Yes, Sir.

November

- Sir, I've come up with something regarding your problem with the Copenhagen conference.

Well you're cutting a bit fine aren't you, Jack?

- As it happens, Sir, no. In this instance timing is crucial and now is just the right time to put our plan into action.

You'd better explain how this is going to work.

- As we discussed, we need to cast some short term doubt on the science behind climate change. We think we can do this by publishing the correspondence between some of the scientists.

But surely these people are committed to the principle of climate change. Why would their correspondence be helpful in anyway?

- If you go through enough stuff there's bound to be something that look's suspicious, especially if you take it out of context.

How can you be so sure?

- Because we've already looked through the emails to check that they'll serve our purpose.

But surely the scientists involved will eventually be able to explain away any misunderstandings.

- Exactly! The important word there is "eventually". If we get our timing right, the news will be out there just before the conference starts. That way there won't be time for the scientists to come up with a convincing response. In fact we are assuming that there will need to be some sort of official investigation into the whole matter.

This sounds very messy, Jack, someone is going to end up with a lot of egg on their face. Make sure it's not me so you keep this well away from here.

- I've already anticipated your concerns in that respect and that's why we're going to use a university in England as the fall guy.

And the email correspondence; I trust that's going to be leaked in the normal way.

- Yes, I have one of our tame hackers lined up ready to go as soon as you say the word.

OK, let's go.

The Next Day

Jack, I've been thinking about this climate conference. I reckon that if it's going to be a failure it would be good idea if I stay clear. What do you think?

- I'm not sure that's a good idea. For instance, until our little plan is made public, we don't know that it's going to fail, or at least we can't be seen to know. Also, once the shit hits the fan, someone is going to have the opportunity to pick up the pieces and make something out of the situation. And there isn't going to be anyone else stepping up to the plate.

But who am I going to cosy up to? The Europeans are not happy bunnies right now, particularly the Brits. They still seem to be a bit upset that we kept our plan to wreck the banks a secret from them.

- Well, Sir, it has caused them more than a few problems, financially speaking. And of course Mr Brown has suffered. He was proud of his efforts regarding the British economy and now it's all gone down the pan. Now he's prime minister he can't very easily blame the person who was in charge of the banks when it was all going out of control; he was that guy.

I also gather that he thinks we gave Blair the heads up on our plan to wreck the world's economy and that's why he handed over to Brown when he did. I trust there's no truth in that rumour.

- None that I know of, Sir, although I have to say Blair did move a lot of money into property over a period of time before the crash.

But as an investment surely property has suffered like everything else.

- Yes, but compared to other investment options it was the best of a bad bunch, after all bricks and mortar will always be there.

As opposed to Collateralized Debt Obligations, Jack.

- Exactly, Sir.

So getting back to Copenhagen, who am I going to be best buddies with?

- There's no option really, it'll need to be the emerging economies and that suits us fine.

OK, I'll go, but not from the start. I'll arrive half way through, knock a few heads together and take all the credit.

- That's normally what we do, Sir.

Really?

- Remember World War 2, Sir?

Is there really no such thing as an original idea, Jack?

- Well there was one I heard some time ago that for some reason sticks in the mind.

And what was that?

- Kill all the chickens.

What!

- You had to be there, Sir.

2010

February

Jack, I have a couple of points regarding DSG. You say that you found it some time ago.

- Yes, Sir, We were pretty relieved since it explained so many things.

So I gather. But what does it do for us regarding STOP?

- Unfortunately, although it helps our cause it does not mean that we can cancel STOP completely. Although nature does seem to be intervening on our side there's too much of a time lag to make any difference.

What do you mean?

- Well nature is working with us to reduce the human population but the effects will come too late to save us.

But if nature was really coming into play here surely the plan must work.

- That depends on what you think the grand plan is, Sir. If it's to save the human population then it's not going to work. If on the other hand the grand plan is to save the planet, and by that I mean sustain the greatest biodiversity, then nature may well have decided that this could best be achieved by wiping us out.

When you say "nature may have decided" Jack, I hope you're not referring to Intelligent Design.

- No, Sir, it was probably a poor choice of words.

It certainly was, but let's move on; there is one other thing. You said that you have tested a great many people to check your theory and it got me wondering.

- About what exactly, Sir?

About whether or not you have tested any Presidents, Jack.

- Now why would I do that, Sir?

We're not discussing the reason here, Jack. And I notice you haven't denied it. So are you going to fess up or what? I bet curiosity got the better of you.

- Well, Sir, part of the research did involve testing previous incumbents, so yes, Sir.

I knew it! I knew you wouldn't be able to resist, Jack.

- I wouldn't put it quite like that, Sir.

OK, so what was the outcome? Someone must have failed the test. By that I mean that they lacked the "sensible" gene.

- I don't think it would be fair to divulge the results, Sir. Some of the people concerned are still alive.

Well at least give me a clue. Were there any failures?

- Well let's just say that the pass rate was not 100%, Sir.

I might have guessed. And I bet it was Reagan, wasn't it.

- Perhaps surprisingly, no, Sir, it wasn't.

Well if it wasn't him it must be Bush Junior.

- Now why would you think that, Sir?

Well just look at some of the things he has said. My favourite is the one about the French not having a word for an entrepreneur.

- Well there are two things to say about that, Sir. First, there's nothing wrong with that statement.

No, Jack, I'm sure you're wrong there. The word entrepreneur comes from the French.

- The comment doesn't say that the French do not have the word, but instead that they don't have a word with the same meaning as the English version. In French, the word entrepreneur means someone like a contractor or proprietor. In France a plumber would be an entrepreneur. In English it means someone who is perhaps an innovator who takes a certain risk setting up a new business. The chances are that your local plumber does not fit the bill and I'm not aware of any other word in French that can be used and has the same meaning. So it's quite possible that the French do not have a word for entrepreneur.

Well OK, if you say so. What's your other point?

- My other point, Sir, is that there's no evidence that indicates Bush

Junior ever uttered those words. He did say some pretty stupid things but that wasn't one of them. You really must stop using the Internet as your main source of information.

Aha! You've admitted it. Bush said some stupid things. He was, or should I say is, the one.

- We all do stupid things from time to time, Sir. That doesn't mean we are lacking DSG.

What, even you Jack?

- Well, Sir, I told you about DSG and right now that seems like a stupid thing to have done.

The Following Day

Jack, after our conversation yesterday there was one other thing that occurred to me. I forgot to ask whether I had been tested for DSG. I know you don't want to talk about specifics but I think I have the right to know.

- I dare say, Sir.

So?

- So you'll be pleased to know that you have Darwin's Sensible Gene.

I was rather hoping you'd say that. And I would like to suggest that in future all presidential candidates are tested before taking office.

- That is already part of the standard protocol before they even stand for their party's nomination. I thought it best, Sir.

What? And that includes Sarah Palin?

- Yes, Sir, she was tested.

And she passed!

- No, Sir, of course not. She failed. There was no sign of a Sensible Gene in her sample, which is why we allowed her to stand against you.

Oh, right, I see. All the bits are beginning to fall into place.

- They normally do, Sir. Eventually.

April

OK, Jack, the Swine Flu epidemic has run its course. Have we learnt anything from the exercise? 'Cos if we didn't, it's been a bit of a waste of time, since we could have been going with the killer version by now.

- Oh no, Sir, it certainly hasn't been a waste of time. On the contrary, we've learnt a great deal.

Like what?

- Well like the fact that, unlike normal flu which mainly affects older people, our one hit the younger ones.

And do we know why?

- We do, Sir. We think it's because we based our flu virus on the one originating in the 1970's and that the older people have a natural immunity from the infection dating back to that time. The young ones don't have that advantage. What this means is that when we do come up with the killer version it needs to be based on a version of the flu virus which pre-dates any living person. That way no one will have natural immunity.

Good point. What else have you got?

- Well many governments, and particularly the UK, have been embarrassed by the amount of vaccine that has been left over. We hope that in future this will have two ramifications. The first is that the governments will be able to order far fewer doses of the vaccine without being criticised.

Well they won't be criticised up front, Jack. But I can imagine that a few heads will roll if we get the sort of body count we're aiming for, but I guess that by then it'll be too late.

- Exactly, Sir, and in fact there is some doubt about whether there would be any production of the vaccine at all.

Why would there not be?

- Because various governments have been trying to avoid paying for the stuff that they haven't used. If I were a drug company, the next time a government asks me to produce millions of doses of flu vaccine in double quick time I'd probably tell them where to go. Either that or demand the money up front and I can't see many governments agreeing to that.

OK, so is there anything else?

- Just a few minor things. The photo of the little kids at the airport wearing face masks was a good stunt which had a couple of results.

Stunt, Jack?

- Oh yes, Sir, one of the things that the ad men came up with. At the time it helped to increase the level of panic in the population at large. But later, with the benefit of hind sight, the whole thing looks at bit silly. Hopefully, when the next one hits, people will be less inclined to use face masks and this will help the spread of the virus. The same principle applies to Tamiflu. A lot of people paid silly money for the drug and will think twice next time.

And were there any down sides?

- Just a couple, Sir. The number of people who refused the vaccine because of the MMR scare was less than expected.

Why was that?

- We think it's because some people are prepared to risk their child's health by not getting them vaccinated. However, when it comes to their own health they're not so stupid. They'll play it safe and get the vaccine. Also, the scare to do with Guillain-Barre Syndrome didn't have the take up rate we hoped for. Next time we'll have to come up with something a whole lot scarier.

And in English please, Jack. For example, let's call it something like "Liquid Brain" syndrome. With that at least you know exactly where you stand.

- If you had something called "Liquid Brain" syndrome, I suspect that standing would be one of the many things you probably wouldn't be able to do, Sir.

No, but you get my drift.

- Yes, Sir.

So overall it was a worthwhile exercise.

- I'd say so, Sir.

And Jack, there is one minor thing. Next time around, should there be a problem with the availability of vaccines, you will make sure that there is a least one dose won't you.

- Of course, Sir, but won't you want one too?

June

- Sir, there is one further issue that's cropped up as a result of the Swine Flu project. It appears that the normal winter flu has failed to appear. We're not sure whether it's connected to our version but it does seem to be a bit of a coincidence.

Well if it's connected is that a good or bad thing?

- Well in the short term it's has a bit of a negative effect in that we didn't get the normal body count from winter flu. However, in the scheme of things, it's probably irrelevant since if we manage to wipe out 100 million people, whether or not there's a flu epidemic the following winter is going to be somewhat academic.

The Future

- Are you ready, Sir?

I think so, Jack. Tell them to start the count down.

- Yes, Sir.

Some Minutes Later

Arghhhhhh!

Later Still

- Are you OK, Sir? Only you were making some strange noises as we took off.

That's hardly surprising is it. Nobody explained to me just how quickly we would accelerate. It feels as though I've left some of my vital organs behind.

- If you mean your bladder, Sir you may be right. Just look at the state of your seat!

Oh dear.

- Never mind, Sir, we'll soon be docking with the space station.

How soon, exactly?

- About two hours, Sir.

Two Days Later

Thank god we're here at last. I thought that we would never make it.

- Well, Sir it was a close shave. Some of the staff at mission control were a bit upset when they found out who was being sent to the space station.

Well who did they think would be going?

- Perhaps two young couples who could breed and continue the human race, Sir?

That would always have been a long shot, Jack. Better it was four people who have, through the years, done their best to save humanity.

- Of course, Sir, in your case it was just two years.

Well, yes, but I represent the position of the President. Anyway, how was the situation resolved?

- As far as I understand it, Sir, at first the controllers refused to dock our craft with the space station. But eventually, the managers persuaded them to proceed as planned.

How did they do that?

- I don't know, Sir, but whatever it was, it worked.

And have we had any word on Monica's condition?

- Not good news there, I'm afraid. When her Zimmer frame got caught in the walk way to the gantry and she fell, she broke her hip. I'm afraid she had to be put down. And of course, there's no way that Rachel would come without Monica.

No, I suppose not. Anyway, now that we're here, I need to eat something since we've had no food since we left earth.

- Well, the trip was only supposed to take a couple of hours. There didn't seem to be any need to pack a picnic hamper.

Now, now, Jack, there's no need to get testy.

- Sorry, Sir.

How much food is there?

- Well, there is supposed to be enough to last five years, but that was assuming that there are four people on board. Since there are only two of us, it should last twice as long.

And did they include a cheeseburger?

- I believe so, but you do realise don't you that it's all concentrated stuff, so it'll just be some sort of paste that tastes like a cheeseburger.

Right now, Jack, I don't really care. Just get me something to eat.

-Yes, Sir.

Two Minutes Later

Ugh, this stuff tastes awful. And why is it a strange colour?

- You mean luminescent pink? My steak is the same. Oh no, I think I know what this is!

Don't tell me!

(Together) Pink Margarine!

Jack, you'd better check to see if all the food is like this.

- Yes, Sir.

A Few Minutes Later

- I'm afraid it looks like it's all the same, Sir.

So where does that leave us? Just how much nutrition is there in this stuff?

- Let's put it this way, Sir. We probably need to find another source of food in the next fortnight.

In that case, we'd better get on our way. Engage warp factor 5!

- This isn't Star Trek, Sir.

I know it isn't. In Star Trek, they had a proper staff restaurant! But then again, if this isn't Star Trek, why do we have a lever with a label that says "Start Warp Engines".

- Er, I'm not sure, Sir. The means of propulsion is supposed to be an ion engine which is designed to get us to the nearest habitable planet within a year.

Well that's as may be. But I don't see a lever labelled "Start Ion Engine" and I do see one labelled "Start Warp Engine". So let's go with that, shall we?

- Yes, Sir.

A Few Minutes Later Still

Is anything happening? How will we know that we're on our way?

- Well, Sir, the fact that I can still see the Earth through the porthole suggests that it is very much the case that we are not on our way.

Well, you'd better start trying to find out what the problem is.

- I'm afraid my training didn't cover warp engine maintenance, Sir.

Well use your common sense and start with the lever. What is it connected to?

- It's attached to two wires, Sir.

And what are they connected to?

- Nothing, Sir!

504

Shit.

- Exactly, Sir. Now we know why mission control let us dock. They knew we weren't going anywhere.

So what do we do now?

- We'll have to radio mission control and see if they'll come and get us.

That's assuming the radio works.

A Few More Minutes Later

(Together) Shit!!

Conclusion

2028

It was in 2028 that matters came to a head and as a result the President was forced to flee to the relative safety (or so he thought at the time) of the International Space Station (ISS). The President and Jack were correct about the food on the ISS; it was all made from Pink Margarine, apart from one pack which really was a concentrated cheeseburger. Whether the President ever lived long enough or had the perseverance to find it amongst all the other items of food we will never know. As for all the other packs, the only difference between them was the label.

In any case the Pink Margarine used for the food supplies on the ISS was but a small part of the stock of the stuff which, contrary to Jack's statements to successive Presidents, had still to be disposed of. By 1990 even the small market for it in San Francisco had dried up. Following the problem with the ozone layer (contrary to what Jack said at the time, only one ton of the stuff had actually been dumped in Antarctica), Jack decided to leave the Pink Margarine in storage. However, the President eventually got wind of this and in desperation, Jack arranged for the remaining stocks to be loaded on to a fleet of cargo ships and it was dumped in the deepest part of the Pacific Ocean. In terms of the amount involved, matters had been made worse and the quantity stockpiled had increased because some States had continued to produce Pink Margarine in order to claim compensation from the federal government long after the market for it no longer existed.

Things started to go wrong towards the end of the twentieth century. Scientists noticed that on average the climate world-wide was getting warmer. Initially, this was blamed on the increased levels of CO_2 in the atmosphere. However, the real reason was not discovered until the early twenties (2020's, not 1920's). For some time the El Nino effect had been getting less predictable until, in 2023, it stopped completely and it took a while for the reason to be established. The first indication was the apparent calmness of the sea, centred on a point near the Mariana Trench. This was the deepest part of the Pacific Ocean and when Jack heard about this his heart sank, since he knew what the cause was likely to be, although he didn't know the reason. For he had specifically instructed that the Pink Margarine be dumped in the deepest part of the ocean, never to be seen again. Or so he thought.

The appearance of the sea in the affected area was as though an invisible layer of oil was covering the sea. An analysis of the sea water established that the viscosity was slightly higher than normal, although it was not thought to be significantly so. However, a subsequent test of water samples from greater depths showed that the viscosity increased as the depth increased and at the lowest point was positively glutinous.

The sea water resembled wallpaper paste (e.g. Polycell Heavy Duty) and was subsequently referred to as "Thick Water". Further analysis showed that this effect was caused by minute microbes which were present in the water in massive numbers. The result was like the plumes of algae which had become increasingly common in the seas around the world. However, in this case, the microbes were invisible and seemed to be multiplying at an alarming rate.

This increase in viscosity caused the water currents which fuelled the El Nino effect to stop. It was thought at the time that this alone could explain global warming, but it later transpired that there was another more deadly effect. Thick water is less likely to evaporate and therefore there will be fewer clouds and ultimately less rain. This effect was not understood for some time, since it is very difficult to measure the total amount of cloud cover world-wide. Also, the lack of an "El Nino" effect changed weather patterns to make some areas wetter but others drier. It took some years for scientists to appreciate the overall global effect.

However, once the seriousness of the situation was appreciated, the reaction of the international community was swift. The United Nations decided that there were three problem areas to be tackled, these being:

1) What was causing the problem?

2) What effect would it have in the long term?

3) What could be done to fix the problem?

It was determined that each main area of the globe (USA, Europe and China) would be primarily responsible for one of these problem areas. On Jack's advice, the President volunteered that the USA would determine what was causing the problem. Jack made this recommendation based on the fact that:

a) He already knew what had caused the problem.

b) It would mean that he could more easily cover up the true situation.

The Europeans chose option three leaving option two for the Chinese. They did this on the basis that they wouldn't have to do anything until the other two questions had been answered and they assumed that this would take some time. In the event they had to act a lot quicker than they thought because the Americans (i.e. Jack) already knew what had caused the problem. Of course, they couldn't admit to the actual cause so Jack came up with the story that a survey of the deep by a nuclear submarine had discovered that there were vents from undersea volcanoes which were giving out plumes of noxious gas and that these alone were the reason for the problem. This turned out to be the cause of Jack's fall from grace. He had managed to cover up any number of things during his time as a Presidential aide, but this was one step too far. Senior naval personnel knew that there had been no such survey, so they instigated one of their own.

It did not take them long to find the cause of the problem. Even in the Pacific Ocean, fifty thousand tons of Pink Margarine is hard to disguise when you know exactly where the problem is centred. At first they did not know what it was but then the periscope got clogged up with the stuff. When the submarine resurfaced they were able to take a sample and send it away for analysis, which of course proved that the substance was indeed Pink Margarine. On its own, it would not have caused a problem, but Jack's invented excuse for the Thick Water was much nearer the truth than he could have expected.

There were indeed volcanic vents on the sea bed, but they weren't giving out noxious gases. They were spouting microbes which against all expectations were able to exist in the hot and inhospitable conditions under the Earth's crust. Presumably it was a tough existence and nutrients were scarce. However when they emerged into an area of the ocean that was covered in an abundant supply of "food" they multiplied at a fantastic rate.

Once the Pink Margarine was discovered, Jack knew it was only a matter of time before the truth about STOP came out. He persuaded the President to use the ISS as an escape route. However, after the launch had taken place, the truth about the cause of thick water reached mission control and initially they refused to dock the launch vehicle with the ISS. However, they were informed by the supply company about the fact that all the food on the ISS (apart from the cheeseburger) was Pink Margarine and the unanimous conclusion was that the docking should take place. (The real reason for the existence of the ISS had been leaked to someone at the supply company some years previously and they decided to sabotage STOP. However, how they found out about Pink Margarine, or managed to get hold of some, is a mystery. It suggests that information was being leaked from the very heart of STOP). It was deemed a fitting punishment that the two of them should spend their last few days eating nothing but the pink stuff.

As for the propulsion system, of course there was never any realistic chance of developing an engine to power the ISS to another habitable planet, but while the government was happy to throw significant amounts of money at the problem, the manufacturers were happy to accept it.

Back on Earth, once the cause of the problem in the Pacific had been discovered, it didn't take long (two days in fact) for the Chinese to decide that things were very serious and something had to be done.

This rather caught the Europeans on the hop, since they were still arguing about how to pay for their part of the job. The British wanted the money to come out of the budget for the Common Agricultural Policy, but fearing a backlash from their farmers, the French vetoed this idea. In fact by 2024 most French farmers received so much money from the EU in terms of grants to look after the land (as a result they were now called "Les Gardiens du Terre"), that they had stopped actually growing anything. Consequently, if the grants were to be reduced or even abolished, the French farmers had no immediate means of earning a living until they learnt how to grow things again.

The situation was deadlocked; however the matter was eventually resolved by the British people living in France, who by this time almost out-numbered the French. They organised a bloodless coup d'état to overthrow the French government and cunningly commenced the operation on a Saturday afternoon, knowing that France is basically closed all day Sunday and Monday. By the time the French people opened their shutters on Tuesday morning it was all over. Unfortunately, as regards saving the planet, it was too late. The microbes had multiplied to a point where they were too numerous to stop.

The effects were rapid. The lack of cloud cover led to a lack of rainfall which in turn led to an increase in global temperatures. A spiral of disaster had started. The first countries to be affected were on the east coast of the Pacific Rim. Food shortages led to mass starvation. People were prevented from travelling to countries that still had food initially by a lack of fuel, then by the fact that countries quickly closed their borders to protect what food stocks they had.

However, it did not take long for the microbes to spread into the Atlantic via the Panama Canal. Efforts to stop this happening, although probably futile, failed when a lock keeper fell asleep on duty and left the sluice gates open.

Within months, the effect had spread across the entire globe. The lack of rain meant that within two years all human and most other life forms were wiped out. Thus, Jack achieved his ultimate aim of reducing the human population but it is debatable as to whether he would have considered STOP an overall success.

www.ingramcontent.com/pod-product-compliance
Lightning Source LLC
Chambersburg PA
CBHW071628260626
47170CB00001B/6